ELECTRIC SOUK

ROSE McGINTY

urbanepublications.com

First published in Great Britain in 2017
by Urbane Publications Ltd
Suite 3, Brown Europe House, 33/34 Gleaming Wood Drive,
Chatham, Kent ME5 8RZ
Copyright ©Rose McGinty, 2017

A CIP catalogue record for this book is available
from the British Library.

ISBN 978-1-911129-82-0
MOBI 978-1-911129-84-4
EPUB 978-1-911129-83-7

Design and Typeset by Michelle Morgan

Cover by Michelle Morgan

Printed and bound by CPI Group (UK) Ltd, Croydon, CR0 4YY

urbanepublications.com

For my family, friends
and the Falcons

The Mermaid

A mermaid found a swimming lad,
Picked him for her own,
Pressed her body to his body,
Laughing; and plunging down
Forgot in cruel happiness
That even lovers drown.

W.B. Yeats.

An eye for an eye

We flee across the border. Sand djinn scratch against the car windows. The Al Shemal storm wails after us. Cramped in the well behind the driver seat, I am covered by an oily blanket, trying to scrawl this last note to you. My head throbs from the petrol fumes and my ribs ache as we jolt over the hard, rocky desert. Patrick swears at the thick road ahead; and at the road we can't see behind, the dark shadows that must pursue us. I cannot bear to think that the truth will be buried beneath the surly, thirsty dunes.

The cold metal of Laila's small gun presses against my hipbone, through my pocket.

 Sun

one

Every line of my palms and fingers is digitally captured. A veiled official snatches my passport. She pushes me into a booth, '*Asre'ee.*' I am blood typed, blood tested, X-rayed, measured, weighed, prodded, examined for all sorts of infectious and sexual diseases, even tested to see if I am pregnant. I can't fight it, the heat, humidity, and all these needles. A nurse warns me that if I am found pregnant or have TB or HIV, it will mean instantaneous deportation, no appeal. All I can taste is dust, red dust. It coats me.

The official returns with my passport stamped. The stamp permits me to work; it also forbids me to leave for six months, '*Yanni*, no turning back now, Miss Aisling.'

I'm used to the Ryanair lifestyle, coming and going as I please across Europe, like a kittiwake on the current. There, beneath our unclipped wings, borders barely exist. Now I am fenced into the desert with digital, medical and actual barbed wire.

The official hustles me around the Immigration Processing Centre, jumping the queues of sullen, male, immigrant workers. I lower my eyes from their cursing stares. Hundreds of forms are pushed at me to sign, none of which I understand, as I'm not allowed to look at them and anyway they are in Arabic.

'Sign, sign', snaps the official, as she hurries me from one desk to another.

At once I appreciate those rights we have at home, that I've never thought about much before. Suddenly they are all gone, with a stamp.

Finally, the day's barbarities are over; the porcelain blue skin of my right arm is blackened with bruises. I am pushed out into the velvet heat. My eyes are drawn to the Arabic moon; full heavy gold, it barely holds itself above the dark horizon of the Bay. Mesmerised, for a moment I melt away from the noise and hustle of the centre into the inky sky, the night that promises ancient dreams.

No one is here to meet me. I look about for a taxi to take me to my hotel but I can't find one. I watch lines of dazed young Indian men in drab overalls line up at the health check queue. One bony body pressed against another. Whole villages. No one speaks; all cower before the formidable immigration officials, guns in holsters at their waists. I am unnerved, my white skin is too luminous. And I am the only woman in the crowd.

I don't know where to turn, where to go next. I am jostled a few paces deeper into the crowd. Bladed elbows jab my ribs, my toe is stubbed against a heavy boot. I gasp for air, my flesh is clammy and strands of hair stick across my face, catching in my eyes. A hand grips my wrist and pulls at me.

'*Yallah*.' A gruff male voice at my ear.

I cannot see his face; he is twisted away from me. He gives me another sharp tug.

A twinkling point catches my attention and above the crowd a Liverpudlian shriek, 'Straight off the plane and already swanning off with a local. I'm goin to 'av to watch you'se.' A set of zebra striped nails slap away the dark hand grasping still at my wrist. 'Ee, kiddo, don't mind them, women are liquid gold here; you'll soon learn to zone it out.'

I am acutely aware of the dark, brooding eyes watching this spectacle. I try to see where the man who grabbed me has gone, but he has disappeared into the mass. His grip was so insistent I can still see the mark of his thumb on my wrist.

'I'm Angie, welcome to the desert.' Angie is resplendent in hair extensions and killer heels, 'Sorry I'm late, the traffic is mad tonight. Come on, kid, there's a bottle of vino collapso with your name on it waiting for us.'

We hop into her startling siren-pink Land Cruiser.

'What do you do at the Health Board?'

'Nurse training.'

'So, have you been here long, Angie?'

'About a year in these parts, but it must be five years now since I came to the Gulf. Was only meant to be for a weekend of retail and cocktails, when that prick of a husband of mine ran off wiv me sister. I just ripped up me return ticket, and I'm still 'ere, gerrin' a tan and lookin' for a Sheikh.'

Neons scream past us at hyper speed as we drive down the airport highway. I can't see anything of the city beyond the dazzling headlamps.

'How do you like it?' I ask Angie.

'I know three roads – the road to work, to the airport, and best of all, the road to the bar, hon. And that's all you need.'

It's to the bar where we are heading now, which Angie says is known as the 'airport lounge', as everyone goes there first for a drink whenever they arrive, 'And before they leave, if they're lucky.' Angie laughs.

'Dick'ead!' Angie swerves sharply, narrowly missing another Land Cruiser in the left-hand lane as a Ferrari bears down on us from the right. I cling to my seat belt. 'Friday night, prayers are over. Look at 'em go. It's like the Grand Prix.' Angie flicks her talons at the sports cars and Land Cruisers racing past, one so fast that as it takes a corner it tips on two wheels. 'Just last week, me mate Mick had his jeep written off in a pile-up on the airport road, and his pelvis is a write-off too.'

'That's terrible. What happened?'

'Fifteen-year old local in a Hummer, completely stoned, but no action will be taken against him. After all, no good Muslim boy drinks and there ain't no drugs in the desert.'

We pull off the highway and enter a small dusty compound of low-rise concrete boxes. A battered sign over the nearest door reads 'Heather's Scottish Club and Coffee Shop'. Balding and paunchy middle-aged British men are queuing, handing over bank notes to enter. Angie's arrival provokes a storm of wolf whistles; she gives an appreciative wiggle and we totter past. Inside, it's all sticky surfaces and choking smoke. The main saloon is almost entirely male, and I feel myself take a step back into a time warp as we walk in. In Dublin, the bars these days seem to be mostly female territory, all wine glasses and wasabi nuts. I don't know where all the men have gone.

Angie has her spot by the bar and a crowd of rough-diamond admirers are lining up drinks for us both, starting with a bottle of Jameson, in tribute to my homeland. Accents from all over the north of England and Scotland boom around me. Perhaps it's the long journey, different time zone, the smoke, the whiskey, but in this muddling noise I can barely make out a word anyone is saying. Mostly the conversation snatches I catch seem to be about football and stories of nights on the lash. I tune out. I want Scheherazade's tales, enchantment.

'He won't be seen alive again, poor sod.' I tune back in, listen to a man talking to Angie. He says a British national has been detained, accused of industrial espionage. He has broken his contract with the national airline early to take a new senior post in a rival airliner. His Royal hosts, owners of the airline, do not approve. Now, they are my Royal hosts too, as they are the patrons of the National Health Board. 'The wife's desperate, no one will tell her where he's being held. All she knows is he's in solitary confinement, somewhere out there.'

I see him, huddled, sweating in the corner of a small, dusty cell.

Mammy, maybe you were right. When I told Mammy a couple of months ago that I'd got a job in the desert she completely lost it. She would rather I had set my sights on the familiar tracks of America. I have a brother, Danny, in Detroit. But there's no work there. Great cities across the Western world have ground to a halt. Danny has lost his job and is even thinking of coming home. He has a notion of being self-sufficient, growing potatoes and all that. He's forgotten the Irish winters after all these years.

'The Middle East though, Aisling, women are covered up there. It's a male society, traditional, and there's them religious fanatics, bombings.' Mammy exploded the cutlery on the kitchen table. I'd put this conversation off all week until after Mass, when I thought she might be more serene. Some hope.

'And where do we live? Mammy, look back twenty years ago. Anyway, the Middle East is quiet enough these days. See these brochures of all the new cities, it's real opulent, the future, Mammy.'

'You go now Aisling, and you'se are lost to me.'

'Woman, let her go, will ya.' Grandaddy roared from his chair by the stove, 'I remember when I was a young' un my mother, and her mother before her, were always covered from head to toe in black. My mother was a clever woman, but she was dead behind the eyes from peeling spuds all day. We had our own Taliban, those fecking Christian Brothers'. Mammy chiseled the Sunday roast in the tin to within an inch of its life. 'Our young 'uns need to travel, mix, change the world. Feck, look at that wee Polish girlie in the chipper. She's a good girlie, gives all the fellas round here a little bit extra fish, and a little bit extra with it!'

'Grandaddy!'

So this morning I was packed off with a box of Bewley's best and prayers to St. Jude, of Hopeless Causes.

One of Angie's admirers, Jimmy, an oil rig worker, half hanging-off a bar stool, lurches his gut towards me and clamps a bulbous red hand on my shoulder, 'So what's a wee Irish girlie like you doing here, if ye donna mind me asking?

'Ah, she's here because she's the Prof's bit of stuff,' Angie cackles.

'Don't be telling me yer here after one of them dreamy-eyed Sheikhs, coz I'm telling ye now they're all shysters.'

'Ee, don't look so mortified,' Angie says, 'I'm only joking, but you do know that's what the Arabs will think, don't you? Probably most of the expats in the office too. We all know you've worked with the Prof before.'

'But he's married.' This causes a gale of laughter.

'Aren't we all lassie, doesn't stop me having a Chinese takeaway tonight though does it?' Jimmy leers. Angie sees the bewildered look on my face and points to two small Chinese women, dressed in leopard-print leggings and silky camisoles, sat at the far side of the bar with a portly older woman, pin-thin eyebrows. 'Sweet young girlies like you don't come out here all alone, no husband or boyfriend in tow. Most of the women out here, expat women, are sunny mummies. You are a rarity, kid.'

'Ay, so why are you here young Aisling? Debt or an ex? Why on earth else would anyone come to this God-forsaken hellhole?' Jimmy asks.

'Ireland's gone bust. I was laid off from the hospital where I worked.'

'Jeez, isn't that everyone's story now?' Jimmy rumbles into his beer.

No more questions, I breathe. A drop of whiskey from my glass glides along my finger, tracing the lines of my palm. I had walked out of the Mater hospital the day they gave me my official notice and over to the bar, ordered a tot, knocked it back. My mobile had buzzed. I'd looked at it, ordered another; but the barman must have misheard me and brought me a gin. I couldn't drink it; my hands were shaking too much. *Mother's ruin*, that's what it's called, isn't it? I left it on the bar. I walked down to the Royal Canal, looked at a pram half submerged in the murk. It couldn't be the usual shopping trolley could it, not that day of all days? My stomach had cramped hard, I'd had to turn away. Looked again at *his* text, 'Take care of yourself, Ash.' Take care of yourself. Was that it, after ten years? Four little words. And how perfectly timed; no job, no fiancé, no ... I hadn't been able to form the word in my mouth, those two precious tiny syllables. I'd leant against the rail on the bridge. A splash on the face of the phone. Another. The bitter wind pinched my fingers. Numb. Barely a ripple as my phone sank. Shite, I didn't feel it slip.

The smoke thickens into smog, men curse, dribble in their pints and slobber periodically over Angie. In a corner a card game seems to be getting out of hand and a scuffle breaks out. Glass splinters across the floor. Before I came here my dreams were of mystical figures riding stallions with silvery manes across the dunes. Through a window I just catch the last golden glow as the moon slides beneath the oiliness of the Bay.

two

I give in to the urge to steady myself, and lean against a cool white wall. It's forty degrees, even the two minute walk from the car to the building foyer has grilled me. Back home the September leaves will be flushed with a russet rash, and Grandaddy will be piling up the turf ready for the winter.

Only half awake yet, my head is sore from last night's welcome at Heather's and the day starts early here. My first day in my new job. Six o'clock and I'm inside a contorting Rubik's cube. My new office is an old marble palace, slightly dishevelled by the standards of the new, thrusting glass shard buildings being forged all over the city. Some time ago the palace became an apartment block and each floor was divided into a warren of flats, winding off long, dark corridors. Coming up in the lifts it is difficult to orient yourself. Each snap of the cube, each turn along a hallway, leads to a different endpoint.

Angie finds me and leads me into a huge office where Joe, my new office mate is sitting at one of the desks, tapping away at a computer, whilst simultaneously obsessively wiping the desk about him with a tissue. Joe looks like an angel fallen to earth and tumbled in a bush.

'Tea, tea?' A small, thin elderly Indian man with a broken toothy grin hurries in behind us.

'Miss Aisling, meet Abdullah, our tea boy. Would you like some tea? Any time you do, just ring this bell,' Joe says, pointing to a switch on the wall.

'You're joking me?'

'No, I'm not. Each flat has its own tea boy. Granted 'tea boy' doesn't seem quite the right description for Abdullah, he must be ninety.'

'I'm really not sure that I can ring a bell and expect someone to come running to bring me tea, it seems so ...'

'Coffee?' By now Abdullah who had shuffled out of the office during this exchange has returned with a small, piping hot glass of a murky, sludge-yellow liquid. He offers it to me, 'Marhabaan bik.'

'Oh, thank you, shukran, but I don't drink coffee.' He hands me the coffee anyway.

'You'll have to get to like it. You'll be drinking at least a dozen cups of this a day,' says Joe.

'Everyone you meet with will insist you drink a cup and won't start a meeting until you do. It's all about the hospitality.'

I try to sip, but it is nuclear hot. The taste is not unpleasant, slightly nutty, and maybe menthol even. It catches at the back of the throat, quite unlike anything I have tasted before.

'*Yanni*, there you are. Miss Aisling Finn?' I start at the sharp, strangely mottled French, Arabic, trans-Atlantic accent. 'Jez, mad Mozah, that's all you need' Angie mutters. Two fully veiled women and a tall, droopy looking man in a long white thawb enter the office. They move like eels. Behind them slinks a woman with an insolent air. She is chewing gum; her pneumatic figure just about restrained by a tight vest top and ripped jeans, all barely hidden by her flapping open abaya. Joe's face flashes boiled sweet cerise as he scrubs intently at his desk, eyes down. She pouts her fulsome lips, leans against Joe's desk, her tamarind eyes spiking, 'You are quiet today Mr Joe, no kiss for Miss Mozah?' Joe mumbles something, grabs a file from his desk and shoots out the office, tripping over his own feet. Mozah laughs after him, 'Live, there is only one life.'

Angie coughs her disapproval. Mozah flicks her a look and turns to me, 'Shufi, Miss Aisling, you need to come with us for official processing.'

'I've done all that, haven't I?' I soothe the indigo bruises, still darkening on my arm. Joe and Angie laugh.

'You'll learn.'

☪

Five hours later and I'm faint from thirst. Mozah has pulled me from one office to another. She does not think twice about personal space; no civil requests to follow, move here, sit there please. I am just manhandled expertly into place. Cameras flash in my eyes for my Resident's Permit, my staff ID, this record, that record. A couple of spivs from the government bank sidle up, dressed in Mafiosi suits, gold chains and dark shades. I know the procedure now, just sign. I do. One hands me a card, 'Miss Finn, if you need anything, just call me. Any time, really any time. Even at midnight. Yes, call me at midnight. I will come to you then.' Mozah snatches the card from my hand and throws it in the bin.

'Your business here is finished.'

'Ah now Mozah, you are not so shy in Beirut. Let's party tonight.'

'In your dreams,'

'Always, baby, always.'

Mozah has pushed me to the door during this exchange. One prod and we are in the corridor. She turns, letting the hood of her abaya slip and tossing her purple streaked curls. The look over her shoulder to the spivs is long enough.

'See you at the Celestine, *chéri*,' one calls after us. Mozah whistles low under her breath for a second.

'*Hallas*, enough for today. I will call you a driver to take you back to your hotel.' She arranges the driver and leaves me waiting in the foyer. She has made no attempt to hide her irritation at having to babysit me all day and is eager to be done with me, and elsewhere. As she walks away her mobile rings, she ignores my thanks and goodbye. It's home time and I watch as streams of fully veiled women, like black magnolia buds, leave the building and find their drivers, all in white Land Cruisers. The pick-up area is tight and countless spats take place as cars scrape each other and the women scream and slap at their Indian drivers. How will I spot my driver in this pixelating scene? My eyes blur. I need water. Mozah's voice pierces above the din. She is biting her words and jabbing at some unseen foe. She flings her phone in her tote bag and turns back to me.

'La, la, Miss Aisling, you look sad. *Yanni*, sweetie, no need. You miss your home. Come, let's go shopping.' She tweaks my cheek and blows a gum bubble.

Long hours of shoe shopping in the ice-cold mall follow, trying on impossible teetering stilettos, adorned with diamante bows and ankle fringes. Several maids drag around after us, carrying Mozah's ever-increasing number of bags. Mozah does not take a breath, 'Those girls in the Professor's office, you know what they do all day? *Mafi, mafi.* That one, Fatima, she's always late, says her baby is sick. Pah! She's lazy. She stays in the mall late, late at night. Shopping, always shopping. I speak Arabic, English, and French. I have a certificate from the American International Global College of Commerce, Kansas. *Yanni*, tell me, why does the Professor not take me in his office? You think I would be a better secretary for him, *yanni*?'

My ears bleed. We stop for mint lemonade at a cafe; it is so sweet my teeth pinch. Mozah wraps her long fingers around my wrist, 'Miss Aisling, you move out from your hotel this week? You cannot live alone in this country. It's not proper. In Beirut, New York, Paris, yes, I can live with my girlfriends in a condo, but here I must live with my family. You will be my sister. Come, I have room in my villa and you'll have your own maid. The Prof will be very happy. I will look after you for him.'

More than my teeth pinch.

After the café, we go to the Electric Souk in search of an illegal mobile phone trader. Mozah insisted we come here to get me a mobile, although the Board is meant to be supplying one. 'La, la, no one will give you a mobile, they are playing with you only. Fill this form, fill that form, your phone come tomorrow, then tomorrow, then next week. *Inshallah*.' Mozah explains that we need to get my phone in the souk as none of the mobile shops will sell expats a SIM card without official paperwork and CID clearance.

I imagined the souk would be a warren of alleys, where merchants in red fez would proffer trays of tarnishing silver trinkets and I would glimpse dark, kohl eyes through an upper floor lattice window. I want to hear a drum or a lute. Instead, the Electric Souk is a vast warehouse, packed with a central ring of corrugated iron booths, where traders sell every kind of hand-sized gadget, from electric toothbrushes to mini DVD players. Young boys in thawbs jump around these booths, arguing over the merits of each beeping, flashing must-have device. The outer ring of the warehouse accommodates boxy shops, piled high with white goods, wrapped and bound in strips of plastic. The men stand about the shops, rubbing their beards, chewing *khat* together and occasionally directing a clip about an ear to a particularly bouncy youngster.

'That's our beloved *Maleka*'s - the Queen's - private hospital.' Mozah points through the doorway to a shiny building across the road. 'She's a great business woman. She's going to open some community clinics next, private, *yanni*.'

'Really, you sure? Hasn't His Highness declared that all the community clinics should be free to everyone, no need for private health care anymore?' This is why I am here after all, to work on His Highness's great healthcare reforms. Mozah smiles, 'There will never be any free clinics, watch.' She taps a finger to her right eye.

'*Shufi*, here's Raschid.' Mozah sweeps us to a dull corner, where a wily looking man with a heavy satchel is shifting from foot to foot, half-hidden behind a stack of microwave ovens. 'Raschid, *Salaam-Alaikum*,' Mozah greets him with a flourish of jangling arms, heavy with gold bangles.

He returns the greeting with a mumble, and a scowl, '*Alaikum Salaam*.'

'*Kaifa haluka?*'

'*Alhamdulillah*.' The greeting over and the mobile phone flutters from Raschid's hands to Mozah's, 'SIM, you stupid man, we need a SIM,' Mozah demands. Raschid mumbles something.

'What's he saying?'

'Oh *mafi miscallah*, nothing.'

'He doesn't look too happy about this.'

'He's never happy, he's from Syria, no visa.'

Raschid is looking at me in a way that makes my skin prickle; I turn my back to him. Mozah continues talking. 'He wants more money for the SIM, and he should know to just give me it, no arguments, I work for the Government.' The SIM card is handed over for the agreed sum. Raschid hands some papers to Mozah to sign, more mumbling.

Mozah flares, '*Akh Fariq*.' She slaps her hands together, in opposite directions as if brushing dust from them. Raschid spits.

'*Akh Fariq*? What's that mean?'

'La, la, no, you must never use that name. No, forget you heard it. Come, we go look for some bags now.'

I look back to see Raschid scuttle out the souk and immediately into a black Hummer pulling up fast, windows dark.

three

A croaking wail shakes me from my sleep, the call to prayer. I look out of my high-rise hotel window across the endless landscape of shimmering sugar cube buildings to the dawn. I curl up in the window seat, lean my head against the slowly warming glass pane and listen, a cry from down the centuries. I'm used to the call of the ocean, where the grey seas course through my blood and sea kelp wraps around my dreams. A dull ache in my stomach. These first days have not been what I expected, although what that was I'm not sure now. Everything is back to front. Day is night and night is day. In this new world, the cursor moves from right to left. Books start from the back. I pick up my glass with my right and not my left hand, as that's an insult. Everyone sleeps during the searing mid-afternoon heat and then goes out at midnight to eat on the cooling grass beside the Bay. As for the joys of trying to get bullet points to align to the left of a page rather than the right, there's no saint to pray to for intercession on that one.

I won't be able to rest my aching head against this glass for much longer, and it's time to head to the office anyway. The heat is already burning through as rose infuses the sky, dissolving away the night lilac. Just time to Skype Grandaddy before I go to work, and before he goes off to fetch his morning paper and flirt with Siobhan in the village shop. I gave him a lesson before I left and wrote down instructions in his notepad, where he records the odds on the horses.

The Skype ring tone repeats a few times. 'Aisling? Is that you?'

'Hiya, Grandaddy'

'Can you hear me Aisling? I can hear you.'

'Yes.'

'Can you hear me? I can hear you.'

'Switch the video on Grandaddy.'

'Ah, there's you'se. I can see you. It's a mighty looking room you're in there.'

'Grandaddy switch on the video. I can't see you.'

'Can you hear me? I can hear you.'

'The video button.'

'Feck.'

We try five times, each the same script. The last has rather more fecks.

At work, it's as frustrating as trying to Skype Grandaddy. No clues. Nothing is written, no reference papers, records or reports. I've been here a week now, searching. My desk and filing cabinet are bare. Joe is no real help as he is responsible for finance and can share with me unintelligible spreadsheets about the budget and pay roll, but nothing else. Anyway, he is far too busy tying handkerchiefs about his mouth in his latest germ offensive.

Oud, ancient fragrances long forgotten in the West, damask rose and musky amber drifts in the dark corridors. Other than Mozah, the women who work here are completely veiled; you can't even see their eyes. Not seeing someone's face and eyes makes you feel blind; even though your eyes look, they see nothing. The men are tall and swaying, in their long white thawbs. They do not look at me, but bow away when they speak. All around me people talk in a lullaby language, words repeated over and over: *yanni, wallah, yallah, habibi, inshallah, Alhamdulillah.*

'Well now Ash. I can call you Ash, can't I?' Tony Morton, the office administrator comes in, drawling in his Texan way, his tongue slipping like a rattlesnake. Before I can decline this familiarity he slithers on, 'You just have to remember one thing in the desert, all rightee. You can't trust nobody, especially A..rabs. They watch behind them veils, there's eyes everywhere. You can't go nowheres before they know down in the *Black Box*.'

I look to Joe, I have no idea what Tony is talking about. 'It's what us expats call the HQ of the secret police. You must've seen the black glass box out by the Bay?'

'They all work for them, Ash.'

I am called to the Prof's office.

'Remember that, Ash, all of them.'

☾

'Miss Aisling, here is some correspondence. Please, write the replies.' I am a speck at the far side of a lake of glass, the Prof sits across from me. He skims some paper work over the table. The door is wide open and our conversation taking place under the vigilant eyes of Yusuf, the Prof's office manager and three of his cronies, all sipping coffee, the tiny glasses doll-like in their meaty hands. It is my first meeting with the Prof since I arrived. I am eager to see him again. Back in Dublin, the Prof had approached me in the Mater hospital canteen one lunchtime. I was reading. He sat down beside me, recited a Heaney poem.

'Professor, where are you from?'

'Miss Aisling, I was born in a book.'

That got my full attention. He laughed, poetic exaggeration was all part of the Arabic sense of humour he warned. The Prof told me what he meant was that from just the age of three he was sent overseas and educated in English boarding schools, where he was weaned with tidbits of Narnia. His next chapters were a scholastic grand tour of the universities of Europe. He lectured on an eclectic range of interests, neurology to Persian poetry. Throughout the time he was at the Mater, we would go to poetry readings at Trinity and plays at The Gate. We knew each other through the books we loved. We both adored Seamus Heaney, and sometimes we would bump into him walking his little dog along the Sandymount Strand. He would give us a quick nod. Our talk was always of verse and very little else. It was a relief to us both from the daily toil, we did not want to litter it with the everyday.

The everyday knows how to shut fast a book though. About a year ago, His Highness called the Prof home to head-up his health reforms. This was a great honour that could not be refused.

I look at the sheaf of dots and slashes, 'What are these letters about Professor?'

'Complaints that the water is making people's hair fall out.'

'Is that true?' I fidget at my long, straggly curls.

'*Wallah*, of course not. These expat housewives have nothing better to do than worry themselves sick that everything here is killing them, except all the G&Ts they drink each day.'

I slump. I haven't come all this way, surely, to be writing placatory letters to housewives in the desert? Before I can even comment, let alone protest, the Prof has stood up and crossed to a pile of folders, the first I've seen here. He pulls one out, 'Please, read these too. Your first major assignment is the publicity campaign for our new free community health clinics.'

'Professor, I am confused, shouldn't the hospital be running the clinics?' The Prof drops his voice a little, peering over his chic frameless glasses.

'Strictly speaking, it should be the responsibility of the hospital, but those fools over there cannot be trusted with a Band-Aid, let alone with a new multi-million dollar health clinic service. His Highness has given personal instruction that the Board is to retain the budget and run the new clinics.' He continues to speak in a low voice. 'His Highness is wounded. He is famous as a great humanitarian and moderniser. But now, the WHO has published a damning, truly damning, report ranking the health of our people amongst the worst in the developed world.'

'And so, these reforms?'

'*Alhamdulillah.* His Highness has consulted with the best advisors in the world, and decided to break the control of the hospital by setting up free community clinics around the country.'

'I see.'

'We need to get this right, Miss Aisling. If this goes wrong and the hospital rebuilds its powers it will set us back years. There's great opposition from the traditionalists, and any mistakes will play into the hands of the Treasury.'

I am conscious that the clinking of coffee cups from the ante-office beyond has ceased.

'Take your time, Miss Aisling, this is my advice to all newcomers here. Our world has a different clock, not Western time with its seconds and minutes. Always tick, tick, tick. Our time is without end. If you try too hard, if you push, you will fail.'

C•

'Angie, my head is a mess! What am I doing here?' We walk across the foyer of a beautiful, luxurious hotel; the pink-veined marble-sorbet slicks beneath our feet.

'Writing billet doux to the sunny mummies by the sounds of it, telling 'em to drink more gin. They'll love ya! No, I'm kiddin you'se. Ash, there's a real job to be done 'ere. That WHO report seriously pissed off His Highness. The day he got it, he went straight over to the hospital. By rights, he'd only go there for official receptions and stuff, see the nice, sparklin' bit they wanted 'im to see. Cut a ribbon, you know, you do PR.'

Angie catches a glance of herself in a mirror in the corridor, plucks at a stray stand of hair, blows herself a kiss, and continues.'Saw it for 'imself that day. Went right into A&E, just like any of us. Saw the queues, the fights in pharmacy to get even basic meds. As for the wards … it's deliberate ya know. They're money grabbing bollocks them doctors, you got a give them a 'gift' for everything. Give 'em a big enough gift and you'll skip the queues and go straight to their private list.'

We descend a staircase into darkness and smog.

'Nothing a voddie won't cure though, babe.'

A motley long line of men slouch under a neon sign, '*Shenanigans*'. We walk past and straight into a lime green Irish bar, complete with sepia scenes of the Easter Rising, Guinness toucans and rusty farming implements hanging from the gloopy ceiling.

Angie is quickly crowded, lots of men clamouring to buy her drinks. I look twice as I see local men, not in their traditional thawbs, but incognito in Western dress, still unmistakable. The rest are sweaty expats. Except for one extraordinary individual, he has modelled himself on Hercule Poriot, pint-sized, a greasy quiff and moustache, and a long stick nose. He is dapper in an Edwardian cream and baby blue striped blazer, canary yellow cravat and massive diamond encrusted Rolex. He takes a fancy to Angie and keeps bringing her shots, draping his arms around her shoulders.

'She's one heck of a gal,' observes a rig worker, squashed up alongside me on the bench. 'Enjoys the craic, eh?'

I squeeze myself into a slither, so there's an inch of bench between us.

'Mm.' Angie is managing to accept three drinks from three different men simultaneously.

'What about you? Are you up for a bit of fun like your friend?' The rig worker gives me a wink and rubs a clammy hand on my thigh. I knock it off.

A roar goes up about the bar, men swarm towards the door. I stretch to see. Severe looking women with death eyes and synthetic pouts, wearing off-the-shoulder leather mini dresses and white spiky shoes make their way to the dance floor. Lots of money is being exchanged, as fast as magic card tricks, notes disappearing before our eyes. My eyes smart from the smoke.

'Ere, let me top you up.' Angie is sloshing a bottle of wine around. She flops down next to me, pushing the rig worker away. 'So the Prof seemed odd, distant you say? It 'appens to everyone. Maybe it's the heat or the frustration of trying to get anythink done. Must be even worse if you're a local who got out and has been dragged back.' A grizzled hand, clutching a shot glass, jabs between us. Angie snatches the glass and knocks back the contents. 'When he first come 'ere he would invite us to his villa, do the whole Arabic hospitality thing.' The hand is tugging at Angie's dress strap. 'Hasn't mad Mozah told ya? You ain't the first. I was accused of being his bit of stuff.' Angie snorts, 'Even got in the local rag. You have to be careful, seriously, these people, they've nothing better to do than to gossip about each other and even more about us. There's no *Hello* magazine. We're it; we're the local celebrities. If the Prof's cold, that's just him protecting you'se and him.'

Five northern lads, who can barely stand, writhe onto the karaoke stage in the corner. Calling themselves the Spice Boys, they hammer out a woeful version of 'Spice up your life'. Angie weaves onto the dance floor, and swings about it with Hercule. Mercifully, the Spices disband when Ginger topples off the stage.

Angie returns, whooping. 'Babe, you just have to have some fun. None of us know how long we're 'ere for, a week, a month or a lifetime. What does the Prof say? "You must remember you are only here as a guest, a privileged guest." Come on, let's dance. They can throw ya out any minute.'

four

Click, click, click, click and a sharp rap at the office door. 'Good afternoon, Miss Aisling. It is Aisling isn't it?' A deep, rich South African voice draws me to look up from my notepad, where I am scrawling ideas for a new logo for the health clinics.

'Mm, pretty,' says the stranger.

'Oh go on, it's terrible. Please don't look, it's a long way from ready.' I shield my scribbling.

'I wasn't referring to your drawing,' the stranger smiles, big white teeth.

'Nice, slick!' Joe bounces up from his desk. 'Hey, good to see you Brian. Where've you been?'

Joe claps Brian on the shoulder, and he promptly mock punches him back in the stomach. Then, he saunters over to my desk, and perches himself on its edge, as if it's his.

'Jo'burg, business trip mate, just back this morning.'

'Cool, you must be whacked man. Heard about the latest caper? The Treasury has just slashed our budget and they won't transfer us any money until the New Year.'

'For real?'

'Sure thing. Price of oil has dropped to seventy-five dollars a barrel. It's getting tight. Been to see your guys in payroll yet? Mayhem. The bank slip for this month's salaries should've been signed this morning, but there's literally not a coin left. I'm off now, going to get a coffee on the way home, want to join me?'

'Sorry Joe, I've a couple of things to finish here first,' I say.

'Yah, same, mate.'

Joe heads out on his daily pilgrimage to Starbucks for his fix. Brian stays, holds out his hand to me.

'I'm Brian Rothmann, thought I'd hunt you out as soon as I got back today. I've been really looking forward to meeting you, girl. The Prof speaks so highly of you.'

I can feel myself flush under his exact gaze. He is tall and muscular, lithe. Something of a military bearing, he stands so poker straight. His suit is clearly designer, sharp. A neat beard and crew cut. He holds my hand just a moment longer than usual, his is hirsute. I shiver slightly, deep inside, and retrieve my hand.

'We're going to be working together, closely.' He pauses with intent.

'Ah, so you must be from Rex Consulting. I got emails from the Prof yesterday, briefing me about your assignment,' I reply.

I don't add that within minutes of receiving the Prof's email I had Tony Morton, also a recipient of the email, in the office, giving me his 'unbiased advice' about how best to handle Rex Consulting. 'Y'all see Ash, I'm the kinda guy who likes to call a spade a spade, and there's something too darn polished about these guys from Rex.' Tony told me that Rex Consulting, a South African outfit, were brought into the Board about four months earlier to give support in putting some of the basic business processes in place, including sorting out the payroll, HR and administrative departments. But their remit keeps creeping and they are now managing a wide range of critical projects. 'There's trouble ahead, mark my words. The locals don't like having Westerners 'snooping' about, as they see it.' Tony rubbed his hands in gleeful anticipation.

'How are you liking it so far? When did you get here?'

'A month today.'

Brian smiles, 'Rather a change of scene for you, I would think? I was stationed for a time in Northern Ireland. Whereabouts are you from?'

'You won't know, a small village on the Atlantic coast.'

'You'd be surprised what I know, girl. Travelled about on R and R. That coastline must be one of the most stunning in the world, so ...'

'Stormy.'

'Wild, free, couldn't be more different to here. The desert conquered. A city in the scrub, it doesn't seem real somehow.' Brian sweeps his arm towards the window and beyond to the hazy line of skyscrapers.

'Ireland's hung-over. Big time. Grey skies, grey people, grey times. That's why I came, for something different.'

'Yah, we're all here for an adventure of one sort or another.' Brian sits on the edge of my desk again, smoothing his hand over his commando scalp. 'Let's have one now, celebrate surviving your first month in this crazy place. Come and try out a speedboat?'

'A speedboat? Really?'

'Really! We can hire one at the marina for the afternoon.'

'Grand! I'd love to, when?'

'Now girl, *yallah*, as they say.'

'My work…'

'It can wait, can't it? *Inshallah*.'

He grabs my bag, and my hand. Am I mad? Thinking of going

off with a virtual stranger? But the rules are different here; caution suspended in favour of exhilaration, or you may as well stay home. Dare.

'Ok, *inshallah*,' I laugh.

He leads me out of the office to his convertible sports car parked out front, opens the door for me to slide in. 'Now, let's arrive in the style you deserve, like a princess.' We roar away, sweeping down the highroad and around the Bay to the marina.

☾

Brian's arm is firmly around me as he lifts me into a speedboat.

'You're driving this?' I ask, as he turns the key in the ignition.

'Of course.'

I learn once we reach a small island out in the Bay, that whilst in the military he learnt to drive and fly all manner of vehicles, on land, sea and air. A real action hero.

Ping. Ping. 'You are drinking champagne! On the beach? You know how to live life - dangerously!' My phone sizzles with white-hot texts from Angie.

'From an Evian bottle, of course.' I text back. It is so surreal, sitting on a deserted scratchy little island, just one lone tree left, beaten by the sand storms. The city is a glowing streak across the Bay.

Ping. Ping. 'So has he snogged you yet?'

I text quickly as Brian chases after his cap, which has blown along the beach. 'No, he is the perfect gentleman.'

Ping. Ping. 'Ha! Give it ten minutes.'

We sit on a rug, me sipping illicit champagne. 'So where next, girl? Where am I to follow in your wake?' Brian smiles. It turns out we have been criss-crossing each other's tracks for years, as

Brian was stationed on military duty in Europe and I spent my summer holidays drifting around Europe's medieval alleyways and galleries. I missed him by days when I sat on the grass beside the Sacre Cour, looking out over the speckled tiles of Montmartre two summers back. In Budapest he knows the same café in the park where I used to read, shaded by the plane trees. And in Prague, we work it out, we must have been drinking absinthe in the American Bar right at the same moment, sheltering from a summer shower. I feel as if I've known him all my life.

'That absinthe bit my throat,' I laugh. He places a finger in the hollow in my throat.

'Right here? Me too. But I still wanted more. I always do.'

I flush and stammer, 'I guess now is the time to explore beyond Europe.'

'Cross the Bosporus and into the East...' Brian scratches out a rudimentary map of the Middle East in the hot sand.

'This is such a brilliant opportunity. I'm not sure where to start though.' I point to various spots on his sandy map and tell him there are so many places I would love to see, the souks of Damascus, Beirut's boulevards, Omani wadis, Saladin's castle, the frankincense trail. My fingers are caked with dust. Brian takes my hand and brushes away the dirt as he says,

'I know just the place to start.'

'Where?'

'Ah, you'll have to wait and see.' He hums, Sting. I sing about rain, the desert.

He claps, 'Your voice is so pure.' Then he lies back on the rug, his arms bent behind his head. I admire his long frame discreetly from beneath my lashes, not quite believing I am alone with this man, in a place where it feels like the end of the earth.

Can this man be real? He's cultured, well-travelled and

articulate. Not like the grunting country lads back home. Deep inside me a little voice is saying this is all too good to be true, but I'm letting the champagne fizzle away that tiny nag. No wedding ring, not that that signifies anything. Too charming? For sure, I'm more than used to Irish blather, and have been out with men who could call the blackbirds out of the trees, but only to turn them into a gory pie, along with my heart. My heart, those shreds, can they be stitched back together? Can I forget all the rules and rosaries here? Go with the flow, as Angie urges, 'Babe, it's the expat mantra.' Aisling, wake up. Don't be stupid, again. I pinch myself, mentally.

'Here, let me have one quick swig of that champagne, and we'll toast new ventures.' I hand him the Evian bottle and he takes a small sip, raising the bottle aloft. 'I've earned my first million or so Rand. A new challenge. Here's to my first million riyals, girl.'

After the romance and singing I am taken aback by this sudden boast. 'How many countries do you operate in then?'

'South Africa, of course. Rex Consulting is one of the largest independent consultancies there, although I've just passed it onto my accountants to manage so I can maximise my efforts here. China, I have a worldwide entertainments and ticketing operation based in Shanghai, India and now here.' He explains that his business in India is something to do with logistics and Craig, his business partner, is heading up that. He is concentrating on the new markets opening in the Gulf.

'It's all for the taking, girl. They're amateurs. Goodnight London and New York. Those places are over. It's China, India, the Middle East, yah. These are the new empires. A roaring future and I'm roaring with it.' He punches the air with the water bottle. Can I really be sitting on a beach with a multi-millionaire? Scratch farmers and civil servants, with just their beer money in their pockets, that's all I know. 'You're a God-send to me Aisling. You know this is the first afternoon I've taken off in six months, but then I haven't really had much of an excuse until today.' He hands me back the Evian bottle, and brushes a stray frond of hair from my face. The wind is getting up.

'I'm amazed you are still sane, Brian. Angie, do you know her? She says that you have to go out every night and take a holiday, break out, every eight weeks, to not go crazy here.'

Brian laughs, 'No, I don't know her well, but from what I hear about her, that sounds about right. You have to be a ball-breaker to come out here. I certainly haven't met any women who aren't. They all scare the shit out of me to be honest.' He kicks the empty Evian bottle into the sea. 'Not going to find my soul mate here, I don't think.' We watch the bottle bob. 'Didn't think.' He says it so softly. Did I hear that? Or was it just the breeze?

I am punch drunk at the confidence of this man and the speed of all this. At home you can spend months mooning over a guy on the other side of Bewley's before you so much as ask him the time, and then he won't look up as he tells you it's half past three.

'But you don't strike me as being a ball-breaker, you're special Aisling, a desert rose indeed.'

'Well, you're not like most of the expat men I've met here either.'

'Now, don't you go calling me a desert rose, wouldn't be good for the manly image.' He holds up an athletic arm and flexes his bicep as we laugh, 'No, I can imagine. They're a rather Neanderthal breed. I assume you've been to Heather's with Angie. But I can't see that should worry you, I'm sure there must be some handsome devil of a boyfriend coming out here to claim you soon. I wouldn't leave you out here alone for long.'

I look down, I am always startled when someone imagines I have a boyfriend, husband, certain that the tattoo of the solitary must be so inked on me, a dark heart. 'No, not at all. I'm here alone,' I pause, 'And you?'

'There's no one here with me.' One, long second passes. 'Come on,' he says, 'The sun will drop soon. I can't get over how quickly it turns to night here.' Me neither, I'm so used to the long, angelic evenings of the Atlantic. He swings me up into the launch again. We bump and skid back over the waves, the wind tearing through my hair. Brian grips the wheel.

five

Now it's all real. While I was in the hotel it was like being on holiday. I start my second month finally in my apartment. It's a dusty box; dark, as I have to keep the blinds closed to stop the migrant workers in the scruffy block opposite gaping in. At least the washing machine sings at the end of its cycle, 'Popeye, the sailorman'. Mozah is utterly dismayed that I have moved into this apartment. She's been relentless over the past fortnight, and she almost wore me down. But I know it would only provoke all sorts of jealousies at work if I moved in with her. Part of me was a little tempted, I would love to live with a local family and see their world; and there is truth in what Mozah says about the importance of being with family. I'm even missing Grandaddy and his 'feckin wandering teeth', which always turn up in the strangest place and at the wrong time, once in the font at St. John's. Mozah heard a couple days ago that the paperwork authorising my apartment had come through and tried to intercept it. This caused grand ructions with Tony Morton, and after a forty-five minute screaming fit she raged out of the office with a headache and has not come back yet. In this time, delicately, I escaped.

The apartment block, Bella Villa, is in one of the older parts of the city called Al Hamsa, these days home mainly to refugees of past regional conflicts. Joe says to live here you have to speak 'Google', just repeat key phrases over and over, as there are no street names or landmarks and taxi drivers can't find it. This part of the city, although forgotten, is shabby chic with an eclectic mix of cafes, patisseries, juice bars, a bookstore, dilapidated cinema, even a pizzeria. There's a whole street of wedding dress stores, the frills completely out-do the cream puffs in the patisseries. Behind the shops is a maze of small streets with traditional villas and surprising green gardens, hidden behind high dusty walls. I wander these quiet streets with their fractured pavements at dawn before the heat, peeking behind the grilled gates to the luscious courtyards of palm trees and blazing pink bougainvillea.

Al Hamsa is ear marked for demolition, and is becoming tattier by the day. As buildings are vacated, migrants from the Indian sub-continent take up residence, despite there being no working facilities. Their mercenary landlords crowd these buildings with twenty people to a room. Nothing stands here for more than ten years and soon more of the metallic and glass towers will crunch over this aging, charming quarter of the city. My apartment block is one of the first in this unyielding march of modernity. Next door is a building site where another block is going up and around the corner is a vast field of rubble, which no doubt will soon be re-developed. It is hellishly noisy. Air hammers pound. I don't think there's refuge from that anywhere, this desert is fast becoming one large construction site. Everyone tells me you get so used to the noise you forget it. I'm not so sure, my ears are marine; hushed by waves all my life.

Knocking; Mozah is at the door now in studded and spiked drag queen platforms. She towers, 'Tsk, tsk, Miss Aisling, how can you live like this? You are a crazy woman living here alone. The Professor cannot know this, he wouldn't let you live here. Come now, live with me. The Professor will be happy and then I can work in his office.' The quid pro quo, I'm learning there's always one here.

'Hello, I'm Tomas, and this is my wife Salima.' Behind Mozah, Tomas is a tall greying man, dragging an over-sized suitcase. Swedish, maybe, I think from his accent. He looks weary. Salima is of Arabic descent, thin, with dark circles under her dull eyes, and her hair covered by a long scarf that she tugs at. She ignores my greeting. She is grappling with a squally baby. Mozah points to the apartment opposite, 'They're staying here until their villa is ready. *Inshallah.*' Several of the expats from work are homed in Bella Villa. Joe is upstairs. I'm used to bowling into people I know on every corner in Dublin, but bumping into colleagues on every staircase is a new strangulation. Mozah takes Salima across to the apartment.

Tomas hangs back a minute, 'I'm sorry; Salima is finding it hard. We only arrived yesterday. It's still all a shock. She thinks the women are giving her looks because she isn't wearing an *abaya*. Today she decided to cover her hair. I wonder if we have made a mistake coming here?'

☾

Tomas' baby screams all afternoon. Her furious wail cracks into every corner of the apartment block. My head pulses in the muggy heat. As the sun falls, Angie calls by and insists I go to Heather's with her. I am glad to go, even though the grungy concrete box putrid with cigarette smoke doesn't hold much Arabian charm. Angie is perturbed to find that she has a rival for the role of Queen

Bee tonight. A modern day Salome is gyrating on the dance floor, a ring of men about her, their tongues hanging loose, ravenous. Her eyes are closed to them beneath heavy kohl. One arm is reaching up above her, its hand siren, twisting and turning. Her hips roll, setting off a thousand flashing darts from the diamante belt slashed across a black silk sheath dress, split to the thigh.

'Mozah?'

'Mad cow. She'd better hope there's no secret police in tonight.'

'What's she doing here?'

'She likes to think she's just like us, an expat. Doesn't like to admit she's an Arab. She pushes it all the time. You've seen how she dresses at work. The rules are the Arab staff 'ave to wear the local getup. She's spent most of her life abroad, so in a way she's right. Her family are Lebanese, some sort of dodgy background, ya' know, Hamas or one of those. Had to leave, went to Europe somewhere and then the States.' Angie knocks back a shot. 'Watch out for the Lebanese girls. They're maniacs. You should see how they drive!'

Angie grabs the nearest drunk and pulls him onto the floor, 'Let's show her how it's done.' They knock about the floor, forcing Mozah to the sidelines. She spots me and comes over, bringing with her a man, reeling at a sixty-five degree angle. 'Miss Aisling, you're here. *Mumtaz*. Please, let me introduce Mr Will.' She nudges her companion towards me and then moves on towards the bar.

'I'm the biggest Willie in the desert,' he slurps in my ear.

In drunken guzzles, he tells me he is on the run from his wife and an acrimonious divorce.

'Mind that one,' Angie warns, 'He makes Casanova look like the Milky Bar kid.'

But Mozah eggs him on in his efforts, 'He's cute, Miss Aisling.' He's twenty years older than me, and has just procured two girls, his 'sweet and sour pork balls'. He is tickled with his own ingenuity at adding further colour to the Chinese takeaway parlance of his Heather's compatriots. Will is a high-ranking official in the British Embassy.

Will stumbles to one of the back rooms with his takeaway, and Mozah renews her assault. She brings over a lanky blonde called Frans, streaky bacon sunburnt, 'Frans, Miss Aisling. Isn't she the prettiest thing here?' Frans cannot focus. He reaches out a hand and grabs my waist, hard. I push him away.

'Frans!' Angie takes his arm and thrusts herself between me and him. 'Frans was just saying how pretty Miss Aisling is.' Angie looks as if she might take a swing at Mozah.

'I need a piss. Get me another pint, Ang,' Frans makes a well-timed exit. Angie turns to order at the bar.

'*Yanni*, shame. Frans needs someone his own age, not an old grannie.' Thankfully the bartender is shouting to Angie at this moment, clarifying her order and she misses Mozah's jibe.

'Mozah, really, I'm not looking for someone. I've had enough of men.'

'Had enough of men?' Angie did hear this. 'Kid, how can you ever have enough of men? And if you have, you've come to the wrong place. Ninety percent of the expats are men, hon.' Looking around me, I'm in the right place. My heart is safe here, without a doubt.

The football goes on the big screen and the men gather round it. I find myself caught in a cat spat between Angie and Mozah, one on either side of me, pawing, each hissing in my ear so the other can hear. 'You're my bessie new mate, Ash.'

'Miss Aisling, you mustn't give up. I'll find you another man, not Will, he is a fool. A husband, a Sheikh for you. We will be sisters.'

'These are my men, my pals, that tart has no right being 'ere.'

'It's past Miss Angie's bedtime. She should go home for her cocoa.'

I look deep into the pint of Guinness before me, seeking the secret ruby red ring in its depths. Brian didn't lunge at me, not like Will, Frans and these other apes at Heather's. No, pinch, pinch yourself Aisling; but desert rain worms away in my ear.

six

It's early the next morning. Knocking at the apartment door has woken me. I groan, who calls by at this time? There's never any peace here, always someone at the door, whatever time of day or night. I open the door, standing in a thin, white cotton nightdress, wiping sleep from my eyes and hangover fumes from my brain. I've had three hours sleep, maybe. 'Morning Miss Aisling, ah, you are not dressed yet?' Brian comes into the apartment,

'We're off on an adventure. I promised you one. Come on, get dressed. No, wait a minute, let me look at you.' His eyes are big, greedy.

'Pervert!' I am conscious of the transparency of my dress, and run off laughing to my bedroom.

☾

My first time out of the city and into the desert. All is grey, gritty but still … My toes tap, I smile, I wish I will catch a magic carpet in the corner of my eye. Brian will not reveal where we are going, but tells me we are looking for an unmarked slip road off the main southern highway, near a petrol station. These are not instructions that fill me with hope, but Brian exudes such assurance. As I sneak small looks at him sideways in the car I decide you'd trust him with everything, your life even. Somehow, I just feel at ease with this man.

Brian points to a road sign with a camel on it. 'Jamels' I cry out, genuinely thrilled.

'Jamels, yah. Is that your first Arabic word Miss Aisling?'

'Yes, I adore camels. There's something so haughty and old maid like about their beauty, but they also look like they could have been hell-raisers in their youth, that knowing look.'

'It's the eye lashes that does it for me.' Brian turns off the slip road and onto a track. 'This looks right.'

'How can you tell?'

Ten minutes down the road and flickering through the dust, a dark spot starts to form. Beetle. Its edges hardening as it approaches. An armoured vehicle. The guard, wearing dark glasses, waves us to stop. Brian slips a signet ring off his little finger and hands it to me, 'Stay here, put this on, say nothing, only smile.' I draw the ring on and a red shawl over my hair. The guard has a large stick and an even larger gun in his holster and of course, the obligatory official swagger. He is not smiling. I watch as Brian shakes hands with him, both placing their right hands over their hearts. But then the man immediately places his hands on his hips, the courtesies over. Brian and the man talk in an animated fashion for a few minutes. The guard's voice gets louder and he is pointing furiously, his face, hariza-red. He steps away from Brian and turns as if about to come over to our car. He raises his sunglasses for a second and glares at me. I breathe tightly.

Brian pats him on the shoulder and fishes out some papers from his trouser pocket. The guard stands still, reading the papers for what seems an age, but is only a minute. He looks up at Brian and takes a step back and bows slightly. He turns to our car and smiles to me. I smile back, wanly. He marches back to his vehicle and takes out a small box and comes over to me. Dust kicks up about his ankles. I open the window and he hands me the basket.

'*Salaam-Alaikum*.' I reply, '*Alaikum Salaam*.'

'Please, Mrs Rothmann, it's hot, have some cola and fruit.'

In the box are three cans and some grapes. I smile and thank him. He returns to Brian, pulls out a pen and starts to draw on a piece of notepaper. I take some grapes and look at the ring on my finger again. Mrs Rothmann. I smile, it surprises me, but I like the sound of it. I catch myself, am I going mad? The heat …

Brian is back in the car. '*Alhamdulillah*, it's roasting out there already, wifey.'

'What was the problem?'

'It's all fine, yah. We are on His Highness' land, a restricted area.'

We drive on. Last night catches up with me, and the monotony of the grey landscape lulls me to sleep. I wake as we pull up to a crescent of parked jeeps. Beyond them, towards a rocky hillock is a cluster of men, white teeth at the jaw of the rock. One has an arm out-stretched. We jump out of the car and head towards them, as we do a shot of gold swoops down to the man with his arm raised.

'A falcon!'

'Magnificent, isn't it? Come on, let's hunt.' Brian marches ahead, greets the men and introduces me.

'*Saleem Alaikum*, Miss Aisling, would you like to hold the bird?' The man with the falcon steps towards me. He hands me a leather gauntlet, while another man pops the little leather hood over the bird's head. The bird bobs elegantly from the man's wrist to mine, one leg ringed. It is beautiful, flecked with the colours of the desert dawn. Its head flicks back and forth, it is primed for the chase. I feel its tension.

'Now, let's see this princess fly. Miss Aisling, hold out your arm like this.' I copy my instructor. He removes the bird's hood. A bright eye fixes on me. The bird's chest is taut.

'Do this.' I roll my wrist as shown and with a screech the bird is soaring. Within seconds, it's just a black dot against the white sky.

The men peer through binoculars, seeking out the dot, teasing each other about from which direction it will return. What will the bird bring? Will it return with or without its prize? The bird's owner boasts it never returns without a gift, 'She's the most generous of princesses, praise Allah.'

'Miss Aisling, quick, hold out your arm.'

A flash of golden red and my wrist bounces as the bird lands, squashing a bloodied rodent to the leather of the glove. The men whoop in delight, while the bird rips at the warm flesh. Acid rises in my throat. A speck of blood catches my cheek as the bird wrestles the corpse on my wrist.

'Well done, Miss Aisling.' Brian congratulates me.

'I think I need some water.' I swallow hard. I hand the bird back to its owner.

'Mr Brian. We have something special for you.' A man brings a box over, opens it and reaches inside. He brings out a white falcon, much bigger than the one before.

'From His Highness' falcon farm. How do you say the word? A mix of bloods, *yanni*?'

'A hybrid,' Brian replies. 'I had heard His Highness had a special breeding programme. She is splendid.'

'A Queen,' the man says.

Brian puts on the gauntlet and the bird strides from its box to his arm. He makes his way to the centre of the circle of men.

They stand silent, awed. Brian raises his arm and releases the bird. Unlike my falcon, which disappeared as a speeding dart, the white Queen circles above us, stellar in the thermals. She spirals over the rocks and is gone.

We scan the skies; all is still. We hear her distant cry.

'Come on, my Queen,' Brian urges.

What will this bird seize? A bigger prize than mine for sure, with its huge claws. I feel slightly faint, anticipating a torn desert rabbit, its fear-frozen eyes. One of the men cries, points. He has seen something through his binoculars. All turn to face the sun. Brian's arm strikes dark across the blazing orb. Her cape of white feathers sweeps hot air into our obeisant faces. She bears a dove in her claws.

'Oh my Queen.' Brian is exultant. I turn away, green. The men are wild in their praise, bloody ecstasy. The sun burns violent.

☾

As we return to the city I ask about how a dove comes to be in the desert.

'The men released a dozen of them earlier, before we arrived. To be sure there was something for the birds to hunt.'

'The dove didn't have a chance, out there, not knowing where it was.'

My hand closest to Brian is resting on my knee beneath my pashmina; softly he slips his hand beneath the silk. His finger curls around my ring finger, where his signet ring grasps still.

seven

'*Wallah*, Miss Aisling, *shufi, shufi*!'

Mozah runs shrieking into my office, brandishing a bouquet of newspaper clippings and papers. I look at the clippings, I can't understand them, except for the word 'clinic'. Mozah sits down heavily on one of the low chairs, her *abaya* billowing out about her with a loud puff. She covers her beautiful face with jewelled fingers. 'This is bad, very bad.' She starts to cry.

'Mozah, what is it?'

She explains that the news clippings are articles about how the Treasury has awarded the hospital several million riyals of funding to launch ten new community health clinics.

'What?' Mozah hands me a press release, in English. It is from the hospital and has lots of brightly coloured artist drawings as an appendix. The press release announces the hospital's health clinics plan. I stare in disbelief. I recognise every word, every drawing. I wrote this press release. It is part of the campaign pack I am in the midst of preparing in readiness for the Board's own launch. All that is different is the hospital logo on the top. 'I don't understand.'

'*Subhan'allah*.'

'Mozah, this is my press release. How on earth did the hospital get hold of this?'

'There are people who think it is right that the hospital doctors run the health clinics. The doctors know best with such things.'

I jump, it is Yusef who speaks, not Mozah. He sweeps silently into my office. 'The Professor would like to see you, Miss Aisling, now, follow me.'

The Prof is pacing up and down his office, talking on his mobile phone. He waves at me to sit down. I can see he has the press release and newspapers strewn across his desk. 'Yes, certainly, your Royal Highness, we will be there.' He finishes the call and turns to me, pointing to his desk. 'Miss Aisling, you've seen this?'

'Yes Professor, just now.'

'They've emptied the bank account clean, again.' He tells me the Treasury has taken the money and handed it to the hospital for the health clinic development. 'Some in the Royal Maglis oppose our plans to open the clinics to the migrant workers.' The clinics are the pet project of the Queen. The brother of His Highness, the Finance Minister has cut across her plans while His Highness is out of the country. He is at the UN in New York, offering his skills as a broker in one of the many vicious wars in Africa, and sizing the trade opportunity at the same time, perhaps. The Prof is wry. The Queen has just called him to instruct him to go to the Treasury and demand the Board's funding back. 'In the meantime I need you, Miss Aisling, to get our press launch underway please. I know we're a long way off laying the first brick, but let's announce it anyway.'

I pick up the press release from his desk. 'You've seen these, we have announced it, just with the hospital's name and logo.' I explain that somehow the hospital's press office has got hold of all my work on the health clinics launch and hijacked it. 'And I don't know how they did it. My files are always locked away and my computer is password protected.' The Prof just shakes his head.

'There's no such thing as secure or private here Ash, you must have worked that out by now? You know when I first came here I had a few altercations, shall we say, with the locals. I had a visit one day from CID. They came in with this file, this thick.' Tony Morton indicates a couple of inches. He has come to my office not long since I left the Prof to see if he can glean any more information, and to groan about how anyone is going to be paid this month, payday is not far off. 'Every damned email I've written since I've been here. They read your email yal'know, and the phones, click, click.'

I think about the lovely, intimate texts I have been exchanging with Brian. I feel ill that a faceless man somewhere is reading these. I shake myself. I am not going to become a paranoid expat, not this quickly anyhow. Really, there must be millions of texts flying about, a locust swarm of words out there.

☾

Later, a knock at the door, again. I open it to Mozah and Tomas. Tomas glances at me with a curious look. His shoulders are hunched, down. 'You ready Missy', Mozah, imperious, it isn't a question. 'Mr Tomas is taking us to the mall to get some groceries.' I've missed the text, too busy daydreaming, Brian standing silhouetted against the white hot sun. He has texted to say he is taking me to the souk tonight. I grab my bag. Mozah is already striding ahead to the lift.

'How are you Tomas?' I ask.

'So, so.'

'You look exhausted. It's very kind of you to take us shopping, really if you are too tired we can go another time. I'm not sure what the hurry is to go today.'

'No, it's no problem, I needed a break from Ella's crying. Teething. And I presume you will need some ingredients for tonight's feast? I should at least take you to the shops as I have a car and you are cooking for us all.'

'Eh? Tonight's feast?' We reach the lift. Mozah is already inside. 'Tonight's feast?'

'*Yanni*, I thought I'd told you. I invited a few people over tonight for a party.' She shakes the keys to one of the spare apartments. 'It's Halloween.'

'Even in the desert?' I ask.

'Who cares? It means we can party.'

I sigh, 'Tonight's not good for me.'

'Why not, what else you got on? A date?' Mozah stares hard at me, eyes peregrine. 'It is! You've got a date, haven't you? Tell me, girlfriend.' She weaves her arm through mine, all chummy. This oscillating between accents and patois sets my teeth on edge.

'No, no, I'm just tired and I want to catch up on some emails home.'

'*Wallah*, you think I buy that? Come on, talk.' She jabs me with a talon.

'No, truly Mozah, I just want a night off after all the madness over the clinics and everything.'

☾

I push a battered trolley around the French hypermarket. Its juddering wheels catch, I kick it, stub my toe. Mozah is skittering off down aisles with her maid; they come back with armloads of crisp packets, buckets of olives and nuts, and hunks of sweaty plastic cheese. I stand by the woeful fresh produce section prodding bruised and ancient watermelons, wondering how lettuce can look so miserable. The smell of mold pervades the store. I text Brian to let him know I am now otherwise engaged this evening.

'Sorry, I should have taken you to Whitey's rather than this dump,' Tomas smiles. We have a grand choice of a seventies-style austere French hypermarket chain for food provisions, with various stores dominating the city centre malls or a small European food specialty store on the outskirts of the city, known by all the Keralan taxi drivers as Whitey's, as only white expats can afford to shop there for their home brands. 'I miss good meat and fresh, green vegetables.'

'Me too,' I answer him, 'I haven't seen a single real potato for sale. Sure, you can buy frozen French fries, but no potato has come within a mile of those packets.'

Tomas, laughs, 'Ah, you Irish and your potatoes.'

'And look, there's no rice.' We walk past the rice aisles. I am curious, normally there are two huge long aisles stacked with massive sacks of rice as it is the staple diet of the labourers, and this is where the gang masters come to buy in bulk cheaply. Today, there's just some dirty old grains on the floor.

'You were out early the other morning.' Tomas frowns.

'Yes, a friend took me to the desert before it got too hot.'

'So Mozah is right, there's a man and you have a date tonight?'

'I did have. Not any more it seems. Please don't tell Mozah, I don't think I can take the interrogation.'

'She's a force of nature.'

'Yes, and here she comes with the biggest tub of ice cream I've ever seen.'

'Aisling.' Tomas places his hand on mine, his touch urgent, 'Be careful…'

Nancy is blaring out of the CD player, her Lebanese heartbreak ballads jarring with the itchy mood of the party. Mozah is prodding the party-goers to form a circle to play a game of spin the bottle when Justin, a huge Cheshire cat of a man and a dentist at the Board bursts into Bella Villa swinging two large bottles of whiskey around and meowing like James Brown, 'Ouwh, cats, come on, there's a wild one going down at Al Rhabb. Grab your jam jars, I've got cabs outside for us all.'

Justin not only looks like the Cheshire cat with his huge grin, but also somehow he manages to be everywhere at all times. He is seen at every party of infamy, whilst simultaneously appearing on stage at karaoke night at Heather's or ripping up the dance floor at the Irish bar. He is singing Amy Winehouse's song about going into rehab right now, chuckling about the name of the compound where the party is being held, it tickles him. Justin hands us all empty jam jars from a box he had brought in with him for us to refill with beer, wine and whiskey. A jam jar is thrust in my hands, 'Stick that under your pashmina Miss Aisling.'

We are hurtling through the night traffic out to the desert edge, beyond the industrial zone and towards the Al Rhabb compound, with Justin singing Amy at full volume the entire way there. Finding the compound as ever is nightmarish as this part of town, beyond the super-sized factories, is just emerging from the dust, and consequently the road runs out within a couple of kilometres of the last towering unit. The track beyond is lined with the most enormous concrete pipes I have ever seen, hundreds of them tracking away into the night like a terrifying monster worm. The night is apocalyptic, with a dust storm whipping up around us. We pay the taxis to wait outside the villas, otherwise there will be no way back.

'Par...teee!' Justin and Mozah, now both wearing witches' hats, run hand-in-hand into the villa. Everyone is coughing, from the gritty vodka, heavy cannabis fumes and the thick dusty air. The cocktails, stirred up in an icy bath, are lethal. Even though it is gone midnight the sky is more white than black. 'Come and meet the lay-deees.' Justin pulls me into the main room, where there is a DJ and disco lights, and a gaggle of blonde sunny mummies. They are dressed part-witch/part-Mamma Mia, high-octane sparkle and spandex. They are trying to can-can, arms round each other's necks, toppling onto the marble tiles every few minutes and slinging their cocktails across the room in perfect time with the laser strobe lights. Three of the women glance at me, then at each other and start laughing. The others just ignore me, how do they do it? They just know instinctively, tuned in to any threat, the unmarried outsider; not welcome.

I walk from room to room, looking for Joe. In the small kitchen a woman dressed in a tiny, tiny emerald puffball dress printed with dollars is slumped against the fridge, while a man is licking beer from her nipples, her cleavage spilling out of the tiny dress. Her eyes are wide, pupils dilate into oblivion. The man, sweaty in black jeans, has an arm moving rhythmically under the frill of her short hem. Another creepy looking man leans back in the corner, swigging beer, rubbing his crotch.

'Perv.' He just laughs at me.

The floor is soaked with beer and fag ends. Some geeks puff on cigarettes and swipe at their mobile screens, seemingly ignorant of the fairground girl being thrust against the refrigerator. I go upstairs, in dark bedrooms huddles of bodies lie comatose as fragrant smoke fills the rooms, an occasional giggle. I come back downstairs and retreat outside.

In the yard, three women dressed in burlesque are rubbing the legs and back of a man bearing only a strategically placed glitter love heart. His face is a mask of white make-up and black kohl eyes and lips, dribbling. Through the patio doors I can see Marilyn Monroe in a disheveled, blonde wig and white flyaway dress stumble down the stairs, crashing into the sunny mummies and Justin, who is moon-walking back and forth across the room, creating a tidal wave of cocktail dregs. They all shriek and then one latches onto Marilyn, now swimming in the waves of cranberry vodka and kisses her full on the lips. Justin whoops, 'Ouwh!'

I take my jam jar of whiskey and find a quiet spot in the alley beside the villa. I sit down, resting against the wall. A man sits beside me, a spliff dangling from his fingers. He takes a puff and crumples sideways. I gaze about me at the carnage of the party. I could be at a student party in Rathmines. I dreamed of nights in a jasmine-scented souk. My phone buzzes. Brian. A text. 'Having fun?'

'Hell on earth, and as hot.'

'How's the devil these days?'

'Deadly, drunk and stoned'

'Need a knight in shining armour?'

'I have no idea where I am'

'I believe Hell is just past the shisha pipe roundabout. Three camels along'

Joe bops round the corner. 'Miss Aisling!' He drags me to my feet and back indoors. Mozah is sitting on the arm of the sofa, hovering over Tomas. They are deep in conversation. Tomas keeps rubbing his neck, every now and then he glances around. Joe twirls me around the dance floor, limbs in every which way. I sense Tomas looking at me, more than once.

Suddenly there is a furore from out the front of the villa. The man in hearts has passed out in the middle of the road. The row of taxi drivers, awaiting their return passengers, are cat-calling and whistling. Someone from another villa is shouting, warning to get the man out of the street. The main room is crowded with party-goers congregating from all over the villa, trying to get a view from the window or doorway, shrieking and shouting their various suggestions on how best to deal with the situation. We are beyond the pale, good reason to fear a raid, away from city eyes.

Too many elbows. I go back outside to the deserted yard, and text Brian, 'It's getting messy'.

Mozah joins me. 'Mr Justin's going soon. He's heard about another party somewhere else. Coming?' I look at my watch, gone three o'clock. I shake my head.

'Aaii. You're no fun. You can go back with Mr Tomas. He's boring tonight.' Mozah is chewing gum, she pops it. '*Yanni*, he's beating himself because of the Rex man. What's his name...?'

I am about to say Brian, but Mozah cuts back in, 'Mr Craig. He came to Mr Tomas' office today and told him that the Professor doesn't think he's, how did he say? Hacking it?'

I seek out Tomas, hoping we can share a taxi back to Bella Villa, but I can't find him. I find Joe instead, who tells me that Tomas has already gone. I wander out to the front of the villa to try to find a taxi that will take me home, but Justin has gathered the best part of the current party about him and they have requisitioned all the taxis, and are already disappearing into the squall of dust. I try calling the taxi firms I know, but none will come out this far, wherever I am. I try to quell my rising panic. I want my own bed. The heat is unbearable and the sand storm is raging. I slump down on the curb, and rest my head in my hands. Minutes pass. I lose sense of time. A car draws up just beyond me and a man gets out, walks towards me. I look up, and blink. It can't be.

'I don't understand …'

Brian pulls me to my feet. 'Smile, the cavalry is here.'

I hug him. 'How did you find me?'

Brian kisses me. 'Ssh, that would be telling.'

eight

I'm washing my hair for the third or fourth time, still trying to rinse out the dust from last night, when this time it's the apartment porter knocking on my door. He presents me with a bag. Inside is a compass, a bottle of water, string, a torch and a beautiful box of expensive imported Belgian chocolates. The card reads, 'Miss Aisling's survival pack'.

I text Brian. 'I love my survival pack, where do I get to test it out?'

'How about my favourite place. Where I spend most nights?'

I'm not sure how to respond. Before I can, another text.

'Tonight, the old souk?'

'Please.'

'Bring your string. I can tie you to me!'

☪

'Hey, Brian, Ash, where are you two off to?' Joe comes bounding down the hallway, Tomas hovering a few paces behind.

'The old souk, fancy it?' Brian calls to him.

'Sure. Tom and I were about to go to the gym, this sounds way more fun.'

We walk along the hallway to the lift. Brian pulls me back gently, 'You don't mind do you, Aisling? Probably best we're not seen alone together somewhere so public, you don't want to be the subject of office gossip.' He kisses my wrist.

The lift doors open just as we reach them, Mozah steps out. '*Aaii*, what's this then, a party? Without me!' Mozah's constant harrying eyes quickly swoop from each of us, lands with a hard dart at me, then moves on and stops at Brian. The eyes dart back to me. 'Miss Aisling …'

Before she can say anything more, 'Miss Mozah, please join us. I know Miss Aisling's keen you come, she hardly wants to spend an evening with a bunch of oafs like us, do you?'

Neatly done, Brian.

Mozah has her arm through Brian's, a few steps ahead of me. Joe, next to me, is whittering on about the price of oil and how we will all be kicked out, if there's an economic crash. Tomas, the other side, offering an occasional remark. I drift. The sky, violet. Strawberry shisha sweetens the air. The souk has been creeping up from the harbour over hundreds of years. Dust scratches around the twists and turns. Sequined fabrics of every hue sway and glitter in the dusky alleyways. Camel cooking pans, the size of tin baths, are piled up in doorways. Bedouins, barefoot with calloused toenails, sit in wheelbarrows, ready to carry shoppers' goods. They regard us with their cataract-cloudy eyes. We pass a cart, piled high with sacks of orange powders, small black nibs, green shards, the pungency tickles my eyes. A scrawny cat slinks into a black corner.

'Pashmina, lady, hundred-percent silk, guaranteed.'

'How much you give me, one hundred riyal, bargain, bargain, pretty lady.'

'Sir, sir, blue pill for you. Make your lady happy, very happy, tonight.'

'Here you are at last! I was beginning to think you were never coming!' We arrive at a tagine restaurant in the heart of the old souk. It is on four floors, rickety terraces looking out over the alleyways and main square, multi-coloured lanterns swinging. A scatter of patio tables and chairs stretch out across the square. Huge fans attempt in vain to cool the terraces. Men in their white thawbs sit drinking coffee from tiny golden glasses, sucking on their shisha pipes. No women, other than foreigners. In the midst of this scene stands a bulky man, grinning from ear to ear. His head looks too small for his wide body. He has huge bulging shoulders and biceps. Hair shorn, ears sticking out.

'Mate, good to see you,' a heavy Afrikaans accent, the man claps Brian on the shoulder. 'Everyone, let me introduce Craig Pollock, my business partner.' Craig rapidly shakes hands with us all.

Mozah seizing the lead, makes our introductions. 'Miss Mozah. Mr Tomas.'

'We've met,' Tomas, curt. 'This is Miss Aisling.'

I step forward, Craig crushes every bone in my hand. 'Pleased to meet you, Brian's told me so much about you.'

Mozah's eyes narrow.

Mozah sits herself between Craig and Brian and holds court with them. Laughing, squealing every few minutes and tapping them on their knees, flicking her crossed leg, her anklet tinkling. Tomas and Joe play dominoes. I am at the edge of the group. The mint lemonade is sickly sweet. I look to Brian, but I am invisible to him tonight. All eyes are on Mozah's cleavage.

Across the square a man stands erect, proud with a falcon, hooded, on his arm. He has a crowd of admiring men about him. Two police officers hurry past hounding a couple of migrant workers ahead of them, out of the souk. Some young boys run by, trailing a kite behind them, a puppy chases. A carpet trader throws the most beautiful teal grey silken rug high into the air, and as it flaps downwards, its colours shift to salmon gold. The sound of the Koran, tender chanting, lingers above stone terraces, from a distant mosque.

'Hi guys. What are you all doing here then?' It is Tony Morton, out of his work suit and now in a shiny blue bomber jacket and tight black jeans, a poke of accusation at the corner of his mouth.

Brian, smoothly, 'Tony, sit. I thought I'd introduce your freshers to the souk. We, old hands, need to look after our new friends. Mint lemonade, yah?'

Tony doesn't know how to respond, he jiggles on one foot. Brian pours another tumbler from the copper teapot.

'Have you been to the Kashmiri carpet store?' Tony asks as he sits down, trying to seem nonchalant. 'It's the best place for bargains. I ship them home, sell for ten times the price. Come with me, I am good friends with Ali, the owner. He'll do you a good deal.' No one moves. 'Or maybe you want spices? Or pashminas, ladies?'

Mozah laughs, 'Mr Tony, you should have been an Arab.' Tony bristles. Mozah clicks her tongue and skips off to the washroom. Tomas, Joe and I look at each other in relief, we had been expecting worse. It's not like Mozah to pass up on the opportunity for some drama. Maybe she's out to impress tonight? On her best behaviour?

Brian asks, 'So what's this I hear about Dr Mouna, Tony?'

'Jumped up little Madam. It's madness, pure fucking madness.' Tony practically spits his lemonade. 'That witch won't last two minutes, mark my words. Thinks she can do my job. What does she know about anything, straight out of college?' Tony has just been demoted, and is now on the same grade as Mozah, to her delight.

'The Professor tells me she is ferociously bright,' Brian observes.

'We will see about that, al'rightee.'

We weave back into the alleyways as midnight draws near, cool air somehow licking at our heels. 'What's that noise?' Tomas asks. We all stop and listen. It is a deep rumbling. A shout, and another.

Tony laughs. 'Football,' he declares. The others laugh and move on. I touch the mud wall; it throbs beneath my hand, like blood thundering through swollen veins.

Mozah slows, she loops her arm through mine now. 'So, Mr Brian, he's cute eh? Is he married?'

'I don't think so; he said he was here alone.'

'I knew there was someone.' She jabs my ribs.

'There's nothing going on.'

'*Yanni*, Mr Craig tells me Mr Brian has a new sweetheart. This must be you.' I can't help but smile. 'You like him for a husband?' She shakes herself free of me and runs ahead to catch up Brian and Craig.

'No, Mozah...' My voice trails behind her, lost to the gathering darkness.

nine

'He is married.'

It's taken her less than forty-eight hours since my slip in the souk. Mozah's tongue nips across her teeth. I blink, a hot blink.

'Don't look like that sweetie, he's divorcing her.'

I look across the room to Brian and think of the times he has seemed distracted, the terse calls when he told someone on the other end he would call back later. It must have been her. Why has he never mentioned his wife?

'What's her name?' Why did I ask that? Naming her will make her real.

'Aaii, she's the past. She's not here, not coming here, and Mr Craig says Mr Brian has a new sweetheart, I told you. He wants the divorce. He should do like our men, just say I divorce you three times and it's over.'

I try to turn my focus back to the meeting. The Prof has called us together. We are sat around a long table in the Board Room, under a sepia print of His Highness, his irises flecked with gold paint. Somehow a petition signed by a large number of staff has found its way to the Board. It condemns the promotion of Dr

Mouna, dares to criticize the Prof for her promotion and calls for her instant dismissal. It is evidenced by a raft of petty complaints about Dr Mouna's alleged unwomanly behaviour. Other more colourful complaints are scratched in the vinyl walls of the lifts. The tyres on her car have been let down.

For the moment there seems to be an unnatural truce between Mozah and Tony Morton. They are quiet today, although Mozah mutters under her breath, 'Ha, her, she's just a Bedouin, she has no right to be here.'

The Prof tells us that this latest jabbering has not impressed the Board, however, thankfully with the health clinic drama taking priority, the Board has barely registered the mutiny this time.

'So Professor, there's not going to be a vote of confidence?' Tony asks.

The Prof ignores him. 'Our colleagues from Rex will now work alongside Dr Mouna.' He nods to Dr Mouna, who has sat removed from us at the end of the long table, impassive beneath her full veil throughout the meeting. 'They will help her discover the perpetrator of the petition, and when they are known then Dr Mouna can decide their fate.' Mozah twitches beside me. Tony is bloodless.

The Prof is called by Yusef to take a call. The tea boys arrive and I take the opportunity to move away from Mozah, and go and sit next to Dr Mouna. Beneath the table she takes my hand, I squeeze it softly.

Brian speaks while we wait, 'Our Royal patrons are tense. The Maglis is disturbed by talk of secret meetings, growing dissidence. There are factions that believe the Queen's attempts to open up the country are corrupting it. With His Highness away...' He pauses, the clinking of teaspoons ceases, the room is still, 'The rumours of rifts in the family have reached the streets, yah. Unease is spreading fast, there are whispers of a coup.'

Tony snorts. Dr Mouna speaks, 'Our people fear change. Democracy is the enemy of stability.'

Brian continues, 'The currency is fluctuating, and oil prices are volatile. Food prices are going up fast, rice is becoming short. There have been some strikes out in the camps and a small protest in the old souk about the rice.'

I think back to our evening in the souk, to the shouts and the throbbing mud wall. Blood thundering beneath my palms, *married, married*.

The Prof comes back but says he has to go, so we leave the Board Room in a somber mood. I am the last out of the door and he calls me back. 'Miss Aisling, I need you to prepare for a major press reception. We're inviting journalists and film crews from all over the region to celebrate the official opening of our first health clinic.'

'But we don't have a clinic to open yet, and I thought the whole project had been handed over to the hospital?'

'If we can show we can do this thing His Highness will order the Treasury to hand back the funding and project to us.'

'But where are we going to find a clinic?'

'Our beloved Maleka has gifted us one of her private clinics.'

'Gifted?'

'She's a very generous woman and is determined to improve care in our community, where it's so needed.'

'Where's the clinic?'

'It's down south, on the coast. *Yanni*, there's a port town just before the border called Ras Latifah. We will sail there on the *Maleka*'s private yacht and hold the reception on board.'

'A glitzy reception now?'

The Prof laughs. 'Face, Miss Aisling, face.'

ten

'Ashley, did you say your name was? Maid, come and get Miss Ashley a drink.' My hostess snaps her fingers at a young Filipino girl with lowered eyes.

I am honoured, finally after nearly three months in the desert, the expat wives have invited me to one of their coffee mornings. Every week they meet at a different villa. Coffee doesn't appear to be on the menu, just champagne. I don't really want to be here. And they don't really want me here. It is the festive season, but there's no generosity of spirit in these women. They're sizing me up, this girl who is seen around town with one of the most newly eligible men. We've been discreet, always out in the company of others, invariably Mozah. Tried not to give the office gossips so much as a lick of scandal, but nothing escapes these women.

The maid steps towards me just as two young boys, the sons of the hostess, rush through playing at being space rockets. They swoosh past the girl, knocking into her hard. She staggers and drops the tray with glasses of champagne.

The hostess bellows, 'You clumsy, stupid girl, now look what you've done. Get this cleared up right away before someone cuts themselves, and those glasses are coming out of your wages.' The girl scurries away to fetch a pan.

'I don't think she could have helped that, the boys knocked into her,' I say.

The hostess lifts her sunglasses. She is morbidly-obese, wafting around in a garish kaftan and the obligatory over-sized Prada sunglasses. She squints, 'Ashley, you are new here. Do you have a maid?'

'No.'

'You see if you did, you would realize that you can't be soft on these girls.' The maid is now at our feet, on her knees scraping up the glass and pools of champagne. 'They are tarts and thieves, the lot of them. You can't take your eye off them for one moment or you'll find your crystal down the souk.'

Another woman shouts to us from across the room. 'It's true, I caught mine taking my diamond pendant. She said she had found it in Jasmine's dress-up box, but Jasmine would never touch my things. I sacked her there and then. You can't trust the sluts.'

'And what about poor Simone? Came home and found her maid under her husband in the utility room. The maid said he forced her, but, really, they are all such shame faced, tit-less liars.'

The hostess replaces her blank, reflective sunglasses.

☾

Brian holds my hand as we hop after his friend, Johan, across the glistening granite slabs that step across the infinity pool, marching out as if into the Bay. On the far shore, the mosque twists into the sky.

'I know Christmas is a few days away, but this is my special treat for you, Aisling.' He slides a pearl bracelet on my wrist.

'It's beautiful, thank you.' We turn our gaze from the tiny beads and to a truly colossal string of pearls, curving around the far shore of the Bay. The pearls are the globe-shaped wings of the new Grand Library of Arabic Scholarship, newly built in homage to its predecessor, the ancient library of Alexandria. At night the string of pearls is lit softly, as if a planetary constellation has drifted down on the Bay. This region was long ago famed for its pearls. Traders in the days of Marco Polo travelled from the furthest corners of China to haggle with the Bedouin pearl divers, causing this remote stretch of sand to become inhabited. The Bedouins settled their caravans and dived for the elusive and exquisite pearls, so craved by distant oriental empresses. But then the twentieth century dawned and the seas turned gritty, and when the scrawny divers prized opened their ever diminishing haul all they found was a rotting, oozing, greying slime, sometimes a black gob clotting in the centre. Soon the pearl divers became nothing more than a breezy myth, gusting about the sands.

'Mate, I'm going to have to leave you to wander. I've got a problem with the leather for the exhibition cases.' Johan marches off, swearing into his mobile. Johan is a project manager on the library build.

'Beer later.' Brian calls after him. 'That's bad news. Last crew was sent home without pay for screwing up the glass.' They were the lucky ones, there are darker tales circulating at Heather's about the flogging of workers for missing deadlines; and then there are the hushed stories of those who fall into the Bay at night as they slave in the hot, humid darkness. The library must open this summer, His Highness has decreed it.

Brian tells me about the glass. One of the most radiant claims of the library is that it will house the tallest cabinets in the world, especially to hang the sumptuous carpets from the time of the

Prophet. Only one factory in the world, in Hamburg, can produce glass panels on this scale and each of the ten super-sized cabinets requires the best part of a year to sculpt and shine to such a finish that the glass becomes invisible to the naked eye. The first three panes arrived on time, unscathed. During a storm in the Mediterranean the fourth pane cracked in two. The fifth pane arrived, but slipped into the Bay during off-loading at the dock, immortalising beneath it the pearly skeletons of the drowned workers. The run of bad luck seemed over with the sixth panel, it was off-loaded without so much as a tremble. Gently it was locked into position, hovering in the great hall. All the cabinets are designed to seem as if they are floating, no sign of fixtures. The glass stayed suspended while His Highness came to see it, clapping his hands in delight. But as his retinue clattered into the next hall a catastrophic hailstorm exploded behind them.

After endless miles of dark corridors we are shocked by brilliant light as we cross into the final pearl. It burns, yet we are immersed. The pearl is all glass, with water running over it perpetually. It offers a teary eye on the city, now no more than a distorting reflection. I feel as small as a dot of grit within an oyster. Shooting streams of water leap and fall around the circumference. Droplets splash onto a floor studded with pearls. In the centre of the lustrous hall is the last perfectly formed pearl, supersized. Brian slips his arm across my shoulder and guides me within. It is astonishingly pitch black, but looking up the pearl is pierced with a hundred tiny star shapes.

'His Highness' very own maglis.' Brian breathes into my neck, 'Really, you shouldn't be in here, yah. Women are not meant to know about the secrets of the maglis.'

I close my eyes, it's as if I am held tight in a pearly bubble, rolling through the firmament on prayer. I feel the brush of his stubble.

'Can you imagine how it will be when the books and art works are in place?'

'I don't think it needs books or art. How can they compete with the marvel of this building?'

'True. Maybe that would be as well. There's shrapnel amongst the treasures.'

We wander back out to the infinity pool.

Brian tells me the provenance of the collection is troubled. The Royals argue, when Western experts question where and how the ancient and rare articles for the library suddenly appear, that to leave these beautiful pieces amidst the wreckage of tanks and detritus of war means they will be lost to the world. 'But how have they come into your possession my most accommodating Sheikh?' Brian chuckles.

'Yes, at first it all seems so glossy.' I think back to the brochures I left on the kitchen table for Mammy. She threw them straight in the bin. It is cool tonight, the mercury only rising to thirty degrees. The desert's short winter is starting. I don't think it's ever been thirty degrees back home. Perhaps just as well, it only has to hit twenty and the women down along the prom whip off their tops and march about in their lacy bras. Anymore and Grandaddy would have a fit.

'Tough week?' Brian strokes the beads about my wrist.

'Sorry, I was miles away, literally.'

'Home?'

I nod.

'And here, girl?'

I tell him about cocktails with the sunny mummies.

'The honeymoon is over, eh? It happens about now. The first three months and everything is so exotic.'

'So possible.'

'Not such a fairytale any more, girl? You get to this point and it all gets harder.'

'Yes,' I agree. 'Only so many champagne brunches you can have before you start to notice how we're all kept in our own little gilded cages. The expats stay in their compounds, the locals behind their veils, and the labourers behind the barbed wire of the camps.'

He soothes my long dark hair. 'Too many of these expats become worse than the locals, loving a pecking order. I know that woman and her husband. He works at one of the camps. She's so high and mighty, isn't she?'

I nod.

'Well, back home he was a security guard in a shop and she was an office cleaner. People come here and pretend they are all that, and they really are not.' Brian draws me to his arms.

'They are all running away from something,' I whisper.

'And you, Aisling?'

I sweep away the question, my hand white across the city skyline reflecting in the still waters of the pool. He stares; he wants an answer, I try to shift the focus, 'I wonder what the future holds? There's something of it here already. Hundred-storey buildings that go up in the blink of an eye.' I point to a dark square. 'This tower, it was just a field of rubble when I arrived three months back. Such ferocity. The West sleeps. Seeing all this, being here has tilted the world for me.' Or is it that the world is tilting? The pool slicks black beneath my fingers, the pearls dissolve. 'Only a djinn could have dreamt this.'

'We should go now.' He is curt; the spell cracks.

☾

ELECTRIC SOUK

Brian takes me back to Bella Villa. We are silent in the car. My evasion sits between us. He is impatient with the traffic, swerving violently in and out of lanes. I grip the sides of my seat. We pull up hard at the apartment. I mumble a thank you and go to get out.

'I will see you on Christmas Day, Miss Aisling. I think we'll take a picnic and head into the desert for the day.' Roughly, he pulls me back to him and kisses me on the forehead.

As I reach my apartment door I get a text, from him, 'I will get my answer.'

☾

I watch the day's news coverage, see angry mobs over a distant border. A young man burns. I do not know their cause. My eyelids grow sticky, and then will not open. I am back in the gallery, running from one tomb-like hall to the next, glass shattering around me, behind a fiery figure. As I run into the glassy pearl the water cascades down the walls, turning dark red. Blood red. Blood. My toes are hot. I look down at them, blood boils, seeping up from the floor and covers my feet, rising to my ankles, my knees, my waist, my breasts, my throat, my mouth.

eleven

'Yo, Miss Aisling, Happy Chrimbo!'

'And you Joe.' Joe is leaping two steps at a time down the stairs at Bella Villa, wearing a pair of flashing reindeer antlers. 'Hey, you look down, hard being away from home at this time of the year, isn't it?'

I do miss Mammy crashing about the kitchen, cursing at Grandaddy to get his mitts out of her sherry trifle.

'Something like that.'

'What are you doing today? I bet you've got some great party going on with those Rex boys, your Arabian Knights.'

'No. I don't know what I'm doing, my plans have fallen apart.' Brian should have picked me up at dawn. It's mid-afternoon and not so much as a text. His mobile is switched off.

'Come with me to Heather's. They're going to fry the turkey in an old oil barrel. That has got to be worth seeing, and the Spice Boys are doing a Christmas-special karaoke.'

☪

'Aisling, babe, you came after all.' Angie squeals as she sees me pushing my way through the throngs of drunken revellers in Heather's. She hugs me and tows me out to the pool, where she has a line of Christmas brews of various luminosities and décor lined up, guarded by Jimmy, who is puffing on a cigar. She shoves an electric blue one in a glass the size of a goldfish bowl into my hands, complete with a silver bauble floating on its surface. 'So, why aren't you off on ya romantic picnic in the desert?'

'What?' growls Jimmy. Angie fills him in on my previous plans while I try not to choke on the mystery drink. 'And you've heard nothing from him?'

I shake my head.

'Bastard,' Jimmy says.

'Aisling, a man who lets you down at Christmas is a shite. You deserve better than this,' Angie adds.

I can feel the tears welling up in my eyes. No, stop, I won't cry over him.

'Brian Rothmann?' Jimmy is scratching his head, 'Tall, baldy fella, South African?' I nod. 'I know him. You're better off out of that one. Likes to think he's some sort of international high flier, a player.'

'Oh, he's a player all right, I'd put money on that,' chips in Angie. 'Hon, I've come across men like him before. They're messers. They let you think you're a princess, but there's always baggage, and normally a wife back home.'

'And several other girlies in his bed in the meantime,' Jimmy snorts. At this moment, the oil barrel across the other side of the pool, just lit by the chef, booms with a huge fireball. Cheers all round. Jimmy staggers off be in the middle of the rumpus.

'Angie, this hurts. I wanted to see him today.' My glass glows like a siren. 'He blows hot and cold, and I never know where I am with him. I thought he ...'

'He's just reeling you in and out, that's how they get a hold of you. Men are men, the world over. Look at me; I learnt that the hard way. Never trust 'em.'

'I wasn't going to do this again. I came here to get away from it all. From Mammy going on about Brendan, over the hill, who's going to inherit all that farm up there. Over the hill, he's thirty years older than me, Ang. And the girls in my flatshare, always trying to fix me up with this one, or that one.' Couldn't they see? My heart was in shreds. Is in shreds, still. I need time to stitch it back together, and a new thread.

'I swear, I'm off men.'

Angie clinks her glass into mine, 'Drink up, have another and spill.' Bitter smoke drifts across us.

'Brian asked what I was running from. I'm running from a stupid, stupid mistake.'

'Don't tell me, yer man back home was married.'

'Worse.'

You wouldn't think it possible, with Ireland being so small and everyone being related to everyone, but he was from the North. We didn't go North so much back then, the checkpoints were only just coming down. I can still see him now, waving madly like a toddler, running beside my DART train as it pulled out of Pearse Street station. The last train of the night.

I had just graduated and was fresh into my first job as a junior press officer at the hospital.

'I met him at a party at the nurses' home.'

He was a junior doctor.

'At the end of the party I left, but I forgot my scarf and he chased after me. I got on my train before he reached me. He spent all the next day finding me. It took me five years to find him out.'

Five years and it was a fine romance. Not one of those with

big romantic gestures. Hurried bags of curried chips on O'Connell Street, before he ran off on call.

He was a live-wire with his studies, ward rounds, on call duties, rugby, and going back home every other weekend to his sick mother. She had dementia, was in a home. He wouldn't take me to see her, as new people upset her too much. If they weren't already in her memories then she couldn't place them and panicked, hit out at the care assistants.

'I don't know how so many years slipped by so easily, but there were always exams for him, every year. And so, every year we put off our plans. "I can't think about guest lists and speeches and all that while I've half the diseases in world to memorise," he would say.'

'And you'se never suspected?'

'No, how stupid. It's all so obvious, isn't it?'

'You poor cow.'

'One morning he came flying into my office at the hospital, "America," he yelled.'

He had been offered a post in a hospital in Boston. Could I get a green card?

'"We should get married", he said. "Go to our new life as man and wife."' He wrapped an elastic band around my ring finger. It was all so fast, he didn't even have time to get a ring. 'That evening I ran back to my bedsit to give my landlady notice.'

When I got there, on the doorstep stood Philomena. Forty-something, a razor-slice of a spinster, medical secretary to the radiology department. She saw through everything. Crucifix at her throat, and righteousness on her lips. She stood on the step under a dripping umbrella. For an hour she had been waiting she told me, no rain could deter her mission.

I mitched off work the next day, took the bus to Belfast and onto a village near Ballymena. I went to the home. Philomena, of course, had the address and had given it to me, written out in neat capitals. His mother was there, giving out to the care assistants. I didn't speak to her. It was teatime and she was far too busy, making sure the patients had their meals. She was a grand woman in her matron's uniform. *She* was there too, cherubic smile, helping the ones on their walking frames.

'It was all they were talking about in the café, where I waited for the bus back. Now I had seen for myself. 'Won't it be grand when young Dr Fergus is back with us and helping his father out at the surgery?' 'Ah, sure, and won't he and young nurse Mariad there make a fine couple? Sweethearts since they were babes in arms. Have you seen the ring? Jesus, you could see it from outer space.'

I twanged the elastic band across the café and got my bus home.

'How'se did he think he would get away with it?'

'Five years, Angie. Five years, he lied to us both.'

'What happened?'

'He chose. They married. He went home to be a GP. Had a baby.'

'And you?'

'I cried every night for a year. Then these last couple of years, I've tried, been on a few dates, but none of them are him. So I just stopped, easier to be alone than look for him in their eyes. I just find it hard to stop wanting, to let go …'

'Aw, babe, he's not worth your tears. Forget him.'

'It's hard to. Even after they married, he kept calling, every time he was in Dublin he'd come round to the flat, saying he'd made a mistake.'

'What?!'

'I know. He even suggested …well, you can guess …'

'And?'

'He told me he would get a divorce, I believed him again. But the day they let me go at the hospital he texted to say he had been offered tenure in a teaching hospital in New York. He was emigrating, for good.'

'So you'se came 'ere. Good for you.'

I had to. The night before that sickening day I had bled, not so much, I wasn't far-gone, but enough. Enough I couldn't stay; I needed a new sky, a new sun, a new moon, stars.

twelve

I dangle my toes off the yacht and over the azure waters of the Gulf. A breather, for five minutes. Today is our press conference on the beloved *Maleka*'s yacht, the day we will stage our coup d'état to reclaim the health clinics. A novel way to spend St Stephen's Day, but infinitely preferable to the usual curried turkey sandwiches and Grandaddy snoring in the chair from that one festive whiskey too many. I am caught up in the chaos of the last-minute finishing touches, my head still banging from the night before at Heather's. The Queen has invited a number of Health Ministers from the region, including the Minister of a neighbouring state. Diplomatic ties with this neighbour are strained, squabbles over islands and ancient insults. The princesses are all of a chatter about the wife of this Minister, who is a real glamour puss and once a one-time contender for His Highness' affections. With her extensive retinue she arrived at the glitziest of the seven star hotels late last night. She was led to her sumptuous suite, only to discover a mangy old Professor of Gynaecology asleep in her bed.

Click, click, click, click. I know that footfall. This world of veils is tuning my senses. Brian looms. I look down into the depths, I don't want his smile today.

'The yacht looks beautiful. The Queen is pleased. You've done a good job. Where do you want this basket of gifts for the guests?'

No mention of yesterday, no apology, 'Rather late to be playing Santa Claus, aren't you?'

'About yesterday ...'

'Save it, I'm not interested in late excuses. Over there will be fine, thank you.' I get up and walk away. I hear him slam down the basket. His step quickens behind me.

'Aisling ...' He holds me tight, gripping my shoulders. His smile, fanged.

'Miss Aisling, please I need you for one moment,' the Prof calls from along the gangway, ahead. I breathe. Brian turns on his heel; I can feel the press of his nails in my skin still.

We set sail soon. I walk about the yacht, checking we are ready. Every deck sparkles, it is breathtaking. A long way from rainy press conferences in the car park outside the Mater Hospital. I make my way to the sundeck. Spiders-web lobster nets are stacked up on the pier below. A line of dark eyes blink on the prows of the moored fishing boats.

'There you are.' He is snarling as he crosses the deck, 'I'm going now.'

'Really?'

'Yah, the Prof has just told me he needs me go back to the Board to resolve the issues with the bank, so the salaries are paid this week and not deferred to next month. Like that's going to happen, it's a joke.' He kicks out at one of the cane loungers. 'He needs to understand.' He laughs, 'Wanker.'

Brian marches off without another word to me. I watch him go in the full glare of the sun.

The sail along the coast to Ras Latifah is smooth. Our beloved *Maleka* does not grace us with her presence. The girls tell me this is the etiquette. The Queen will remain in her cabin and the most honoured guests will join her for a few minutes at a time.

The Prof comes over to me, 'Will you take this to Her Royal Highness' cabin please?' He hands me a blue envelope.

When I reach the cabin I knock softly, no reply. I wait. A door behind me opens, I turn, the door almost immediately slams shut, but I am sure I see a Sheikh with a goblet of red wine in hand. And beside the Sheikh, a tall, bald man? I blink, tiny black dots swim. Too much sun. The Queen's door opens, and a woman in the veil holds out her hand. I give her the envelope. I walk back along the corridor, fiddling with my bracelet. It was just a clip of the eye. A queasiness pulls, my throat is taut. I turn the corner and as I do my bracelet breaks and beads bounce off. I must have been tugging at it, not realizing. I scrabble about on the floor trying to retrieve the pearls. Some of the beads have rolled back around the corner. I stick my head around to see where they have gone, as I do the Queen's door opens and the veiled girl comes out holding the blue envelope. She doesn't notice me on the floor. The door opposite opens and a man's hand reaches out, hairy, and takes the envelope from her. I slide back quickly.

The health clinic is positioned just a few paces back from the shore. If I didn't know it was a clinic I would have mistaken it for a small shopping mall; and it does house a few designer outlets selling sunglasses, watches and trinkets. Our guests are impressed and the launch is going well. After our tour of the centre we gather in the atrium to hear our beloved *Maleka* give a welcoming address, which I have written for her. Suddenly a shower of stones ricochet off the atrium's glazed roof. Everyone jumps. I can hear a man shouting outside. The guests all strain to hear. I can only make out '*Allah Akbar.*' The shouting stops. The guests murmur amongst themselves, but before the murmur can rise the Queen enters. She stands awkwardly beneath a grandiose portrait of herself and His Highness. High cheekbones, almond eyes, swan neck, in the painting she is every inch a deity. I look at her squat figure in the gleaming, jewelled abaya below. Her eyes and mouth are all downturned, hard. Her cheeks pucker and jowl. The heavy kohl pulling her royal face down further, everything about her seems to be sliding in a slightly muddy way. Her voice rasps.

The speech is short and suitably gracious, but then, one by one, the Health Ministers from around the region stand up and give speeches of congratulations. Some of our guests rather like the sound of their own voices. I look at my watch, this is going to cause a problem. The grand finale of our event, due in just fifteen minutes is meant to be the arrival of a brand new air ambulance on the clinic's helipad. This is our big surprise, as it was for us too when we were told. Only yesterday we received word that His Highnesses' brother had purchased the air ambulance through his sovereign fund.

I need to get everyone outside within the next few minutes, but now an immensely jolly Professor of Public Health stands up, 'Your Royal Highness, esteemed colleagues, what more praise can I add to the commendations that have already rightfully been spoken here today. There really are no words, instead let me sing.'

'Am I dreaming?' The Prof turns to me, amusement playing in the sheen of his eyes. The jolly Professor starts to sing.

'Whatever is …?' A voice at my shoulder, I turn to see Tomas standing behind me.

'You won't believe me if I tell you. What are you doing here?'

Tomas tells me he has driven down with some paperwork for

the Queen about the leasing and contractual arrangements for the clinic. The papers have to be signed today.

'Leasing? I thought she had gifted the clinic?'

'Come now Ash, of course she has gifted the clinic space, but all these retail units? Now, they make a tidy profit for her Highness.'

'Fair enough, I suppose.'

'Sure, but what is clinic space and what is retail? And what about the empty units, the pool, the atrium, all the other floor space?' I look about me at the acres of marble foyer.

'We now seem to be signed up to renting that space, and at a Royal premium. Clever Queenie.'

The stirring noise of the approaching helicopter is enough to draw the guests out. It swoops about a few times before landing on the helipad to a round of applause. The journalists are jabbering at high speed into their Dictaphones, voices thrilling to the whirr of the helicopter blades. I hand out our press releases about the new service. The photographers are clamouring for pictures of the crew with the Queen, which she obliges, grudgingly.

'*Mumtaz*, Miss Aisling. *Mabruk*! This has been a great day. Good publicity for once, that's what we need.' The Prof bows.

'The shouting?' I ask.

'Ah, *mafi*. A poor mad man, that's all.' I want to know more, but the Prof waves away any chance of questions and laughs. '*Yanni*, now we have our own madness to deal with. We have to make sure the Highways Ministry doesn't build a motorway right through the building.' The Prof tells me that he received notification earlier in the day that the Highways Ministry is intending to build a road to the new port at Ras Latifa right through the middle of the health clinic.

I look about us, all around the clinic is scrub land. 'Surely, they could move the road, there's enough space here?'

'Ah, but that would be too easy and would not require us to pay a sizable fee to have the road relocated.' Tomas whispers to me. 'Clever Queenie indeed.'

'Professor, a word please.' It is one of the Queen's advisors.

A few minutes later the Prof comes back. 'I'm sorry Miss Aisling, Tomas and I are going to have to leave you now. We have been summoned to the Royal Maglis.'

thirteen

A crackle. Joe and I start. Every day it is the same. The PA system groans, crackles again. Then the call for prayer, sadly not a soft beautiful chant but an ear shattering bawl that reverberates through the walls, the floor, every fixture. It grates on the soul. Angie arrives with coffee and pastries, wearing a Starbucks cap. While the local staff go downstairs for prayers, the expat staff gather in each other's offices to catch up on gossip. Joe is wiping at his desk, his screen, his keyboard, scraping incessantly between the keys. Tissues pile up on his desk. His cleaning more manic than usual today. He came in to find anti-Semitic leaflets on his desk. The tone is vile and vitriolic. At first we can't understand why Joe has been targeted, but then we find a leaflet haranguing Jew lovers who buy coffee at Starbucks. Joe's trips across the road are observed.

Tomas arrives. He tells us what happened the night before when he and the Prof were summoned to the Royal Maglis. 'We were taken to the Blue Palace and led through marble corridors until we reached a large tented courtyard. Men sat around on carpets and cushions, smoking shisha.' Tomas says the men were agitated, concerned about the troubles across the border.

Tomas and the Prof sat on the carpets watching for hours, passed endless thimbles of coffee and plates of hard pistachio jelly by their hosts. 'We were asked to join a game of draughts.' Conversation stilled as the game progressed. With every move another man joined the throng around Tomas and his opponent. 'They clicked their tongues every time Abdullah lost a piece.'

The final disc in place. 'Abdullah groaned, and then from the back of the crowd a tall man clapped. The crowd around us parted. The man came forward, congratulating us. He had only one eye. He rubbed noses with the Prof.'

'Who was he? His Highness?' Joe asks.

'Sheikh Fariq.'

Tomas continues. 'The men went and he signalled to us to sit.' More coffee arrived. 'Mr Tomas, I congratulate you on your game.' He said and called me a clever man. He asked us if we were enjoying the festivities.'

Tomas and the Prof thanked the Sheikh for his excellent hospitality.

'Then he asked us "How are your family? Your wife and baby? They enjoy our country? Let me know if there's anything I can do for their comfort. Anything, my friend." He was insistent.'

Next Sheikh Fariq rose and walked away, bidding them to enjoy the night some more.

'What was that all about then?' Joe asks.

'I've no idea, but this morning I received a business card, a gift of the finest Cuban cigars and a message from the Sheikh commending the name on the card.'

Angie coughs.

'And you'll have a new colleague too, Aisling. We learnt last night from the Sheikh's Chief Secretary that Sheikh Fariq will be joining us as a special media advisor.'

While I take in this news, Joe comments that he wants to go to the Royal Maglis. Angie rolls her eyes, 'Watch what you wish for, kiddo. You don't know what you're getting into. It's better to steer clear of the locals.'

'I suppose you would rather us all spend every night drinking at Heather's, never seeing anything of the country, only the bottom of a pint glass.' Tomas retorts.

Angie glares, takes her coffee and goes back to her office.

I want to see more, I just don't know how. It's all so elusive; intense and real for a moment, like the oud, thick in the air, then beyond grasp. I long to see beyond the malls and compounds. Angie says everyone is like this at first, but in all her time in the Middle East she has never been inside the home of a local. No one she knows has. We keep apart.

Mozah pushes into the office moments after Angie leaves, 'Aiee, what's wrong with her? Her face is like sour milk.'

'Headache.' Joe responds quickly, diplomatically, not wanting to expose the tiff between Tomas and Angie to Mozah, who sucks the marrow out of any gossip. She is too excited today to stop and question.

'Miss Aisling, you'll come with me at New Year to the dunes. We'll stay in a Bedouin camp. Mr Brian has arranged it. For you.'

I am promised a night of traditional music and a feast of a hundred dishes, all beneath a shawl of stars. At last. But with Brian? I'm torn, can I resist?

We can hear the pummel of footsteps along the corridor, prayers are over. Yusef bows at my office door and calls me to the Prof's office. Mozah asks if she should come with me, any opportunity to get to the Prof. Yusef tells her no, but she comes anyway. We reach the Prof's office and he waves me in. Mozah attempts to follow, but he dismisses her curtly. She does not go though, instead hangs about in the lobby area, pretending to be asking Yusef about something. The Prof sits at his desk, looking at his computer and does not speak to me while she loiters. We cannot simply close the office door, it would be too scandalous. After a few minutes of silence Mozah finally gives up and goes.

The Prof tells me I am to join a small delegation from the Board that is going to a summit with Treasury officials. He has been instructed that the delegation is to be assembled, after receiving a memo from the Under Minister at the Treasury. The memo orders that Treasury restore all the funding previously transferred to the hospital, by the will of His Highness and the Prophet. The network of health clinics must be established with urgency across the country. Moreover, His Highness wants, post-haste, a policy granting access to all employees. In one move of the ebony disc, free health care has just been extended to the maids and labourers. The invisible million have at last one human right.

☪

Tomas, Joe and I spend the next couple of days locked away in our offices preparing for the summit. Once the crowd has left for the afternoon and we are the only ones left in the building, we decamp to one or the other's offices and work together. On the third afternoon we are working in my office when Tomas needs to retrieve a file from his office.

He comes back a few minutes later looking incensed, 'Someone has been in my office.' He explains that the papers on his desk all looked the same as when he left, but something didn't seem right. He looked about, trying to find evidence for his intuition. Everything was where it should be. He checked twice, not a paper was out of place, not so much as an inch. He sneezed and reached for a tissue. After he finished with the tissue he threw it in the bin.

'That's when I saw it, a lump of sticky grey chewing gum.'

'Cleaners,' says Joe.

Tomas reminds us that the cleaners come in the hour before work. He was the only person in his office all day and he does not chew gum. Only one person we all know chews gum.

'But why? And how did she get into your office?'

'Rex.'

Joe and I exchange looks. 'Rex?' I ask.

'Craig or Brian come by my office every day now. Innocent questions about this or that.' He pauses, 'They want something.' Tomas is stony.

'What could they want?' I wonder.

Tomas tells us at first he just swatted at them, but like mosquitoes they buzzed back all the more persistently. He wonders if the Prof has asked them to check up on him. I assure him this is not the Prof's style.

'Tomas, it's just gum.' I try to restore some perspective.

'The gum, it's where they have slipped up.' He responds, sharp. 'They let Mozah in, an amateur.'

'Mate...'

'Careless, because otherwise it's a precise, professional. A military operation.'

'Tom, you are working too hard,' Joe says.

'But don't you wonder about Rex?' Tomas has let the genie out of the bottle.

I glance out of the window. A long black V-shape crosses the darkening sky. I point. At this time of year, just for a few weeks Yusef told me, this solitary V formation visits the city, once every night. A lone flock of no more than thirty birds. I do not know what the birds are and Yusef does not know their English name. They are just a bit bigger than a crow, but are not a crow. You don't see much wildlife, only the burbling starlings that perch on our window sills for a few pecks of seeds which Mozah feeds them early in the morning. The mystery of this scrawl of birds, quilling their way across the sky for a minute, beguiles me. Dark wings of history, an echo of an earlier age before the skyscrapers. For a moment I can almost sense … then that hairy arm stretching out from the cabin on the yacht reaches across my mind. I jolt back.

At nine o'clock we call it a day. Joe and Tomas decide to go for a game of squash, shake their bones up after a long, hard day. I just want a soak. They leave me to wait for a taxi. I try to flag one down, but they pass by. It's chilly tonight. Yusef said it would be, one last night of cold before the heat returns to swallow the brief winter.

A car pulls up. 'Hop in, doll.' Craig shouts to me.

I explain I am waiting for a taxi.

'You'll be waiting all night. You know what it's like trying to get one once the malls open. Just as well I spotted you, eh?' We weave through the crazy traffic. 'Brian is waiting for you.' How does he always seem to know where I am? Craig swears and honks his horn every few seconds, 'Animals, savages, these fucking Arabs.'

He's like gum, I can't get him off my heel.

'Cristal,' Brian orders, 'Only the best for my princess, princesses.'

Brian is sat on a gilt throne, Mozah draped beside him, popping gum. We are in Fizz. Every week a debutante hotel graces the city, each newcomer vying to be the most sensational, this one has Fizz, the very first champagne bar. The walls are powdered in magenta silk, the carpet an inch thick, deep rouge. Marie Antoinette tasselled lamps and tea lights sprinkle the low glass tables. A waiter in fuchsia pink tails, with an illuminated ice bucket that changes colour every few seconds, approaches.

'You look tired, you shouldn't push yourself so hard. Call me, I can help you. What does the Prof has you working on now?'

'It's fine, time flies past when you're having fun. And Tomas and Joe were there, and we work well together.' Quick dodge, did I get away with it?

Brian rubs his stubbled chin, 'Tomas. I'd like to get to know him. He seems a sound guy, but henpecked yah? We should get him out one evening, show him some real fun.'

'*Yanni*, fun, yes? I wanna dance.' Mozah grabs Brian by the wrist and pulls him away to a square of parquet flooring. She slithers around the floor, around Brian. She casts me a look from the slant of her eye.

Craig pulls me forward, 'Come on, they're not going to hog that floor.' Craig blunders onto the dance floor, with his champagne glass in hand. Mozah is splashed. She shrieks and storms off to the bathroom. Craig follows trying to apologise. Brian and I are alone on the dance floor. For a moment we both stand there.

Then Brian puts his arm around my waist, 'This is our first dance Aisling.' He holds me close as we sway to Elvis, 'Love Me Tender.'

'This is how it should always be, girl. This was my dream back in South Africa, the good life.'

'Mm.' It's true; this is a million miles away from the curried chip dinners on O'Connell Street. The closest I ever come to glamour back home is wandering the perfume counters of Brown Thomas, pretending that I can waste the electric money on an expensive bottle of chemicals. Dublin is lashing rain, puddle-splattered tights and umbrellas shredded by the banshee winds. And tears, nightly, as I try to forget. Now, here with my new silky red pashmina, I glitter.

'But that's all in the hands of the accountants.' He holds me tighter to him. 'Nothing and no one is going to stop me this time.'

I look up at him, I can see my glitter reflecting in his green-flecked eyes.

fourteen

'We never get to see you'se these days, babe. You are always with those Arabian Knights. What time are you off with them tonight?' Angie asks me.

Hefty gas workers, led by Justin, are strutting around the pool at Angie's villa in skimpy bikinis stolen from the washing line. Another contingent, dressed in Union Jack boxers and bandanas, are inventing a new sport that involves attempting to run the length of the pool, leaping from one lilo to the next. Angie is dishing out jam jars of a fatal punch. Last night, Heather's was raided and shut down by the morality police. The expat community is convulsing. Heather's has managed to stay beneath the radar with the police for many years; despite the fighting, carousing and prostitution. An eminently positioned Sheikh has been kept entertained, friendly. Someone though has tipped off the police that a number of the glass-washers do not have the right work visas. The bar manager is in jail, charged with people trafficking. The workers were deported this morning. The friendly Sheikh is nowhere to be seen. And Angie tonight is hosting the alternative Heather's New Year's Eve party.

'So things are back on with you'se and Brian then?'

'We danced, we drank champagne.'

'Well, good on ya, that's what it's all about.' Angie points to her T-shirt that is lying on the sun lounger beside her. On it is emblazoned "Sex and drugs and sausage rolls".

'Don't know which offends more here?' I giggle.

'I could murder a sausage roll,' Angie groans.

'He said something strange though. He said his dreams were in the hands of the accountants.'

'Bankrupt.' Angie smacks down her jam jar in a 'told you so' way.

'He can't be. How could he be working here?' Any contractor working here has to prove their financial standing and stability, and pay a sizable bond as proof.

'He's not all he seems, Jimmy's on the money on that one. But you milk it, just don't get involved. He's worth a fling, that's all.'

The doorbell rings and Angie sloshes her way back into the villa and over to the door, a trail of oily splashes following her. 'Lookey who's here, talk of the devils!'

'We heard there was some craic going down here tonight,' announces Craig, tipping his head to me and depositing a crate of beer.

I call to Brian, 'You're early.'

'Just wanted to make sure you didn't get up to any trouble without us.' Brian starts dancing and playing the air guitar as he comes out to the pool. He quickly has everyone jumping up and down. Laughing, he seizes me and wraps me into a tango hold.

☪

I look at my watch, more than an hour has passed. We have danced to all the party classics and Brian has not let go of my hand for a minute. We need to leave soon but Brian and Craig strip to their boxer shorts and leap into the pool, competing in a new round of Olympic lilo. They are defending South African sporting honour, having divided the competitors into national groups.

Angie falls down beside me on a sun lounger to watch, 'Nice pecs.' The doorbell rings again, 'Oh, bloody hell, I've just got down here.' Angie attempts to clamber up from the sun lounger, but slides to the ground in cackles.

I go into the villa and slip my way across the floor to the door.

Mozah is on the doorstep, 'Miss Aisling are you ready for a night of Bedouin magic?' Mozah kisses me on both cheeks. 'Come, and where are Dumb and Dumber?'

☾

We arrive just before midnight after a terrifying drive where Land Cruisers, lights on full beam scream past us at two hundred-plus kilometres an hour. Worse, are the ones coming at us on the wrong side of the road. Friday night. After prayers, the local boys pumped up on alcohol and coke spend the night tearing up the desert highways, playing their favourite game of trying to force other drivers off the road. Brian's experience of war zone driving comes into its own. For once, no one speaks much. With every swerve my nerves fray some more.

All is silent at the resort as we arrive. We are spending this night in the desert's one and only holiday resort, at the edge of the dunes. Tomorrow we will take the ride in Land Cruisers out remote. Mozah rings at the bell impatiently. And again. After about ten minutes a porter slouches in, he takes our bags and nods for us to follow. We are shown to modest chalets. Mosney, the Irish Butlins, circa 1972, in the dust. After the nightly pounding of air hammers in the city, the silence at the edge of the dunes is strange. I try to read until my eyes grow too tired and then I sleep fitfully, dreaming of sea serpents and storms.

Thunder rolls in my dreams, the sea crashes with jet-black waves. I shake. A man stands over me. I'm about to scream when I realize it is Brian.

'What the hell?'

I am startled, positive I locked the door last night.

'Mm, delicious,' he bends down to me and kisses the line of my collar-bone, his teeth graze my skin. I push him away, still shaking.

'You really scared me. How did you get in?'

'Calm down. All the keys fit all the locks, don't ask.' Brian laughs.

'I guess it doesn't matter in a country with no crime,' I grumble, my pulse still racing.

'No, not when the secret police can get through any door in a trice.'

I take a deep breath, trying to restore my mood and stretch.

'Come on then sleepy, we've an adventure to be chasing after today. And tonight, ah, Miss Aisling, then ...'

'Then ...'

He places his forefinger on my lips and then softly traces it over my chin, down the line of my neck, to my breast-bone. It rests there a second.

A bawl at the door, 'Mr Brian, where are you? *Yallah*, let's get going,' Mozah, full throttle. 'Mr Craig, where's Brian? Have you seen him?'

Brian slumps down beside me on the bed. He groans quietly, lying flat on his back. I sit up, swinging my legs out of the bed and start to rise, Brian pulls me back into his arms. He kisses me fast, fierce, on my lips, collarbone, the curve of my shoulder. He jumps up, 'Tonight' and slips out the back door of the chalet.

☪

Mesmerising, the sand ripples in purples, slithering to the horizon. The desert near the city is mostly hard, rubbly, one dreary granola colour, flat, with scrubby trees. But now, deep south, it is ethereal. So many soft honey hues sweeping together, peaking in immense creamy waves. The sky so often colourless in the city is ozone blue. I gaze out over the oceanic desert, my eyelids grow heavy. Sand dreams of ancient caravans, lines of camels, bright tassels jangling. Epic warriors, faces shrouded in turbans, just their eyes glinting. Women swathed in tattered cloth, rough silver bangles at their ankles.

Suddenly the Land Cruiser stalls sharply. My gaze is drawn back in an instant to the scene about me. At the resort an hour earlier we were picked up by our guide in a tank of a Land Cruiser, positively war mongering. Mozah and Craig sit up front with the guide. I am in the middle and Brian has stretched out in the back. A couple more tanks with other tourists in our convoy follow. Craig is singing to Elvis songs on the radio. Mozah, as ever, is on her mobile. Brian is quiet in the back, sometimes retorting to an insult lobbed over by Craig, sometimes discreetly stroking the back of my neck. Whistling with the singing. Heartbreak Hotel. I draw my gaze from my dreamy warriors and perfumed girls and turn to look at what has silenced the singing. To the right side of the car is the sea of sand, mile after mile. To the left, across the car I can see nothing.

'Shit,' Craig. Silence in the car. I raise myself up so I can see past Mozah and gasp. We are poised inches from the edge of a hundred foot dune. As I day-dreamed, we had driven up and along the crest of mountainous dune. It is a sheer drop down. I have no time to take in the scale before the car in front plunges over the edge, in an eye blink, disappearing before us. Mozah screams. Our guide laughs and presses his foot to the accelerator. I am thrown back in my seat, my shoulder banging against the metal of the car. We sail down, zig-zagging from side to side, rolling on two wheels. I hold onto the headrest of the seat in front of me for dear life. Mozah shrieks and shrieks as Craig spits out every obscenity imaginable. My stomach bumps somewhere behind us. We land with a thud, and skid in a figure of eight, our guide yells out and punches the air. The boys are leaping up and down in their seats and whopping. I breathe again; the thrill still electric through my body.

Mozah is slapping at the driver, '*Wallah*! My nails, my nails.'

We look at her hand; several of her false French polished talons broke off as she gripped the car fixtures in terror. One finger is bleeding. From the fuss she is making you would think she had lost a leg, but I won't let her whining spoil the moment.

We watch as the last car in the convoy helter-skelters down the dune, silenced again by the utter madness of the feat. Our guide smacks the dashboard and we shoot off, driving at some ridiculous speed. It isn't much longer before we encounter our next cliff dune, this time with no warning. The drivers don't stop for dramatic effect as before, but just hurtle straight over the edge. My heart. By the fifth such dune we are starting to understand how best to brace ourselves for our violent descent, anticipating each stomach lurch with whoops. It is then that the car ahead of us, halfway down the dune, rolls.

Mozah's scream is ear shattering. Our driver brakes sharply so we slide at a ninety-degree angle to the rolled car, avoiding it by inches. As we come to a halt we all jump out. My knees are so weak

I can barely stand, tears in my eyes. Our guide and the boys roll the up-turned car back to an upright position. We can hear crying and moaning coming from inside. Gently the boys help the party of three French tourists out of the car. The two women are bruised and have a few small cuts, but the man has a gash to his head. One of the women vomits. The other is shaking. The man just leans against the car, dazed, blood trickling down his T-shirt. Their driver is laughing, praising Allah and hugging our guide. I go to our car and find some water bottles. I give one each to the French tourists. Brian is ransacking the boot of our car. He pulls out a first aid box and finds a bandage. While Brian and I tend to the French man, the three guides argue and gesticulate, by now the third car has arrived, cruising down the dune in a flurry of sand. Mozah is still muttering about her nails and demanding that as he has the first aid box out Brian dress her finger with a plaster. The French tourists are insisting on being taken back to the city and to a hospital. Their shock has turned to full fury. The other tour party in the third car, a mixed group of Europeans, who witnessed the car rolling and our car's dramatic swerve, are green-gilled, shaken and also demanding to go back. The two parties head off. We continue.

☪

We arrive mid-morning at our camp. It fringes an ocular lagoon, behind us a cowled dune. Across the waters the low-lying mountains of our nearest neighbours. The hills are spiked with military masts and satellites, state-sized knuckle-dusters. Our camp consists of half-a-dozen long, open tents. The floor is a patchwork of crimson and indigo patterned carpets, worn and dusty. The tents circle an open fire pit and there are more rugs and cushions around this. Partly obscured behind this ancient scene are signs of modern life, a bank of portaloos, generators, some sheds and a Winnebago. Two bowing Indian servants scurry out from the Winnebago as we pull up and greet us with cans of ice-cold cola and plates of Turkish Delight.

We take our colas and walk over to the lagoon, where we paddle as we sip our drinks. We spend a lazy morning and lunch in the camp. After lunch the boys doze, while Mozah flicks through some magazines and I read a book.

'Ash, what are you reading?' Mozah asks me.

I show her the cover.

'*Girls of Riyadh. Wallah!* This book is banned.' Mozah takes the book from me and fingers it as if it was printed with poison.

'Where did you get this?'

'One of the expat wives. It's doing the rounds of the coffee mornings.' The book is thoroughly thumbed.

'Would you like to read it? I'm nearly finished. You can have it after me.'

'I can't read this.' She tosses the book back to me.

'I wouldn't think you would be worried about reading a banned book.'

'No, it's not that, *yanni*. I know of this book, my cousins talk about it. You like it because it shows you our secret lives. I don't want to read of my life in the pages. It makes me die inside. See, I read *Vogue*. This is what I want.' She lets the magazine flutter through her fingers and sighs. 'I'm so tired of the life here. It can all go in a moment, as I'm not one of them, not born here. Anytime they can send me back to Beruit.'

'I worry for you Mozah. You push too hard sometimes. It looks like you want them to send you back.'

'La, la. I have to stay. I can't go to Beruit. But it's so hard; it makes me crazy, makes me do crazy things. Sometimes I think it's better to be thrown out. Perhaps, the Americans will take me then … Aeii, but then I think, no Mozah, be good. You have to stay. The life here is safe. I have to wear the *abaya*, be useful to them; and, this is why I must work in the Professor's office. Or maybe, Mr Brian's? *Yanni*, maybe he can get me a transfer to his firm in Cape Town. He is the big man. I can be useful to him, very.'

'Maybe … but …'

Mozah picks up the book again.

'What's this book about? Being a modern, liberated woman?'

'Yes, and it's about friendship, the power of female friendship.'

'Pah! These girls, they pretend they are so modern, and *they* chase after the boys. Still, it's all about the boys for them. *Yanni*, that is how it is, our lives are about the men. We must have a strong man, Aisling; it is the only way.'

'Mozah. You of all people, don't believe that, do you?'

'It's all so easy for you, Aisling. You can have a good job, wear what you want, choose the man you want. You pity me.'

'No, Mozah …'

'I don't want your pity. I want your life.'

Mozah rolls away from me, my friendship and turns back to her *Vogue*.

☾

We settle to a game of cards when three Land Cruisers pull up in a blaring of horns. Several local men jump out, there is much back-slapping and hugging as our guide greets the men. They take little notice of us. The men down some colas and then amble off to the sheds. Within moments the sheds are roaring and the men reappear on quadbikes, racing around the tents. Crud showers into the tent where we are sitting.

Mozah yells out to them. '*Yallah, yallah* beauty lady, let's ride.'

We are pulled up onto the back of the quads.

I cling onto a man in a thawb as he tears over the dunes. I can see the speedometer and we are racing at fifty kilometers. I try not to think what will happen if I lose my grip. My teeth are rattling in my head. We are high in the dunes behind our camp, all I can see are walls of sand ahead. We are heading straight at the wall. I close my eyes and bury my face in the back of my driver. I snap backwards as we ascend the dune.

'*Shufi,shufi, jamillah.*'

My driver stops. I emerge from the folds of his thawb and look. The dunes behind our camp rise and then fall away to a vast grizzled plain, across which are even greater dunes than those we had sailed down in the Land Cruiser this morning. The plain swarms. Hundreds of local men race around in every which way, demented, their quads roaring like a blood fest of hornets. Explosions of dust, gritting the hot air. With a war cry my driver swoops down to the plain.

We screech up to a line of quad bikes. My driver leads me to one. The others are arriving and being led to quads also. When we talked about quad biking back in the city I was excited, as I have never tried it before. Now though …

The boys are already racing around. My driver flicks the ignition and my quad shudders to life. Hot saliva chokes at the back of my throat. We are miles from anywhere. No safety helmets, and the plain is strewn with rocks. With the roaring whirlwinds of crazy youths in every direction, a bolt surges through me. I am sure I must be white as a ghost. Please don't let them see.

Brian waves to me, 'Aisling, follow me, yah, we're heading across the plain to some quieter dunes, it's mental here.'

The others are already heading off across the plain. Tentatively, I squeeze the accelerator and I am off - in completely the opposite direction. Soon I am bumping along well enough. The hard plain desert is rough work, every bone in my body feels it is being rubbed raw. With each rock I judder over, I think I've lost a tooth and I can barely keep a hold of the steering wheel. And this is meant to be fun!

We reach the soft sand, the dunes. I find some speed and leap across peaks. At last, now it's fun.

'Are you sure you haven't done this before?' Brian calls out as I overtake him and whizz into the air across a hollow.

I love reaching the crests and looking out to the plain, seeing all the dots of quads below, while in the distance majestic waves of dunes bank and reef. The boys are performing stunts, trying to out-manoeuvre each other. Brian is now at the top of a dune so high and sheer that the rest of us turn back from it. He is standing up on the back of the quad, silhouetted against the platinum sun. He fills the sky. Magnificent. He punches the air and plunges. The dune collapses around him. We clap and cheer.

'Yah, what a ride!' Brian cuts the motor to his quad and leaps off it as he pulls up beside me and jumps onto the back of mine, 'Come on Ash, you have got to feel that, it is a-ma-zing!'

I can't drive up there, I squeak inwardly to myself.

Brian presses my arms, 'Afraid?'

'Of course not,' I retort. St.Jude, where are you now?

'Good girl, like this,' Brian leans over me, helping me steer and control the speed as we scramble upwards. Before I know it we are at the top. Brian pulls on the brake, 'Let's wait a moment, just look.'

A slow pink wash is creeping across the sky, the dunes in the distance are mauve, tinged at the crown with gold.

'It's so beautiful,' he whispers. His body tenses behind me. The plain below is greying. 'A shame to go, girl. I'll drive us down.' We swap places on the quad and rocket down the cliff; sand and the dusk rolling after us.

It is dark on the plain. The ants are now a hundred shooting, colliding stars. The black of the night absolutely no deterrent to the bikers' fun. If anything they are all the more crazed. Wild wails, a pack in the night. We return to the sanctuary of our camp, where the fire bowl is burning and the camp is lit by lanterns and flaming torches. A feast is spread out on the carpets; huge basins of rice, platters of flat bread, and towers of fruit. Fish grilling over the fire. I am hot and dusty. While the staff prepare the final dishes and the boys boast about their driving tricks, I slip away to the lagoon. A little moonlight skims the water. I shake my clothes off and step into the pooling shades. Small unseen creatures scatter about my feet. The water is shallow. The moon tugs the tide, tight to the far side of the lagoon. I feel the lunar tow.

When I return to the camp the others are already devouring the piles of food. Mozah, wearing an almost translucent sarong, sits in glory on a nest of cushions at one end with Craig and Brian either side. She demands Craig and Brian hand-feed her, popping morsels into her gaping mouth, while she cradles her bandaged hand. I sit further along with our hosts, their friends and a couple of bleached prostitutes. I follow the etiquette of our guides in abandoning cutlery and scrunching the food into balls in the palm of the hand. Only Mozah, distancing herself as ever from her heritage, refuses to join in as our guide introduces us to camp customs.

'Aiee. I don't know how you can eat in that way Miss Aisling, like a dirty Bedouin. But European women are so grubby.'

I bite my tongue. I know from the flicker in her eye that she wants to pick a fight. I am not rising to it, not willing to be the plaything for her claws this evening. The boys laugh and Brian pops a grape into Mozah's mouth, saying, 'Not like our gracious Cleopatra?'

He strokes her long bare leg, uncurled in front of him. He hasn't spoken to me throughout the entire meal.

I cannot sit here. I go over to the Winnebago, where the staff have set another small fire. The teapots huddle in the hot stones around the edges. One of the maids bends down beside me and helps me pour the mint tea. The sharp fragrance stings my eyes, unleashing my tears. The woman wipes the tear from my cheek. I don't understand. I may as well be invisible. When I'm alone with him he's another man. Attentive, gentle, caring. But tonight, he laughed with her, at me.

While I've been pouring the tea, our hosts have brought out an assortment of drums, tambourines and whistles and the two Russian girls are on their feet, swaying and rolling their hips, passing a spliff between them. The men are clapping and whistling. Several bottles of vodka are doing the rounds. Shisha pipes bubble, the sickly strawberry smoke circling about the heads of the smokers. Mozah, encouraged by the avid audience whips off her sarong and holds it high above her like a flag as she leaps, in her bikini, across the fire. A huge cheer. One of our hosts tosses a vodka bottle to her; she takes a slug and then leaps back, landing on top of Brian. She kisses him full on the lips and puts the bottle to his lips. She rolls onto Craig and repeats the move. Craig snatches the sarong and jumps up, wrapping it about himself and attempts the dance of the seven veils. Everyone is rollicking around in gales of laughter as this huge, clumsy, drunken oaf stumbles about kicking over plates and bottles. Behind them in the flickery shadows of the fire Mozah is sitting on Brian's lap, and he is kissing her ear.

I stumble back to the lagoon. The moon's hard half-shut eye scorns me. Not the gold-drop moon of my first Arabian evening. That sensuous moon promised so much. Turning away from the cruel eye I walk on, slow tears falling down my cheeks. 'Tonight' he had said. I climb upwards, seeking the summit of the dune that looms over the camp. Craving sanctuary from the tawdry scene, with each tear, moments from the past three months, my stupidity, blot and fall. Every kiss, spent.

Down below, the lagoon is black, still, silent. I yearn for its indifference, but my heart is like the stringy sand-grass, it locks away and is quenched by its tears, forever. The desert's cruelty is that it never lets go.

I lie down, worn out from the climb in the soft sand, chilling in the night air. I look up at the thickening sky. The howls wane, just an occasional yelp, sound of a bottle smashing. Fireworks, must be midnight. I see Mozah and Brian kissing in my mind, locking together.

I tune my ears to the tiny sounds about me, the swoop of a night creature above me, the rustle of grains of sand against my clothing. Minutes, an hour, more, pass. Darkness. In three months I have been out of the skyscraper city three times. My yearning for the red forts, smudgy desolate villages, white sails of fishing dhows gliding back into the northern ports gnaws at me. These images tease me in my guidebook, but the expats I know scoff at venturing out of the city,

'It's too hot, Ash.'

'It's too dusty.'

'Another day. *Inshallah.*'

'Here, have a voddie and let's chill out by the pool.'

They have all they want in the seven-star hotel bars and designer malls. But somewhere I let my dreams slip away, as I got caught in

Brian's glamour. I want there to be something beyond the alcohol, shopping and sex. More than 'Essex with sand', as Angie calls it. I see the girls at work, the 'princesses', Joe calls them in awe, hurry in each morning teasing each other. What stories are whispered at twilight in those villas behind the high walls in Al Hamsa?

That rumbling adobe wall in the souk; I still feel its thrum in my hand. Spring will come early. Earlier than home, where sometimes the handfuls of snowdrops Grandaddy plants along the pathway only poke their innocent heads through in April. The sand folds about me. A lone star chokes in the syrup sky.

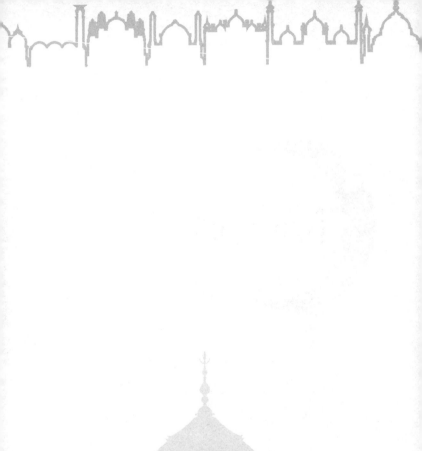

Moon

fifteen

I will forget Brian. I walk as long as I can in the clammy night by the Bay. I can't sleep. So I walk. Every night, for the past fortnight since New Year's Eve. I tell myself Brian is just another sleazy expat. Angie was right. My hard tears splash into the dark night water. The fast swelling currents swallow my hurt. But my mind wanders back to the dunes, to that flickering flame-lit kiss. Mozah's triumphant toss of her head. Everyone is at the Bay at night. The heaving pathway and the heat suffocate my spirit. I gasp for cool air, but first I must loosen Brian's bite on my life.

I scoff at those expats like Tony, who are convinced they are of such importance that they are spied on, bugged. But I recognise in the anonymity of the Bay crowd that I have been under surveillance: Brian's. I realise since I have been here I have hardly have time for anyone else. My social circle, Brian's gang, has been tight; more than tight, brace like. Now, alone at night, by the Bay, looking out across the endless black ocean I feel such release to be free from his constant watch. Soon the release should be complete. The Prof told me today he is going to break out of the Rex contract. The squawking about expensive foreigners prying about the Board is near deafening. Dr Mouna is bending his ear daily, fearful Rex will draw the attention of the National Audit Board for some dark reason. So, the mercenary air seizes the tears on my cheeks.

Tonight, after not many so many paces along the Bay pathway my ankles refuse to go further. They are swollen from walking night after night in the heat, back now with vengeance. I sit on a bench, but everywhere I turn I see shadows of Brian and Mozah. To the left of me, a couple sit beneath a palm tree, her laugh like Mozah's. Rattling my tears again. To the right, Brian, with his clipped military walk struts past me, calling out to a woman ahead, she turns, smiles, he takes her arm. 'Brian', the greeting dying on my lips. My phone buzzes. A text, short. 'Let's have dinner at the Celestine. I miss you.' Deep jugular.

☪

I get a taxi back to my apartment. The stub of a cigarette catches my eye, tucked behind the porcelain basin in the hallway washroom. I don't use this washroom, it's for visitors. I haven't been in here in a while. What prompted me to walk in now? Just a feeling.

I pick it up gingerly, trying to work out somehow how fresh it might be. I can't tell. My fingers are cool, despite the heat. It could have been there since before I moved in, but I'm sure I would have noticed it when I first arrived. I cleaned the place from corner to corner, removing endless layers of dust. Surely I would have seen it? No, it is new. I just know it. Someone has been in the apartment. No trace of smoke, but the aircon has sucked any incriminating traces away. Still, I can feel their stale breath in the air, sense their footfall. His footfall.

I walk around the apartment, testing the locked windows, opening cupboards and drawers and checking their contents, my hands quivering. Everything is as it should be, and yet it isn't. I am being stupid, getting as bad as Tomas. Nothing is missing or disturbed. I just haven't noticed the cigarette before. A careless visitor must have left it there. All the same, I don't want to be in the apartment. I ring Joe. No reply. Angie, the same. I knock at Joe's door then remember he isn't there any more; one of Justin's lodgers found himself suddenly on a plane back home and Joe's moved into the spare room at Justin's villa. Tomas and Salima moved out over Christmas. I am alone.

☪

'Sorry Miss Ash, I'm moving out of here too.'

The next morning at work I arrive to find Joe packing up his files. He is moving down a floor to Tomas' office. Meanwhile, there is great commotion in the offices in the corridor around me. A reorganisation. Someone must have upset someone else, and now everyone is moving offices. This happens regularly, normally provoked by Mozah.

'Hallo Sister, I am your new translator.' A pair of very twinkly eyes peer at me as a veiled woman glides gracefully into the office and lands her large Prada bag on what, until a moment ago, was Joe's desk. 'I am Laila, close the door please.' Laila starts taking items out of her bag: a small box of tissues in a gilded cover, a poesy vase, a Teddy bear, a string of glittery butterflies, some pens and a bag of sweets. My very own Arabic Mary Poppins, I await a lamp. She shuffles the various items around the desk while talking non-stop to me. 'How old are you Sister?'

'I am thirty-three.'

'*Wallah*. Same as me. But this is not possible. You look like a child. So young. Where's your husband and children? How many children do you have?'

'I'm not married. I don't have any children.'

'No husband and you are thirty-three! *Aiee*! This is not good. Allah be praised he'll find you a husband very soon. So your family is here?'

'No.'

'*Wallah*! Alone! Alone! La,la,la,la. No, this cannot be. How could your family let you? Where's your older brother? He should be here with you to take care.' I shake my head. 'But why are you here?' The eyes intense with wonder.

I tell Laila I want to see the world and meet different people. 'Ah, yes, like me. I like to work with foreign people. I taught myself English. Me and my brothers. We watch the American movies and learn to talk English.'

Laila tells me her brother, Sami, has an American accent and sounds like Patrick Swayze. She has worked before with many Westerners in the hospital. She used to be a secretary there with the former Chief Executive. He went to America and her job was gone. But the former CEO had a cousin at the Board, so Laila came to the Board three years ago. For the last year she has been working for Mr. Justin.

'*Hallas*. I tell Dr Mouna no more. Mr Justin is a bad man. Aiee, every morning his breath smell bad, the other secretaries tell me this is the drunken smell. La, la. *Subhan'allah*. It's *haram*. Forbidden. I can't work for a bad man.'

She trills on telling me this man has no control, no respect for himself or how can he smell of the drunk smell? No, she says, she has to be cautious. Her brothers will be crazy if they hear she works for a bad man and they will forbid her to work.

'I like to work. Dr Mouna tell me about you and we decide I should be your translator. She says you have a clear heart.'

A goldfish bowl comes out of the bag next, 'For my frogs. I bring them tomorrow.'

Did I just hear that? Frogs? 'And you're a beauty like me. I am a great beauty.' She tweaks my cheek. 'You see my *nikab*? When I work at the hospital. When I was twenty, twenty-five, I did not cover my face, only my hair. But the doctors there! *Wallah!* Some of them are bad men. Very bad men. Even if they are married. Worse, if they are married. One doctor he liked me very much. He sent me flowers and sweet-things every day. He was an old man. He was forty. He had two wives and children and he thinks I will marry him. Be third wife. No, no. What does he think? I am twenty. I will be wife number one to a young husband.' She pauses in her high speed rattle for a moment, makes sure I am listening. 'One day he came to my office. He begged me to 'go' with him. He tried to kiss me. I screamed and fainted. Allah, be praised, a nurse heard me and stopped him. After that to thank Allah and be close to my God, who saved me, I wear the *nikab*. But here in the office, we close the door and I take it off and you see. I am a great beauty.'

Laila removes her veil and indeed she is a great beauty. Pale, luminescent skin. Soft, chocolate curls framing her heart shaped face. Fine, deep cheekbones, causing a permanent smile and warmth to her facial expression. A sweet smile that belies her feisty words.

'But still the bad men they know. They can tell you are a great beauty even when you wear the *nikab.*'

A knock on the door.

'Wait, wait,' Laila calls as she hurriedly puts on her veil.

When she is once more covered I open the door. Brian walks in, 'Miss Aisling, my text about dinner at the Celestine, let's go tonight. I'll pick you up at seven.' Before I can answer he turns and leaves. Now Laila pulls out a walnut-sized lump of what looks like coal from her magical bag and a lighter. She places the lump on my desk amidst my various papers and, before I realise what is about to happen, lights it. The lump explodes into a cloud of fragrant smoke. Oud. My papers singe.

'There, now we are Sisters,' she says, gently wafting the incense into my hair.

☾

Brian is frowning at me. Why couldn't I resist, delete that text? Instead, I agreed to meet him and he picked me up earlier in the evening and brought me to the Celestine, where we are sipping champagne and eating supper at the beach cafe. Now I am with him in the flesh, all I can think about is Mozah's display at the Bedouin camp and how he kissed her. This is a mistake. I told myself the long afternoons and evenings can make you feel very alone, and it's only supper. The truth – I have to prove to myself, this time I am first choice, not second.

'Why not, girl? What else have you got on?' Brian has asked me to join the gang this weekend at the Golf Master's tournament.

My resistance to him may falter, but I can't bear to be a part of that gang. I have declined, with no real excuse. I loose the brace. He frowns, but his phone rings and he steps away to answer it. This has happened three or four times already in the course of the last hour. I wait.

I am diverted by the news on the plasma screen in the beach bar. Rioting in desert cities elsewhere. Deaths as protesters clash with security forces. Public buildings under attack. Reports of police opening fire. Cars blaze, clouds of acrid black smoke.

Suddenly a burst of laughter and loud voices behind me, approaching. 'Ash! So this is where Brian's got to.'

It is Craig and Mozah, I point to where Brian stands, talking on his mobile. They don't stop but head to the bar, Craig as he passes me saying, 'The wife again, I bet. She's going to bleed him for every penny she can get.'

Brian comes back. 'Sorry about that, Ash. Did I see Craig and Mozah? Before they join us, I just want to talk work with you for a minute.' He asks me how my work on the press campaign for the clinics is progressing. I have got the princesses tweeting and our Facebook page is due to go live in the next few days. 'Good, good.' He isn't listening.

'What's wrong Brian?' He sighs and strokes my thigh beneath the table, resting his hand on my knee. 'No, Brian.'

He's not touching me like this anymore. I move, cross my legs, so that his hand has nowhere to rest and falls away. He puts his hands to his forehead, casually ignoring my snub.

'Tough times, Ash. I was warned.' He says it is always the same in the desert. The Royals bring in foreign contractors and then never pay up, always finding some way to wriggle out, most graciously of course. This happened with the firm that was brought in before Rex. They worked for six months and every month their cheques bounced. In the end they walked out.

'These Arabs are rich for a reason; they don't like to see a riyal leave the land. Bastards.' He tells me he was meant to meet with the Prof earlier in the day to discuss the payment issues and a potential new contract extension, but the Prof cancelled and he has not been taking calls since. Brian is overdrawn. He can't pay his staff again this month. Craig is threatening to bail out and return to South Africa, as his wife is nagging him to return. 'So Ash, you're probably closest of us all here to the Prof. What's he going to do?'

I'm not even second choice; how vain, how stupid am I? No more. I will not betray the Prof. I don't say anything. This will infuriate him, more than anything. Sometimes, silence is the only weapon. I hold it; hold him in the jaws of the brace, just for a moment. It stretches. Music booms out, Mozah has persuaded the bar man to turn up the stereo.

'Jesus, Aisling, I can't fail here too. You are either on my side or you are not.' He jumps up and marches off.

sixteen

'That man yesterday, who is he?' Laila asks.

'Which man?'

'The tall one with the strange accent.'

'Brian Rothmann, he's working on the payroll project and some other projects. He's from South Africa.' The call to prayer growls around the building. 'He is a rude man. He did not say hello to me. He thinks I am a nobody because I wear this veil? No, he should show me respect. *Yanni*, that man will play badly with you.'

A knock at the door, Laila covers up and opens it. A rancid looking individual stands there.

'*Salaam-Alaikum.*' He introduces himself as Tarek and says he is the office manager for Sheikh Fariq. They are moving into the office next door. The mysterious Sheikh Fariq again, but before I can ask any questions there follows a fifteen minute tale of woe about how hard Tarek is finding it to get their files moved to their new office. Laila stands aside loftily, even when Tarek wrings his hands and pleads with her as his 'Sister' to intercede. He obviously thinks she is in charge in this office. Exhausted by his storytelling, he finally leaves.

'This man, this Tarek. He's another bad man. You mustn't let him into this office Sister. You see his eyes, all red with blood. He likes to drink and this is forbidden by Allah. He goes with bad women too. Now I must pray.' Laila goes to the bathroom to wash, returns, closes the door, rolls out her prayer mat, takes off her shoes, her veil, and kneels down. She begins to chant softly under her breath and prostrate herself. Such serenity in her face. The office, for once so still.

Her prayers finished, Laila takes my arm and tells me we are going for breakfast. She leads us down the corridor to the office of the girls who issue press releases and manage our corporate events. Joe's princesses are always pleasant to me, saying hello and being helpful when I need anything, but we have not got beyond to a more intimate level of conversation. In truth, like Joe, I am awed by their beauty, elegance and confidence. They click around the floor, snapping their fingers, yapping out instructions. This is the first time I have been in their office. It is festooned with sparkle, Hollywood-style posters of our beloved *Maleka* on the wall and tables heavy with bowls of sweets. The great surprise is the enormous, two-foot tall wine goblet, in which swim three goldfish, and beside this, another bowl with tiny frogs, which Laila duly claims back for our office. Frogs!

I sit on a low chair amongst them as they giggle and chatter away, top speed. Every morning they order in an array of dishes from a local patisserie. Spinach and cheese-filled pastries, wraps, falafel and honey cake. Laila reminds them to talk in English. One of the girls has just found a phone number scrawled in the dust on the bonnet of her Land Cruiser. The girls are teasing her about the identity of her secret admirer and egging her on to call the number.

'*Yanni*, Miss Aisling, why do you have no husband?' If only I knew. How to answer this one?

'It's hard these days to find husbands. There are other choices for men.'

'And women? In your country men and women live together without being married?'

'Yes, we have choices.'

'You can try first, *wallah*!' One of the princesses shrieks with laughter and wriggles her little finger, 'We should do this in our country. No more maggots.' The others giggle and clap. 'Ah, Miss Aisling, you look shocked. But we're like you Western women, *shufi*.' The girls take off their *abayas* to reveal jeans and T-shirts. 'We watch Sex and the City. We love Carrie. See I have shoes like her.'

I don't ask how they watch this show, Tony Morton has told me you can get pretty much anything you want with the right connections from illegal DVDs and fake Rolexes to anti-psychotic drugs and hand guns. 'But Miss Aisling, what if the men just keep on trying? Each time with another woman.' Laila looks at me with sorrowful eyes. 'So this is the problem, Laila.'

'La, and this is choice? There is always another date, for men.' She pops a chocolate-coated date in her mouth, 'Another taste.'

Another princess speaks, 'For us too, it's hard to find a husband. Our mothers all married by eighteen and had ten, eleven, sometimes as many as twelve children. But our men, do they want this now? No, they want to go to America and marry a blonde woman with big...' She points to her bosom.

Laila adds, 'Now, really it's a big problem in our society, we have three times as many women as men. And those men, what do they do?'

The princesses spit their answers;

'Pah, gamble...'

'Aaii, drink...'

'Go to the Celestine with bad women.'

One of the princesses whispers, 'They only want to play with us. They tell us, come now, let's do these things and I will marry you. But after they play, they go. They do this until they are too old, then they marry their fifteen year old cousin.'

The girls sit silently. 'This is the life now. It is all about money. Do you think this will make the people happy? No. Will it make the God, Allah, happy? No. But do the people care? No. They care only for themselves,' Laila concludes.

The princesses all kiss me on each cheek, softly holding me in their arms and invite me to join them each morning hereafter. I am so touched. We return to our office to find Tarek in there with a young Thai man. Tarek explains this is my new translator, especially provided for me by Sheikh Fariq.

'Eh?' Only yesterday I gained Laila with no prior warning or negotiation. And who is this Sheikh Fariq to be sending me a translator?

Laila screeches, 'No, no, I'm Sister Aisling's translator.' An almighty row breaks out with words fired out by all parties at machine gun speed. Laila's screech brings the princesses running along the corridor and they are now all shouting and gesticulating wildly. Laila is crying hysterically. One of the girls slaps the poor Thai man who stands wordlessly.

Joe arrives in the midst of the bedlam. 'Whoy, what's going on with the princesses? Come on; let's leave them to it. This looks like it's gearing up to be a biggie. The Prof wants us.'

One of the princesses hears this and tells me to go, she will fetch Mozah to calm the situation. I doubt very much that this will be the case, more like fuel to the fire, but I know that in about half an hour, as ever, everyone will simply walk out for the rest of the week and this will at least restore some peace. I leave them to it.

Tomas, Brian and Craig are already in the Prof's office. The Prof's face is inscrutable. As soon as we sit down he quietly reports to us that he received instruction this morning from one of the royal advisors that the Queen wants her reform programme to advance with far more pace. She is dismayed that critical projects are delayed across all government departments. She has set a new timeframe and for us this means that all ten planned community health clinics must be operational within the next six months, brought forward by more than a year. We gasp. The previous timeframe was ambitious, given all the bureaucracy and political interference. This is impossible. The Prof tells us that he is determined we will deliver on time and to this end has signed the contract extension for Rex. Brian will now manage the project. Brian speaks, 'Sheikh Fariq is concerned. He is clear that there can be no bad news staining our beloved *Maleka*'s good name.'

I wonder when I will ever meet our elusive Sheikh. He is fast becoming a thorn in my side. 'I'm sure this will be a help to you Miss Aisling as Mr Brian tells me you are worried and cannot cope with the press campaign. Brian will take responsibility for your office and the campaign now.' I am stunned. This is not the truth at all. How could the Prof credit such a lie? I can feel a flush at my throat, and Brian's eyes on it. But the Prof is continuing to outline how the new arrangements will work and I can see he is in no mood for any interruption. Deep inside, something slumps.

☪

Screeching can still be heard from my office. I am too dazed by what has just happened in the meeting with the Prof to go back to that pandemonium.

'Shops, now!' Angie catches me in the corridor, it's almost home time anyway.

We head for a vast mall, complete with fake canal and gondoliers. Angie buys yet more Jackie O sunglasses, and then, sitting on a tacky plastic bridge over the canal she orders us a Chinese meal. It features boiled belly and fried bittern, delicacies I decline; and a pot of tea with huge sad daisies bobbing in it. I have no appetite.

'That bitch.' Angie has just received an abrupt email from Mozah, demanding that she clear her diary the next morning so that she can have a supervisory session with her. Mozah is her new line manager. Up until this point Angie has reported directly to the Prof and she has no intention of reporting to mad Mozah.

'What is goin' on? Has the Prof gone barking?'

I relay what has just happened to me.

'I know you've a crush on Brian, Ash, but I don't trust these Arabian Knights. They seem to have got the Prof wrapped around their little finger now. I wouldn't be at all surprised if they are not behind what's happened with Mozah becoming my line manager.'

'I think you could be right. Brian and Mozah seem ...' I poke at the daisies in the teapot with a spoon.

'I've got this sinking feeling, kiddo, they means to have me out of my job. And to think they had the cheek to come and lord it up at one of me parties too.'

'So, what are you going to do about Mozah?'

'*Mafi miscallah*. I'm off to Cyprus tomorrow for a week on a training course and to party. She can go swivel on it.'

I laugh, 'I love your style Angie.'

'And what are you going to do about that pointy-headed project manager? You can't let him get away with making out you've failed.'

☾

If only I knew. I cannot sleep tonight. I switch on the news. In another desert land, another young man despairs. Mohsen Bouterfif cannot find a job or a home. Mimicking the vegetable seller from Sidi Bouzid, he lights a match. In the middle of the market square he runs, he burns. Across North Africa, hundreds more are fighting and dying right now.

Straight this way, a dictator flees.

seventeen

'I know where your loyalties lie now.' I look at the text on my phone, it pulses rage.

Brian had texted me the day after the meeting with the Prof saying he was with Mozah at that moment, arranging a night out for his 'gang'. He expected I would come and show some loyalty. Mozah would confirm the details with me later. I deleted the invitation and called Angie in Cyprus.

'Aw, it's classic bullying tactics, Ash. First the abuse, then when they think they might lose ya, they start love bombin' you. Wait for the flowers, the grand gestures. He really is a git.'

'Angie, when are you coming back?' I was missing her; she'd been gone two weeks.

'When the voddie runs out, chick.'

The Rex pack is everywhere. Brian is even in the Prof's office, as suddenly the Prof is sent to America for a congress. Tomas comes into the office, shaking some papers; he is seething. Laila is with the princesses down the corridor, talking about the latest episode of the massively popular Turkish soap opera 'Noura', which has all the Arabic female staff quite hooked.

'Here, there's one for you too.' He slams it on the desk.

I look at the memo. Brian orders that I meet with him and Mozah the next day and brief them on my work, and then he will decide if he still requires my input.

'Feckers, excuse my Irish,' Tomas lightly punches my shoulder, trying to make me smile with his attempt at an Irish accent.

'So, I guess I won't be working on this with you anymore, Tomas. Brian is bound to trash my work and throw me off the project, no doubt putting his name all over everything I've already done.'

'No, I think Brian will keep you on, he needs someone who can deliver and a pretty cover at that.'

'After he's made out I've failed with this project and I've blatantly snubbed his little tests of loyalty?' I pace up and down the office. I look out the window, the sky is a thick porridge today. 'I don't understand what's going on here? One moment the Prof tells me that Rex are out, the next they are in charge of everything and Brian is acting like he's the CEO.'

'I see Sheikh Fariq's hand behind this, but what's his connection with Rex?' says Tomas.

Something nags at me. 'What do you mean Brian needs a pretty cover?'

'To cover the affair. With Mozah. They're lovers. You know how people gossip in these offices. Watch every tiny move.'

We can't really talk about this any more at work, we are conscious of too many ears about the place. We agree to meet for dinner in the souk.

Not long after Tomas leaves there is a knock at the door. 'Brother, this is Miss Aisling,' Tarek squirms his way into the office, a tall swaying Arabic man following him.

I know immediately this stranger is a Sheikh. He stands majestically. He has an immaculate black shining beard and moustache. An expensive perfume engulfs the room. In one hand he compulsively turns prayer beads. His white thawb gleams. Strong one-eyed gaze, haughty brow. The other eye is hidden by a black patch.

He slips the beads into a secret pocket and then stretches out his hand to me. We shake hands and then he touches his hand to his heart and bows slightly to me. Next he raises his hand and clicks his fingers. Behind him an Indian youth appears with a crate, wrapped in pink cellophane and a large ribbon.

'For you Miss Aisling. I am Sheikh Fariq and I've been very much looking forward to meeting you, my dear. I regret there's been some misunderstandings over your translator, Miss Laila. Tsk, please this is over now and Tarek will speak with Miss Laila to put matters right. Let's be like family now. Please accept this small gift. I want to help you people who come so far from your homes to make ours a great nation. We need you people, you do us a great honour and are our dearest guests.' He bows again.

The youth sets down the box on my desk, which I can now see is carved intricately. 'You're busy now I am sure. I'll come back later. But, please I have a paper for you to read. I'm going to send it to His Highness. I would be honoured to receive your view and also the view of the Prof. He's a worthy man, you will show it to him?'

Tarek hands me a file. Sheikh Fariq bows once more and walking backwards, leaves the room.

Sheikh Fariq. He is not at all as I imagined, so humble and sweetly spoken. I look at the file. What will it contain? There are three pages, typed in English, 'A plan to alleviate the problem of aged spinsters.'

☪

'Did you find any good ideas on not becoming an aged spinster?' Tomas laughs.

We are sipping mint tea in the souk. Brightly coloured lanterns swing in the dusk, gusting in the breeze of the massive fans cooling the terrace. The souk is bustling tonight. Drums pulsate somewhere down an alleyway.

'After that crate of chocolates he gave you I think this Sheikh Fariq might have his own ideas to prevent you falling into ancient spinsterhood.' That's my fear too. 'What happened about Laila? I see she's back in the office now.'

I pour us some more tea and take a breath before relating the latest turn in the office saga. 'Sheikh Fariq has re-instated her and apologised, and made Tarek apologise too. He gave Laila a bottle of perfume, which she promptly threw in the bin once he had gone, saying she wanted nothing from a dirty man.'

'Sensible girl. She's obviously very perceptive when it comes to men. What does she make of our friends, the Arabian knights?' Tomas rattles the spoon in his glass.

'She doesn't trust Brian.'

The lanterns flicker as the electricity drops for a second or two. 'Like I said, sensible girl. And what about you, Ash?'

'I should have listened to you in the first place. I was stupid.' I push away some damp strands of hair at my neck.

'You are not foolish Ash. You thought he acted in good faith, why wouldn't you? But you shouldn't let men like him turn your head. You're worth more than that.' Tomas pats my hand kindly. 'This is an easy place to find everything starry, but Brian's behaviour is typical of the wide boys who come here hoping to make a fast buck. It's cut throat and securing the next deal at whatever cost is what it's all about.'

I hope I'm not part of a deal. As if he's read my mind, Tomas says, 'He's playing the long game with you Aisling.'

'What do you mean?'

'From the moment you stepped off the plane he's been seducing you, but he's playing it carefully. He hasn't quite got the measure of you. None of us have. You're a steel fist inside a velvet glove.' I don't know how to respond to this. Tomas continues, 'You're alone, in a role senior beyond your years. You are cool, calm, competent. You are not an easy lay like Mozah. For now, she is easily bought and he can use her to get where he needs to inside the Board.'

'Well, at least he has turned his attentions elsewhere.'

'Don't believe that for one minute. Mozah's not bright enough to be much use to him long term. He wants something more to hold over you than a quick shag, he wants you to fall in love with him.'

An animated group of young local men stride past our table, with greater purpose than you normally see in the dreamy souk. Their *dishdashs* and *thawbs* are different somehow, not so pristine, and their beards are longer and wilder. Altogether, they are more austere looking. Tomas agrees with my observations and speculates that they are followers of one of the new, more fundamental branches of Islam that are a growing presence in the city.

For the past two weeks protests have been whipping across the Arab world like the dust storms. Tunisia, Algeria, Egypt, Palestine, Jordan and Yemen. Ever closer. Mammy is worrying. But so far, it is quiet here. Yes, the princesses are no longer talking only about '*Noura*' at their breakfast gatherings, instead they tut and exclaim about the protests. We watch on the news as Cairo becomes a war zone. The princesses are amazed to see women protesting alongside men in Tahrir Square. They wonder how the governments in these countries allow the protests to continue, why they do not protect their citizens better from these unruly elements. 'It cannot last long, by tomorrow the police will have sent people home. Their president is a strong leader, he will defeat them. Look, they have nothing, no guns, just placards. Who are these small people?'

They see the protests as unholy, stirred up by students, outsiders and criminals. They have little sympathy with the people who are suffering in these countries. This is Allah's will and they should live with their destiny and pray for better circumstances, not set fire to cars, buildings, themselves. Several young men have now followed the example of the vegetable seller. Only Laila asks if it really is Allah's will for children to go without rice when governments spend billions on weapons, which they are turning on their own people. The princesses are sure that His Highness will quell any dissent here, it will not take hold. And the people love His Highness too much, he is a descendant of the Prophet and the people cannot revolt against him, for fear of invoking the wrath of Allah. Even so, there is a notably increased police presence everywhere. In the souk tonight there is most definitely a pulse in the air, it puts me on edge.

'Things are about to get difficult, Ash, with or without all the ructions elsewhere. It's been a honeymoon so far. The pressure will start now. Most expats go home in the first three months, homesick or sick of the heat and dust. Or they do something brainless and get thrown out. Those that survive, that's when the locals will start their tricks.'

'What makes you think that Tomas? I'm finding the local people far friendlier than the expats. The princesses are so lovely.'

'I don't know. I can't put my finger on it yet.'

We sit in silence for a while, just drinking our mint lemonade.

'What are we going to do about Rex, then?' I ask after some minutes pass.

'Something bigger is going on than we can see right now.' He pauses. I wait. 'I went over to their offices today. I had a meeting in the same tower block, so I thought I would call in. Have you been there?'

I shake my head. I haven't, although Brian has told me all about his office with its magnificent view over the Bay. One time we went to the souk to buy some artwork for his office from one of the galleries. I was surprised by his choice. I expected him to be drawn to some discreet monochrome abstract prints, but he had chosen a massive piece, the biggest painting in the gallery. It was a good ten-foot tall and four-foot wide, and was painted in vibrant yellows and blues. The painting buzzed, nothing was still or stable about it. It featured a cat, sitting with its back to the viewer, on a shaking stool. The stool had many legs to give it the appearance of movement. The cat was a petrol blue colour, sat on the indigo whirring stool. The painting's taut energy made me nauseous.

I tell Tomas about it.

'I know the painting you mean. I saw it in the gallery too. The one just down there?' He points to a building tucked away in the shadowy arches of the souk's main throughway. 'You know who painted that cat? The Chief Scientific Advisor to Saddam Hussein. His Highness gave him refuge after the Americans invaded Iraq. He was responsible for developing the nerve gas that massacred the Kurdish people in the north of Iraq. Now he is here, leading His Highness' genetics research. Come with me, I think we should go to the gallery.'

'Why?'

'You will see.'

The gallery has a beautiful exhibition of hadithas, gorgeous golden calligraphy representations of the Prophet's wisdom. It is enchanting. While I gaze on the golden swirls Tomas talks to the assistant in the gallery.

'Aisling, over here.' The assistant pulls back a curtain in a corner of the gallery to reveal a staircase. 'This is where the finest art is kept for private view by members of the Royal Family.' I ask Tomas how he knows about this as we ascend the stairs. He tells me that one of the men, a minor Royal, at the maglis told him about it, and the treasures it contained. We walk into a simple room, painted white, with a wooden floor. All along the walls are paintings and photographs. I barely note these, as on the far wall, directly opposite where I stand, a fury of yellow. The chemical killer cat.

I turn and descend the stairs. Tomas follows, 'I had this suspicion, and you know, I was right. There are no offices. Rex has a postal box, that's all, in the tower block.'

A business address, it lends an air of legitimacy. Just what kind of operation is Brian running? Tomas tells me he has been scouring the internet for traces of Rex Consulting. Strangely for a company that Brian claims is one of the largest management consultancies in South Africa, there is little to be unearthed. The only bytes are half a dozen blogs from disgruntled tourists in Shang'hai who bought pop concert tickets from a booth, registered to Rex, and found their tickets were worthless frauds.

'A tout,' Tomas jeers.

Angie is right, but how is Brian, clearly a bankrupt, able to function in this country? The authorities are paranoid about foreigners with debts. Any expat who wants to return home at the end of a contract has to prove they are leaving no debts before gaining their final exit permit and this entails giving two months notice to the bank so that a file can be prepared to demonstrate no unpaid bills will be left behind. Only recently there was a heartbreaking account in one of the smuggled-in foreign newspapers about an elderly, cancer ridden Nepalese man who came to the desert twenty years ago and had spent the past fourteen years, forgotten, in the debtors' camp in the desert. He had opened a little tailors business, but his Sheikh landlord kept putting up the rent, far in excess of his earnings. When the business failed he wanted to return home, but he owed a few hundred pounds to the landlord in rent arrears. His family, back in Nepal was poor and had no way to raise the money. He was thrown into the camp, where for fourteen years he had been undertaking punishing hard labour, chipping rocks, earning just a few pounds a month, while all the time the interest on his original debt escalated. Chip away as he did at the rocks, he could never chip away at the debt and it now stood at twenty four thousand dollars. In all this time he had no contact with his family, who assumed him dead.

Now he is dying of cancer, just a bag of bones, and cannot pay his medical fees. Somehow word of this terrible story got out and a Nepalese charity is trying to raise the money to pay off his debts and medical bills and fly him back to Nepal.

'All I can think is that Brian has a patron in high places, and if that is true he could be more dangerous that we think.'

'Dangerous?'

Tomas nods.

'Don't you think you're overestimating him?'

We have left the gallery and are winding our way through the dusty narrow alleyways. We turn into one that is all severe shadows. 'Why is Rex snooping about the Board? Taking over all the major projects? Getting a stranglehold? How do they keep getting their contract extended even though Dr Mouna and others have tried their best to block it?'

Tomas reminds me there are vast sums tied up in health care provision. All the new health clinics, the air ambulance service, new research centres, there is even talk of building a new state-of-the-art million-dollar hospital. 'Kerching. It's bonanza time and Brian means to cash in, along with his patron no doubt. Nothing and no one will be allowed to stand in the way of that. Like he said to you, you need to know whose side you are on Aisling.'

It is late now. The stalls in the souk are packing up as the browsers settle down at tables in doorways, playing dominoes and sucking on their shisha. The music drifts away. This hour is slow, sooty. As we pass a clutter of tables a figure leaps up,

'Miss Aisling, Miss Aisling, *Salaam-Alaikum*.' It is Tarek. He stumbles over to us. 'Miss Aisling. Are you having a pleasant evening? Ah, good, very good. You look very nice tonight. Would you like some golden fish? I think you would. Sister Faria tells me you like her golden fish very much. Tomorrow I'll get you these fish. And a bowl, a big bowl for your office.' Tarek is waving his hands about wildly. His speech is slurred with shisha, and maybe more. I notice there are two burly Russians at his table, one who is surreptitiously sipping a clear liquid from what looks like a vodka bottle, into the small glass coffee cups on the table. 'How many fish? Sister Faria has three so you shall have twice as many! *Wallah*! You'll come with me after work to the aquatic bazaar. And Sister Angie will come too and then when we have the golden fish, we can all go to dinner. I'll take you and Sister Angie. Sister Angie is a very great woman, no? Tomorrow. We get golden fish.' Tarek stumbles back into the shisha cafe and the arms of his friends there.

Tomas steers us away. 'Oh no, we'll be the talk of the office tomorrow; and what have I got myself into with these golden fish, and Angie's not even here.'♀

Tomas chuckles, 'Golden fish!' It is just all too unreal tonight. 'Don't worry, he won't remember anything tomorrow.'

I wish I could forget everything too, but the blue cat skulks about my thoughts.

☾

The next morning as instructed, Tomas and I sit in the meeting room for over an hour at the appointed time to meet Brian and Mozah. They do not show up. As the hour strikes Tomas swears and stomps out. I gather up my files to follow and as I do a tea boy arrives with another memo. It is from Mozah. It tells me curtly that I am no longer required to provide any PR support to the health clinic project and should send all my files to her office without delay. Brian is reviewing my position and will confirm my next assignment, if any. If any!

'*Hallas*. This is all? Yes,' Laila signals to the office boy to pick up the files. 'Now let me take these to that bad woman. You stay here and never speak to her again. I'll slap her nicely if she's rude to me, really she dare not. *Yallah*.'

I smile, Laila has been crackling with rage like a fluorescent strip light since I came back and showed her the memo. At first she demands I go and harangue Mozah, make it clear to her I am not to be "played with". When I decline to resolve this in Arabic fashion, she then changes tack and recommends I take the other and polar course of action deemed appropriate in the Arabic world, ignore Mozah and her note totally. 'No, you should not help this woman. You think she means anything in this life? She's nothing. Look at your shoe, she's less than the dirt on your shoe. Ignore her. You see her in corridor, turn away. She call you, you close the phone line. Allah says we should not look on rubbish, we must turn our eyes away.'

Secretly, I would love to take the Arabic way and completely ignore Mozah's demands. However, I do not want to give Brian any ammunition with reports of my unprofessionalism, so Laila has offered with great glee to deliver the files to Mozah. She will slam the files on Mozah's desk and sail out, clicking and shaking her fingers in disgust.

The air con in our office is not working properly and my head throbs from the sticky heat seeping in. Outside the sky is claggy. It seems to become more oaten and pastey with the thickening troubles at the Board. The endless sweep of dirty white box buildings no longer look so mystical to me, just narcoleptic. I want to go and talk to Angie, lick my wounds, but she is still in Cyprus. She has decided to extend her leave as she is having such a wild time, as the occasional text from another outlandish bar where she is drinking with another outlandish man testifies. She says she deletes every one of Mozah's texts insisting she return immediately.

Laila returns from prayers. I ask her how Mozah reacted.

'She wasn't there. Her secretary tells me she has gone somewhere with that bad man, Rothmann. All the people here, they talk about those two. They say she's living with this man. She'll be lashed if the police catch her. She's not American. She forgets her blood, we do not.'

My phone beeps. While Laila was out of the office it sprang to life and over the course of the last half an hour or so it has beeped continually. This is the thirty-fourth text from Tarek.

'Ah, Tarek, la,la,la', Laila wrings her hands and then sinks her head into them, her elbows sliding across the desk until she ends up prostrate.

I ring Tarek and try to tell him to stop texting me about the golden fish and more to the point, Angie's hotel number in Cyprus, which he is determined to get from me. It does not work. The texts still come. Laila calls him and in cat-claw sharp Arabic reiterates the message.

But still; beep, beep.

'*Hallas*, Laila. I can't take any more. This is ridiculous. I'm going to see Tony Morton, this has to stop. Now.'

'Sister, he's crazy and we'll be crazy soon too. We'll go to the psychiatry ward for this man? No, no, I don't think so. Tony Morton must slap him properly. It's bad, very bad, to act like this, like a drunk American boy. It's *haram* for a man to treat a woman like this. If he did this to me my brothers would beat him, kill him.'

'I think I need to meet your brothers, fast.' We laugh.

Two of the princesses tap gently on our door and pop their heads around the door, 'Girls, girls, what is the joke?' They giggle too as they come in, throwing off their *nikabs*. Both kiss us, wrapping us in heavy night-jasmine scent. Laila rapidly explains the situation as the princesses gasp, and cluck, their huge kohl-heavy eyes pooling ink. Amna brushes my arm lightly with her diamante talons, while Faria calls the other princesses on her mobile. Within moments the office is a nest of starlings, cawing and clacking as the princesses flap about in their bejewelled and embroidered *abayas* and the story is repeated over and over, all the time my phone still beeping. Each beep elicits a chorus of screeches.

Then hush, Amna answering her mobile, signals frantically for silence. The princesses now all stretch to hear the conversation. Amna is closely interrogating over the phone, her finely threaded brows twisting. Finally she slams down the phone and takes a full second to survey her audience before in slow, carefully declaimed English for added effect and gravitas, declares to her enrapt listeners, 'Tony Morton, *hallas*, terminated today.'

The room erupts, as if a farmer has fired a shotgun, starlings squawking in every direction.

'Immoral behaviour, *yanni*.' Hands clap.

'He used bad words with Dr Mouna.' Fingers snap.

'He touched Mozah, *wallah*!' A foot stamps.

'Money missing.' Tuts and a low whistle.

'CID coming to arrest him, downstairs, now.' Gasps.

The princesses, as one dark screeching flock, take off from the office, to rip at the flesh of the spectacle.

eighteen

Mozah, bangles jangling up a storm, calls around in the evening with all the rumours and gossip now circulating about Tony. I keep her standing at the door, barring the way in. What is this call really about? Let's not pretend we are "Sisters" now.

'*Aiee.* We got such a fright when they came in. Mr Tony was at his desk, asking me why his email had stopped working. "How should I know?" I told him. You think I am the IT department! The police, they shouted at Mr Tony to stand up and before he could say anything they handcuffed him. They dragged him along the corridor and down the stairs to the lobby. Everyone was there, clapping and laughing. It was a party, *yanni.* Mr Tony, he was very angry. His face was red, like the Dutch cheese. He shouted and swore. Someone threw a shoe at him. It hit him, right on the nose. Ah, I laughed.'

The rest I knew from the many texts I received all afternoon from the other expat staff. Tony was bundled into the back of a dark transit van. No one knows where he is now. We have been warned not to call or text him, lest it implicates us in any of his troubles.

'*Yallah*, Miss Aisling, we have an apartment to see. Mr Brian says you can't stay now you're the only Board employee left here. It's not safe for you.' My colleagues have all moved out, driven away by the noise and dust. In a way it's a relief, before there was never a moment's respite from someone knocking on the door. I am not strictly alone anyway, as the apartments have been filled again quickly by expats, this time from a gas company. These are tough men who spend long hours on site, then spend all their free time drinking and come back to their apartments for a few hours sleep every now and again, or to bring back a prostitute. They can sleep through anything, building work or a blowjob.

'I'm fine here Mozah.' It's not true. I hate the men hacking up phlegm in the hallways, and I only take the stairs now, as being squashed up against hot groins in the lift is too much to bear. Yet, it's better than being in Brian's hands.

'La, la. No, Mr Brian has cancelled the contract on your apartment.'

'What? How dare he?'

'We have to go see an apartment in Mr Brian's tower, then he can look after you.'

☪

The apartment is a tiny one-room studio, it must have been designed to be a maid's room. The room is on the top floor and it does have a grand view out over the Bay going for it. Just as well, as it is an odd layout, all corners and angles, you would want to be looking out rather than in. Mozah for once is speechless as the agent, an ultra-cool Lebanese guy in leathers, nods to the view and satellite channels on the plasma TV, great features. He snaps the TV on and starts to flick through the endless porn channels.

Something is missing.

'Where's the kitchen and bathroom?' I ask.

The agent pulls back a cupboard door on its runner to reveal a rail for clothes and then a tiny sink with a cupboard beneath it, and next to it a washing machine with a fridge stacked over it. Above the sink on a shelf is a microwave. Wires are dangling everywhere. 'Everything you could ever need.'

'And the bathrooooom?' Mozah shrills.

The agent saunters across the floor and swings open a wardrobe door on the other side of the room, where there is a toilet with a showerhead swinging above it. Mozah simply slams the wardrobe door shut and we leave.

I hail a taxi in the street to go back to my apartment, but when it pulls over Mozah hops inside and demands we go to Fizz for a medicinal glass of champagne. There is no arguing with her. Ensconced in our velour pink thrones in the bar, she continues to groan about the bijou delights of the apartment, while extolling the lynx-like sleekness of the Lebanese agent. I barely listen. I am furious with Brian and as much as Tony makes my skin creep, I am wondering what has happened to him, if he is all right. Drinking champagne tonight seems wrong. Various texts are flying about from the expat staff, but no one really knows Tony's fate. Some speculate he is under house arrest, others that he is in the *Black Box* being interrogated; more, that he has already been deported.

Completely tipsy, Mozah rings Brian and leaves him a somewhat hysterical message about the apartment viewing. She slaps shut the phone and slings it across the table. 'There's only one thing.' I know I'm not going to like this. 'Mr Brian has a spare room in his apartment. You'll have to move in there; then I can come and visit you every day. We'll be Sisters again.'

A pretty cover indeed. 'You know that's not possible Mozah, it would be illegal.' I shiver, what is going on here? I feel Brian's grip again.

'Pah, who cares? We'll just get you a ring and say you're Mr Brian's fiancée. And, Mr Brian is the big man now, *yanni*, no one can touch him. The Board and everyone else will soon learn that.' A sly smile on her lips, 'Miss Angie's got a nice pool, yes.'

'What do you mean?'

'*Yanni*, just that I heard her place might be coming free soon. Mr Brian should have a villa with a pool.' Mozah's phone rings. It is the Lebanese agent, inviting us to his place for a night of karaoke. I want to go home, too much has happened today. Brian's prints clear. But this is a good distraction and has stopped Mozah's scheming and whining for a moment. The agent's place is near my apartment. I say I will go for one quick drink, to stop Mozah wearing away at me.

☪

Really I go because this is my chance to glimpse the secret world behind the high walls of the dusky Al Hamsa quarter. The agent's villa is on one of the oldest and consequently greenest compounds and is somewhat dilapidated, cluttered with geraniums in pots, Matisse prints and African statuettes. A couple of ancient torn chaise longue slouch across the room, one propped up on a pile of magazines and huge squashy cushions are scattered around. Church candles, in huddles on tabletops, provide a weak gleam of light here and there. In the corner of this gloomy room there is a Grecian urn, which could easily accommodate a full-grown man standing. Water trickles over the ridged shoulders of the urn. The agent pours us each a beaker of gin and hands around the customary dish of creamy dates.

Over the course of the next hour guests arrive, each more Adonis-like than the last. All exceptionally groomed and clad in designer T-shirts and jeans. Mozah and I are the only women. The karaoke machine cranks up. We sit beneath a palm tree, jasmine winding its way up the trunk and over the walls of the villa. The fragrance of hashish hangs in the garden's deep corners. Kasim, the agent's lover, arrives at the party and joins us. His wife has discovered she is pregnant with twins this morning. Kasim is six months married. Somehow he manages to live both lives. But what he really wants is to take his babies when they are born, go abroad and live his life openly, but he has accepted that will never happen. He is the eldest son and it is his duty to support his ageing parents and numerous siblings. Mozah, who knows the wife, whispers to me he chose a bride who she says is older, ugly, no one else will marry and she is so grateful she doesn't question his nights and weekends away.

Kasim cries, he can only ever be himself for an hour or two at parties like these. And these parties are a huge risk. Although men walk hand-in-hand in friendship in the souk, homosexuality is still a crime. Punishable. Dark murmurs of electric therapy. Rape with truncheons and worse, far out in the desert compounds of CID. The secret police will cure your evil urges.

'Soon it will all change. Revolution is coming, even here.' A young man comforts Kasim. 'There will be liberation. We will be able to live. This time they cannot deny the people.' Kasim punches the air. 'We'll not oppress anyone. Everyone will be free to live his life.'

And his wife, I wonder?

'Look, see here what is happening.'

We crowd around Kasim's iPhone and watch clips posted on

Twitter from protesters in Tahrir Square. The crowds have swollen over the past couple of days. There are people there of all ages, not just young students now. At first the atmosphere was carnival-like, with fireworks and families carrying homemade banners. Now as night falls, a dark python of riot police coil about the square. Shouts. Bangs. People begin to run. Fire. White smoke.

A young British journalist files a report online, I read aloud:

'I am running from the square, something is in the air. This is about to turn bloody, and everyone knows it. White smoke drifts over me, tear gas, people around me choke and double over. As I run down the street, trying to cover my mouth, two or three burly young men in ordinary clothes run towards me. One punches me to the floor. The secret police. I am dragged to my feet and battered some more by the police. I tell them I am a British journalist. An officer comes over and hits me hard, twice in the face, 'Fuck you and fuck Britain.'

I pause.

The Lebanese agent has sat down with us during this discussion. 'Don't pray for war. You've no idea. I was just twelve when the bombs began to fall. I spent the nights of my teenage years living in a basement of my uncle's pharmacy. We read in the basement by torch light. I have read all the classics, a war education you could say. They were all my uncle had, a collection of Reader's Digest classics. Blue leather-bound with silver gilt. I can smell them now, the old leather. Dickens, Austen, Hardy, James. And Shakespeare. I was reading *A MidSummer's Night Dream*, Act 2, when the bomb hit the pharmacy.' He pulls up his T-shirt and shows us a curving white scar. 'My sister was reading the Sonnets, she took the direct hit. Don't pray for blood, it's always the blood of innocents that flows.'

Mozah, flounces into the garden, trailing a pink cerise and sequined scarf about her and caterwauling some song. 'Miss

Aisling, come and sing with me.'

How can I sing? Pain passes in a moment here, everyone is back to the party; and yet, it lasts an eternity, ground into the desert.

Mozah grabs another party-goer and they sing together. Kasim joins me, watches me watching Mozah.

'You wonder how she can be like this, dancing on a night like tonight?' he asks me.

I nod.

'She was dancing when they took her child.' He says.

'Her child?'

'Mozah was married, when she lived in Lebanon. It was an arranged marriage, of course. Her family married her to a fool, with the brain of a baby. But her husband's family were high ranking. She couldn't live like that, even after she had his child. She would sneak out to the nightclubs. It got known. One night, while she was out, the imam was called, the divorce pronounced and the family took her child. It was their right. She'll never see the child again.'

'Poor Mozah.' That loss, the worst.

'She screamed for two days. And then she went dancing.'

We moan at home that we are slaves to mortgages, bills, the taxman. Control, what do we know of it really? We are so lucky.

Kasim goes to get a drink.

I lie, lost in my thoughts, on a pile of cushions. The stakes are so high in this world, just to get through each day. The party smears about me. Someone brings out a guitar, and another, an oud. The party hushes as people fall onto cushions and carpets, and listen to the mournful strains. Mozah falls beside me,

'Mr Brian is heart-broken.' My heart starts, I look up. Mozah's face is hidden in the shadows. 'He says he never sees you now. I told him to beat Tarek and get you some golden fish.'

'Don't remind me about the golden fish!'

Mozah reaches for my mobile, which is in my pocket. 'How many texts now? Forty-six! Wallah! What's this? Look at this one.'

I read. 'I win big at camel beauty pageant. I am millionaire. Gone to Cyprus to marry Miss Angie.'

'What!' I leap up from the cushions, find a quiet spot in the villa and call Angie. It is true Angie tells me. Tarek has just won a small fortune, something in the region of two hundred thousand dollars, at the camel beauty pageant. His camel has won third place in one of the more minor rounds. Every year His Highness holds a huge festival celebrating the camel, the desert version of the Cheltenham Cup. The pageant goes on over several days and there is camel racing, camel decorating and several rounds of beauty contests, judged by His Highness' most-trusted advisors. If your camel wins the ultimate prize, you will be awarded with an eye-watering monetary reward, while His Highness requisitions the camel beauty queen for the Royal stud.

'What's the criteria for camel beauty?' I ask.

'Blowed if I know!' Angie laughs. 'Are you sure Tarek is on his way here?'

'That's what his last text says.'

'Just what I need. Think I'd better move on.'

'And that's the least of your worries.' I tell Angie about Mozah's veiled threats about her villa.

'I told yer, didn't I? You can't trust these bloody Arabian Knights. And that mad Mozah ...' Angie sighs. 'Aw, what am I goin' to do? Bet they were behind whatever's happened to Tony. Now they've got designs on me job and me villa and knowing that Mozah, on me wardrobe too? I guess I better get back pronto, kid.'

nineteen

I barely sleep for the next few nights. I have to watch the news. Egypt burns. The tanks roll into Tahrir Square. But whose side is the army on? Children clamber over the mighty vehicles while everyone holds their breath and waits to see. Men on their knees, in a moon crescent, pray before the tanks. Rubber bullets fire. Live rounds too? Rocks are thrown. Constant clashes, and reports of over a hundred people dead and two thousand wounded. Mubarak dismisses his government. The wealthy leave on jets for the Gulf. Everyone is on the streets, inhaling vinegar to try to combat the tear gas. It's the first Twitter war, tweets flying like bullets in every direction; and where they hit, hashtag: Revolution. Hastag: Jasmine Spring. Riots spread throughout Egypt. In Lebanon, Palestine, Jordan, and Yemen, thousands are on the streets demanding change. Egypt shuts down the Internet and mobile networks.

'Come home Aisling.'

'Grandaddy, it's fine here, promise.' Yes, we jump if a car backfires. Yes, when a block of flats for migrants starts to smoke, we ask, quietly, is this the first sign? But, flats burn here every day, the electrics are so shoddy. Everyone, Muslim or Christian, prays and a barricade of prayers locks out the fire of protest as it rages across the Middle East.

☪

Tomas storms into my office. Rex has submitted a report that Joe has written to the Board with their logo all over it. Joe has no idea how they had got hold of it, and is convinced they must have found a way of hacking into his email system. He knows it is his because it isn't quite finished and there are a couple of silly typing mistakes in it, which are in the Rex version too. How brazen or how stupid they are to not even check or tweak the report, cover their tracks? Then Joe bumps into two of the new boys Brian has just brought over, barely graduated, and they snigger like the couple of snotty teenagers they are, as he passes them in the corridor. This sends him into a rage and he returns to his office to fire off an email to the Prof and a copy of his report, only to find it is no longer in his electronic files. Just gone, completely, without a trace. I am on my way out of my office, 'I can't talk Tomas. Sheikh Fariq wants to see me.'

'*Salaam Alaikum*, Miss Aisling. My humble apologies for my unforgivable interruption. Please, my dear, only one moment and then you may continue with your writing. Your work is important for the good of the people and we thank you,' Sheikh Fariq greets me in the corridor as he sees me approaching his office.

If only I had any work. Now I am no longer working on the health clinic project all I have to do is write staff bulletins praising our beloved *Maleka* for her generosity and vision for pioneering the health improvements in the country; and these are far from appreciated. Thankfully Laila intercepted the latest newsletter before it went to print. Somewhere between my office, Laila's translation and the graphics department, the article I wrote inviting the staff to give their ideas about the new health clinics encountered some meddling, and I had apparently asked the staff for their views on piss and shit.

Tomas and Joe nearly fulfilled this request on hearing of this trick, laughing themselves until they rolled on the floor. 'It is all piss and shit here,' Joe gulped.

Sheikh Fariq continues to praise me in elaborate terms as he ushers me into his office. 'Miss Aisling, you work so hard for our country, I was only telling His Highness' Chief Advisor this last night. I spend many evenings at the maglis with the advisors. We know you are far from home and your people, so I would like to show you my country's hospitality.'

The Sheikh invites me to join his family at the weekend at his camel farm. It is far into the desert. He promises I will see the real country, away from the city and roads. He says he will have his people prepare a special feast. They will kill and roast a whole sheep and there will be many great dishes for me to try. 'You like camels, I have many baby camels. *Mumtaz*!'

Before I can even attempt to think about how I can graciously decline this invitation, Sheikh Fariq sweeps me from his office as various of his cronies arrive for coffee.

In a daze I return to my office to find the princesses and Laila sampling some Turkish Delight that a secret admirer has left for Laila. Evidently from their assessment this is a particularly expensive brand. I tell them about Sheikh Fariq's invitation.

'What do you think Laila? It's not proper for me to go to the camel farm, is it? Would you go?'

Laila splutters, 'La, la, la, you are very funny, Sister. My brothers would never let me go to the house of a married man. But for you Sister, this is a great honour. He's from a family of princes. It would be an insult to not go, you have to, but *yanni*, you shouldn't go alone.'

Thankfully my dilemma is resolved the next day when Sheikh Fariq sways into my office first thing and explains that as he has ordered a grand feast now there will be more guests. He says he is going to invite the Prof. I breathe again, the Prof will be my chaperone. I've always had a fondness for camels and also the thought of attending my first desert feast is a real privilege.

I go round to the Prof's office, now that he is back from overseas. I linger, shifting from one foot to the other before the ante chamber, I almost think better of it, he seems even more distant since he came back. He has made no comment on Tony's situation, other than it is a matter for the authorities now. I have not been able to talk to him about my work; he just brushes this away telling me this is Brian's remit.

'Professor, I have an unusual request, I hope you don't mind me asking. Sheikh Fariq has invited me to a feast at his camel farm. Will you be my unofficial brother for the day?'

For the first time in ages, the Prof chuckles, 'Ha! I think I will have to Miss Aisling. It wouldn't surprise me if our eminent Sheikh doesn't have it in mind to make you wife number four.'

I turn to leave the office and as I do, I think I hear him speak, so softly I almost don't hear him, 'Maybe we will get time to talk too, Aisling? We should.'

I am thinking about these words and how for just a moment I thought I had seen a glance of the old Prof, when at home time Mozah slouches into my office. 'Come for some food with me? Don't tell me you are working late again today.'

I have been fobbing off Mozah and her renewed sense of sisterhood all week. I do not want to find myself in a situation where she can pressurise me about moving into the Rex apartment,

'*Yallah, yallah habibti*.' Laila cuts in, 'La, no, Sister Mozah, many sorries, not today. Sister Aisling is coming to my house now to meet my family. It's arranged, our cook is already making the luncheon.' Laila grabs my bag and arm and bustles us towards the door.

Mozah looks put out. 'But we have important things to discuss, Miss Aisling. I've talked to Mr Brian. He has a proposal for you. He wants to talk it over this afternoon.'

'*Yanni*, whatever that is, it doesn't sound important to me, it can wait and luncheon cannot, *yallah* bye.'

'No, Miss Ash...'

I shrug my shoulders and smile as if to say, "What can I do?" 'I'll call later, sorry.'

Mozah catches my arm. 'Really Miss Aisling, you must come, Mr Brian has a surprise for you too.'

My stomach contorts. I want nothing from Brian and certainly not a proposal or surprise of any sort. Laila's eyes are flashing. I feel her tense, her grip on my elbow tightens, I nearly yelp.

'No, Sister Mozah, you know this cannot be. This is *zina, haram*, it is not right for Mr Brian to surprise Miss Aisling. You must tell him to respect our ways.'

Mozah pulls herself up to her full height. I sense a spat simmering. 'Mr Brian does respect Miss Aisling, he only wants to tell her he has booked a *dhow* on Friday for her birthday, for a party. I'm sure he would be very happy for you to come, Sister Laila. It'll be a very respectable event.'

Laila harrumphs with such volubility I am fearful the plaster will splinter and crash from the walls. I can see her gathering herself together to launch a diatribe no doubt about the wickedness of Western men.

'I'm already busy Mozah. I'm sorry I'll have to decline. If only Brian had checked first.'

Thank god he hadn't. With his usual arrogance, Brian has just taken it for granted that I will fall at his feet. He is the last person I want to share my birthday with.

'*Wallah*! What do you mean, you are already busy?'

I don't want to tell her I am going to the camel farm with the Prof; something inside tells me not to.

Again Laila speaks first, her voice like honey, 'My family is holding a party for Sister Aisling. She should have her birthday with her new family here, my family. She is my Sister now. Now, we'll be late, we must go. Good day Sister Mozah.' And with that we dance out of the office and Mozah for once is speechless and thoroughly put in her place.

We are both shaking with silent laughter as we race down the stairs. Once we reach the car park, breathless, I finally laugh out loud and thank Laila.

'It's nothing. These Rex men, I don't like them. They are godless. Wicked men. You are my Sister now and I'll protect you, even if I told a lie, save me and forgive me Allah. Let's have lunch in the mall and then you can come to my home and be away from these men. Would you like that?' Laila takes my hand and squeezes it.

'How could I not? *Shukran*. My Sister too.'

We drive to the mall where we meet with two of Laila's sisters and some of their friends. And briefly, just for a moment one of Laila's older brothers, Hisham, who has brought the girls to the mall. He is tall and has a sultry elegance like many young men here. But his eyes are atomic. Laila introduces us and he bows his head, before saying a few words in Arabic and then leaving us. As he walks away he looks back; it is just an instance.

The girls are delighted that Laila has brought me along, this cross-cultural outing is as novel and exciting for them as for me. Moreover, they want to go to a new Italian cafe that has recently opened, as they haven't tried Italian food before and were too nervous to go before, without having a European with them to explain the menu. They are so welcoming, stroking my arm and playing with my long hair.

The mall is quiet at this time of the day as the locals do not shop in the daytime. Night is when it all happens and the shops stay open till two-in-the morning to accommodate the massive crowds who come to parade. I love the mall at night, it is so social, with as much of a buzz as Temple Bar of a Friday night. Like going to the pub, people don't shop alone, they go out in groups, the women dressed in their most sparkling *abayas* and for the men, huge Rolex watches. Flirting across the expanse of the mall hallways, rather than the dance floor, the odd flick of the *nikab* to reveal a coy smile and a kohl rimmed eye. Every now and then, a strategically dropped receipt with a phone number scrawled on it.

During the day none of this thrill is likely, but instead we have the originality of macaroni. The girls are ecstatic with all the different pasta shapes and sauces, as well as the exotic names, fusilli, tagliatelli, spaghetti. Almost as enticing as Versace, Prada and Valentino. The questions about how to cook pasta come thick and fast, along with invitations to various houses where the girls promise they will cook me lasagne and cannelloni. Each girl purchases several bags of swirling shapes from the delicatessen counter as we leave, delighted with their new sophistication. I now have a month of pasta to look forward to, but I smile broadly, as this was why I came here. Even if I hadn't bargained on eating spaghetti bolognese in the desert, I am getting to make friends with local women at last.

As we leave the mall we bump into Tomas, Salima and baby. The girls ignite with joy and in an instant have the baby out of her pram and are cuddling her and cooing. Tomas pulls me aside and to my relief tells me that Sheikh Fariq has invited him to Friday's feast. Tomas tells me he is thankful as all week Brian has been calling him and suggesting they go for a beer. He keeps putting him off, troubled by his interest and insistence. Brian says he will swing by on Friday, now Tomas will not be there.

But although one problem is solved, Tomas scratches his head, 'I can understand why the Sheikh would invite you, Ash, ha. And the Prof, that's the boss. But why me? He barely knows me, we just exchange greetings in the corridor.'

'I think Sheikh Fariq is just being hospitable. Let's just go with the flow, as they say here, and see what the day brings.'

twenty

A roar went up across the Middle East last night. We even heard it here behind our barricade of prayers. Mubarak resigned. People in Tahrir Square fell to their knees and prayed, chanted and wept.

Saturday morning, early and the city is squally with dust. Not a sign of life anywhere. I was woken at three o'clock by the screaming wind and grit. Metal ball-bearings, hurling against the window. After watching the coverage of the exultant partying in Cairo, and the nights of gunfire, fire-crackers, Molotov cocktails, the sound at the window half-scared me to death in my early-hours grogginess. Above the roars across the Middle East, the infamous Al Shamal storm has shrieked into the city once more. Every year, at about this time, the desert tries to claw back its lost land. Scrapping at the tower blocks and choking everything in a crematorium coating of dust. Stern edifices that only hours earlier struck out to the sun, shining in their armour of steel and glass vanish, shrouded. Only dark phantoms remain.

I lie in bed listening to the grazing sound, my teeth on edge. I can't return to sleep. I lie waiting for the dawn, hoping it will chase away this night tormentor. It doesn't come. As the muezzins start the call for prayer at about half-past-four I slide out of bed in the gloom and pull back the curtains. It is as if I have woken on a hostile, brutal moon.

☪

Tomas and Salima pick me up a couple of hours later to go to the rendezvous point, where we will meet the Prof and Sheikh Fariq. It is the last petrol station to the west, before the city scatters into the desert rubble. The wind batters at the jeep, a huge chunk of machinery that is starting to feel like a dinky toy. Inside we swelter, despite the aircon. The storm sucks out every last gasp of air. Tomas sings 'Happy Birthday' to me in Swedish and cracks terrible jokes and we giggle at them, our laughter edged with a shred of hysteria,

'We must be mad going into the desert in this weather.'

At the petrol station a small convoy of Land Cruisers await, headed up by Sheikh Fariq in a tangerine Landrover. He waves at us to follow.

'At least we won't lose him in that,' Salima observes.

'Who are those other guys? They look 'shady', is that the word Aisling?' Tomas asks.

There are about seven vehicles in the convoy, other than us and the Prof. Swarthy men, with dark reflective sunglasses, chewing on cigarettes, are at the wheels of these cars. They look at us blankly, except one who smirks, and throws a heavy comment to other unseen companions in his vehicle. All the cars have blacked-out windows.

We follow the highway to the west for a few kilometres and then suddenly the convoy swerves sharply off the road. Now we bump on the hard desert, no roads, just rocks and the bleached bones and ragged carcasses of ancient goats. I cannot fathom how Sheikh Fariq can find his way in this endless apocalyptic panorama. After a few more kilometres we reach a barbed wire fence and straggling array of shacks and tents. We are at the camp.

We are welcomed by a crowd, the 'men in black' as we name our convoy companions, as well as some women and children who emerge from the tents. It is a confusion of greetings, and people and names, into the midst of which Sheikh Fariq leads out a tall, leggy camel with a great deal of attitude. It is distinctly bad tempered and toothy. I stand admiring the camel.

'Hello, I'm Hanna. Here let me take a picture of you with the camel.' Hanna takes the photos and then commandeers me, putting her arm through mine and marches me, followed by the rest of the party, around the camp.

She tells me she is studying international politics at Henryville American University. She says that she is going to be a diplomat. We see some scrawny red and white fleeced goats, dusty sheep and lastly, the baby camels. Hanna, with schoolmistress confidence, tells us that the camels with thin ankles are racing camels, and not for eating.

Tomas mutters to me, 'Please don't tell me camel is on the menu today.'

Hanna points out the blue markings on the fine faces of the camels, with their long lashes making them look all the more like moody, ancient ballerinas. The blue paint is used as branding to denote ownership. The baby camels are affectionate, and keep stretching out their necks to be patted, eyelashes fluttering.

'Hey, Aisling,' Tomas whispers. 'Those baby camel remind me of someone.' His smile impish. This is the first time, after all these weeks of the stress of settling in, that I have seen his boyish charm. He chuckles and says, 'You, my darling, you have the same gorgeous eyes and lanky legs.'

'Tomas!'

He laughs. 'Sorry, I can't resist. Thought I'd drop in a woeful Brian Rothmann-style chat-up line, in case you were missing your day on a *dhow*. You do have nice eyes, but not as pretty as a camel.'

'Charmed, I'm sure.' I am so glad not to be on the *dhow*.

'Now to the tent.' Hanna, arm through mine again, marches forward to the largest tent.

To us, the as yet uninitiated, it looks worn, scraggy and frayed, grey like the rest of this world. Two Indian servants hold open the tent flap and then inside we find ourselves in rich colour. The tent material is woven in warm scarlets and indigo, with cream and cobalt blue threads here and there marking a zig-zag pattern.

'Come, my beloved guests. *Shufi*, our desert women weave this by hand. Every thread has a story. Our tents stay with our families for many generations. This one is many, many years old.'

Hanna shows us peepholes secreted in the wall panels, for the women to look through and choose their husband. The floor is scattered with mats, fleeces and cushions. In the middle there is a tall, sturdy, gnarled pole, 'This is the family pole, '*al wasser*', as it holds us all together,' Sheikh Fariq says.

Hanna leads Salima and me to one end of the tent, where she takes the coffee pot from one of the servants, who bows and backs away. She serves us, shooing away the attempts of the servants to do this for her. The men sit at the other end of the tent, talking about the momentous events in Egypt the night before. Hanna explains that normally a woven wall would separate the two ends of the tent, so the men cannot see the women. But today in this company, with Western guests, there is no need. Even so, there is still an invisible wall.

Hanna chats to us about her studies, her tutors, her next essay. Henryville American University is a branch of a great Ivy League academic institution, recently opened in the desert as part of the Queen's cultural exchange mission. Hanna tells us her favourite teacher has just left to go to teach in London. He is an American and one day in class attempted to argue that although chronologically Mohammed had lived after Christ, this does not mean that Islam, as a later religion, is the more modern or advanced faith. He referred to women priests as an example of how Christianity is more progressive than Islam. Contract terminated. Although it is a shame to lose this tutor, Hanna is certain that he is wrong in his analysis and asks us what we think. Thankfully Gabriella squirms, rolls over and knocks into the coffee pot. No harm done.

'My brothers,' Hanna waves as two hulking young men enter the tent and with them, hardly noticeable at first, a slight, grey-haired man, unsmiling. The men nod to us and a tray of dates is sent our way. 'My uncle, Sheikh Fariq is a poet, but I have to go through his desk because he throws everything he writes. He writes about love and the moon with great beauty.' At the other end of the tent a trunk is opened and a fuss is being made of dressing Tomas in sumptuous gauzy robes, edged with thick gold silk ribbon and a tinselly head-dress.

Hanna springs to her feet, seizing my camera. 'Selfie,' she squeals and runs off down the tent.

We follow, Tomas approaches.

'Do you know who that is?' he asks, his eyes signalling towards Hanna, 'One of His Highness' nieces.' We are in the Royal Camp, being served coffee by a princess.

Everyone is gathered around Sheikh Fariq, where he is holding court with grand flourishes of his arms.

Hanna yawns. 'Tsk, business, business, that's all they talk about in there. Boring. Let's go to the other tent.' She takes my arm and walks me round to the back of the first tent, where there is another smaller tent. 'This is our private tent.' A servant, eyes down, pulls open the flap to the tent. In the centre of this tent there are two highly carved wooden thrones. Hanna throws off her *abaya* and flops into one, leg lolling over the arm. I sit in the other, look about me, not wanting to look at Hanna. When she threw off her *abaya* she revealed she is only wearing a flesh coloured silk camisole and jeans. The camisole is too loose for her and her puppy breasts are rolling out. Hanna is a large, flabby girl.

'Do you like my bracelet?' she asks, jangling a heavy ornate bangle. Not waiting for a reply, she stands up and steps in front of me. Her lolling breasts now level with my eyes, 'I like your hair clip.'

My scraggily hair is tied back with an antique silver clip, *he* gave it to me, and even now after the heartbreak, still precious as my only memento of that cherished hope. Hanna fingers the clip, 'Pretty.'

I tell her a good friend gave it to me.

'I like it very much. I like European antiques, we don't have such precious things here. Everything is new.' She continues to finger it. 'Your hair is too thin for this clip.' With that she pulls it from my hair, puts the clip in hers and sits back down. I open my mouth, remember where I am, close it.

She yawns, 'Excuse me, we're all tired today. We were watching the news about Tahrir all night. *Yanni*, what's happening to this world? My Uncle Fariq's angry. He says our fingers stand together on our hand and we should stand together as Arab Brothers. He thinks His Highness should be with Mubarak, show these criminals in Cairo real fire. Instead he says, does, nothing. This isn't our way.'

Hanna tells me Sheikh Fariq has met Mubarak a few times, has visited his palace in Sharm El Sheikh one time with some of His Highness' cousins.

'Mr Blair, you know the British President, was there.' Hanna says Sheikh Fariq is alongside the Prime Minister, who is pressing His Highness, to offer Mubarak sanctuary. His Highness seems reluctant this time, even though he has welcomed so many unsavoury fallen idols in the past. Laila has whispered to me in the office during prayer time, when we could be sure of being alone, about the people's unhappiness with the bounty of His Highness in these matters.

'Maybe, he thinks such an act will bring trouble,' I say.

Hanna takes my hand. 'Don't worry, there'll be no trouble here. You'll be safe, we all will. Sheikh Fariq will make sure. He's high up in the CID, he can do anything he wants and the people know this.'

CID. The secret police. Oh God.

Everyone, expat and local alike live in fear of CID. Most expats are convinced their office phones and mobiles are being tapped, as the phones often click and buzz. I cannot believe the expat chatter about beer and sausages is that riveting. Still, there are lots of rumours about who works undercover for CID. Everything is rumour, and rumour is everything. Tony had warned me, it is a well-known 'fact' that the CID had operatives in all government departments. Certainly there are shadowy local staff who none of us expat staff are ever introduced to, and who seem to do nothing but wander the corridors, looking balefully in on us at our desks. I asked Laila about one soulless character who mopes along our corridor every day at about nine thirty, she just dismissed him as 'nobody'. But she does tell me not to talk about CID or speculate who works for them in the office, '*Yanni*, there are things best not to know about.'

Bunkers in the desert, interrogation suites where no scream can ever escape, be heard. Surgical masks, splattered with blood dug into deep holes. That's what the regulars at Heather's say. The missing? In Dubai, on a bender perhaps? My thoughts shift to Tony Morton. Arrested on whose orders?

'Ah, so pale, I know how to bring colour to you, come, let's have some fun and find my brothers.' Hanna grabs her *abaya* and runs out of the tent.

As I follow, the Thai maid waiting outside stands briefly in front of me, 'She's a cruel one, watch out Missy, and the brothers too.' She draws back her sleeve to show me an arm bruised with bites and pinch marks. Tears come to my eyes.

'Ssh, tell no one.'

'But I must help you.'

'This is a good job.'

Before I know how I can put my offer into action I say, 'Come with us when we leave.'

I know even as I say these words this is a hopeless proposition. The girl shakes her head, and casting a scared glance over my shoulder, slips inside the tent. A roaring of engines drowns out all further conversation. Hanna indicates to me to follow her. Her brothers fire up two quad bikes, and Hanna pushes me towards one the greasy hulks. He is grinning broadly as he eyes me up and down. Before I can object, not that it is possible over the din of the engines, he pulls me to him and I am clinging on for dear life and he slams his foot on the accelerator and we shoot off after Hanna and her brother on the other bike.

My stomach pitches. We are going so fast and over very rocky ground, no soft dunes here. I have visions of me bumping off and ending up a gory, bloodied wreck of bones. I dig my nails into the ample girth of the hulk, who is whooping with joy as he flies off boulders. This is a mistake, as it seems to arouse him all the more. I can barely open my eyes and all I can see of Hanna is a shadow of dust someway ahead of us. We reach a rocky hillock. I cannot see where Hanna has gone. The hulk cuts off the engine. Now just an eerie silence after the roar.

'Some water?' He hands me a water bottle. 'Shukran.'

'You have a good accent.'

'Laila, a girl at work, is teaching me.' He spits. 'What can our women teach you Western women? You should teach them some things.'

I pull my shawl closer. He reaches into a bag strapped to the steering wheel and pulls out a can of beer. 'Shouldn't we be catching up with Hanna? She'll wonder where we are.'

He laughs. 'Don't worry about her. It's hot out here. We should go into the shade.' The hulk nods to some boulders in the shadow of the hillock. I hold back, '*Ta'alee hona.*'

We walk over to them, sit and drink in silence for a few minutes. My nerves ease. The hulk scrunches up his can and kicks it to the distance. He turns to me and grins, lunges at me, trying to kiss me. My head slams against the rock; but I don't feel the pain, he is heavy against me, panting, his lips slobbering over my face. His sweat, acidic. I feel a sharp wave of nausea. He has me pinned hard against the boulder with his knees, as he opens the fly of his jeans, his penis, mottled, furious, thrusting. His hands pulling at my clothes, but I push with all my might at him.

'I'm going to be sick.' He jumps back, as I double over and throw up.

Stray strands of my hair stick to my wet face, my head throbbing now. My stomach grips, again I vomit. The hulk watches impassively and turns away to the bike, fumbles with his zipper, he switches it on, revving the engine.

'*Ta'alee hona*'

I don't move. He revs the engine again.

'*Ta'alee hona.*'

I shake my head.

'We'll go back to the camp now.' He gets onto the bike.

I don't move.

'Miss, this is the desert.'

I get on the bike and he roars away.

The minutes on the bike seem like hours. Every now and then I squint through the dust, but I can see nothing. I have no sense of whether we are heading back to the camp, or elsewhere. I am taut. The hulk doesn't whoop now. Spine iron. Finally we screech to a halt, I open my eyes, we are back at the camp.

The hulk jumps off the bike, 'She's sick, get her some tea,' he snaps at one of the servants.

Sheikh Fariq approaches, a concerned look in his eye, 'Miss Aisling, you're sick, you're shaking. 'Ah, the bike is too much for you. You,' he clips the hulk across the ear, 'You ride too fast, you have to be gentle with a lady, not a peacock.'

I take the tea that is handed to me and say nothing. The hulk lights a cigarette, shoots me a menacing look and shambles off.

'Come now, I'm going to show you how to cook fish over the fire,' says Sheikh Fariq.

I follow the Sheikh, my knees liquid, my head sore. It is getting dark and I just want to get home now. Through the shadows of the mighty tents I can see the fiery figures of children, djinn, wailing. The Prof is poking a stick in the flames. Baby Gabriella is grizzly in her mother's arms. I can't see Tomas or the Sheikh's retinue. In the distance, by one of the animal pens, Hanna is hugging the hulk.

Sheikh Fariq shows me a large platter of skinny silverfish and fist-sized crabs and then gives me a lesson on how to grill them properly. A hundred eyes pop and crackle. I sit on a large stone and play with one of the grilled fish on my plate. I have no appetite. Tart bile keeps rising, and I have to swallow hard.

The Prof joins me, 'So, what do you think will happen next Miss Aisling? What have you learnt about our people in your short time with us? Will there be revolution here?'

'I don't know. All I know is that I don't want to wake and find tanks in the street.'

The Prof nods.

'It seems quiet and calm, for now,' I say.

'For now. How fast life can change in this world? *Hallas*.'

'But after last night?'

'Yes, a few days ago we were all so sure the army would crush the protest, and instead they are the heroes of the revolution.'

'What do you think will happen, Professor?'

He shrugs his shoulders, '*Alhamdulillah*, only Allah knows.' He pauses, 'I'm … I have to tell you Aisling …'

Aisling? His irises contract, the whites luminate. No 'Miss?' Formality driven off.

'Prof?' He hears the query, quiver in my voice and moves closer to me.

'Everyone, our feast is ready, please be welcome, my honoured guests and friends,' Sheikh Fariq comes over and leads the Prof to another large tent before he can finish his sentence.

Tomas and the men are already seated, the Prof and Sheikh Fariq sit with them. The Sheikh presses huge slabs of meat on their plates. Hanna comes into the tent. She frowns at me and sits at a distance to Salima and me. Sheikh Fariq looks down to the women's end of the feast and calls to her. She points to the servants, but her uncle snaps at her again. Sulkily she heaves herself off a pile of cushions where she is reclining, chomping on a bone. She grasps a couple of bowls and with a spoon slops their contents onto our plates, whether we want this morsel or not. Salima tries to stop her, saying we are happy to serve ourselves, but Hanna ignores her. Once she has slammed down the bowls she retreats to her cushions, scowls at the Sheikh and pulls out an iPod from her jeans pocket. I push my bowl to one side, it is too much. My stomach is hollow. I ache all over.

The Sheikh whistles and a drummer and two pipers appear. Between bites to eat, some of the men in the retinue get up and clasping their hands high above their heads, stamp about to the music. After what seems a massacre of meat, Sheikh Fariq gestures to the men to go outside. He clenches a cigar in his teeth.

The hulk, smoking a cigarette, shambles in and points to me, 'My uncle wants to talk to you.'

I can barely rise from the cushions.

The hulk leads me to the fire where the men are now sitting around on old boxes and oil cans. 'Miss Aisling, Miss Aisling, you enjoy our banquet tonight, yes, here sit next to me.'

I balance on an oil can, hardly breathing.

'Hanna, Hanna,' he shouts to the tent. No response.

The hulk trudges back to the tent. The Sheikh sits across from me, he leans forward and gazes with his one eye with such deep intensity into mine. This is something many people do here, it's as if they want to swim in your soul. His pupil slicks to the outer corner. He laughs and sits back again.

'You must be a Capricorn, you're such a nice lady.'

Surely, I have misheard him, so I don't know what to say.

'I am right, am I not? You're a Capricorn, or maybe Taurus?'

No, I did hear him right the first time.

'Aquarius,' I reply.

'Of course, the free spirit, yes, I am right. My favourite sister is an Aquarian. Yes, you're like her. Indeed, the best people in life are of the Aquarius sign, they're the thinkers and peace keepers. I like these people. They're loyal. I'm sure you are loyal.' He laughs. 'I speak seven languages. What unites us Miss Aisling? Tell me.'

I shake my head. 'What makes me and you, brother and sister? Not DNA, genetics no; it is words, poetry. You come from the land of poets, I know. I admire your poets, William Butler Yeats, the greatest.' He pauses and looks at everyone around the fire.

They all nod agreement, although I am sure most have never heard of Yeats.

'I speak these many languages because I can chase words across them all, like a hawk with a dove in sight. You see that?' He signals to the moon rising in the sky. 'Poets love the moon because everywhere, everyone sees her. Do you know the Arabic word for the moon when it's like this?' He curls his small finger into a crescent, it curves like the scarred void of his empty eye. 'It's called 'hal', like your word 'halo'. The moon is our angel, watching us.

'And our women are of the moon, watching us.' One of the men adds, they all laugh.

The Sheikh raises his hands for silence, '*Shufi*, words bring us together. This is why talking is the life to us, why we sit together like this in the desert. We talk about everything, we share our words, our secrets, like you and me share the moon now, tonight. You understand, my dear?'

He dives deeper with his gaze, to the fathoms. My soul folds, foetal.

Hanna approaches with a small silver casket, fragrant smoke twisting from its latticed lid. She roughly takes hold of my loose hair and lets the incense drift through it. Sheikh Fariq stands up and claps his hands.

'The hour is late friends, time for us to drive back to the city.'

There is much slapping of backs as we make our farewells, and the convoy prepares for the trip back into the gritty darkness.

Just as we are about to get in the jeep, Hanna runs up to me, 'You should have shown my brother respect. For him to look at one like you is an honour.' And with a toss of her hair, she runs off. As she runs something silvery flickers in the moonlight; my precious hairclip tossed to the desert rubble. Lost to the sand.

twenty-one

'Are they following us?' Tomas asks fast.

We are back on the main highway heading to the city. The convoy had split off once we reached the road. Tomas is ashen.

'What's wrong?'

Before he can answer Salima's mobile phone rings. She answers, but seems confused about whom she is talking to, asking for the caller's name repeatedly. 'He keeps saying he wants me to go to the villa.'

'Hang up Salima, it's just a crank call,' Tomas instructs.

She starts speaking in Arabic to the mystery caller. She thrusts the phone at me, 'It's for you. They want to speak to you.'

'What? I don't understand.' I take the phone. It is the hulk. Meanwhile in the background Tomas and Salima are arguing about how the hulk has got hold of her mobile number.

'Miss Aisling. Are you better now? Did you enjoy the camp? I want you to come to our villa tonight. It's too early to end the party.'

'Thank you, but I'm very tired.'

'You'll stay the night.'

'No, that would not be proper.'

'I want you to stay the night. You will.'

'No.'

'I want you in my bed. You have to do what I say. I'll kiss you.'

I drop the phone.

'Who is it Ash?'

'Sheikh Fariq's nephew. He wants me to go to his villa. He wants to have sex.'

Tomas explodes. 'Sleazy little bastard, give me that phone.'

I have never seen Tomas like this before. Salima takes the phone and screeches in Arabic, before opening the window of the jeep and throwing the phone out.

'*Hallas*,' she says, 'Now he can't call. I told him he was shaming his mother and never to call again.'

'That was a little drastic, but thank you.'

'I can get another phone. He will not stop you know, he will ring every minute. This way is best.'

'This whole day has been a disaster,' Tomas groans.

'You don't know the half it.' I tell Tomas and Salima about my encounter with the Sheikh's hormonal family. They are horrified. Quickly they work us all up into a frenzy, playing out more and more far fetched scenarios of what will happen next, now I have snubbed royalty; and speculating how the hulk had got Salima's number, which he evidently believed to be mine. They must have rooted through our bags at some point during the day; it would have been easy enough as they were in our unlocked car.

We pull up to Tomas' villa. Tomas drops off a thoroughly wired Salima and the baby, and then drives me home. He is silent during the drive. I am riven with exhaustion. The traffic is heavy, everyone out for their Saturday night socialising.

'We need to talk Ash, there's more happened today than you know. I didn't want to speak in front of Salima and worry her. She already hates it here.'

'You're scaring me now Tomas, what's going on?'

I can't be seen to have a man in my apartment at this hour, so we arrange that Tomas will come up in a few minutes, entering by the lift from the garage below, rather than through the front reception area.

I pour us some whiskey while I wait. A soft tap on the door. I let Tomas in. He takes his glass and begins, his voice stiff, 'Sheikh Fariq said today, with these troubles in North Africa, more than ever our country needs strong leaders. Big men who will be heard, seen, at the front, telling the people how it must be. Like in the army.' Tomas pauses, sips his whiskey. 'The people say the country has gone soft, they want a return to the old ways.'

'What does that mean?' I ask.

'No more of the Queen's reforms. People are going on Twitter and complaining about the Queen. They're calling her all sorts of names because she is obsessed with building the health clinics for the migrant workers, rather than improving care at the hospital.'

'I can imagine Fariq was furious, he worships the Royals.'

'He told us that last week a young mother haemorrhaged to death giving birth in the hospital; she was treated by an Indian doctor. He called him an 'inferior' and said it's a scandal, what's going on in the hospital. People wait for hours to see a doctor.' Tomas wipes sweat from his brow. 'He poked his finger at us and shouted 'Brother, you are the leader, you must stand up to the people. We cannot allow the people to criticise His Highness and our beloved *Maleka*. They say she's a crazy woman and has no idea about running the health service, and should stay home, look after her family.'

'What did the Prof say?'

'He didn't get a chance. Fariq was ranting. He told the Prof that he must be seen every week in the maglis, where the imams attend, where he can have influence.'

'It sounds awful.'

'It was embarrassing, Ash. The Prof is the CEO, not Fariq, after all. And here he was being told not to shut himself away with emails and spreadsheets. Fariq even asked if all the years he had spent abroad had made him soft, like a woman. In front of me. The loss of face. I didn't know what to do.'

'Poor Professor.'

'Then Fariq's friend, the Scottish man spoke. He said there must be no chance for opposition forces to form around an issue like poor care at the hospital. And Fariq said this mustn't be the fatal spark for the country.'

'It's as bad as that? We just don't see what it's really like here.'

'No, all we see are the malls and the tourist souk.'

'Will there be trouble?'

'I don't know. But we're already in enough trouble.'

'What do you mean?'

'That salty little Scottish man is the Sheikh's personal financial advisor and CEO of Blackheath & Company.'

The name rings a bell with me, but for the life of me I can't think why.

'He asked me how I was enjoying working in the desert. He said most Westerners find it hard, adjusting to the climate, the culture. There's such pressure here to succeed, after all most of the expats can't cut it back home, he said, and can't go back with their tails between their legs.'

'I'm not sure I like his tone.'

'No, I didn't. He lit a cigarette. Made a big show of it. Flicked the ash at me. Then told me it isn't sensible to get too comfortable. I had a lot to prove. He said people are watching, watching everywhere, at the office, the mall, the gym, even at the villa.'

'What!'

'"Every wee mistake is noted", that's how he put it. And I'm making too many mistakes. The Sheikh's disappointed with me.'

'I don't understand?'

'They don't like our Western style of management, too consensual. Asking staff for their opinions in newsletters. It will bring revolution to the country.'

'My piss and shit newsletter will bring revolution? Please, this is a joke.'

'No joke. He said we should learn from Tony Morton's sudden departure. We're only here because the Sheikh is such a benevolent man. But they'll give us one more chance.'

'What does that mean?'

'He said we need to work out who our real friends are, and Blackheath & Company will be delighted to help.'

Of course, that's where I had heard of Blackheath & Company, they are one of the Gulf's major recruitment agencies, specialising in supplying financial advisers.

'Aisling, they want you.' Tomas looks deathly.

'For what? You're scaring me.'

'He asked if you were close to the Prof. They think you must be because he brought you over.'

'And?'

'They want the Prof to help their cause.'

'Their cause? What's that?'

'He didn't say and I knew better than to ask. He said if I can get you to influence the Prof, then I will get a bonus.'

'Tomas, you look sick. What kind of bonus?'

'He said he didn't understand what the Prof sees in you. You are just a scrawny girl from the bog.'

'Charming!'

'He likes Japanese girls, with flat chests and flat hips. Fariq likes bums and boobs and big hair. He said he can procure anything, black, white, male, female, juvenile.'

'What a scumbag.'

'Then he said, Ash, "Let us be clear, the Professor may have brought you both here, but it will be Sheikh Fariq who decides if you stay. Let's not talk about the alternatives in this heat, miles from anywhere. Remember, only the vultures come here, to pick on the bones we leave behind after we feast."'

We sit for some time in silence after Tomas finishes.

'I'm frightened Tomas, really frightened. I can't believe all this was going on today. I thought I had enough problems with the hulk, and I put that down to teenage hormones, nothing worse. This is on a whole different scale.'

'If I tell Salima, she'll have us on the next plane out of here.'

'With no exit visas?'

'Shit, Aisling, what are we going to do?' Tomas sits with his head in his hands.

'I don't know, what can we do? I want nothing to do with any of this. I certainly am not about to become Fariq's agent.' I pace up and down the lounge. Tomas looks up at me, through his fingers. I can't keep still, every fibre of my body twanging. This is madness, stuff like this does not happen to ordinary people like us. No, I am not going to get caught up in this paranoia and craziness. I breathe again as rationality sets back in, 'This is a shock, and it's been a long day. But let's look at this calmly. Fariq didn't actually say any of this to us did he? He was the perfect host. It was that Scottish man, he's just another fierce crazy expat with an over-inflated ego and I reckon he's over stepped the mark. They're hardly going to do anything to white Westerners. It would cause too much of a scandal.'

'Brave words.'

'What's the worst they can do? Deport us? So what?'

'I hope you're right, for both our sake's.' He puts down his empty glass and goes back to Salima.

After Tomas leaves, every bone trembles. For all my bold talk, my body betrays me.

twenty-two

At dawn, before work, I go to the Celestine for a swim in the indoor pool. The pool is empty at this time and I can swim up and down, with no curious eyes watching me. The hulk's heavy weight still presses against me. I can smell his hot, sour breath. On my body purple bruises are starting to bloom. I cry.

☪

I can't concentrate at work today and stare at my screen. Laila is watchful, finally mid-morning, she breaks the strain. 'Sister, Sister, we have to buy you a dress.'

Life rackets on.

'Why?'

'Shuhailah is getting married and you're invited to the wedding.'

Laila's cousin, Shuhailah, also works at the Board as a secretary, although she can't type. She spends her days comparing nail designs with the other secretaries; none of who can possibly type with such highly garnished talons. She is a sweet, pretty girl of twenty-six, but is utterly convinced she is cursed. She believes firmly that some of her jealous female cousins, who resent her prettiness, have put a curse on her so that she will never find a husband. At the grand age of twenty-six, and still unmarried, she is certain she will never marry. So this wedding has come about out of the blue.

A few weeks ago a woman, who works in another office at the Board, visited Shuhailah on a work errand. A couple of days later the woman's family contacted Shuhailah's family to ask them for her hand in marriage for the woman's brother. The princesses, Laila and I were eating our mid-morning pastries, when a tea boy brought in an envelope for Shuhailah. It was her proposed groom's photograph. We all craned to look at the picture, but Shuhailah, held it up high and out of reach.

'No, no, I can't look. My eyes will not look. They stop me. They burn. Aaii.'

'*Wallah*! It's her curse.' The princesses ruffled around Shuhailah.

'Shuhailah, Sister, stop this talk. The Prophet forbids us believe in curses. You must look, for Allah.' Laila jumped up and snatched down the photo, 'See, how handsome he is. Your babies will be beautiful.'

After some persistent cajoling Shuhailah was persuaded to meet her suitor. The meeting was brief and held in the presence of the elders from both families. The groom presented Shuhailah with a gold and diamond necklace that Elizabeth Taylor would have been proud to wear.

Showing me the necklace in the office, Shuhailah kissed and kissed Laila, 'Sister, when I met him my heart was doing this,' she thumped against her chest fast.

'I thought I would die. *Whallah*! It was the curse breaking.'

And so Shuhailah agreed to marry this man she had just met. That was it, five minutes. The girls here spend longer in the malls pawing over which dresses to buy. But Laila told me that often a couple will only have met once, if that, before the marriage contract is signed. They will not meet in person again until the wedding ceremony. For the past few weeks Shuhailah has arrived later to work than usual with dark rings round her eyes. People have so little private or personal time that romances can only be undertaken by phone in the still of the night. The phone lines buzz all over the Middle East as newly engaged couples get to know each other and fall in love by mobile.

☾

We walk through the mall, festooned with hearts for Valentine's Day tomorrow, to the floor where all the wedding dress shops are situated. Laila finally asks me about my day at the camel farm. She questions me in detail about the array of dishes presented and seems content that sufficient honour was extended. She walks in silence for a few steps.

'Sister, you are not telling me everything. I can tell. Something happened?'

I cannot fool Laila's sharp eyes. I tell her about the hulk.

'*Wallah*, this is very bad. How can that young man behave like this? He brings shame on his family.'

'When I think about it, I was so lucky Laila, he intended so much more. I know I was sick, but I don't know what stopped him.'

Laila holds me. 'Allah is always with you Sister. I pray for you everyday and for his protection as you are here without your family. Allah hears my prayers. And now I will teach you a prayer, some words to say over and over if you are ever in trouble.'

Laila teaches me the prayer; as she does, a pure light shines in her eyes.

'But all will be fine for you, my dear.'

'How so?'

'Sheikh Fariq would be so shamed if he knew what this boy did. He will not do this again. He will think better of this today.'

'Truly, Laila?'

'Truly, and if he does come after you, then I will talk to Hisham. He knows this family a little, he will stop this. Don't be afraid, Sister, he's just a foolish boy.' Laila pulls off a sparkling ring from one of her laden fingers, 'But you should wear this. It means you have a fiancé, no?'

'Well, yes, but I don't.'

'That doesn't matter. We'll make one up for you. I had an expat friend at the hospital. She did this; it's best here for Western women. And it will keep that Rothmann away too.'

I put the ring on, 'I'll keep it on at all times.'

'*Alhamdulillah*, it looks real. Keep it, I have many.'

I kiss her in thanks. 'Feels odd though.' I try not to think of the last time I had done this, with Brian and the falcon.

'One day soon, I hope you'll wear a ring for real, Sister. And me. We are not so young and should find our husbands before the next Shamal wind. Last night I dreamed of my husband. Allah brought him to me. He was no prince, *wallah*, but a poor butcher in the souk. He gave me a knife. It was dripping with blood. What do you think this could mean? I am to be a poor man's wife?'

'I don't know, Laila, but it maybe better than a prince.'

'Allah chose him, so I will be happy. I will always be rich in his love.'

We reach the dress shop floor and I forget everything else at the wonders ahead of me. I am delighted with this shopping expedition as it means at last I can have a foray into the miles of Lebanese dress shops in the lower floor of the mall. I have walked, breathless, along the long stretch of shops, where each shop seems to out-do the previous for sheer sequined audacity. I have longed to go into one of these boutiques, but you never see Western women in them.

Frills, silver foil, cerise feathers, seashells, rhinestones, and lacy trains. Each shop must have several hundred of these triumphs of corsetry. At first I find them gaudy, but as Laila and the shop assistants drool over bows, fake lilies and swathes of iridescent silk I succumb to the bling, and by dress eight I am twirling in and out of the dressing room trying on more and more outrageous frocks. In the fifth shop, the air opiate with a deep musky oud, and about twenty dresses later, Laila eventually settles on the most gorgeous backless, crimson silk dress for me. As I stand in front of a mirror I smile, this is the world, the magic, the colour I craved. Laila sees me smile and takes my hand.

☪

The week can't pass quickly enough, with each day adding a new decibel level to the volubility of the princesses in the office at the prospect of the wedding on Thursday evening; and also the news of my engagement, which times beautifully with Valentine's Day, such a bonus for my cover story. I am hugged and kissed to within an inch of my life, and virtually every girl on our floor tries on my ring. Luckily they do not press me too much for detail about my fiancé, as I guess it is usual that they don't ask these questions as few brides here know much about their grooms, but they all want to see the ring. That is the most important thing.

It is a good diversion and, as the days sparkle with wedding talk, I all but forget the camp and the threats. Laila is right, I hear no more from the hulk. The sandstorm eases. The city shards glimmer once more. Tomas hears nothing from the ridiculous little Scottish man. All seems quiet for once.

Mozah screeches into the office. She grabs my hand. 'Sister, how can you?'

'Who is this fiancé? When did this happen? How is it we know nothing about him before? This is fast, very fast, Miss Aisling.'

'Oh, I didn't mention him, because I came out here to forget him, Mozah. We broke up before I left. I didn't like to talk about it here, it hurt so much. But he Skyped me on Valentine's Day and told me how much he missed me. Then he proposed, just like that.'

'And the ring? He has been here?'

'No, it's an old one of mine, until I see him next.'

'An old one! Do you learn nothing from us? You have to have a new ring!'

I'm learning.

☪

It's mid-week, Laila and I are going to the home of Dr Mouna for lunch. Shuhailah works for Dr Mouna and she is hosting a lunch to celebrate the imminent nuptials this weekend. Laila tells me I am the first expat at work to ever be asked to one of Dr Mouna's luncheons. Dr Mouna lives in a large gated villa in a part of the city I haven't been to before, where local families of high status live. The villas are even more palatial than I have become accustomed to, but, as elsewhere, these marble visions shimmer as capricious islands in a sea of rubble and sewerage pipes. The city is expanding so fast that the utilities are already inadequate and everywhere is dug up.

We are ushered into the front room of the villa, the family maglis, the public part of the house. Visitors never venture further into the villa, that is private territory, behind a heavy, ornately carved wooden door. The room is large with several green and gold sofas and chaise longues arranged around small tables, laden with many dishes. A maid dips about the room offering delicate pastries and dates. About twenty women from work arrive in time, some with older female chaperones, all coming in fully covered, some, in fact, with their eyes covered too. Laila and Shuhailah's family are very traditional and their friends come mostly from the more traditional families. At work about a quarter of the women now don't cover their faces, but they are not amongst these women. So I am taken aback when the *abayas* come off and rather than the jeans I am expecting to see they are dressed as if for a nightclub on Leeson Street. There is a lot of cleavage on show. The older women taking in every curve, each sign of potential fertility, ready to report back to families of eligible bachelors.

But the conversation, so dull, safe, unlike the lacy lingerie on display. These highly educated women speak only about cooking and children. It's different to our little office breakfast soirees, where there is a lot of giggling about the size of male 'bananas'; but also serious, whispered conversations about the mounting unrest in neighbouring countries and brothers itching to fight. With the grandmothers present, the talk is formal and restricted. I expect a clamour about Libya. Our eyes have all turned now to Benghazi, tinder-dry and ready to crackle with the fire of revolt.

Instead, the main preoccupation is finding the most flamboyant superlatives to pay compliment to the swaggering caramel tart and strawberry mousse cake, one cake never enough and this second especially in my honour. Soon everyone is on a sugar-high, compounded by the sugar-syrup mint lemonade. My head is spinning worse than on a conventional Temple Bar hen night.

The older women take it in turn to come over to me and stroke my white skin, giggling all the while. Shuhailah has brought her gold engagement jewellery with her and after cake, the women hand it around to be examined and the groom's worthiness calculated. Dr Mouna comes to sit beside me. I thank her for inviting me.

'I am pleased you came Miss Aisling. As a Sister to a Sister I must speak to you. For all our education, our beloved *Maleka*'s work for equality, this is still a man's world. You must be careful.'

'I'm trying.'

'Our life is changing. And there are those who would stop this. My husband, he goes to the maglis.' She whispers in my ear, 'His Highness' maglis.' Dr Mouna's husband is a leading surgeon at the hospital, a man of rank. 'The maglis talk of turning back. They seek to persuade His Highness that his reforms, letting in Western experts, are unwise. He shouldn't listen to the *Maleka* and her American Professors. Business is best kept within the maglis, not in the glare of the sun, like these Westerners would have.' Dr Mouna pauses, while we are passed a slab of the caramel cake, lavished with cream and glitter. I appreciate her bravery, no one speaks of the secretive Royal maglis, the men's world.

'*Yanni*, they say all these new ways of working with open books, letting the world see into our affairs, keeping records, is dangerous. It is best if we keep our knowledge in our heads, not on computers. Our enemies, as well as friends, can see too much now.'

Dr Mouna sighs, 'Ach, Miss Aisling, we're all afraid there are too many foreigners, spies, like those men in their smart suits from Rex. All these foreigners must go. Tony Morton was the first; there are others on the list. You see, the Sheikh will bring in his own men to the Board.' Dr Mouna seems to read my worry. 'People who don't know you, don't know you have a clear heart, they will say bad things. Take care now, and don't be open on your phone or in the email.' Dr Mouna pats my hand and goes over to look at the gold. I feel cold; *a list*.

twenty-three

Once more I'm as thin as rice paper and I should be joyous, it's the weekend and the much anticipated wedding party. But I cannot take my eyes away from the television reports of 'A Day of Rage' in so many cities across the Middle East. More strikes, tear gas, violence, killing. I slip on the crimson dress but I look like a spectre, wrapped up in a bloody sky.

Laila picks me up. It is late; weddings, like women in their dark *abayas*, are of the night. As we drive, I am conscious of a heavier police presence at key junctions and roundabouts across the city.

'Laila, why so many police tonight?'

'Our leaders fear a Day of Rage tomorrow. After prayers today the people went to the Libyan and Egyptian Embassies to show solidarity. This isn't allowed. We, the people, we can't gather, we can't be out in the street like this, it's illegal.'

'I see.'

Laila flicks her hand at a building site as we pass it, still in full throttle despite the black night. 'Ha! Our people want more than shopping malls of American stores.'

'But will they do anything? The people seem so compliant.'

'Hisham says the Twitter is full of talk about taking one of the roundabouts, maybe the Electric Souk roundabout. But, hush, we must not talk of these things tonight, it will bring bad luck to the wedding.'

The party is being held in the grand banqueting hall of the Celestine Hotel. The ceiling dangles with thousands of lines of smoky crystals. All the roses in the world must be in this hall. As we walk in we leave our phones at the door, security is tight. Laila tells me no cameras are allowed as the women will take off their *abayas*.

'Our weddings are everything. People judge the family from the wedding celebrations. This, this is a small wedding, only five hundred women. Some weddings have thousands of guests.'

Women billow past us in the most gorgeous jewelled *abayas,* and when these come off I suddenly feel very drab, the only white woman here, in my simple sheathe dress. The younger, still marriageable women are glorious in fantasia gowns, all plunging, clinging and slit in every which way. Heavy with egg-sized gems, and the gold souk is on parade, all clanking. The hair and nails! Laila has spent the afternoon in the salon and now has nails that are red glitter, budding with ivory-ceramic roses. The salons must have been a blast of powder and perfume all day: curls, extensions, jewels, hairpieces, crowns. The make up is 'tiger eyes', lots of kohl and ruby lipstick and henna filigree all over the hands and arms. Many of the older women keep on their *abayas* and veils, gorgeous dresses just peep out, in brightly coloured flashes, from beneath the dark swathes of fabric. The older women wear traditional gold facemasks, they unnerve me with their sharp *djinn* contours.

I have never seen such beautiful women in my life; without exception, they are all exquisitely gorgeous. And how they move; a slow, gentle, rolling dusk tide. Suddenly it is clear to me why there is an insistence on being covered, why the men are so fearful of the women. Women are of the night, with its deep mystery and power.

A figure in a short tacky scarlet prom dress stands out sore amongst all this grace. Mozah, always flaunting her contempt.

'What's that woman doing here? No, this will bring Shuhailah bad luck, very bad luck.' Laila storms off to speak to one of her relatives. While she is gone one of the gorgeous creatures steps onto the illuminated catwalk that runs the length of the hall, and starts to gyrate slowly along the glass, slinking to the drum beat and rhythmic sounds of the band, hidden behind curtains. She is dressed in a gauzy rose-coloured dress, banded in gold leather, with curls to her waist strewn through with strings of diamonds. This is Shuhailah's sister. Another woman, in wisps of silks, joins her as they inch towards the throne. Then an older woman strides onto the stage and throws handfuls of dollars over them. Four maids, on their knees, snatch up the money as it falls, into old, crumpled shopping bags. The women in their fabulous heels walk over them, not even seeming to notice. I look at the maids' worn out loafers, still dusty. Gradually more women join the dancers and more women come up and throw money into the air, sometimes first touching it to the heads of the dancers or dealing it like cards into their faces. Over the next hour different formations of the same twenty or so women, the close relatives, come up and dance first in twos or threes, a few more join them, and then the older women come and throw money. A woman sitting beside me whispers to me that the money throwing is to ward off unwanted male attention, the evil eye.

Laila returns, telling me that Dr Mouna invited Mozah, and Shuhailah could not refuse her boss. 'But we'll just ignore her. What's it you say? Give her the cold shoulder, yes, I like that.'

Thankfully Mozah shows no sign of intending to join us anyway, she is ensconced on a throne on the far side of the hall with Dr Mouna. It is curious that Dr Mouna has invited her, as the women at work despise Mozah with her brash Americanisms and Lebanese liberalism. She is not fish, but entirely fowl, to them. Bringing her to this wedding is a risk as it will offend many of the women. I can't help wonder what malice is afoot, even here? The vast glittering hall starts to close in around me. The air hammers thud in my forehead. But, no, I can trust Dr Mouna, surely? I shake the suspicion away.

An extraordinary Bedouin girl, as slight as a reed, her body waving and quivering like a bull rush in the wind, takes to the stage. She sings a beguiling fusion of a haunting Arabic lullaby with hip-hop, and some tongue clacking. The effect is hypnotic. Some of Laila's cousins leave the room to wait outside; Laila explains they are strict in their faith and will not be anywhere that music is played. But their mother, unveiled at all times, stays and in broken English wails to me about her eight daughters.

'Ach, tell me, why they throw everything away? They have so much, but they want none of it. Don't they know how hard it was for us? We couldn't go out of the house. We couldn't work. That one, seven years, we gave her everything to become a *doktora*.' She points towards the back of one of her disappearing daughters, 'No, it is too hard Umma. The hours are too long. I'm so tired. I'll not be a *doktora* any more. I'll stay home. And that one.' She points to another black back. 'She had a high position in the bank, very good job. But Umma, she says, the nanny is playing with the husband. Of course, this is what the nanny is for, men have so many needs. You can't give up your job for this, I tell her. But, Aaii, she does.' She wipes a tear. 'The little one, she brings pain to my heart. She won't go to college. All the time reading the Koran.

No, no, only the mosque, every night for lessons, meetings. What are these meetings?'

All the time the singer whirls around and around, a dizzying swirl of old and new. The drums clamour, now all the older women ulate their tongues behind their teeth as with midnight the bride arrives. The hall is bathed in a lustrous light as slowly, so slowly, Shuhailah takes one stiff step at a time along the catwalk. We gasp, she is a woman made wholly from gold and diamonds. Pressed under the weight of all the layers of bejewelled lace and gold, it takes a full ten minutes for her to falter along to the far end where a pearl-encrusted throne awaits. She sits rigid as the women, in procession once more, weave towards her throwing bank notes. A swelling galaxy of twinkling gems. She doesn't smile, only looks down.

Laila hands me a shawl. 'Are we leaving?

'No, no, wait, it's time.'

The grand doors to the ballroom fling open with a fanfare of trumpets as the groom bounds in with a brace of male relatives. They are dressed in gold full length robes and bearing swords. A tremendous cry erupts in the room. The men charge along the catwalk until they are met midway by a fan of Shuhailah's sisters. The men bow, and the women guide them, swaying their hips, to the throne. Shuhailah is concealed behind a tall, frilly screen. Her sisters pull it back at the last second to reveal her to her handsome husband. He bends over and kisses her shyly to roars of approval from his male entourage. Hesitant, the groom lets the sisters dance with him in front of his wife, until they tug him back to sit beside Shuhailah. Hand in hand, they watch as the sisters dance with the entourage, who are swishing their swords high above their heads and leaping and whooping with joy. Laila discretely points out her brother, Hisham. He is pure energy, acrobatic. He feels my eyes on him, he looks across and grins.

It is late now. With a final drum roll the men bounce out of the room. It is gone three in the morning. Not too long after this the older women start to leave. I make my excuses too, as I know Laila wants to chatter with her cousins. As I leave one of Shuhailah's sisters approaches me with a golden lily from the bride.

'For your wedding,' she says.

I leave, twirling the lily between my fingers, wondering if I will ever marry, the fake band on my finger nipping.

'Miss Aisling, what a pretty dress.' It is Brian, Mozah beside him. 'Do you need a lift?'

I decline.

Mozah walks off towards the car park. 'Suits you, all this glamour. But you're not there yet. Where's your bling, girl?'

Other than my ring I am not wearing any jewellery. I was so tired when I dressed I had forgotten, not that I have jewellery to speak of for this sort of occasion. Laila has already told me off for this oversight, but I am surprised at Brian commenting on this.

'Stop, I forgot, you have this rock,' he takes my hand in his mean grasp for a second, pressing my fingers hard into the stone,

'Becoming quite the Arab princess, aren't we?'

twenty-four

'Tomas, what am I going to do? I don't see how I can get out of this.'

I am at Tomas' villa. We are both fretting today. Brian rattled me awake from my siesta earlier,

'You looked cute, girl, at the wedding. Look, you missed out on the *dhow* trip on your birthday. It was awesome, yah, seeing the city all lit up at night from out on the Bay.'

He told me he had booked the *dhow* again for next weekend, for just a few special friends. Craig was leaving, his wife had issued an ultimatum.

'You'll come this time, won't you? You have to say goodbye to Craig. Spend some time with your old friends, your real friends. I, um, we, miss you.'

'What could I say Tomas? I've made so many excuses, I just didn't know what to say this time.' And I got the sense a refusal this time might be too provocative; I heard the bite in Brian's voice.

I rub the ring on my finger.

'Watch what you do there, Ash. The evil genie might appear.'

'I suspect he already has.'

'True, a man like that, that ring is a beacon, it makes you a challenge.'

I groan.

'Brian needs allies at the moment, and you have the favour of Sheikh Fariq. He must have learnt of the maglis' plan to get rid of Rex. If only they wanted rid of me.'

Tomas is pacing, one eye to the television which has been on all the time we have been talking. Yesterday, Salima was called urgently to Morocco to look after her father, who had just had a heart attack. Salima managed to get an emergency exit visa, after haggling with the immigration office. Now Tomas is ruing that decision and beating himself up for letting her go. Today the Rage spread to Morocco. Public buildings burn, people are fighting in many towns and five are dead.

'I should be there with my wife, Aisling. These bastards won't let me go. I'm being held against my will.' The immigration officials refused Tomas an exit visa.

☾

I knock back some Irish whiskey, it burns in my throat. The weekend has come too quickly for me. The *dhow* looks ancient, gnarled old wood, but it is fully motorised, no romantic sails. A sticky pungency gives away that it has been varnished lately. Brian comes over and hugs me.

'Good, you're here, come and have a beer.'

There are a handful of people on board, mostly the Rex boys and their girlfriends, and Mozah. Craig has brought a guitar with him and as we set sail he starts to strum on it. We pull away from the dock into the swarthy bay, and within minutes the ugly tangle of skyscrapers seen from the sea becomes a gorgeous, glittering tiara. Where on land there is no coherence to the jostling concrete giants - each thrusting for the best spot, fighting to be closest to the sun, flashing their glaring windows at each other - at sea, the city attains elegant order. It is captivating, dashes of green, red and blue flaring off the tiara spikes. We set off across the Bay towards the curley-whirley mosque and the library, tiny opalescent seeds in the distance.

'Aisling, a song, sing with me,' Craig calls over.

I am about to refuse when I see the grimace on Mozah's face.

I cross the deck to Craig, I whisper in his ear and he declares, 'Wonderful, wonderful, perfect choice.' He plays and I sing '*Sail away with me honey.*' The words just so right for this gibberish night.

Brian who is at the bow talking to a girl of about eighteen turns and looks at me, leaning back and listens. Mozah crosses to where Brian and the teenager are standing, she says something to the girl and nods towards me. I sing on.

'More, more, *bravo.*'

For the next half-hour Craig and I sing a selection of old favourites. Throughout, Brian just leans back and smiles at me. Mozah and the teenager glower. Eventually Mozah comes over to Craig, while he speaks to her I check my phone and decide to give Angie a quick call as I have been trying to get her all day, but with no joy. Her mobile just keeps going to voicemail. Mozah is pestering Craig for something.

'Ash, Mozah wants a song, up for it? "*She moves in mysterious ways*"'. I know it, but there's no way on this earth I'm singing it.

'Sorry, Craig. Not in my range. But, hey, I'm leaving Angie a voice message. Let's sing 'Angie' to her, such a classic.' Craig starts to sing, I join him. Mozah stamps off.

As we finish this time Brian comes over. 'You have such a haunting voice. We're almost at the old city, take a break, girl, and sit with me, I want to talk to you.'

We walk out to the open deck. We are floating beside the library. I remember our day there, cringe.

'It's splendid isn't it Ash, I knew you would love it, that's why we had to come out here again.'

We sit in silence as the curley-whirley mosque shimmers past. 'Thousands of people are fighting for their freedom as we float here Brian, it's all so surreal, don't you think?'

He says nothing.

The Middle East roared again yesterday. Muntadar al-Zaidi, the Iraqi journalist who threw his shoe at George Bush, was arrested in Baghdad after travelling from Beirut to take part in this Day of Rage. Razor wire wraps itself around the desert lands. Bullets rain down after prayers. Tahrir Square in Cairo is thronged with protesters once more. No one can wait any more.

From the corner of my eye I can see the teenager is crying and Craig and Mozah look like they are arguing. 'Who's that girl with Mozah? She doesn't seem very happy?'

Brian doesn't even give her a glance, 'Don't worry about her. Don't worry about anything tonight. Forget what's going on in the world, yah. How are you, Ash? We don't seem to have had a proper talk for a while now.'

A salty squall of wind blows my hair in my eyes. He brushes it aside, letting his fingers linger on my cheekbone. Stung, as if by static, I jump aside. He snatches his hand back, coughs, shuffles.

'It's a long way from Tipperary, isn't it? You must miss all those green places. I've always wanted to see Ireland, one day I will visit.'

Careful Brian, you are slipping. I hide my quick eyes, curled under my lashes.

'Are you enjoying work, Ash?'

'Of course, it's great. Everyday there's something new to amuse me.' I am lying, all I do now is write the staff newsletter, and flick through the one English newspaper.

'Are you sure? The Board pisses the shit out of me. You can't get anything done, someone always makes sure of that. If you get one small task in a day done I count it a good day. I wonder why the hell I'm still here. We haven't been paid yet, you know.'

'Maybe you should cut your losses. Why give away any more of your time and talent?' The words chewy like fudge in my mouth.

'You're right of course Ash, and you must be reading my mind. I'm going to cut my losses. Enough is enough, *hallas*, right?'

I stifle a sigh of relief, but too soon.

'I want you to come with us, Ash. Our business is going to expand elsewhere in the region. I have a new business partner. He carries some weight in these parts, access to the highest levels, if you get my meaning. We have some major deals in the pipeline. I need a good PR, he likes you, will like you I mean, and I know you'll fit the bill perfectly, girl.'

I need Laila's prayer.

'Look, now isn't the time to discuss the detail, but give it some serious thought and let me know what you think, yah.' He pauses. 'I don't want to scare you but things could get difficult for you at the Board soon, for all the expats. You should consider my offer very carefully, you won't get a better one.'

I don't say anything.

He taps his foot. 'I think we would make a great team Aisling, and in more than one way, but it looks like I was too slow off the mark there.' He lifts my hand, and fingers the fake ring. 'It seems rather sudden, but I hope you're happy.'

'I am, very.'

'He's a lucky man.' He laughs, my skin prickles. 'How about you sing me a song then, girl? What's the one, '*Irish Eyes are Smiling*'?'

I return to Craig and we sing Brian's request. Brian joins the tearful teenager, sitting on a small bench. He barely sits down when Mozah pushes herself between them. The girl almost falls off. Mozah places her hand on Brian's knee. We sing a couple more tunes and then Craig says he wants to dance and on goes the stereo. He drags Mozah off the bench to the dance floor, where she is soon grinding like a professional pole dancer around the mast pole. One of the Rex boys catches my hand and we dance. I have Brian in view still, he has his back to the dance floor and his young companion and is looking out to sea. The child is weeping quietly, dabbing at her eyes. My partner swings me about and accidentally I bump into Mozah.

'Watch it. Oh, it's you. You're having a good time tonight aren't you, Lady GaGa.' She pokes her fingers in her mouth as if about to vomit and then pokes her finger at me.

'Ignore her, she's drunk,' says Craig. 'Mozah, come on, tonight's all about letting loose and having fun,' Craig is trying to drag her away.

'Like she does, breaking up marriages. Slut! *Sharmuta*!'

'What are you talking about?'

'Ohh per-lease, don't come the innocent with me Miss Aisling. *Yanni*, I know exactly what you've done. That ring is worthless to you. Shame on you.'

I gulp, she knows the engagement is a fake. She will broadcast this high and low and make a fool of me.

'I'm surprised you could bear to tear yourself away from his bed to come tonight.' Mozah smirks.

'Are you looking for a slap?' My fingers tingle in readiness.

'Tomas. It has to be you. You two are always together, and now

Salima's left him,' she shouts triumphantly for all on the *dhow* to hear. No one is dancing now.

I laugh hard. 'You really do have a nasty, bitter view of everyone don't you? Judging them by your own sordid standards. That's the real scandal here, isn't it Craig?'

I walk away as Craig wrangles Mozah spitting like a wild cat, and I go back out to the deserted deck. We have rounded the Bay and are heading towards the skyscraper city again, back out in deep sea. My dance partner brings me a drink. I look over at Brian.

'Who's that girl over there with Brian?'

'Her, that's Brian's fiancée, oh shit we're not meant to tell anyone that.'

'Fiancée, that child?'

My dance partner tells me the girl arrived two days ago from South Africa. He goes back to the dance floor.

'He got his divorce?' My words just a hush above the spray. I look out on the sparkling buildings, welded together with Indian blood. *I miss you, too slow off the mark.* I look at the teenager, her eyes puffy. Mozah is on the dance floor with Brian now, arms around his neck, anaconda. He sees me looking and smiles, his hand on Mozah's rump.

I want off this boat.

twenty-five

We come into dock. Mozah has her arms around both Brian and Craig as they descend the gangplank, but I slip down behind them, looking ahead to see if I can spot Laila. I texted her from the *dhow*. She replied that she would send a driver to pick me up. Brian is meant to be driving me home. A man jumps up from small gaggle of men fishing off the quay.

'Miss Aisling, it's me, Hisham, Laila's brother.'

'*Salaam-Alaikum*, Hisham.'

'*Alaikum Salaam*. Laila sent me.'

'I'm so glad. Please, can we go quickly?'

He looks at my stumbling companions. 'I understand.'

Brian turns at this point and sees me walking away with Hisham. 'Ash, where are you going?'

'Don't worry, I will get myself home, you have your hands full there.'

I turn on my heel before he can answer. Hisham's car is parked close by. We get in and he revves up and put his foot down as Brian, who has slumped Mozah over Craig, marches towards us.

I give Hisham directions to Bella Villa, but he drives in the opposite direction.

'Where are we going?'

'The traffic is crazy on the road to Al Hamsa, let's get some mint tea.' We drive around the Bay and head along the coast road. Maybe I should feel nervous, but so long as I am not with Brian, and am getting as far away as possible from him, that's all I can think right now. Hisham switches on the car stereo and sings softly to Arabic music. We pull up to a petrol station where there are a few small shops. Hisham calls out to a young lad on the forecourt who brings us some mint tea.

'I need to get out of the city.'

'Me too.' I reply.

We drive along the road until the city is just a glowing golden chain behind us. Fire flares overhead. The road is sewn on both sides with barbed wire fencing. Just through the fencing I see oblong tin after oblong tin, all lined up in perfect symmetry. 'What's this place Hisham?'

'Arab Auschwitz.'

'I don't understand.'

'A camp, for the labourers. This is the far edge of the industrial city, you see those flares. Gas.'

Hisham tells me that the labourers live in the aluminum boxes, stacked three high on narrow planks, forty or more to a box. No facilities, no air con, just a tap outside. Rice twice a day. Sixteen hour shifts, through the night.

'Those cabins must be like ovens in the heat.'

'This is how the West keeps warm in winter, how our Royals get rich. For this we will shed blood. This is our shame. We'll have our Day of Rage, *Inshallah*.'

The flares diminish to guttering matches as we drive on, the road becomes a track and then bumps along a couple of kilometres until some shadowy tumbled-down adobe shacks come into view. We pull up next to a pile of crumbling blocks.

'I'll show you our old village.' Hisham finds a torch in the boot of the car and we stumble around the rocky alleyways of the village.

The adobe houses are small, just one or two rooms big. The roofs are caved in. No doors. Graffiti is scrawled on the walls, and empty beer cans and syringes lie scattered about. I step carefully, wary of hidden needles.

As we walk Hisham tells me this is the fishing village where his family once lived for generations, until oil was found. Now no one lives in these villages, everyone has moved to the city. The only life here is weekend parties of young playboys. At the edge of the village a small mosque tower, like a stubby muddy child's thumb sticks up. No door to bar the devoted, we climb the tiny staircase and at the top look out from a small slit window on the lights of fishing *dhows* bobbing away in the warm sea. The close walls of the tower press us together.

'Laila is so fond of you.'

'I'm fond of her too.'

'Our lives here are small. It's good for her to have a friend from overseas. Before you came she was so alone. It's hard for her to be a woman of her age and no husband or children. And I can't be with her as much as she would like. Her life is inside the home, mine is outside.'

'She told me she has never been outside of the city, except to go on pilgrimage to Mecca.'

'*Yanni*, true. There are parts of even this small city she has never been to. She can go to work, the mosque, the mall, the souk, but beyond that, then me, or one of our brothers would need to go with her. You cannot imagine this?'

'Maybe not, but my Mammy has never left Ireland and only goes up to Dublin once a year for the Christmas shopping. It's not so long ago ours was a small society, a small world, if you stayed and did not emigrate. In Ireland, you either stay close, or you go, far.'

'*Wallah*, we are the same. The Irish are the Bedouins of Europe.'

'No camels.'

He laughs, 'And you, was your life so small?'

'Yes, in a small village; like this by the sea, but ours is a cold, harsh sea. I couldn't wait to get out, go to Dublin to study.'

'Dublin is a great city?'

'The fair city, we say.'

'But the rain …'

The rain. Cold, grey water ran through my days, the granite streets and the slithering, slatternly Liffey. My city life was long hours in the cold, clinical greens, blues and sterile whites of the Mater Hospital. And a sterile love. By the time I was laid off, I felt that there was no colour left; even the greys and greens had washed to translucency.

'Aisling?'

'Sorry, I was miles away, talking like this takes me back there.'

'We have no rain, I promise. Come.'

He guides me down the dark steps of the mosque and keeps hold of my hand once we are walking along the beach.

'And your life?'

'We have everything now, villas, cars, computers, mobile phones, but life before was simple. I would have liked to live here in a small house and fished every day. Be free.'

The dark sky above us roars, the grit of the beach slashes around us. I am nearly blown off my feet but instinctively, Hisham and I pull together.

'Harriers. The base is over there.' He points out to the desert, where red lights squint in the distance. 'Our government prepares; they will send support to Libya. Airlifts of the people have started.'

I had watched the news for as long as I could bear earlier, heart-rending scenes of families being wrenched apart in the chaos, children screaming for their fathers. Worse still the reporters warned mercenaries were on the scene. Gaddafi had contracted with brutes from the Sub-Sahara to attack his own people; they were already seeking out and massacring people who had fled the conflicts in the Sub-Sahara.

'Gaddafi has threatened the bloodiest of wars, thousands and thousands of Libyans will die if the West intervenes,' Hisham says.

'I don't think the West has any great desire for another Iraq. But how does the world sit by and watch this horror?'

'*Yanni*, how do we sit by and watch this horror?'

'I have seen people die before my eyes on the TV screen, beheaded, actual people.'

'People think this is a movie, but one day it will not be on their TVs in their homes, but for real in their streets and homes.'

He kneels. 'I must pray.'

The first faint streaks of milky gold stream through the sky. I walk beside the shoreline, watch flecks of the dawn glisten one by one on the waves, as the stars pale. Hisham, his prayers said, falls in with my step beside me.

'I like talking with you Aisling. Please can we come again and talk some more. Of our futures, dreams, next time.'

I smile, 'My name means dream, in Irish, so yes.'

'I shall call you Mounia. It means dream come true.'

'And Hisham, what does that mean?'

'Hisham, it means destroyer of evil.'

'I think I might need a destroyer of evil.' I tell Hisham about

Brian. His eyes are dark. 'You must take my number and if you need me, call, any time.' He presses my hand to his heart. The morning heat is seeping through the sand. A ruby red comet announces the dawn.

twenty-six

The enemy lines are drawn.

I sit by the window in my apartment, looking out across the rubble, dreaming of the sea lights of last night until Tomas calls. He tells me he was brushing his driveway free of the piles of sand that gather overnight when a car cruised by slowly, something about it caught his attention. He looked up to see Mozah peering at him. The car drew up and Mozah and Brian got out. She claimed they were there to check on work at the villa next door, which was to be assigned to a Board employee. Tomas knew there had been no workmen there, despite her excuse. She invited herself in and promptly wandered about, making a show of commenting on the décor, asking stupid questions about the utilities. Nosing around.

I tell him about her accusations the night before.

'Bitch.'

I tell him about Brian, the child fiancée and the job offer.

'The man is a psychopath, Ash. He was laughing at me in my own home.'

'The only comfort I can give is that they might be gone soon. He said he was thinking of cutting his losses.'

'Let's hope that's true. If not we'll have to find other ways to make sure he goes.'

'What do you mean?'

'I'm sure the authorities would take a dim view on his friendship with a local woman, who also happens to work for a government agency where he is contracted.'

'I don't think involving the authorities is a good idea. It will turn into a huge drama and how will that look for the Prof? We'll have Fariq breathing down our necks before you can blink.'

☪

Instead, we have Rex breathing down our necks all week. Me especially. I want to shake them off. I call Brian and politely refuse his offer. I take a deep breath as I speak to him, I fear he is not a man who will take rejection well. He is predictably tight-lipped about it and tells me I am making a tremendous mistake. 'You'll soon see, girl.'

Now Rex are everywhere, in every office, every meeting. Joe says he feels as if he is being stalked. Justin complains that a stack of files has disappeared from a locked cupboard in his office. Laila is sure someone has been in our office overnight, despite it being locked. She knows that some of her ornaments have been disturbed. Brian takes over Angie's office and usurps her as Chair of a sub-committee, Rex now apparently leading her project too. I still cannot get hold of Angie and am starting to really worry about her. Why has she not returned from her leave? It does not appear that Brian is cutting his losses after all.

The atmosphere grows tetchier by the day. My throat starts to burn, a ball of fiery, wire-wool lodges in my chest. Always in the background, the sound of rocket-fire in Libya. I receive a memo from Sheikh Fariq's office at the beginning of the week instructing me that I am to hold a workshop on Thursday for the senior management team to discuss the setting up of the new executive consortium. This is a bold move as the Board has not delegated any of its powers or approved this move; in fact a proposal about such a development has not even been brought before the Board. The Sheikh will furnish me the day before with a report setting out a new management structure for the executive consortium.

The workshop is to be held in one of the new seven-star tower hotels. It has gone up in the short time I have been here and is now in its soft opening phase. I am a little reluctant to use this hotel, but at such short notice there is no other option. It is perfectly beautiful, but we had used this hotel once before in the previous month and there had been an unfortunate incident. The conference rooms are on the same floor as the spa, at the very top of this fifty-storey building. At lunchtime someone decided it would be a lovely idea to hold the buffet around the indoor pool. The pool is an infinity one, curved and slightly sunken, so it appears to float in the sky and out to the Bay.

I did not attend this particular conference, but the princesses were there to give event management support and came flying back in fits of laughter to tell me what happened.

'Miss Aisling, Miss Aisling, stop, stop, it's too much!' Faria was doubled over, clutching her ribs.

'Faria, whatever is the matter?'

'The Chief Docktor from Azerbaijan, a greedy man. You should see how he piled his plate high with food, every dish he tried. *Yanni*, no wonder it happened. How could he see over that stack of meat?'

I had a horrible feeling I knew what was coming, but had to ask all the same, 'Faria, don't tell …'

'The splash, Miss Aisling. Straight into the deep end! With his whole plate of food. What a belly-flop!'

Drowning delegates is the least of my concerns on the day. Of course, I don't receive the Sheikh's report. I expect this. As the senior management team starts to arrive it still hasn't been faxed to me. A number of the team are running late. The workshop is forty minutes overdue. Mozah, amongst others is not here. I watch the grand crystal clock on the wall but its long, tendril hands seem not to move. The sickly scent of lilies overpowers the room, beneath it the sharpness of chlorine. There is no excuse, this is a deliberate snub. Finally she arrives, a smirk on her scarlet lips. However, still no word from the Sheikh, although his office keep saying 'soon, soon' when I call. The Sheikh's office text, the report is on its way with a messenger. Tomas comes over to me saying he has to go, please give his apologies. His features like concrete. He says he will tell me more later, but for now says he has a sudden headache. As he leaves he passes Brian in the doorway.

'Aisling, are you sure you won't reconsider my offer?' Brian asks, looking over my head and across the room to Mozah.

'Brian, this is hardly the time or place for this.' I croak. 'I'm about to give a workshop for the Sheikh on the new structures for the executive consortium.'

'So that's still a 'no' is it? Shame. You see girl, I don't see you fitting into the Sheikh's new plans.'

He strides into the centre of the room and claps his hands, 'Ladies and gentlemen, may I have your attention please. The Sheikh has sent me here to day with his new plans, which he would like me to take each and every one of you through on a personal basis. I suggest you all retire to the coffee lounge downstairs, yah, take some refreshment and I will see you each in turn.'

The senior management team immediately start to disappear.

The Prof and Brian speak in a corner. Brian, hands on his hips while the Prof raises and waves his hands over his head. I pack away my papers.

Mozah makes a detour across the room to pass me as she leaves. 'You can clean up the rubbish,' she laughs loudly and points to the platters of half-eaten pastries.

Brian comes over in her wake and in the next breath to her insult adds, 'Apologies Aisling, but your services are not required in the new PR department of the executive consortium.'

They both leave, snorting.

I sink beside the pool, I feel feverish. The Prof paces and glares out across the heavenly Bay. Everyone has gone. The Prof tries to call the Sheikh's office, but the phone just rings off the hook.

'On whose authority? Whose authority?' he growls. I stand up to go. 'I overheard what Brian said to you. Has he offered you a job?'

'He has at Rex, but I turned it down. I don't think he's taken that very well. It seems I'm no longer required at the new executive consortium.'

He sighs, 'Aisling, I have something to tell you. I tendered my resignation earlier this week.'

'What?' I can barely rasp.

'You are a clever woman Aisling. I think you have seen something of the pressures I'm under here, so you will understand. My position has become untenable.'

'I don't understand. What's happening here? I thought Rex were gone.' After the camel farm, I had fully expected Rex would be told to pack their bags in favour of the wretched little Scottish man and his firm, Blackheath & Company. The Prof just shrugs his shoulders, 'Alhamdulillah.'

'Where will you go Professor?'

'Away. Please, do not mention this to anyone. I have my arrangements to make.'

I nod, swallow hard. My throat hurts.

'I'm sorry to let you down like this Aisling. I know you thought you were coming here for a grand adventure. It would be best for you to go.'

My turn to shrug my shoulders, 'There's not much hope back home these days. I guess I will have to try America?'

I don't want my Arabian dream to be over, not now.

☾

Tomas comes over in the afternoon, with a bottle of Swedish 'firewater' he has brewed himself, in the garage of his villa. My head is heavy, I am struggling to breathe.

'The expat initiation test, desert throat. Everyone gets it. It's the worst throat infection you will ever have. Here, drink. Kill or cure. Skal.'

I tell him about the workshop. He gives a hollow laugh. He tells me he saw Yusef when he went back to the office to pick up some papers after he left the workshop early. Yusef was angry because he was about to leave to go to the hotel with the Sheikh's plans when Brian intercepted him and took them. 'I'm not so sure he has the prerogative to do that, and Yusef certainly knew nothing about the Sheikh asking Brian to see the senior team.'

'If that's true, then that's a bold strike on Brian's part,' I say.

'He is flexing his muscle in ways that don't seem to be sanctioned. What I don't understand is why doesn't the Prof stop him? Maybe he's doing his dirty work. Someone's pulling Brian's strings that's for sure.'

'Not the Prof. I think Brian is just cocksure of himself.'

Tomas whistles in agreement. 'Tell me, why did you leave the workshop early? What was wrong?'

'Mozah.'

Tomas recounts how she came over and asked how his father-in-law was recovering. He told her Salima was still in Morocco with her father.

'Still?' she asked. He knew what she was insinuating.

Tomas quickly rebutted the implication that Salima had left him, telling her that Salima's father was very ill and she would need to stay with him for some time, but she would be back. Mozah told him he didn't need to keep up the pretence with her. Why didn't he come out for a drink with her and Brian tonight? They would cheer him up and if he needed some company Brian could arrange that too. Tomas gave her short shrift, and she said he was a fool to turn down their generosity and support. No wonder he had left in a fury.

'Tomas … I … It's … too much… where are Tony and Angie? Still no news on either of them.' My voice dries out.

Tomas has a match with Joe to go to and leaves. I huddle under my blanket on the sofa, fending off the freezing aircon. I want to hear Angie say 'Fuck them all, let's go have a voddie, kid.'

It's no good, I'm too cold, the fever is taking hold. I boil some water and crush some *nana* leaves that Laila has given me for my throat. Their minty aroma oils my fingers. I breathe the scent in, and it's as if we are back by the shore, *his* warmth around me.

twenty-seven

'Your exam certificates, Miss Aisling.' Mozah followed by the drippy eel man comes into the office without even knocking first; Laila hurriedly pulls her *nikab* back on.

'Mozah, you need to knock to give Laila time to replace her veil.' I cough, my throat better but still raw from the recent infection. It's taken the best part of the week to pass. She ignores me.

'Your examination certificates, now,' she snaps.

'Why do you need them? I submitted copies when I was offered my job and those were checked and validated then.'

She puts her hands on her hips and shouts, 'I'm not arguing with you. I need the originals today.'

'Sister Mozah!'

Her face purples and crinkles up like a sultana. I shoot a warning look to Laila, I don't need a cat fight right at this moment. 'You still haven't given me a reason why, or on whose instruction you're working,' I reply as calmly as I can.

'I don't need to explain myself to you. I'm working directly for the Sheikh now, and I don't have to account to the Prof or you or anyone else.' She clicks her fingers at me.

I click mine back. 'Well, I don't have my original certificates here. I wasn't told I would need them. They're safe at home in Ireland. If you want them then you'll need to pay for me to go home and get them, business class.'

Laila clucks approvingly in the background.

Mozah whistles. 'Tut, tut, this won't look good for you. I promise you, you'll be going home, but on a one way ticket ... cattle class.' With this she minces back out of the office, eel man slithers at her trail. Laila hisses after her.

'Laila...'

'Let me go see Dr Mouna. She's in charge of all these HR matters, we'll see the truth from her.'

Emails pop up on my computer. Tomas and Joe have also received similar visitations and demands from Mozah today. But Justin and other expat staff have not. Why are our credentials being questioned now? I am certain this is building up to a confirmation that we are about to be terminated, following Brian's declaration that there is no place for me in the new executive consortium. Tomas and Joe expect they will be told similar news. Laila dismisses Brian's threats as hot desert air.

'He has no right. You must show him you are strong. Who does this man think he is?'

Who indeed.

Laila goes and returns with Dr Mouna, her voice behind her veil strangled with fury, '*Yanni*, my dear, I apologise from my heart for this terrible wrong that has been done to you. It's not done in the name of the Board or our people.' Dr Mouna assures me my job is not and has never been under threat. Brian has no right to speak to me in this way. I do not need to supply my exam certificates.

'But Dr Mouna, Rex seem to think they're running things now?'

Dr Mouna's veil swishes. 'Aaii, one more month only.' She

tells me that the Sheikh has only signed a temporary extension to the Rex contract. The National Audit Department will not countenance it being extended any further. The extension has only been agreed this time as a matter of expediency. The Sheikh is buying some time, keeping Brian occupied with setting up the new executive consortium, while the Board's lawyers find a way of dealing with Brian's legal threats about non-payment and contract breaches. There is so much noise now about Rex from the local staff, 'The Sheikh's ears aren't closed, but he needs to find a clever answer, exit.' One that would mean not a penny more being paid to these sharks.

'Why would the Sheikh tell these bad men to set up the consortium?' Laila asks.

'There will be no consortium.'

Dr Mouna will say no more and waves a finger to indicate we should not either. 'Sister, you're very much valued at the Board. We see how hard you work for the people. We'll not lose you.' Dr Mouna hugs me.

'Dr Mouna, I hear there's a list of people who will be terminated, and Tony and Angie have both gone, and we don't know where?'

'I don't know about them, but your name isn't on a list.'

☪

It is prayer time. I go to find Tomas to tell him about Dr Mouna's reassurance. Tomas and Joe jump as I walk into their office.

'You two look shifty.'

They beckon me over to the computer at Joe's desk. The screen is filled with a spreadsheet. Joe points to some figures. My eye trace along the columns. I know this is a set of accounts, but don't understand what I am looking at. I can see nothing wrong, other than one strange figure, which just does not reconcile with any of the others. It stands out like a sore thumb. Joe flicks through a few more similar sheets, all with their own sore thumbs.

I look at him and spread my hands. 'Why don't they add up?

He smiles wryly, then he hits a few keys, changing the formulae, and the figures in the boxes start to change dramatically, and the sore thumbs gain many sore fingers. Suddenly deficits are appearing throughout the various sheets. Joe hits a totalizer button. Forty million riyal deficit.

'That's almost five million euro,' I whisper.

'Coffee,' says Tomas.

We leave separately and meet in the coffee bar across the road, safe to do this while prayers are still on, although we only have a few minutes before we may be missed, all of us so conscious now of peering eyes.

'That's this last month alone,' says Joe as we sit down. He explains that the Rex boys, who for the last few months have been running the payroll and accounts department asked him to supply them with some financial data. The files were too large to email over the Board's creaky system, so he put them on a memory stick and took the stick to their office. A couple of hours later the tea boy came back with the stick. However, when Joe opened it he realised it was the wrong stick, but being curious he took a look. This is when he discovered the peculiar accounts and payroll ledger. He fiddled about with it, seeing the sore thumbs and realised the formulae looked odd. He copied the stick and went along to the Rex boys' office on a made-up errand, and managed to slip the stick back onto a desk under a pile of papers.

'I then went into the archive and took a look at some of the historical accounts. No such spreadsheet trickery there, just hand-written ledgers that made no sense and never added up, constant deficits, but hidden in the scrawls.' Joe pauses for dramatic effect. 'By my quick and dirty reckoning, over the past five years something like a hundred million dollars has not been properly accounted for.' Joe explains that this money has been paid out in a variety of unusual ways, to contractors who never existed; or to contractors who did exist, but were never contracted for such vast sums.

There was one contract account for four million US dollars to go to an American military intelligence company. What would they be working on at a Health Board? I shiver, during the past few weeks armed forces have been posted throughout the country alongside the police; and the Prime Minister has strengthened the legislation banning public gatherings. The Council of Clerics declared that 'reform and advice should not be via demonstrations and ways that provoke strife and division, this is what the religious scholars of this country in the past, and now, have forbidden and warned against. Political parties are banned, as they are not in keeping with the ways of Islam.'

Vast sums of money are just streaming in and out of these accounts, nothing to do with the Board's formal budget. 'Money laundering?'

'At the very least, wholesale fraud and corruption by the looks of this,' says Tomas.

'And if this month's accounts are any indication it's still going on.'

'Rex...'

We look at each other, no need to answer. The formulae that have been used to hide the true accounts are highly sophisticated and divert money in ways that are difficult to trace, unless like Joe you are a trained in forensic accountancy. We all doubt that any local at the Board can have constructed the formulae; and certainly Joe adds, the old ledgers do not hide the crimes nearly as well. The ledgers present their own flummoxery, in that they are such a mess, but the fraud is not so deliberately hidden there.

'What do we do now?'

'We sit tight and dig around some more. We need to get definitive proof first. And we need to work out where all this money is going.'

We head back to the office. The Prof has asked everyone to gather in the Boardroom after prayers. He breaks the news that he has resigned and will be leaving in the summer before Ramadan. Within minutes there is uproar in the building as the news shoots from office to office.

I go back to my office and sit at my computer, unable to focus on anything. Nothing to do anyway. Who needs a staff newsletter, the news will always be ancient history. Even email cannot speed like an Arabic tongue. There is a knock at my office door. It is Mozah.

'Are you worried now Miss Aisling?'

I ignore her, keep staring at the dark screen.

'First Mr Tony, then Miss Angie, now even the Professor is going in these sudden circumstances.' She emphasises the 'sudden'.

I turn my eyes to her, slowly. 'A three-month notice period, which the Prof has just confirmed, Mozah, as you well know is hardly an abrupt departure.'

'*Hallas*! If it's that long. You know his successor might not need or want the Prof around.'

'My understanding is that the Sheikh will be advertising across the region for a replacement, and that will take some time.'

'Pah! There are exceptional candidates close by, real close, who could start tomorrow, even today.'

'Perhaps.'

I turn back to my computer to signify the conversation is over.

'You're going to need some protection when the Professor goes. All alone at Bella Villa, and soon you'll be all alone in the office.'

I sit rigid.

'You know, you are only, what is it the Prof says? A 'guest' here; and there's a queue of natives ready to take these posts. I'm sure Miss Laila would like your job.'

'Go, Mozah.' Before you choke on your own spite. Or I choke you.

'Ha! There're enemies everywhere, behind every veil, ready to betray.'

twenty-eight

Laila and her sisters chew over the curious machinations of the last few days with me in the tented maglis in the yard of her family villa. Many villas have these tents, an echo of the Bedouin times. Heavy yellowing plastic on the outside, but inside, the tent glows with patterned woven walls. It is air-conditioned and even has a plasma TV that can pick up satellite channels. We rarely watch it though, the sisters cannot bear the rolling coverage of the Arab Spring. 'We'll not look on such bad things in the world,' they cry, as if by closing their eyes the troubles will go. Laila and I would like to watch, as we both know you cannot run from the troubles, and day by day they seem to be blazing this way, faster than we could ever run.

The West has started air strikes in Tripoli. Over this past month across the Middle East more protests, every day more people are shot, rounded up, imprisoned. Disappeared. Everyone lives under the curfew. Even in countries like Egypt and Tunisia where the revolution has been victorious the rioting has not abated, people desperate for the revolutionary promises to be made good today. Despots are sacking their puppet governments and handing out oil money to public servants in a frantic bid to ward off regime change in their states. Every week the fervour takes hold in a new country. This week it is Syria, where President Assad's forces fired on a peaceful protest at a mosque in Deraa and killed six. Insurgents and terrorists, the government state. Amongst the dead, Ali Ghassab al-Mahamid, a doctor from a prominent family who went to the Omari mosque in the city's old quarter to help victims of the attack.

We lie on cushions on the floor, tired out by the afternoon heat, even though the aircon is on full blast. Tiny nieces and nephews run in and out. Laila has been quiet for a while, when she says most definitively, 'You'll come live with us, then this bad man Rothmann can't hurt you. You shouldn't be alone now.'

At night I still wake, with stabbing in my stomach, rubble gripe.

'Bella Villa's a dirty place. You'll have a better life with us. *Yanni*, I'll ask my brothers. They'll say 'yes' and make the arrangements.'

'*Akide*, this is best,' agrees one of Laila's older sisters. 'But this we don't need to talk about. It's done now, praise Allah, we just have to bring your belongings.'

The tent flap opens and Hisham walks in. His sisters spring up to each feed him a different delicacy or pour mint tea, he is the favourite brother. He joins Laila and myself on the floor and asks why we all look so troubled.

He listens and nods, 'There's wrong at the Board.' He tells us there is much talk of this on the blogger sites and Twitter. Many rumours. People are very angry about the hospital, the health clinics, the health insurance plans. They are blaming the Prof, saying he is a traitor, no more than a Western saboteur who wants to ruin his country. The talk is getting violent. The Day of Rage drawing closer? I shudder to hear this.

'Please don't worry Sister, our words are more violent than our actions. It's easy for people to say bad things on the Twitter, where no one knows who they are. We're a peace-loving people. We obey Allah and are good Muslims.' Laila seeks to reassure me.

Hisham continues, 'It's good that the Prof is going now, it's best for him. We have known for some time this would happen. The journalists have been saying he's been terminated for the last two weeks or more, and they're also saying that the Board will be closed down. There must be calm.'

'He resigned, and Dr Mouna said the consortium would not happen,' I counter.

'There will be lots of stories about the Prof. It will be hard to see the truth. The consortium will not happen and the Board will be replaced by a new Ministry of Public Health.'

Smoke and mirrors, always.

'The Prof is already yesterday's news. All the talk is about who will be Minister, Sheikh Fariq or the Queen's brother. This will be a big fight. So much trouble now at the top of the house, but behind heavy doors.'

'Allah protect us, if it spills out …' says Laila.

Hisham tells us that there is hushed talk in the mosque of a power struggle between His Highness' sons. The Queen's son has been named Heir Apparent. The first son of the first wife smoulders. Fierce debates about the merits of the Queen's social reforms split the Council of Ministers. Now all the more so, with the first buds of the Arab Spring, the Queen wants to invest heavily in sports and cultural facilities to build a healthy society for the future, to channel the energies of the youth that can easily be drawn to more rebellious pursuits. The old guard think the money should be hidden away in gold, property overseas and in increasing the internal and external defenses of the state. There are causes, capital is required.

'Today the Tweeters claim that His Highness' first son has been given special gifts by his father. A multinational bank, an English football club and the state airline.' Hashtag. Appeasement.

'This first son, he favours the Brethren, he is forging strong links in China and Russia. In his maglis every night there are foreign intelligence operatives.'

'Men like these Rex,' says Laila.

'No, Rex are just expats on the make,' I reply. 'There's no need for foreign operatives in a health service.' I push away the memory of the sore thumbs from my mind.

'The make?'

'After money.'

'Let me see.' Hisham asks me to spell out Brian's name. He taps it into his phone. '*Mafi.*'

'Let me try.' I tap in Brian's name, Craig's, Rex into various search engines. Hisham is right. Nothing. How can this be? Even Grandaddy's scrap of a terrier has his own Facebook page, where he dresses in different lurid neckerchiefs. Everyone has something about them on the Net, somewhere. How do you hide from the Net? Acrid cigarette smoke overwhelms me.

'Someone is smoking?'

'Sister?' Laila and Hisham look at me curious and then at each other.

'Can't you smell it?' I can taste it, my tongue furs.

'Aisling, you're tired. I've frightened you with all this talk.'

'No, I ...' But the smoke has gone.

The tent flap batters open and in runs the cheekiest of the nephews carrying a heavy ceramic dish of bright green pasta, 'Macaroni Weez', he yells.

It was St. Patrick's Day earlier in the week and the pasta has been dyed in my honour. Laila's sisters are now addicted to macaroni cheese since their introduction to it at the mall. As we eat they promise me we will eat it every day when I move in. I hope it won't be bright green next time. I can see Hisham twitching a smile as he spoons a mouthful.

After our late lunch, Hisham gets up to drive me back to Bella Villa, despite Laila's entreaties that I stay. But tonight I need to think, to pack.

We get into the car and drive. 'Aisling, now you know our secrets. The world the West doesn't see. Don't reveal it to others. It wouldn't be wise. I tell you of our maglis because it will help you to understand our country, and I want you to understand. I nod. 'Our ways run deep through the generations. But, I also want you to know why our young people are ready.'

We pull up at a red light at a crossroad.

'Aisling, let's not go back to your apartment yet. You're worried. It's better for you to be with me, not alone in that place all night.'

He places a finger across my lips to stop me arguing, reaches across kisses me.

☪

We leave the city behind. The packing can wait. It's nearly dusk.

'The singing sand dunes are about an hour south of the city.' Hisham tells me as we speed along the highway.

'Singing sand dunes?'

We drive along a highway full of thundering trucks, passing three freshly smashed up juggernauts and a couple of mangled cars at one place. We pass an army base. The sign is painted out white, although you can still make out the embossed words 'army base' and the road is lined with wire fences and watchtowers. We drive deeper into the desert going by signs warning us not to take photos, not to trespass, and that we are in a secure military area.

'Are you sure we should be here?'

Hisham laughs. 'The desert belongs to itself.'

☾

Towering golden waves above us, we stand at the foot of the dunes, amongst a litter of single boots, sandals and trainers. Where are their other halves? The curve upwards looks gentle enough. Hisham smiles at me.

'I'll race you.' And he is off. If ever there is going to be an unequal race. But soon he is staggering as he sinks almost to his knees in the soft sand. I gain on him, lighter on foot across the shifting terrain. 'This is impossible.' We both pant and laugh.

The summit is close, my knees feel as if they are going to snap. Then, suddenly the gentle curve becomes a narrow vicious precipice, with razor edges and vertical plunges forty or fifty foot on either side. I can hardly stand, every footstep just seems to slip me backwards, my sandals are pulled off me by the sucking sand.

Hisham takes massive leaps forward. 'Come on, it's easier the higher you get, the sand is getting firmer here.'

But nothing can stop me sliding, sinking. It is like being in one of those gulping dreams you get just before waking, slipping further and further. I reach out, there is nothing to hold. Hisham is a blur, off at the top of the dune. I can't even call; my mouth is sticky. The glare of the dipping sun in my eyes makes the world around me bleed away too, all is white, and scorching. Then ... a low almost metallic hum, from deep beneath me. I can feel the panic stirring. I shut my eyes tight. I grab, needle sharp-nails blister through my fingers. Deep, metallic groan. A slash of hot grain across my face.

Suddenly, rocks and waves of sand shower around me as I roll. The groan fills my ears, every corner of my mind, the sand around me throbs. I hear a scream. Mine?

'*Habibti*, I've got you, I've got you.'

The falling stops. I open my eyes. Hisham is brushing sand from my face and hair. '*Wallah*! That was some tumble! What happened? Did you hear the *djinn*? She sang to you.'

'*Djinn*?'

'An old story. The Bedouin believe there are evil spirits in the dunes, the *djinn* disguised as elderly crones looking for young flesh.'

'She sang for her supper as she tried to devour me.' I splutter and spit out sand.

Hisham is now sweeping sand vigorously from off my body. His hands, hot. 'No harm done. Sorry, I nearly smothered you myself. You gave me a fright. One minute you were there and the next you were gone. *Hallas*!' He stands behind me, enveloping me in his arms. His chin resting on my head. 'Don't worry, the *djinn* isn't going to have you this time. I'm not letting you go, the dunes can hunger.' Far across land and time, as the seas of grey sand drift, murmuring their song, we stand at the edge holding tight together.

twenty-nine

Bella Villa is gloomier than ever as the hall lights are not working. Hisham has dropped me off after our evening at the dunes. I said I would be fine, with fingers crossed behind my back. I stumble up the stairs and along the corridor to my apartment. I fumble for the key in my bag, as I do so I lean against my door and am surprised when it swings open. I am certain I locked it before I left this morning. I flick the lights; thankfully they are still working.

'Hello,' I call out. No reply, what do I expect? Still my heart is in my mouth. I stand for a moment, transfixed. Then, I run back down the stairs, trying not to trip in the grey light. The greasy doorman is chewing tobacco and watching porn on his mobile TV. I explain what has happened and that I am afraid there is an intruder. He doesn't look at me; eyes glued to the screen where two naked women are frolicking in a swimming pool, instead farts and declares this is impossible, as he would have seen them enter the building. I ask him to accompany me to be sure there is no intruder. He rubs his crotch and rolls his eyes towards me. I change my mind. No need, I must have forgotten to lock the door, silly me. He turns back to the TV.

I go upstairs. On tiptoes I walk from room to room. No one is here; nothing seems to have been touched. Yet in my mind there are invisible smeary fingerprints everywhere. I remember the cigarette butt. I sit down on a sofa and cry. Had I not shut and locked the door properly this morning? How else could the door be open? Nothing is gone, touched, surely if there was an intruder then the place would have been rifled? The heat, this country, everything is getting to me. Mozah has got to me.

I want to ring Hisham, but what can I say without sounding like a paranoid expat?

I ring Tomas instead. I tell him about the unlocked door, then Mozah and her threats. He hesitates and then weakly tries to reassure me, it is all too easy to leave a door unlocked. He doesn't sound convincing.

'Aisling, do you want me to come over and stay tonight if you are nervous? I am happy to do so. I am rattling around this villa on my own while Salima is away.'

'No, no, that really will bring us trouble. I'm being stupid, it's nothing.'

My nerves are just strained.

'It's a shame you can't come on this trip to Ras Latifa. You could do with a couple of days away.'

Tomas and Joe and a number of others are going to Ras Latifa later in the week for two days to attend a series of meetings about the health insurance plans. I say goodnight and walk around the apartment one last time, making sure all the windows are locked and the door locked and bolted, with a chair pushed up against it.

It is from Ras Latifa, later in the week and April Fools' Day, when I next hear from Tomas. It is late when he rings, gone midnight.

'So how's Ras Latifa?'

'Dull. However, the nightlife is making up for it. You won't believe what happened to us tonight. Joe is here with me, say "hello" Joe.'

I hear Joe calling out in the background.

'We met a very interesting character in the hotel lounge. We were about to call it a night when he came over with a bottle of Bollinger and offered us a glass. We couldn't really say no without it seeming rude. Turns out he is a Count and an advisor to various Middle Eastern governments. He chain-smoked Cuban cigars and told us some sordid tales. You won't want to hear those.'

'Not really.'

'Anyway our Count friend offered a prostitute each to Joe and me for the night. Of course we refused. He took some persuading that we were not going to go off with these girls. Joe's eyes were popping out of his head.'

'Mm.'

'See you tomorrow. We'll tell you all then.'

☪

Tomas and Joe pick me up the next evening and we go to the tagine place in the souk for dinner. As we eat and talk about their surprising encounter Joe receives a call from Justin. Tomas and I can't make much sense of the half-conversation we are overhearing, but Joe looks worried. Rose-water sorbet, the delicious local specialty, arrives as Joe finishes the call. He puts his mobile on the table and groans, rubbing his temples. He tells us that Justin has called to say he has been visited at his villa by the police and required to relinquish his passport. He wants to know if any of us have had similar visits, and if not, to warn us to expect this as he gets the impression that all our passports are to be taken. We are alarmed. Our sorbet seeps away.

My phone rings. It is Laila, she is shopping in the souk, ordering new furniture for my room in her villa, and knowing I am having dinner there, she rings to see if I want to join her. I leave Tomas and Joe to go to see Justin, and wander through the souk to the falcon store where we are to meet. Laila and her sisters are outside, they all hug and greet me as enthusiastically as ever, looping their arms through mine. Hisham and a couple of Laila's cousins are in the falcon shop looking at the birds, perched at ankle level around the store. Hisham smiles and nods to me. The girls soon sweep me off and we bustle from one shop to another looking for hairclips, ribbon and rhinestones to decorate the sleeves of their *abayas*.

We meander into a cramped, dim alleyway, and an even more cramped and dim shop selling cheap plastic toys. Once inside one of the girls pushes aside a curtain of sweet strips to reveal a hidden staircase. We slip down into a cool basement, which is bursting with every kind of fake designer handbag imaginable. Laila explains that this is an illicit shop, which, true Bedouin, every few weeks moves from the basement of one shop to another. Finding it twice is always a problem unless you have contacts. Occasionally an expat woman stumbles in by chance, but she will never find her Aladdin's cave again. I had heard about this mythological shop from several expats, all who had tried and failed to locate the treasure trove. It had become a holy grail for the bored housewives, but without an entry to the local women's circles they will forever hunt in vain. Laila decides she likes a Chanel label and tries out several immense tote bags. Bags, like sunglasses, are super-sized in the desert. Next, the girls take me to a cupboard of a shop teaming with strings of amber prayer beads. They take the beads between their fingers and rub them. The richest aromatic scent slowly wafts between their fingers. We buy some strings at a fraction of the tourist price.

'This has cheered me up Laila, *shukran*.'

'My pleasure, but why are you sad?'

I tell Laila about Justin's news.

Her eyes deepen beneath the slit in her nikab. 'Aaii, not here,' she whispers, 'Let me call Hisham.'

We purchase our bags and wait for Hisham. He arrives a few minutes later. 'Let's go to the Bay,' he says.

Laila's sisters decide they will go home, while Laila and I drive with Hisham to the grassy knolls that buttress the Bay. At this time of night they are thronging with families picnicking and young boys chasing balls. Seeing families enjoying the cool grass at night, as if it is the middle of a summer's day, always makes me smile; it is just too incongruous for a girl from a rainy clime. We find a patch of grass away from the crowds, looking out across the Bay, where the lights of party *dhows* speckle the dark waters. 'Something has happened,' says Laila.

'Yesterday His Highness went to Switzerland.'

'He's ill?'

'Tired.' Hisham sighs.

'So?'

'The first son of the first wife, he's now the Prime Minister.'

'But there's been no election? I thought there was already a Prime Minister?'

'Yes, but he's tired as well.'

'Ha … he is gone to Europe too.' Laila claps her hands.

'Will they come back?'

'*Inshallah*.'

'The maglis is appeased. The Prime Minister he holds with their ways, the old ways.' Hisham's lips are pursed.

'And you, Hisham?'

'These shouldn't be our ways. These old men would keep us from the world, and the world from us. We must be able to see, think, speak for ourselves. We're not children, and soon they'll find we have grown and have the beards and muscles of men. But, already, it's started.'

'Last night many people from Syria, Iran and Yemen were taken away.' Laila starts to cry. Hisham continues. 'We have a friend, from Sana'a. All day I've been trying to call.' I take Laila's limp hand. 'This happens,' she says. 'Our governments and leaders like to play cat and mouse; only the people, like us, we are the mice.'

Hisham speaks, 'You see, there's trouble in all these countries. Protests. The police fire on the crowds.'

'And poverty. Food prices are high. No work,' says Laila, 'Like here, rice costs twice as much as last month. How are the people meant to live? Everything costs so much. We are dying inside. This is not the life.'

'But the rich grow richer, fatter. See how our Royals and their friends are buying London, eating up European cities,' Hisham warns. 'Our Ministers grow fearful, this is only a warning. Anyone who could be a troublemaker, *hallas*, they will go. Our government will hold tight on you foreigners now.'

How tight?

'Tony, Angie, Justin …' I could not say the word, *me*.

Laila whispers, '*Inshallah*, I will talk to Dr Mouna and find out, for now we pray.'

thirty

'Miss Aisling, are you in contact with your Embassy?' Dr Mouna closes the door to my office and removes her veil. Even before I see her face I know something is wrong. She has not greeted me with any of the obligatory niceties, just straight to her question.

Laila rises from behind her desk, 'Sister?'

Now we see that Dr Mouna's face is drawn, wrung out.

I stutter. 'No, I've never given it a thought. I don't think there's even a consulate office here anyway.'

'Tsk, dear. You must call. Today. The police have sent me a list of ten expat staff. I have to confirm that they work here.'

'Sister, what does this mean?' Laila's voice is stringy.

'They will come for the passports. Today.'

'Dr Mouna …'

'Yes, dear, your name is on the list.'

Before Dr Mouna can say anything more, the door opens and Mozah comes in.

'I'm looking for Mr Brian.' I want to laugh at her excuse. Why would Brian be in my office?

'Well, clearly he's not here.' No one says anything; we are all waiting for her to go. Dr Mouna breaks first. She looks at me, dips her head, replaces her veil and leaves. Mozah follows fast, slamming the door. I feel faint.

'That woman! Laila, I'm going to see Tomas and Joe, warn them.'

'Not now Sister, I fear you're being watched. Sit here quietly, with your work for now.' I collapse back into my seat, Laila is right.

I sit staring at some papers, but they are a blur before me. I can't quite take in the meaning of this. I can't go home. Can't just go to the airport and get on the next plane. I suddenly feel the desperate urge to leave. I didn't know until this moment how precious my passport is, that square of burgundy cardboard, it is my freedom, my safety, more than just a set of stamps from exotic places. I want to feel cool rain on my face.

The morning drags by. Laila and I say nothing, both lost in our thoughts and fears. One o'clock. I pick up my bag. A rap at the door. The eel man slides in. He casts his eyes down while he hands me a memo. It's in Arabic, of course. He slides back out as Laila translates it. The police order. I am to bring in my passport tomorrow and surrender it to the immigration department. I scrunch up the memo and throw it in the bin.

☪

Back at my apartment, I am restless all afternoon. I try to sleep but all I can hear is a mewling prostitute through the walls of my apartment. I cannot read, the dust itches at my eyes. I pace. Tomas calls me and invites me to meet Justin, Joe and himself in the souk. We plan to eat and then the boys want to go to the souk square and watch a European football match that is to be shown on the big screen. Justin is putting on a brave face after the unpleasantness of the night before and is insisting we go out and 'show the bastards we don't give a fuck'. Tomas and Joe got memos too.

I meet my friends at the grand gateway to the souk. It is thronging with expat men, the match has drawn everyone it seems. It is forty degrees tonight, everything is fuzzy in the heat.

The boys are arguing. 'No, Laila is far more likely.'

'What's this about Laila?' I ask. Justin mumbles. 'What?' I ask again.

Joe replies for him. 'The office spy.'

'What? How can you think that? Laila is my friend.' I want to slap Justin's sweaty Cheshire cat face.

'And don't you wonder why?' His fat lips twist. 'She's a clever one, you can see that.' Tomas rubs his chin.

'Tomas! Not you too. Stop, we can't let this happen. We mustn't doubt our friends. This is what always happens here, and I am not going to be eaten up with suspicion.'

'Aisling …'

'No.' I walk away from them and into the souk, ignoring their calls after me.

I don't want to go back to my dusty, comfortless apartment. I hate being there. And I can't watch another night of bombings in Libya and shootings in Syria. There is no end to this Spring of pain. I wander, not really knowing what I am doing, seeking cooler air in the alleyways. Thoughts dart about my mind scorpion fast, everything blurs in their frenzied wake. I cannot grasp onto a single one, instead I let my worries scuttle as I turn away from the main thoroughfare in the souk, which is crowded with noisy football fans and tuck myself into the alleyways. I let myself be soothed by these soft glowing tunnels, where exotic fabrics glitter at every corner, and I can lose myself in the thick musk. The heat overtakes me. I sit down at the Lebanese ice cream parlour and sip on a pot of clementine sorbet. I watch a pair of small tumbling boys play with a ball and a souk cat. The cat slinks over to me and rubs itself against my ankles. I bend over to stroke it.

'What a touching sight. Two flee-bitten strays together.'

I swing around. Brian, in the red strip of Manchester United. He comes over to my table and sits down. I stand up.

'Not going to stay and entertain me?'

'I'd rather entertain Satan himself.' I step away fast.

'Go on then, run. Oh no, I forget, you can't go anywhere can you?' he sneers.

I turn into the first alley I see and despite the heat I pick up my pace. I start to jog, I know he is following me. I begin to run, deeper and deeper into the labyrinth. I think I can still hear his laughter behind me. I look over my shoulder, my eyes are smeary with the heat, all the faces in the narrow passage way look like his. Voices call out to me, all like his. All eyes, lupine, his. I turn a corner and bump into a tall man, him. I want to scream, but no sound comes out. I shake myself free, it is only a tourist. He tries to apologise but I just run on, and on. I am getting lost. I don't know this part of the souk so well. I am away from the tourist stalls, the fabric merchants, and deep amongst the shisha and spice sellers. Sweat beads on my body. The heat in my throat is choking. Whistles and claps ring out. 'Slow, slow.'

'Crazee woman.'

'Pretty lady, come this way, I look after you.'

'Run to me, darleen.'

'*Yallah.*' Arms and hands stretch out at me, I tear my way through.

A deserted alley. I gasp for air and slow my steps. The night is so close, binding me. I lean against the adobe wall for a moment, desperate for cool oxygen. There is none. I close my eyes. I rub the prayer beads in my pocket. I hear that deliberate clicking of the heels. I keep my eyes shut, wishing that when I open them he will be gone. Closer. Closer. The clicking halts in front of me. I can feel a monstrous heat from his body just an inch or two from mine. I can smell his sweat: smoky. I open my eyes. He stands in front of me. Neither of us speak. A cruel smile and he licks his teeth. He leans over me and places a finger at the edge of my mouth and draws it across my lips.

'Tomorrow.' He strides away.

thirty-one

Next day, my passport is in my hand. I go to the princesses' office as I know they won't be here so early. No one is around yet, except the tea boys clattering in the kitchens. In my other hand I clutch the number for the Irish embassy, it's over the border, no office here. I ring it now. A bright Irish voice answers.

'Patrick MacMahon speaking.' I gulp and nearly cry. It is the first time I have heard my home accent in months.

'So, now, tell me again. Sorry, I'm not getting this down fast enough. Feck, my head. Last night was wild. Those international school teachers.' He whistles. 'We won, y'know.'

'Won?'

'The rugby. You should come over, we've a ball at the embassy to celebrate this weekend. It'll be great craic, we've a class host for the night. I wanted Dustin the turkey, but the Ambassador was having none of it. But we've Graham Norton, for real.'

'Patrick, that's what I'm trying to tell you, it's a nice invitation, but I can't. I have to give over my passport today. I'm trapped.'

'Ach, don't you worry about that. Go and buy yerself a dress. I'll have you at the ball by the weekend. We need some new faces.

I'm bored with teachers, they do things with chalk and rulers that make your eyes water.'

'As easy as that?'

'Sure, this sort of nonsense happens all the time. It will just be a squabble, some procedural crap.'

'Mm, I hope you're right.'

I replace the receiver. A goldfish gulps at the surface of the goblet. Poor thing.

I go to my office. Laila has just arrived, laden down with a large bag, full of material swatches. She orders me to choose the ones I like, as her sisters will go to the souk this evening and buy the necessary linens to ready my room in the family villa. Laila told Hisham about the passport demand yesterday afternoon and he has ordered his sisters to have the room kitted out by the end of the day, no more delay, he wants me safely with the family no later than tomorrow.

'Laila, I can't.'

'*Yanni*, why not?' Laila tweaks my arm.

'Brian. He's not going to leave me alone. I don't want to bring trouble to your family.'

'Pah! What can that small man do to us?'

'I think he's capable of anything.'

'Ha! Let him try. I will kill him. Please, please come and be my Sister. It is better for you and for me too.' Laila hands me some fabrics. 'Choose.'

I pick a cool cotton, I can't bear another night alone at Bella Villa.

☾

Mozah scratches at the door with chipped talons. 'Passport.'

I stretch out my hand with my passport, too tired to argue today.

She flicks through it. As she does this, Laila swipes it from her.

'I will take that for you to the immigration office, Sister.' Before Mozah or I can say anything she sweeps out of the office with it. Mozah for once is dumbstruck and follows Laila.

A few minutes later Laila returns. 'How could you give your passport to that woman? Are you crazy? Who knows what she would do with it? Feed it to the dogs and you with it?'

'I wasn't thinking.'

Laila hugs me, and stroking my hair says, 'Ssh, I know, we'll look after you now, me and Hisham, and these bad men and that one, you must have nothing more to do with them. Pah, they're gone now from your life. We will shut the office door to them.'

If only I could take Laila's simple and direct approach to life's troubles. We are interrupted by sounds of a commotion coming from the front of the building. Our office is at the back. I want to see what is happening, but Laila holds up a hand. 'Stay.'

We don't have to wait too long to discover the cause of the ruction. One of the princesses bursts into our office, handbag lashing into everything, her veil sliding to one side. Her eyes are magnificent with the drama.

'*Wallah!*' she cries. 'The police are here. CID.'

Tomorrow, he said as I clung to the souk wall.

'*Hallas, hallas,*' she sinks into one of the chairs. As we let her get her breath Laila and I exchange uneasy glances. 'Mr Justin's going to be arrested.' She claps her hands. My stomach spasms. 'It's on the Twitter.' She shoves her phone at Laila, who swipes at the screen frantically.

'Yes, yes. It says one of the greedy Westerners will be … no, I can't say that. *Yallah.*'

Laila grabs my hand and we run down the stairs to the foyer. The Tweet has flown about the local staff in moments. The foyer is a heaving, nauseous chequer board of black and white veils and *thawbs*, for once the restrictions on proximity between the sexes completely abandoned. The princesses are all perched along the reception desk, in prime viewing spots. They call us over to them, we squeeze our way through. The noise is unbearable, from the far side near the door some women start clacking their tongues. Four stony-faced CID officers arrive, guns at their hips, dark shades covering their eyes. The building security guards meet them, twitching, officious. They bat people out of the way, stamping on toes, knocking elbows and lead the CID officers to the elevator. The doors snap shut. The crowd roars their approval. Laila holds my hand, I can feel her trembling. We watch, barely breathing, the red arrows above the elevator. Floor five. Minutes pass. I cannot take my eyes off those arrows. Everyone is watching. 'Ah!' A collective cry, the arrows tick past floor four, three, two, one … zero.

The doors snap open. Women shriek. Two of the officers march forth, following them, Justin his hands at prayer in handcuffs and gripped firmly between the two remaining officers. As he sees the throng ahead of him Justin howls, 'This is a mistake, a mistake. I've done nothing wrong. You have to believe me.'

Those nearest him taunt back. Quickly the throng takes up the jeer. Justin's face flushes, sweat pours off him. I try to pull forward, to reach out to Justin, but Laila holds me back. Someone spits at him. The crowd slow claps. More spit, as he is thrust out the doors and is shoved into the back of a white van. The crowd screams.

thirty-two

Too many eyes are watching. The email is still. We all remain in our offices, none of the expat staff visit each other to exclaim over this turn of events. During prayers my mobile phone rings. It is Patrick, his banter gone.

'Something about this doesn't smell right. I can't get any dirt on why they've taken your passport. No one's saying anything. Usually someone will say something, right. You know how the Arabs love to gossip. Nothing. Zilcho.'

'One of my colleagues, an Australian, has just been arrested at the office.'

'A grand show?'

'Of course.'

'Fuck.'

He hangs up.

Laila comes back from prayers. The rumours are swarming locust-like. Justin has been fired variously for drunkenness, taking bribes, having a criminal past, and most luridly, for having relations with young, migrant boys. If all this isn't enough, now there are even wilder rumours about accomplices.

'Sister, there's a list of names.'

Another list. Dear God, give me strength.

'Who next?'

G

Ten minutes before the end of the workday the sounds of jeering echo once more through the marble corridors. Laila and I wait until the clamour dies away before leaving, neither of us wish to witness any more scenes of humiliation. Tomas texts me. Another expat colleague is the latest arrest. The list. My mind whirrs. Is this a list of passports to be confiscated or expats to be arrested? Or is it one and the same?

'Laila, am I going to be dragged from the building next?'

'The mall,' Laila orders.

G

Technicians lavish vivid colours onto our nails. 'Now shoes,' Laila orders. We both quickly find the sparkliest sandals in the store. Their price tags make us wince.

'Well, if I'm to be deported, I'm going in style' I say as I finally give in to the bling. 'These can be my deportation shoes, and if and when they come to arrest me I'll walk out with pride.'

'Now you are like us, truly.' Laila kisses me. We buy the sandals, and head back to Laila's villa so she can show me my new room, my sanctuary.

As we pull up we can hear screaming from within. 'Aaii, what now?' Laila leaps from the car and runs up to the front door. As she opens it a torrent of water rushes around her ankles. Inside, a minor geyser, in the ensuite to the room set aside for me, is gushing through the building and everyone is splashing around in flood water. The maid had decided to test to make sure the plumbing in the ensuite was working. The shower was just a trickle. The sisters called a workman in, he banged on the pipes. Two hours later, the pipes started to groan. A rumble. Whoosh. Laila is spouting invectives about the shoddy workmanship, almost as much as the geyser is spouting forth water. I tell her not to worry, I can manage another day or two at the apartment while this little disaster is set right. As Laila sets about the workmen returned to fix the pipes, I return to Bella Villa.

Worn out, in the sallow afternoon light, I fall asleep. The heavy dark door of my apartment opens. A man dressed in white walks along the hallway towards me. His shadow precedes him. Tall, long. I can see him in the hallway although my eyes are tight shut, locked in sleep. He turns into the room where I lie on the sofa. He smiles as he crosses to me. He places his hand on my heart. Its beat stills. I sit up. I open my eyes. Only atomic darkness and frankincense.

☾

I feel sick as I walk into the foyer; I didn't get back to sleep after I woke from my dream in the early hours. I am wearing my new sparkling purchase. Normally, as I get to work a few minutes early most days, when I arrive there is no one except the security guard in the reception area. Today there is already a horde, several of the coffee cronies amongst the mob, leering. The princesses are ready and perched, they smile and wave to me reassuringly. I press my way through, climb the stairs, leaden. I reach my office and switch on my computer. My email is working, so they can't be coming for me yet. The tell-tale sign is when your screen goes blank. At seven-o-clock the roar goes up. I put my head in my hands.

The sound of heavy footfall outside my door. The door lashes open. A man in uniform comes in. I lose my breath, the world spins. Keep a grip. Don't show your fear. He says something in Arabic to me. He hands me a yellow form, all in Arabic, it makes no sense. My hands are shaking visibly. Abdullah, our tea boy, dives into the office. He says something to the officer and takes the form from me. He gestures to the officer to follow him. As he leaves the room he turns to me and says, 'Everything ok, Miss.'

I start to cry as he shuts the door. My stomach in knots. Laila comes in and immediately runs to me and holds me tight in her arms. 'Hush, hush, Sister, there.' I tell her what just happened. She wipes the tears from my cheeks and goes to find Abdullah. She comes back in smiling, almost giggling.

'*Shufi*, the police man came for Sheikh Fariq. The papers were for him, a traffic fine. The police man thought you were his secretary.' We both start to laugh, hysterically.

'So who was arrested this morning?'

'Three in HR. They worked with Mr Tony, Egyptians.'

For once the corridors are deathly silent. Now that not just white Westerners are being arrested, everyone seems much more jittery and people stay in their offices. I ring Patrick and tell him about the latest developments. He listens quietly and tells me to leave it with him. At midday Laila is sick, a migraine. She goes home reluctantly. I know she doesn't want to leave me.

'I'll be fine, Laila. They've had their fun for today.'

I sit alone in the office, praying my words will be true. The clock on the wall ticks too loudly.

'Miss Aisling, you look tired. Come, my dear, you need good food and good company. I see we are neglecting our duties as your most tender hosts.' Sheikh Fariq, turning his prayer beads, stands at the doorway with two of his secretaries behind him.

There is no arguing with him, and with the secretaries as chaperones, even though they speak no English, I cannot use propriety as my excuse. If only I had the migraine. As we reach the reception there is a crowd waiting, ready to see if there is to be any entertainment this home time. Sheikh Fariq claps his hands and waves his arms at the crowd, he shouts at them in Arabic, then looks to me and shouts again.

'For shame, for shame. Is this how we behave? Waiting to laugh at the wrongs of weak men. Mercy. We show mercy.' The crowd mutters, but disperses. 'Come, I will take you somewhere very special for lunch Miss Aisling. Maybe, we will see our beloved *Maleka*, I pray.'

☾

Sheikh Fariq opens a door in the shadows of the souk to reveal a spectacular Persian palace. All surfaces are gilt with tiny mirror mosaics, dazzling in the sunlight streaming from the open roof. The palace is on two levels, with a wooden upper floor, built as a balcony overhanging a square courtyard. In the centre of the courtyard is a towering fountain of tumbling horses and stars. Rugs and piles of cushions are grouped in alcoves around the fountain. Sheikh Fariq leads us through the courtyard opens a door to a glitzy jewellery box.

'Welcome, Miss Aisling. This is His Highness' dining chamber. For use only by the Royal Family and,' he pauses deliberately, 'Closest friends.'

Every inch of this room is flecked with gold. A magnificent gold table, with many gold thrones about it, dominates the room. The table is dressed, of course, with gold cutlery and sparkling ruby crystal plates and glasses. The opulence is breathtaking, even for this city.

Sheikh Fariq sits at the head of the table, with the secretaries on one side and me on the other. Waiters bring in a flotilla of little dishes. The secretaries do not eat. To try to do so would mean removing their veils. I just pick at my plate of vine leaves, and sip some water instead.

'Eat, eat, Miss Aisling. Do not mind them, they wish you to eat. You think this is a feast? 'Ah, Miss Aisling I will take you to palaces where you will taste the best, the absolute best. We will go for *Eid*.'

The Turkish Delight in my mouth clags my teeth. Its chalky sugar-flour grips the back of my throat. My breath sticks. I choke a little, cough. The waiter hands me my glass of water. Sheikh Fariq does not seem to have noticed, he is continuing with his promises of the experiences he will share with me.

'You'll meet my dear friend, Prince Hamad. He's a great man. He calls me to him. I help him with his Western businesses. Do you know the secret of business Miss Aisling, do you?'

I shake my head.

'No, no, of course not, you are a writer, the business it is not for you. I will tell you the secret.' He beckons me to lean in to him. I do before I can think. 'Your eyes, so blue.' I pull back, and he leans back in his chair too. 'Ach, the secret.' He expands his arms, 'Wait, you wait, time brings you everything you desire.' He smiles, 'This is what the West doesn't understand. Everything now, now, now. No! Wait, and you will see. Allah provides. Do you see, Miss Aisling?' I do not know what to say.

My skin is flushing, I know. I say nothing.

'One time, my dear friend the Prince asked me to take the deal for him with an American. The man had no patience. Every time we met he would do this.' He shakes his hand vigorously as if shaking on a deal. 'Listen, I tell him, hear my poetry today. The next day, I tell him, come, fish with me. Day by day, his face gets red, so red. Some days I send him a note, I don't meet with him that day. I have other business. After three weeks, my dear friend the Prince is very happy. I have the best deal for him. No one has ever bought at this price for guns, bullets before.' I start. 'I shock you, I see, Sister, but we have to keep our people safe, there are too many who would undermine our society. Always these foreigners stirring up trouble. You feel this in your life with us, am I right? There are those who would cause you trouble?'

What should I say? Before I can answer, he goes on. My answer not necessary I see.

'*Yanni*, you shouldn't worry about the small troubles at the Board. You'll have your passport soon. This is an unfortunate formality; some new security measures. Forgive us. We have to be careful these days. Make sure we know our friends and our enemies. But you of course are our very dear friend, and our beloved *Maleka* is much pleased with your work. I tell her of it. She will thank you herself very soon.' He pats my hand, the veils twitch.

A knock at the door to the dining chamber. The Sheikh clicks his fingers and a waiter opens the door. I look, almost thinking to see the Queen. He stands there, a dark shadow against the glitter.

'Mr Brian, come in. Sit.' The Sheikh flicks his hand to the waiter to offer Brian some sweetmeats. 'Mr Brian, thank you for coming here today. I want you to meet the new Head of Communications for the Executive Consortium. I trust you will support Miss Aisling with her every request.'

'Of course, Sheikh Fariq. You know I hold Miss Aisling in only the highest regard.' Spittle at the corner of Brian's gash of a mouth. Delicious, how I've longed for a moment like this.

'Good, good. Now tea.' The waiters bring us mint tea, poured from golden kettles while a musician playing a lute-like instrument enters the chamber. He sings a mournful song. The Sheikh closes his eyes as he listens, a tear seeps down his cheek. Brian fixes his eyes on me throughout, ready to pounce.

The songs wavers and stills. The musician bows and leaves. A waiter approaches the Sheikh and whispers to him.

'My friends, I must leave you. I am called to the maglis. Please dine, enjoy.' The Sheikh and his secretaries' leave and I stand to follow.

'Stay, let's do as the Sheikh said and enjoy some time together. When will you ever be somewhere like this again?' Brian blocks my exit. 'We are to work closely together now, Ash. Let's be friends again. I miss our times together.'

'You have your fiancée.'

'She's gone. Couldn't hack it.'

I step closer, determined to make him move out of my way, but he catches my hand, winds his fingers in mine. 'She doesn't have your spirit.'

'Ah now, I'm sure you've more than enough spirit with Mozah, so.'

He snorts and lets go of my hand. 'She had her moments.' His eyes glaze, he seems to forget me.

I try to make good my escape, but he pushes back in front of me. 'Please Ash. Just a minute, yah? We expats need to stick together after everything these past few days. You obviously have great support from Sheikh Fariq, but he's away a lot on business. If the revolution comes, you may need a friend, girl. It will be ugly. These activists don't only despise the regime, they despise everything and everyone that represents progress, the West. They want to take this land back to the age of caves and tents. Stand outside the mosque behind the electric souk, you will hear the hatred in the imams voice over the tanoy. Blah, blah, George Bush, blah, blah. Mark my words girl, they're preaching hell's fury and they'll unleash it everywhere. You won't be able to rely on that one in the veil in your office then. Even the Sheikh.' He pulls a piece of paper from his inside jacket pocket. He shakes it at me. 'You see this? You know what it is?'

A list. It's a list. I can see that. The names are upside down. I cannot read them.

'You're pale. You know what this is then.' Those teeth, glint gold. 'You see the top two are crossed through?' He pushes the paper up close to my eyes. It's a blur, but I see the thick, angry lines. 'Weren't pulling their weight. An embarrassment to the Board and the State. We don't need sleaze like them. Gone. Scratched.' He puts the list back in his pocket. 'Now people will see who's in charge. What's happened so far? Nothing, nothing to what's to come.' He laughs. 'Those pathetic bean counters, I'll teach them to poke around.'

I take a breath, 'I don't know what you are talking about Brian? You're talking riddles.' I shove past him. At last, he doesn't stop me.

'Go then. Just remember, I tried to help you Aisling.' My hand is on the doorknob. 'The Dutch woman, girl. It wasn't in the papers here. But all the expats talked about it. It was in the foreign press, on the internet. Last year, before you came.' I stop. 'Adultery. That was the charge. Five years she got. Took her embassy seven months to get her out. Seven months in prison. It was too late by then. She had to have it, abortion wasn't an option.' His shoes click on the tiles. He's right behind me now, 'She was lucky though. She didn't have to marry the bastard. Her embassy got her out. Do you know what they do to unmarried pregnant women? Ha!' His breath is hot on my neck. 'There are no rapists here Aisling, only adulteresses.' I turn the handle to the door.

thirty-three

He doesn't follow me this time. No need. He's under my skin and he knows it. I run out of the Persian jewel box and flag the first taxi I see. I ring Tomas and Joe to warn them. No reply, from either. I try again. I text. And again and again, once I am back in my apartment. An hour passes. Another. I pace, stirring up little clouds of dust that glint in the air like Brian's prowling irises. Eyes, eyes everywhere, all the time. Why aren't they responding? Are they in the back of a van already?

My phone pings. I snatch it up. I look.

I can look after you Aisling. I mean it.

Ping.

Miss Ash. Wots wiv all yr calls. U ok?

Joe, where are you?

Gym. Just thrashed T at squash. Loser. Wots wrong?

Brian. He's put your names on the list.

Shit. How do u no?

I saw him. He told me, showed me the list.

Shit. On our way. U at home?

Yes.

I pace again. The minutes pass. Then an hour.

Ping.

Traffics murder. T.

Ping.

I wouldn't ignore me. You're trying my patience.

Brian. I fumble at the keys on my phone.

Please get here soon. We were right. Brian is behind everything. And he's scaring me.

I hit the send button.

Ping.

Traffics 2 bad. Givin up. Soz. Signal shit. Call u l8rz.

Ping.

I scare you. Ha!

Oh God. What have I done? I have sent my text for Tomas to Brian. I drop the phone. It screeches across the floor. It starts to ring. I can see the name flashing. His. I can't move, can't pick it up, can't answer it. My heart thuds. I let the phone ring and ring. I just stand there, looking at it writhing on the floor like a cockroach on its back, kicking up filthy dust globs. I want to stamp on it, crunch it to bits.

The cockroach crouches at my feet all night as I sit, unable to move, beside the window. Every hour it starts to writhe again. His name flashes red across its belly. I wait for him. I watch the world outside the window as if it is a film, unreal now. I see the creeping grey light of dawn, the migrant workers shuffling off into battered minivans, the morning fighter jets tracking across the sky. My alarm clock buzzes. He didn't come. Not this time. I dress in a trance for work.

☪

The crowd is dark this morning, growling. I am jostled through. Laila is in the foyer already, she sees me and takes me by the elbow. We climb the stairs.

'Whose turn today?'

Laila shrugs. 'This is a bad place now. With too many bad people. My brothers say I should resign. But I cannot leave you alone here, Sister.'

Screams reach us up the stairwell. Tongues clacking and whistling. Tears wet my face and Laila is crying too. We reach our office and shut the door behind us. We know it will not be long. One of the princesses will come flying in with the news. We wait in silence. No one comes. The noise dies away. Still no one comes. We hear the swish of *abayas* go past our office and hushed voices.

'Laila?' Laila nods and slips quietly out of our office.

I wait. The door bursts open. Tarek comes in wailing, stumbling, drunk. I can't understand, but I know the words Sister Mozah and Sister Angie. He is beating his breast. Laila comes in behind him, ashen faced. She shouts at Tareq and pushes him out of the door.

I run to her. 'What's he saying?'

'Mozah has been arrested.'

'Mozah!'

'They say she sells her body to wicked men.'

'He's thrown her to the pack.' I whisper.

'We must pray for her.'

My knees sway. There was more. My mind pitches, releases. What was it? Yes. 'Angie? Tarek, he said Angie.'

Laila is shaking her head. 'I can't say. It's too bad. They're saying very bad things about Sister Angie. I won't say those things.' Laila is crying and jabbing around in her bag. She hands me a mobile phone, 'Ring your embassy. Tell them. They must help Sister Angie. She's in prison.'

I sink to the floor.

'Please Sister, you can't cry, we must help Sister Angie,' Laila says, brushing back her own tears.

I tap in Patrick's number. Laila listens intently as I speak to him.

'I can't promise anything, She's a British citizen, but I will call the Brits. Let them know. But don't hold your breath. The feckers, they don't get involved.'

'They have a duty to.'

'They have a Prime Minister touting for a cheap gas deal.'

'But…'

'One middle-aged woman. Will make the papers for a day or two. Twenty-five million homes to heat. But don't worry. The Irish government doesn't like its citizens being bullied. I've got a plan. I will get you a temporary passport. It will take me a few days. Hold tight.'

'I'm … Patrick, you know.'

'I'll drive over the border and come and get you myself. I'm a car ride away, that's all.' A nine hour drive.

I hang up and hand the phone to Laila.

'Keep it. They'll listen to your phone. Use this one, you will be safe.'

'Laila, I know my room isn't ready yet, but can I stay at your house tonight? I will sleep in the tent. I don't want to be alone.'

'I'll call Hisham. We'll go to your apartment straight after work and bring your belongings.'

☪

Hisham is dressed in jeans and a baseball cap when he arrives. He explains he doesn't want to draw attention at the apartments and people will be less interested in seeing a Western man accompanying me. Much to her ire, Hisham takes Laila home first, as he wants my flight from the apartments to be quick and unremarkable. He drops me off a street away from Bella Villa. By the time I have walked to the apartment in the burning heat he has already parked and found a way into the building through a fire escape and he is inside my apartment. I am confused. I didn't give him my key.

'Hisham? How did you get in?'

I see it. My few belongings, books, a couple of framed photos of Mammy and Grandaddy, clothes, are strewn across the floor. Drawers are hanging out, the sofa cushions thrown to one side. All urine-drenched, faeces smeared up the walls. I run to the bathroom and am sick. I go to run the sink tap. My make-up and toiletries are smashed into a mush in the basin. A used condom sticks out of the centre of the mess. I stare at it.

Hisham is working fast, stuffing a few dry clothes into my case, 'We don't have much time. They'll come back. Take what's important. Leave the rest. Is anything missing?' I can hardly tell and can't answer. Hisham looks at me. '*Hallas*.' He grabs my hand, 'We go now.'

He hurries me along the corridor to the fire escape, 'This way. The traitor on the front desk will call them. He mustn't see you leave.'

In the car Hisham hands me a veil and we pull away. My stomach grips, 'Hisham, I can't come to your home. They'll hunt me out there.'

'No, he won't dare. Please, put on the veil, just for now.'

I do as he asks. My world turns black, blind. The cloth is stifling. I can't believe I have put the veil on. I feel trapped, but less so than without it, at this moment.

'You don't mind wearing it? I know this must be hard for a Western woman.'

'Hisham, I cannot put you-'

'Ssh. You are all the more beautiful to me now. I have to remember your smile. I have to listen only to your voice. It's like bird song to me.'

I miss April's bird song; the ripe morning call of the robin, the collar dove's gentle cooing evening lament. We drive through the city and out along the coast. 'We're not going to your villa? We're going back to the village?' I recognise the way.

'Tonight I want you to feel completely safe.'

C·

We stand barefoot at the water's edge. No seam between the night and the sea. Beneath the pitiless sky we do not speak. The tide starts to lap about our ankles. A dark moon. Just the universe clotting around us.

'I long for rain.'

Hisham unfolds his arms from around me and steps back. I hear the rustle of cotton. I turn around, he pulls me to him, naked. We stand a breath away from each other.

thirty-four

My priority today is to find out what is happening to Angie. How terrified she must be. I don't want to think about it, yet it's all I can think of. The four pressing walls of a cell, the pregnant ceiling. Angie likes to seem as if she is a tough Scouser, but really, when the mascara comes off … I call Patrick.

'Lie low, act normal.'

Hisham drives us back from the village and drops me at work, hesitant. I have to carry on, show *him* he does not intimidate me. Laila and the princesses will be with me every minute of the day; no one will dare come near me.

The lobby is empty, the crowd gone. This unsettles me more.

I reach my office and unlock the door. The room is fluttering with a thousand snowflakes, only it doesn't snow in the desert. The snowflakes are slices of paper. Every file and folder in the room has been shredded.

Click, click, click.

I stand, unflinching, with my back to him. I know he is there. He whistles. I turn to face him and hold his eye. My scorn burns. He turns now, and leaves.

'Brian,' I call after him, 'Would you ever just grow up.'

Laila organises a small army of tea boys to clear up the mess. As they clatter around she draws me to one side, 'This is more than just trying to frighten you and destroy your things, Sister. They're looking for something. What do they think you have?'

Yusef comes into the office. 'Miss Aisling, what's going on here? No, no, don't tell me, I don't have time for this now. The new Under Minister wants to see you right way. Please bring your notepad.'

I follow Yusef to the Prof's office, as we pass the elevator, the doors close, but not before I think I see a glimpse of the Scottish advisor as the doors clank shut. I slow, that stab to the stomach. The stabbing comes with more frequency every day.

We reach the Prof's office, but he is not there now. Instead Sheikh Fariq sits at his desk. Yusef speaks with him in tones of consternation, Sheikh Fariq answers curtly and smacks his fist on the desk. Yusef comes out and apologises to me for the trouble I have experienced in my office. He grumbles in Arabic as he calls for the tea boy and barks orders at the poor man. Meanwhile Sheikh Fariq waves me into the room.

'My dear, dear Sister, come sit here with me. Today is a great day for our country.' The Sheikh directs me to the large chaise longue now positioned in the centre of the room.

'Her eminence, Her Royal Highness, our beloved *Malek*a has graciously given me the great honour of serving as the new Under Minister.'

'*Mabruk*, Sheikh Fariq.'

'*Shukran*. This is a very great honour and it's the express wish of her Highness that I carry out some big changes. Only the very best people will work here. The rest will be thrown away, they're worthless, rubbish people. No more foreigner trouble I promise you, my dear. We will start today. You shouldn't be afraid, not any more. Not here, not anywhere in our land. With our new Prime Minister we will once again be strong, stable, no Jasmine Spring here, you will see. *Yanni*, you will write a press release for the Western press about me.'

Sheikh Fariq paces the floor as he dictates a long and glowing testimony to his many talents and special qualities, all the time rolling his prayer beads as ever. 'You're impressed, I see, Sister. It's a great honour for you to work with me.'

I return to my office, tidy once more, although not calm yet as now a flurry of tea boys are filling the room with life sized, trailing arrangements of glittering roses and peacock feathers.

'Sheikh Fariq wishes to mark your promotion and thank you for your special work, and friendship.' Laila reads a card.

Ten arrangements of every colour now stand to attention in rows across the office, leaving no room for us. Right now, I can't take in this craziness. I ask Laila to find out where the Prof's office is now located. It turns out the Prof no longer has one; he is squatting in Tomas' office. Persona non grata.Tomas and Joe send a message asking me to meet them at the Irish bar that evening. We have to find Angie, get her released.

☪

In the Irish bar, Will balances a particularly wriggly lap dancer on his knee. Joe attempts to have a sensible conversation with him about Angie. Will's eyes roll with whiskey. We don't hold out much hope for Will being of any use in freeing Angie. Not only is the British Prime Minister about to arrive any day now to beg a bail out from the Royals, a fact the Arabic media is gloating over, meaning Will is not going to rock the boat; but Will's ever-complicated sex life has taken a new turn. His latest mistress, irritated by a previous mistress, has filmed them in a threesome and emailed it to his estranged wife, just in time for their next divorce court hearing. Will is spending most of his time in the Irish bar downing Scotch and slipping into one of the shabby back rooms with a different girl every few hours.

It is an unfortunate sight, given Tomas' news. One of Brian's henchmen called in on Tomas at his villa in the afternoon, where he demanded he pack up and be out by the end of the week, as the Rex boys have plans to move in at the weekend. Tomas told him where to go. He replied that Tomas would be leaving on the next plane, once the local rag published headlines about his sordid orgy with Russian prostitutes in Ras Latifa.

'I don't like this, Aisling. Angie in prison, your apartment and office trashed, and these threats. Those wankers from Rex have been strutting their stuff about the building all day. They think they're untouchable.'

'It's them that will be out of here on the next plane, Tomas, now Sheikh Fariq is the new Under Minister. He's no great fan of Rex.'

'I'll believe it when I see it.'

'But that's the thing here, Tomas. You look out the window on the same white sky every day. Nothing ever changes, and yet somehow everything is changing all the time. Nothing stops still, it's all a mirage.'

'You are right of course ... Sheikh Fariq ... nothing will stop still.'

Tomas stands up from the table, he gives a half-wave goodbye and pushes his way out though the crowd.

'Tomas?' I call after him, but he doesn't look back.

'Aisling, Will says Angie isn't in prison. He's made some calls. She never came back from Cyprus,' says Joe, returning to our table.

'So where is she?'

The Irish bar regulars have their theories, which they care more for than their missing mate.

- Maybe she's back home in Liverpool, caring for her demented mother?

- No, she's got a new contract in Ibiza, she's been seen skinny-dipping there with a Russian entrepreneur.

- Her! Rodney's wife gave 'er her marching orders once she found out about their lock-ins at Heather's.

I step out of the smoggy bar, desperate for air. It hits me. How did we not realise? The desert devours time, a year is but a day, a bite. Angie's been gone for nearly three months.

thirty-five

'Where are you Tomas?' I am in the office, my head polluted from the rank wine at the Irish bar the night before. A number I don't recognise has flashed up on my mobile. It's Tomas, but ringing from an unknown mobile number.

'Car park. Call you later.'

'What?'

I can hear rumbling, 'Are you in a car, Tomas?'

'Yes.'

I can hardly hear him above the noise of the engine, 'Going to the Celestine, getting it sorted, for once and for all.'

My mouth is dry. 'Who are you with?'

The signal fails.

☪

The morning passes, no word from Tomas. At home time Hisham comes to pick me up in a friend's car to take me to the villa by a circuitous route, in case we are being watched. Hisham is quiet in the car.

I stroke his cheek, 'Are you not talking to me today?'

'I don't like you going to *that* place.'

'I had to go to the bar, to help Angie.'

But he will not speak to me. Finally, we pull up outside the villa. Laila and her sisters are in the front yard playing with the small children and some kittens. Hisham lets me out and then drives off at speed.

Laila leads me to the tent. She sits me down and starts to brush out my hair. 'We should oil your hair and rub some musk in it. This is what we do for our men.'

We sit in silence as she continues to brush. She reaches into a tin and brings out a cube of flaky, amber musk that looks a thousand years old. Its aroma immediately fills the tent with sweet warmth. Laila rubs the musk between her fingers and pours some deep green oil into a small copper bowl.

'When you are here it is so easy to imagine you always here. You are like one of us. Our Sister. When you go to Western places it reminds him you are different to us. And then he remembers.' She starts to rub the oil along the waves of my hair. Tress after tress. 'Soon he is to marry our cousin. He has known you for so little time, he wants more time. This is why he is angry, and today you reminded him of this, of our difference.'

Laila kisses my forehead and leaves the tent. My heart scrunches.

I lie amongst the cushions, the musk melting between my fingers, just numb. The sounds of the children and kittens hush over time. The hour for mosque comes, a gentle chant in the distance. The tent darkens. When I wake Hisham is beside me, my musky fingers clasped in his.

'You are awake now?' he whispers.

'Hisham you cannot …'

'Ssh.' He cradles my fingers and then runs them through his

hair. 'Mm....musk, jamillah.' We stretch together, supine.

'You are getting married.'

'Ssh, *inshallah.*' he kisses me.

'I'm sorry about going to the bar.'

'You're a good friend to your friends. This is only right.' My conscience needles.

'Tomas! It's so late. How did I forget?'

I reach for my phone, no messages.

'This is weird.'

I tell Hisham about the call from Tomas that morning, how his voice was so charged.

'Who do you think he was going to see?'

'Sheikh Fariq.'

'Ach.' Hisham rolls onto his back.

'Call him.'

I try, no answer.

'Text.'

Hisham pulls my long curls across his chest while we wait and holds me tight.

'*Habibti*, I like the feel of your hair across me when we lie together.'

Five minutes pass, a beep. A text from Tomas.

'I'm ok. Tell you tomorrow.'

I roll back into Hisham's arms.

☾

Tarek is waiting for me the next morning in my office with instructions from Sheikh Fariq that I am to take a delegation of Chinese doctors to see the new children's hospital that is nearing its build completion. The group is large and only just arrived after a rough flight. Many of the delegates are ill tempered and the interpreter is petulant. As I attempt to corral them through the building and out to their coach I see Tomas. I wave to him, but he blanks me. While the group argues about who will take the lift first, I walk over to Tomas and say hello.

'You can't talk to me, never, not ever again.'

He won't even look at me. He is crumpled all over, pasty-faced. His eyes bloodshot.

'What's wrong? Are you ill?'

'And don't call me either. It's too dangerous. They're tapping our phones.' He shuffles.

'Who is Tomas? This doesn't make sense.'

'Not now. I have to go. Leave me alone.' He tries to walk away, but I catch his arm.

'Something happened yesterday. Tell me.'

His eyes, the terror.

'I'm leaving, you should too.'

'What? We can't. Our passports. Tell me, Tomas, why are you so scared?'

'No, no, go away.'

'If we can't talk here, please meet me after work. You must explain this to me.'

'No.'

'Tomas. I'm scared now.'

His face softens, 'Ok, I'll meet you at La Piazza, near the gondola ride kiosk at three o'clock. Come alone, mind. Tell no one and don't ring me.' He hurries away as the interpreter chews on my arm with a thousand more complaints about the day's itinerary.

☪

The children's hospital is like a space ship, pulsing green and blue light. It is the central focus of a new science park of sharp-shaped buildings on the eastern edge of the city. All the buildings are constructed of futuristic, shiny materials and the whole impression is that a giant child's box of toys has been scattered in the desert. The Chinese delegates are suitably impressed and forget their moaning as they poke at various gadgets on the wards. I can barely pay them attention. That look in Tomas' eyes is haunting me.

☪

Tomas isn't at the kiosk at three o'clock. I lean against the railings surrounding the fake canal and watch a young local family glide away across the shallow water in the motorised gondola. The canal, lurid blue. Nothing here is real, and I'm getting sick of all the plastic.

'Come with me, we can't meet here. Those Rex thugs are in the upper mall.'

I jump. His approaching footfall was silent behind me.

We head out into the roasting heat of the car park, instantly my hair sticks to my neck and my dress is like wet tissue.

'Are you sure it was them?'

'Don't doubt me, Aisling. Not today.'

We decide to go to another mall in the north of the city. It is older, smaller and less popular. As we approach his car, Tomas pulls out of his pocket a small yellow and green twisted wire that fans out with five copper prongs at one end. He hands it to me. 'Look.'

'What is it?' I turn it between my fingers.

'I found it at the villa. They're listening.'

We reach the car. 'Don't say anything inside. Watch, see if we're followed.'

I get in the car and even though Tomas' request that I watch the mirrors is ridiculous, I can't stop myself from looking. It is impossible to tell in the dense traffic if we are being followed or not, there are too many white jeeps zipping in every direction. Trying to keep an eye on the flashing metal is making me nauseous. Tomas doesn't look at me, only stares at the road ahead.

We park in the mall basement and make our way up to the shops by escalator. Tomas remains silent, lost. He nearly misses the step off the escalator. I catch him as he trips.

'Tomas, what's this all about?' I ask as we pace up one of the aisles. I hate the stickiness of my hair, clothes, aircon-dry. He starts to cry, heaving sobs, whooping. The violence of it is shocking. 'They know everything, everything.'

He is broken.

'They? Fariq?'

'I thought he would help. I went to his office. He was angry. He'd just taken a call from a cousin at one of the newspapers. Aisling, they're going to run the story. The prostitutes at Ras Latifa. They're calling for me to be lashed and thrown out.'

'Oh Tomas.'

'It's worse. They're accusing me of corruption, taking a bribe over the clinics, getting the highway moved. I told him, this is Rex, Brian. Framing me. Fariq wanted to know more, asked what I knew about Rex.'

'But Tomas, the camel farm…how could you trust him?'

'How could I not? He said he'd take me to the Celestine for a real drink. We could talk freely there, as Brothers.'

'Oh God.'

'We didn't go to the Celestine. We took the airport road. That's when I knew I'd made a mistake. He wouldn't say where we were going. I thought I was going to be kicked out there and then, put on a plane. We went through the industrial zone. He turned the aircon off. Shit, it was hot. I was dripping. He pointed at the trenches, you know those huge ones where they are putting the water pipes in? We turned off the road, went across the desert. I thought we were going to the camel farm again.' He sobs.

'Tomas, this is too much.'

'We went a few miles. Pulled up at an old villa, barbed wire all round it. He took me inside. It was empty, just dirty, nothing there. We went into a room out back. There was a TV and some sofas, and blood, black blood across the walls. Fariq put the TV on. He ignored me. Talked on his phone.'

Tomas sits down on a bench under an artificial palm tree, he bends over and puts his head in his hands. 'We have to leave, resign, get out somehow. I'm sick of this fucking country. It's evil here. All evil. And they know. They know everything. They know where Salima is, where her father's house is, where she goes to the market. They know who her friends are, when she goes to the nursery. They've been watching. They could be watching now. We must keep walking.' Tomas jumps up and strides off, he is mumbling now. 'I told them I wouldn't say anything. I would just go home quietly, so long as they left my family alone. But he wouldn't let me. Fariq kept yelling at me.'

'About what, Tomas? You're not making any sense?'

'He said not to worry about Rex, not to worry about work. Family is everything, worry about your family.'

Tomas grabs my arm tightly. 'I see it all now. They work for Fariq. Why didn't we see it before? We're being followed.'

I look around. 'Where? Who? I don't see anyone Tomas.'

'He's watching. He said to me. I am your Brother and I will

watch you always.' We turn down a different aisle. 'Come this way.'

'He's lost too much money. The air ambulance deal. Should have been *hers*. He can't, won't lose any more. He can't lose *her* favour. I have to make sure this doesn't happen. I have to help him.'

'Hers? Who? What does that mean?' His sobs have stopped, but he pants for breath.

'Tomas?'

'You. They're going to say we're having an affair. You'll be in big trouble. They told me you must resign and go. They know you know.'

'What am I meant to know? You make it sound like I know more, something more, something big?'

'Yes, exactly, that's exactly it, they think we know something more.'

The sore thumbs stick up in my mind. 'The money Tomas, the missing millions on the spreadsheet on that USB stick.'

Tomas is looking around, his eyes wild, sweat dripping off his brow.

'I shouldn't be here. This is a mistake. They're coming.'

'Calm down Tomas, you're safe here. What can they possibly do to us somewhere so public?'

He stops stock still, 'Shoot us. They can shoot us.'

'What?'

He runs off, I chase behind him.

'Tomas, stop, please.' I pull on his elbow. His face is wet with sweat and tears.

He whispers, 'No, no, no. I'm not allowed to say. He said he would make sure I never saw Salima again.' Tomas makes the shape of a gun with his two forefingers and puts them to his temples.

'Fariq put a gun to your head?'

I can barely say the words. The mall is spinning around me,

all the noises that seemed so human a few seconds ago, children chattering, music wafting out from one of the shops, high heels tapping on the tiled floor, now coming to me as one dull boom, as if through thick water. This cannot be true. Surely.

I look into Tomas' eyes. I see it. He has seen death; thought he was about to die.

I will never forget those eyes. Never.

'They *will* kill us. I know it.'

We walk in silence, up and down the same aisle twice. I don't know what to do, to say. I can't take it in. Time judders, I look about me, my surroundings bend, as in a warped mirror. I feel elastic, my steps distant. The marble moves.

'I need a coffee,' Tomas says, he looks so shrivelled up. We walk towards the centre hallway of the mall where there is a coffee shop on the mezzanine floor.

'Why Tomas? Why?'

'I don't know. He said the people must be protected. It's a dangerous world.'

'Tomas, I just don't get this. How can they know anything about Salima? And really, how can they hurt her? She is miles away. And why would they threaten me? What have I done?'

'Bad things happen to people everyday. They have car crashes, men are stabbed by random muggers, children get lost and are never found. He said so.'

'It's crap.'

'Women are dragged into alleyways and raped.'

I catch a glimpse of my face in a shop window, wraith-white. We walk on, reach the main hallway. I see a small girl skipping ahead of us with two helium-filled balloons. It's all so achingly normal around us that it seems abnormal, hyper real. I want to run over to the girl, skip with her, hold balloons, let them drift up, out, away; but they would only get caught in the glass atrium.

'What do they want us to do?'

'I don't know. He said he would tell us.'

Grandaddy is at my shoulder. '*You feck 'em, my gal. The Virgin Mary be with you.*'

'I'm not doing anything he says.'

'You have to.'

'No, never.'

'We have to get away, go somewhere where no one knows us. America, I'm going to America.'

'Stop Tomas, this is nonsense. So Fariq has his fingers in the till. What can we do? Nothing, he knows that.'

'We know, that's enough. Fucking face, he can't lose it.'

'None of it makes sense. No, there's more to this, I am sure, even if I don't know what.'

'Maybe it's best we don't know.'

'I think that's too late now.'

We take the stairs up to the mezzanine coffee shop. It is empty, no one but bored housewives comes to the mall in the afternoon; and, it's getting late. The mall will shut soon for afternoon prayers. We order our drinks and sit down.

'He left me there, alone. It was so hot. No water. He went off. It was dark when his men came back. They dragged me out to a car. Threw me in the boot.'

'Tom …'

'I thought they were going to kill me, out there, burn my body.'

The waitress brings our drinks. 'They dumped me outside my villa. I didn't know where I was, as it was dark. I was just so glad to be alive. When I figured it out I went in. They'd trashed the place. I got a knife from the kitchen and I sat all night on the balcony. They drove round and round the villa all night.'

Tomas' mobile rings. We both jump. He answers it, 'Hello. You!'

'Who is it?'

'Mozah.'

'I thought she had been arrested.'

He speaks to her. 'Fine.' He hangs up.

'What did she want?'

'She asked how I was, how was Salima and the baby? She hung up.'

There is nothing to say, this day is already too crazy, without wondering about Mozah and her games. Tomas stares at the marble floor, I look too at its bleeding veins. A waitress mops tables about us. Tomas doesn't touch his coffee. Slowly, I sip my water.

A tall local man comes into the coffee shop and smiles at me as he approaches. His waist looks bulky, a holster beneath his *thawb*? Madness, why am I thinking these things? There must be twenty or so empty tables around us, but he comes and sits at one just behind us. He clicks his fingers for one of the girls to bring him a coffee and takes a call on his phone.

Tomas turns green. 'Let's go.'

We leave. I look back. The waitress is bringing the man his drink. He puts some notes on the table before she reaches him. He gets up. He is following. I steer Tomas to the nearest shop, a homeware store. I hide us behind a tall display, and watch him come into the store. He looks around, passes further into the shop. Tomas is shaking. I tug him after me. I hurry us out into the open of the wide entrance way to the store. No cover here. I look to our stalker, just as he turns about, looking for us. Our eyes meet.

'Come on, Tomas.' I pick up the pace. I head towards a jewellery shop, but swerve us quickly into the shop next door. It sells lingerie. 'He won't follow us here.' We watch as he walks past, scowling.

'The game's over. He knows we've clocked him. He'll give up now.'

We head back to the car. 'Where shall we go?' I can't think. I'm so tired. 'I don't know, I really don't know.'

'I don't want to go back to the villa,' says Tomas. It will be prayers soon.

'I know where we need to go. Drive. I will point.' As we get onto the highway I text Hisham. 'I'm coming to you now. Don't call.' I point the way. Now my eyes are glued to the mirrors as I watch, frantic to see if we are being tracked. Every car seems to squint back, malicious.

I direct us off the main high road and into a suburb of small compounds and a large warehouse, the Electric Souk. I point to a piece of scrubland beside a small parade of buildings. One is a petrol station, there are the obligatory couple of fast food joints, a pharmacy, and a small Indian convenience shop, watermelons piled up outside. On the scrubland there are probably over a hundred white, seemingly identical Land Cruisers parked. It is easy to hide here. We slide the car amongst the others. Beyond the cars is a mosque where men are gathering for prayers.

I can see Hisham standing a few feet in front of the mosque looking about. I raise my hand. He nods and walks off towards the back of the parade of shops. We catch up with him around the back of the Indian convenience store, hidden by a couple of shacks. In low voices we briefly explain the situation. Hisham says nothing while we talk. As we finish he softly brushes my face. I am crying, and I didn't even know.

'Wait here one moment, keep hidden. They'll be here soon, if they aren't already.' Hisham walks away.

'Who is he? Where's he going?' Tomas asks.

I can't answer, I have a desperate need to feel Hisham's arms about me. The wail of the muezzin begins. My tears flow at its haunting beauty, the anguish of the centuries in its never-ceasing refrain.

'What if he goes and gets them? This is a bad idea, Aisling.'

'I trust him.'

'With your life?'

thirty-six

A car pulls up, a few minutes later. Hisham signals to us to get in.

'We go to the Gatsby. He can stay there. He must not leave the room. Understood?'

Hisham has a friend, a manager at the hotel, who will cover for Tomas. Hisham has told him Tomas is in trouble with his wife and has left her. The friend has accepted this. In the meantime Hisham will try to get a fake passport and exit visa. Tomas is quiet as Hisham outlines the plan, all his energy drained. He closes his eyes in resignation. Hisham tells him not to switch his phone on or use it, promising to bring him a new one the next day.

'Mozah …' Tomas mumbles.

After we drop Tomas off, Hisham takes me to the villa and leaves me with Laila as he wants to go to the souk immediately to find a man who might be able to help with the fake documents.

$$C^*$$

I soak in a bath, while Laila sits on the edge, we go over and over Tomas' story. I expect Laila to not believe me, say it is all lies, crazy.

She pours cool water over my body and rubs a rich cream into my skin.

'Our Royals have their own rules. When I worked in the hospital one time a Royal Sheikha came to the maternity rooms. She gave birth to a baby girl. Her husband, a Sheikh, came the next day. He brought the baby out of the room and gave it to the nurse. He said it was not his baby. He asked for his baby. His son. The nurse explained his wife had given birth to a girl. He struck the nurse, and walked back into the room where his wife was. We heard a shot.'

'No.'

'We were told never to speak of it.'

'But?'

'The Royals deal with things their way. The Sheikh was sent to a special hospital in Europe, maybe. But no one talks of these things.'

After the bath, we retire to the tent. Laila reads the Koran and I let my mind roam, anywhere but the desert. It takes me to the tumbled-down church on the clifftop at home, and I crave to take Hisham there with me, where we could find freedom. I can almost feel the ripping Atlantic wind that wrenches every breath from your body, blows out every thought, gives wing to every hope, carrying them away on the sea spray.

My phone rings.

'It's you isn't it? They said someone told them everything. It's you. I know it is. You told them where Salima lives. You tricked me brilliantly. You're the spy.' I nearly drop my mobile, his voice so brutal.

'Tomas, what are you saying? How can you say this? I'm your friend. You know I am. I've been helping you. Is someone making you say these things?'

'Helping me! No, not you. You've only ever been helping yourself. How you must have laughed at me?'

'I've never laughed at you.'

'You and him. Whore!'

'What? Tomas?'

'It's all too late now. He doesn't love you. You stupid bitch.'

'I don't understand.'

'Don't lie to me Aisling. I know. You're Brian's whore.'

'That's ridiculous. How can you say this to me?'

'I hate you. You put my name on the list. He showed me. It was your writing.'

'No, no, you are wrong.' My voice weakens. How can he think this of me?

'Aisling, I thought you were my friend. I trusted you.'

'I am, Tomas, I am. Where are you?' I can hear noise, shouting, in the background. 'Are you still in the hotel?'

'It's not safe there. They'll find me.'

'Where are you? It sounds like the souk?'

'I can't tell you.'

'I'm worried about you.'

'Aisling …' He sobs. 'I'm afraid.'

'Please tell me where you are. I'll come to you.'

'You are my friend?'

'Of course.'

A gulp. 'Souk. By the gallery.'

⸺ C ⸺

I see shadows everywhere in the souk, long fingers tearing at corners. I have come alone, worried that if Laila came it would frighten Tomas off. Something scurries round a corner and I jump. I take a breath for a minute and go deeper into the labyrinth. It's busy tonight and I am jostled past barrows. A new shipment of spices must have just come in, there is such a hum around the spice stores. The mix of ground cardamom, pepper, za'atar, ginger and chilli powder burns my eyes. I rub them, worse. I can't find my way fast enough through to the main passage way and along to the gallery. It's over an hour since I spoke to Tomas. He hasn't answered any of my calls or texts since. A dark blot smudges against the far pillar of the gallery arcade. I walk towards it and it shifts a little.

'Where's your wire?' He barks at me, emerging from the smudge. His eyes are wild, dilated. His damp shirt is hanging out of his trouser top and he is wearing bright blue hotel flip-flops. 'I know you're taping me. They're listening. They're watching out for me, always.' He sits starts laughing manically. 'Go on, do it, do it, kill me. That's what you are going to do, isn't it? Do it quickly, please.'

'I'm not going to kill you Tomas.'

'You're the assassin. I know you've signed my death warrant. I've seen it. You signed it with your own blood.' He must be drunk. 'He just used you and tonight he's going to rape you. He will slice you up, out there in the desert. Whore.' He shouts the insult.

'Tomas, ssh. People are looking.'

'They were looking. Looking for you. And now I've told them. They know you're here. You're going to die tonight. You'll never be found. We'll burn your body.' His voice blisters with hatred. I don't want to believe this. I don't want his fear. 'There, there they come.' I look around despite myself. I know it will be Brian and Fariq's thugs. I feel *his* finger on my lips, hear *his* howl. But, it's just some locals, heading to a shisha café probably. They smile at me. I want to slap myself. 'There, no, there.' Tomas is pointing frantically in one direction and then another, and another, at any man in a *thawb*,

'Hush.' He sinks to the floor in a heap, weeping. I kneel down beside him and put my hand on his shoulder.

He flinches. 'Please tell my family I love them. I'm not a monster. Brian is saying I abused Gabriella. He says if I go home they will arrest me. Lies, lies. But no one believes me.' Sweat is pouring off him, his very hair is drenched and his eyes roll.

I've seen this before. Those wild souls in the A&E at the Mater, destined for St Ita's and high doses of lithium.

'Aisling. I am so sorry I forced myself on you. Did they make you do it? It must have been horrible for you.' He curls in a ball.

'Tomas, listen to me, you're not well. Really not well. We need to get you to a doctor. You've had a shock. Your mind isn't coping. Let me help you.'

'You're not going to kill me?'

'No, no, how could you ever think that?'

'Aisling, *habibti*.'

Hisham.

'Laila called me. Said you had come to the souk to find Tomas. She was worried. You shouldn't have come here alone. What's wrong with him?'

'We need a doctor.'

☾

We take Tomas, crushed, barely able to walk, back to his room at the hotel. Hisham's friend, the manager, calls the hotel doctor, who gives him a sedative to help him sleep. We tell the doctor he is having a breakdown over his wife leaving him. I call the Prof to tell him what is happening and ask his advice on what we should do next. Tomas is sleeping for now, but he clearly needs treatment and there is no psychiatric ward in the small private expat hospital.

The Prof invites me over to talk the situation through and sends his driver. It is late, but I go. We cannot speak on the phone, I know this now.

At the Prof's villa I recount the day's events. The villa is musty with flaking leather, every wall lined with ancient books. The television, on silent, streams pictures of men, all with one arm raised, chequered *ghutras* hiding everything but their eyes. That skyline, I recognize it. It's the next city across the border, so close.

I feel foolish, telling it out loud, and I doubt everything now. The phone taps, the wire, the cars following us, the conspiracies, Mozah's call, the gun for heaven's sake. How could I have been drawn into the delusions of a man having a breakdown? Why did I believe his crazy tale so easily? I am becoming worse than Tony Morton. The Prof reassures me, in this climate, a strange place and with all the recent unsettling events, it is easy to jump to fanciful conclusions. People live in a state of dread in the desert. Something about it, its malice gets to expats and locals alike, and of course that rubs off on even the most level-headed.

'But that doesn't mean, Aisling, that we take people out into the desert and put guns to their heads.'

'I know. I'm sorry.'

'You're tired. We're all tired. The last few weeks have been trying. Now, do you have Salima's number? I'll call her and we'll find the truth there, I think.'

'You think she has left him?'

I give the Prof the number and his driver takes me home.

☾

I can't sleep. Even though the aircon is on in the tent, I am clammy. I keep looking backwards for clues in Tomas' recent behaviour, trying to trace the steps to his mental collapse. How did I miss it? Was Mozah right, as well as mean, how irritating? Has Tomas broken up with Salima? Has he been so ashamed, so distraught he has hidden all this from his friends here? The arrests, the passports, the list. It's all torn at our nerves. Brian's bully-boy tactics, the last straw? But no, he was furious with Brian and Rex, but no more than any of the rest of us. Then again, the threat of exposure in the press, so public, so humiliating. Did he fear Salima would believe the stories?

Something scratches in my mind.

I get up and pace the yard. It's still over thirty degrees. I can't think in this heat. How can a man become such a gibbering wreck so fast? Breakdowns don't happen like that, do they? Breakdown. The very word implies something more entropic. This is so… explosive? From nowhere. In the mall he was distressed, but lucid. He was lucid. I tell myself that again and again. Maybe, some paranoia? Yet, in just hours he has become a wreck. Could he be so shredded by paranoia, so fast? Is that possible? What is possible in this desert?

This is a modern country, the host of weekly summits for world leaders and home to multinational companies in skyscrapers. The Prof said it, 'We don't put guns to people's heads.'

And Fariq. He's only ever shown us kindness. He is a poet, a man of words, not bullets. Surely? Tomas' account, its blood wrath, is from an ancient, bygone time. From a mad mind. Fariq is an influential man, he does not need to resort to this petty terror.

And the man, with a holster under his thawb? Did he follow us?

'*Yanni*, you are a beautiful, white woman Aisling. Of course he followed you. Men must do that always. You just noticed this time. It means nothing. *Mafi*.' The Prof's explanation.

He did follow.

But the terror in Tomas' eyes. Where did that come from? I saw it.

And before, that night at the camp, when Fariq penetrated my soul, I felt it then too. Sharp, the evil.

thirty-seven

The next morning on my desk is a huge wooden casket filled with chocolates. Sheikh Fariq. I push it to one side. Not long after the man himself puts in an appearance. Much to Laila's dismay he dismisses her from the room, with a wave of his prayer beads. He asks me where the Prof and Tomas are today. I say I don't know where the Prof is, and Tomas is ill. Is it me, or does the Sheikh seem different today? Not his usual assured self. Uncertain. Shifty even? Or am I looking for this? I observe him acutely, every angle of his shoulder, every move of his eye.

'Maybe Mr Tomas should go home to his own country if he is ill? I, we could, arrange this. Get him an exit visa. Do you think it would be best if he went home?'

How curious. I have not said what is wrong with Tomas, it could just be a bout of flu or upset stomach, and yet here is the Sheikh suggesting he is so ill he should go home. He doesn't wait for me to answer.

'Yes, yes, I think it is best if Mr Tomas went home. I will call a Brother at the Ministry and make the paperwork. I told him on

Monday that he should not worry anymore, that he is my Brother and I will watch him always.'

Like a crack across my face. Those are the very words Tomas used. But, the Sheikh says them so softly, gently and with what seems like concern. Has Tomas mis-interpreted him?

'Miss Aisling, you will have seen these things in your country more than we do here. Here, when someone is sick in their head the family keeps them at home, so we do not see these people. We have no experience of how they act, they talk.'

The Sheikh knows about Tomas' mental state? How?

'Have you seen Brother Tomas? When I last saw him he said some very bad things. I think there is something wrong with him.'

Sheikh Fariq sits down and tells me how Tomas stormed into his office shouting about Brian and Mozah. It sounds like he created quite a scene, claiming they were lovers, saying Brian was robbing the Board, a story about Tomas and prostitutes. Sheikh Fariq thought Tomas was drunk. He offered to take him to the Celestine for a coffee to sober him up and get him out of the office, no need for gossip.

Plausible.

On the way to the Celestine Tomas got even more manic, making accusations about Fariq's involvement with Rex and alleging that he was presiding over massive corporate fraud and theft.

'This hurt me very much, Miss Aisling. How could he say such things? I am his Brother, his dear friend.'

Sheikh Fariq decided that Tomas was sick in his head, something more than drunkenness. He took Tomas to the airport as he thought the pharmacy there would be open and he could get something to calm him down; it wasn't. This is all mirroring Tomas account, but this reflection is not cracked apart.

Sheikh Fariq's concern seems genuine. Is the Sheikh's narrative too crafted, too careful? But, Tomas accused me of all sorts too. Spy, assassin, whore.

Fariq decided to take him to his home to calm him down. His wife was not happy when she saw the state Tomas was in, as their young nephews were in the villa playing, so Fariq took him through to the servants' restroom at the back. They gave Tomas a drink with some sleeping tablets crushed in it and left him to rest. He slept for a few hours and when he woke seemed better. The Sheikh told him not to worry, he should take a break, go on holiday, go to America maybe?

'Tomas, do not worry about work, family is everything, worry about your family.'

The Prof is right, fanciful conclusions. Sheikh Fariq did not hurt and threaten Tomas, he is trying to protect him and avoid a scandal at the Board. I curse the sand *djinn*, you will not play with my mind. Each vertebrae of my spine let's go and my jaw softens. I agree with Sheikh Fariq that Tomas is sick in his head, that he needs proper help and I urge him to make arrangements for Tomas to go home to Sweden for some rest and treatment.

The Sheikh thanks me for my advice and stands up to leave, 'It is so sad to see this happen to a family man. My nephews liked Tomas, they had fun playing soldiers on Monday.' Playing soldiers; static hisses.

'I thought Tomas slept?'

'When he woke up and was better he played with the boys. I got them an old gun in the souk that morning.'

The prayer beads click.

thirty-eight

'He is seeing a psychiatric doctor this afternoon, for now he is sleeping.'

The Prof tells me he has been to the Gatsby and arranged, through expat circles, for the wife of one of the expat bankers to see Tomas discreetly. She is a psychiatrist back in her own country. I tell the Prof about Sheikh Fariq.

'I feel so stupid, how could I have believed any of it? Of course Sheikh Fariq wouldn't harm anyone. He's such a kind man.'

The Prof agrees it is best for Tomas to go home and get some professional help, but the Prof has not been able to make contact with Salima. He says he will go and see Sheikh Fariq and support him to make the arrangements for the exit visa.

☾

I can relax now. I am bleached raw after the last forty-eight hours. I need to get out of the city, away from the heat. Get some perspective back. I meet Hisham after work and we go to the deserted village, our favourite place. The day smoulders, we slip out of our clothes and into the molten sea. The desert cannot reach us here, although it salivates at the shoreline. We float together. I lie back in Hisham's arms. The sky darkens from dirty white, to grit, to black, and sea and sky melds.

'He said they would burn my body. No one would find me.'

'Hush, hush, forget these troubles.' He kisses my fretting away. 'My Mounia, tell me about the mermaids of Ireland.'

In the monochrome stillness I whisper briny fables to him.

'*Houriyyat el baher*, my mermaid, I want to always lie here like this with you.'

'Mm, Hisham, it's a lovely dream.' He feels silky. A wave slides across him like mercury.

'No, it's more than a dream. My company has offices in Manchester. They need someone to go over for a year, *yanni*, more. I have requested a transfer.'

'But your family … your wedding?'

'This would be a promotion, my family will approve. I will tell them to delay the wedding until I have been to Manchester, so I can prepare a home for my bride.'

I bleed out into the black.

'And in that time you will come to me.'

'You want *me*?'

'*Mounia.*' He takes my hand and places it over his heart.

'Your family will never agree.'

'Overseas it can happen. It's not so unusual. Our men go abroad, to study, to work. They don't come back.'

'You could do this?'

'Yes, but there is a price. I'll not be able to return here for many years, and you, you'll never be able to come here. You will never be family. Laila won't be able to cluck like a hen over our children.'

I stay in his arms, but I do not speak. I think of all this means, for him. Long minutes pass by, the water wrinkles.

'Aisling?'

'I cannot ask you to let go of your family, all this, everything, your world ...'

He kisses me, *'Enti shamsi, enti qamari.'*

☪

We return to shore. We both find many missed calls on our phones.

Mine is the Prof. 'Tomas has gone missing. He wasn't at the Gatsby when the doctor called to see him.'

Hisham tells me the first of his calls is from Ali, the Gatsby manager. Tomas has gone and so has a passport and travel documents belonging to another guest, a tourist, passing through on their way to Thailand. There was a scene, some confusion at reception involving Tomas just as a party of overnight tourists checked in. Ali fears Tomas took the tickets and passport.

'Oh God.'

'That's not the worst.'

'Hisham?'

He doesn't answer, 'Hisham, tell me.'

'It starts tonight.'

'What does?'

'The Rage. Our Rage. Tonight we cut off the city, we take the Electric Souk roundabout.'

'We?'

'Do not ask more. *Yallah*, we must get back to the city.'

☪

We race back, aiming for the airport. It seems the most likely place to find Tomas now. My phone rings, I don't know the number.

It is Tomas. 'This is your last chance to tell me the truth, Aisling,' he says.

'The truth about what Tomas? Where are you?'

'You already know that because you are coming to kill me. Now tell me, have you killed Salima?' It is noisy wherever he is calling from. Tanoys, it must be the airport, I guess.

'Tomas, you know I would never hurt you or your family. I'm sure Salima is fine. You're hurting me saying these things. You're not well Tomas.'

'Not well?'

'You need to see a doctor.'

'You think that is best for me, then do it, just come and get me, kill me, get it over with.'

He sounds so crippled. Then suddenly he yells, 'But you can't, you won't get me. I'm getting on a plane. Right now. I'm going.' He hangs up.

I call the Prof and let him know that Tomas is at the airport with a stolen passport and ticket. He tells me there is nothing we can do now, just wait for the inevitable, *inshallah*. The traffic is crawling on the outskirts of the city. 'Our people are making their way to the roundabout,' Hisham says.

'Why now, Hisham?'

'In truth, we are not ready yet. We plan for a little later, but last night one of our Brothers was arrested at the home of his grandmother. His sister lives there, she has, how do you say, a mind of a child?'

'Learning disability?'

'Yes. The CID men burst into the home, broke up the doors. It scared her very much and she screamed and hit the men. One of them hit her back. He smashed open her head. This morning in the hospital, she died.'

Hisham and I drive on in silence, wondering what will happen next, both expecting a call from the police. It takes us nearly two hours to get to the airport. I tell Hisham he should go to the roundabout. I don't want him to go, but I know he needs to be there. He refuses, 'The Rage will last many hours, days maybe. It's early yet, there is time. You need me first.'

We walk about the terminal, but can see no disorder anywhere. We check the board, a flight to Bangkok left about an hour or so before. Was Tomas on it? We wander for another twenty minutes, not knowing what to do. Where is he? What madness? He is so vulnerable. I should have prevented this happening. Should have realized he would do something insane like this. We go home, there is nothing more we can do.

☾

Laila and I lie in the tent. The night is deep now, Hisham goes into the city, to the Rage. He has forbidden me from saying anything to Laila. I hold his arm, but he shakes free and kisses me, 'Allah will protect me.'

Laila rolls over. 'You're quiet, Sister.'

'I wish I knew what's happening to Tomas. He's out there alone in the world somewhere.' And I wish I knew what was happening to Hisham.

'There's more, Sister?'

I cannot lie to her, I say nothing.

My ears keen for the sound of trouble, but this suburb is a long way from the city centre. All I can hear is the usual thrum of traffic.

It is gone three o'clock in the morning and we don't understand why by now we have not heard what is happening to Tomas. Laila switches on the television. It is a sizzle of white dots and dashes. She flicks through the channels. All are the same. 'Aaii, the satellite is gone, again.'

I say nothing. I know the government will close down the TV station first. We all know the pattern, we've seen it stretch across North Africa. My mobile still has a signal, for how long? The waiting is killing. Laila and I gather some blankets and settle down and try to sleep in the tent for the night. It is our safe and special place and we don't want to leave it. My mind is cavernous tonight and every fret is roosting there, darting back and forth into the darkness and always returning with more morsels of grief.

Laila lies beside me, still. I know she is not sleeping either, her breathing too shallow, her body too rigid. How can I take Hisham away from her? Her favourite brother. And I will never see her again too. This tent, our shared secrets and intimacies. Laila will drown in her tears. Our lives so far apart, but our hearts the same. I don't want the cold, wet nights of Manchester.

I feel Hisham's lips on my forehead. My eyes are heavy with sleep. One kiss. I listen to his soft footfall retreat across the yard. Next time I am woken it is my phone vibrating. I can't find it in the dark and while I scrabble around it stops. I slump back into the pillows. I doze off again, but ten minutes later it buzzes. This time I answer in time. At the other end of the line there is a lot of noise. 'Hello?' but no answer, just noise, then the phone cuts off. I groan and roll over. The phone buzzes again. The voice is clear. 'The man in glasses, is he your man?'

'Tomas, where are you?' Now I am wide wake.

'Tell me, the man in glasses, he's a secret agent isn't he? You sent him to follow me.' He hangs up. Laila wakes.

'It was Tomas. I don't know where he was. He was crazy.' She takes the phone off me and looks at the dial history.

'Dubai.'

The Far East flights all stop at Dubai. Now I cannot sleep. What will happen to Tomas when he reaches Bangkok? It is so far away. He won't know a soul there. I have flashes of Tomas lost stumbling around in the sticky, bustling streets. How has it all come to this? I sit by the tent flap and wait for the light.

The dawn is grey as the night flees and before the sun stretches. The only relief is that it is Friday, and I don't have to face the office gossips. Without a doubt Tomas' plight will be the dish of the day, and there will be great mastication of every morsel of his pain and humiliation.

Laila and her sisters leave for the mosque. Hisham has already gone. Is the Rage happening? There is no way I can tell. Maybe not? Surely Laila will have heard and the sisters will not go to mosque. All must be quiet still. I long for Hisham to be with me. Nothing feels the same this morning. Every minute sweats heavy. I need a long walk, but there is nowhere to walk. I rattle about the yard for a few minutes, but it is like a kiln and the dust is thick today. It smothers my lips and I choke. I return to the tent and lie back down on the cushions and let my eyes follow the stitch of the fabric, I let its repetition numb me. Tony, Angie, Justin, Tomas, missing in the weave. An hour passes, two, more.

'*Yallah, yallah*, come quickly, he's here, Tomas is here and he's making very bad threats.'

thirty-nine

'He says he has come back.'

'If he ever went!'

Laila had coming running into the yard, waving her mobile at me. Now as we speed in her car towards the airport, Laila tells me that while she was at mosque she had a call from Tomas, from a local number. 'He wants to go to the police, the Royals. He wants me to translate. Tell them he is innocent, that Sheikh Fariq is the thief. He's crazy.'

'This is crazy, this whole thing.'

'He wants to warn the Royals that Sheikh Fariq has an army and will shoot them. He says Sheikh Fariq wants to be *Caliph*. He has a gun.'

The roads are crushed with traffic, '*Whallah*! What's this? It's Friday. Why so many people?' Laila asks.

'Laila, I think there's trouble in the city. Look people have flags and banners in their cars.'

'*SubhanAllah, SubhanAllah*, la, la, please, not here.'

We reach the airport, just as we are parking my phone rings. A local number, but not one I know. It is Tomas. He is in a taxi. He says he is heading for his villa as he needs to find a belt to keep up his trousers, but he can't recall where he lives. The driver has stopped at a petrol station and now he wants me to find him so I can take him to get his belt. He has no idea where in the city he is. Laila takes the phone and asks to speak to the driver, who is from Kerala and new in the country this week, speaks little English or Arabic, and also has no clue where he is either.

'Aaii, this is crazy, Sister.'

We tell the driver to take Tomas to the Celestine and we will meet them there. If we can get there.

As we edge through the city we see hundreds of men, of all ages, their faces lit with fervour, almost skipping through the streets. The banners say theirs is a peaceful protest. They call for reforms, an end to corruption, power for the people. Chanting thrums like a thousand drums. Laila tries to call Hisham. There is no answer.

'He'll be at mosque. It will be fine,' she says. I can say nothing.

At the Celestine I leave Laila in the car, run in and scan the plaza lobby for any sign of Tomas. I can't see him. There are plenty of expats gathered here, ready for brunch. Are they oblivious to what is going on outside? Stiff upper lip, nothing is getting in the way of 'Champagne Friday'. A shadow flits across the foyer. I catch it, but not fast enough. Tomas is out the door and leaping into a taxi.

I run back to our car. 'I lost him.'

'Come, let's go back to our tent, Sister. It's not safe to be out.'

We drive back to the villa, passing growing crowds. At the villa we get out of the car. The heat is terrible. The leaden sky pressing down just an inch above our heads. Laila is still trying to get hold of Hisham, as we walk round the tent behind the villa.

'He is there, isn't he, with the protesters?' She starts to cry. 'Call him, Sister, please, he will come back for you.' She grabs my bag from me and rifles through it, pulling out and throwing in the dust anything that isn't my phone.

'Hey!'

She finds it. 'Call.'

I look at my phone. My fingers itch for the keypad, but I can't. I look again at my phone. It is real. 'Laila, look.' The signal symbols on our phones are gone. We both try to dial. Nothing.

'La, la, Aaii.' Laila runs into the villa.

'Dear God, please let him be safe,' I pray.

Moments later, Laila comes back into the tent, tears streaming down her face. 'The Net, it's gone. What will they do to us now the world is switched off?' One by one her sisters and the other women of the family join us. All the men are gone. Softly, the women chant.

☪

It is late when the men return, noisy, shouting about the march; tents are up, the roundabout occupied. It is a confusion of bodies and noise. I search amongst the flailing arms and yabbering women, flapping *abayas* and hurtling children, for Hisham. Where is he?

Hisham has stayed. Dear God. He is in one of the tents. My breath puckers. Sami, one of the brothers, comes over to me with Laila. He tells me he will go over to Tomas' villa and see if he is there. Tomas. I had almost forgot. Where is he in this chaos? What if by now he has gone to the police and related his wild allegations? Stirring up trouble on today of all days.

Sami returns within the hour. There is no sign of Tomas at his villa. The suburbs are still quiet. My phone rings. I jump. I didn't realise the signal was back. It must have been a temporary blip, not so unusual then. The government has not cut us off, a good sign, it must be. It is Tomas. He is out of money and the taxi driver has dumped him at the Irish Bar, no doubt thinking he is just another drunk expat, which is where he is ringing from now. Sami takes me, calling Hisham on the way.

At the Irish Bar we find Tomas slumped outside, despite the heat. He looks drunk.

'Tomas,' I call to him.

He looks up, dazed. 'Salima?' He climbs up with difficulty, swaying.

His white shirt is grubby and torn, hanging out of his trousers. He is holding his trousers up, as he has no belt. He also has no socks on and no laces in his shoes. His eyes are not focusing and there is spittle at the corners of his mouth. He has a black-eye, haggard. Only a few days ago he was a healthy, smart man. Is this possible?

'We have to take him to a doctor, he looks sick,' says Sami to me beneath his breath. 'Tomas, you can't sit here, it's too hot. Come with me now.'

He shambles over to our car. 'I'm thirsty, so thirsty.'

When did he last drink, eat, sleep? Sami hands Tomas a small bottle of water from the boot of the car, as he drinks it a figure comes bounding over to us. 'It's not safe for you to be out Aisling. Sami, there's a curfew.'

Sami speaks hurriedly with Hisham. They hug and Sami runs off into the night. 'Come, we must get to a doctora while we can.'

'Sami?' I ask.

Sami is going to the tents to replace Hisham. We get Tomas into the back seat of the car and go. For a few minutes Tomas is quiet but refreshed by the water, he starts speaking loudly and aggressively, as if in tongues. It makes me shudder, this voodoo sound. He grabs my hair and pulls on it hard. I cry out. We are on the highway so Hisham can't stop.

'Let her go.'

Tomas laughs manically, 'She injected me you know, at the airport, while the man in glasses watched. I tried to run away. I threw a chair at the window, two soldiers jumped on top of me. They were kicking me. They made me take a tablet. Poison, poison.'

He talks in tongues again.

'I call my friend, the doctora.'

'You, Salima, you told them to poison me.'

'Shit, shit, no network.'

'She gave me this bottle of tablets and told me if I didn't take them all they would make sure I never saw my family again.' He takes out a small bottle of pills from his pocket and shoves a handful of the tablets in his mouth. 'Look, look, here I am taking them.'

I try to reach him to stop him, but can't. He grabs my hand and twists it, viciously. 'You, you're the true evil one. I have to kill you. Fariq told me to. He says you are the enemy.'

He is really hurting me. Hisham yells at him to let me go, but he won't. He bites me hard on my wrist. I cry out. Hisham pulls up onto the pavement and gets out. He drags Tomas from the car and wrestles with him, eventually punching him out.

He slings the prone body back in the car. 'Forget the doctora, we're going to the hospital.'

We skid through the backstreets, avoiding the main roads. The city is quiet, holding its breath. As we pull up to the hospital, Tomas begins to groan in the back. Hisham calls out to the security guard at the casualty department to help him and between them they manhandle Tomas into the hospital. I follow in behind them and a stern German nurse who appears to be in charge of the casualty department stops me and says I have to fill out some forms. She thrusts a raft of papers and a chewed-up biro at me, pushes me onto a bench. Hisham and the guard, with Tomas between them, disappear down a corridor. The scene around me comes into focus. Bloody focus.

Broken men. Bandaged heads droopy, like battered snowdrops. I can see men with shards of bone tearing through their dirty thawbs and jeans, men with blood seeping from gashes and others leaning against each other moaning in pain. There are only a handful of chairs, with occupants collapsed on them, some barely conscious. The smell of blood, metallic.

I sit on the bench, motionless. I don't want to look. The casualty department reception is a small, dusty concrete box, with taupe paint peeling off the walls. No aircon, just some noisy fans, all squealing at different pitches. One wall is completely glass, smeary, with the automatic doors sliding back and forth. They chop together loudly every couple of minutes. A hatch in the far wall is surrounded by a cage, through which I can see the receiving clerk, who at this moment is cursing at an old man, clinging onto the cage and refusing to move, blood splattered. Blood, I can't shut out the blood.

The forms in my hand wilt. Another nurse, a wiry Filipino, comes over to me after a few minutes and takes the pen and forms, even though I have not completed them. A young man throws up, his vomit splattering the floor within an inch of where I am sitting. The Filipino nurse starts to scream at him. The room swings. I cannot stop here on this bench. While the nurse is screaming at the man, I slip past her and run along the corridor. I pass small cubicles where men are groaning, and the stench of flesh and faeces brings me even closer to gagging. I find Hisham and Tomas at the end cubicle. Tomas is sitting in the corner on a chair, his head in his hands.

'The guard is bringing us the doctora.'

'This place is terrible.'

'It's all right, he'll be moved quickly to the psychiatric hospital. I had to come here first, it was closest and he was hurting you.'

Hisham takes my wrist and looks at the deep purple wheal forming where Tomas bit me. He kisses it. 'Hisham, out there, those men ...?'

'Not now, I'll tell you about it later.'

We wait for some time, listening to the moans from the neighbouring cubicles. Tomas does not move, he is like a deflated jack in the box. Finally the doctor arrives. He speaks in a perfect cut glass English accent and is tall and noble. He explains he is the on call psychiatrist. Hisham describes the situation and the doctor nods from time to time. He ushers us out into the corridor while he briefly assesses Tomas. As we wait a man runs screaming past us, trailing blood and pursued by two brawny guards. Nurses are haranguing each other at the nursing station. A phone is ringing loudly and incessantly at their desk, which they ignore. Paramedics arrive with a corpse- like figure on a trolley, they leave the body without a second glance, outside one of the cubicles. Greenish urine streams from the corpse, no one notices.

After a few minutes the doctor joins us, looking grave. He tells us he is concerned about Tomas and needs to perform a full assessment, but cannot do this here today. He wants to admit Tomas to the psychiatric unit, however there are no beds. He proposes giving Tomas a sedative and letting him sleep for the night in the cubicle, then he will move him to the unit the next day, '*Inshallah*.'

I tell him Tomas has already taken a handful of pills. The doctor asks Tomas for the bottle. Just vitamins. He tells us to come back in the morning.

'I can't leave him like this. Not here.'

'I'm sorry Miss, but you cannot stay. It's the rules.'

We look in on Tomas before we go, he is lying on the trolley in the cubicle, asleep. His face still furrowed with torment. I stroke his clammy forehead. Hisham pulls me away.

'Come, there's nothing more we can do, let him sleep.'

As we return to the villa Hisham hands me his phone and I watch a video he has taken of the day's events. I can see crowds of men at the roundabout. Over a thousand, Hisham says. Prayers are said and then the crowd begins to chant its demands. Fists are thrust towards the sun. Placards held high. Men sing and laugh. Young boys scamper about, waving flags. It could be a football crowd, there's excitement, a thrill, but no menace.

The video cuts. Starts again. The sun is higher. The police arrive, wielding batons and shining riot shields. They encircle the protesters. There is jostling at the edges, but the police slap the backs of men they know. It's jovial. Cans of cola are even shared across the line of police. Another cut. It's dusk. Tents are being pitched. Laughter, as some fall down as soon as they are put up. Banter. One policeman has his eyes shut. Is he sleeping? The crowd dwindles as some men leave for the mosque. What is that rattling noise?

A scream.

The stamp of feet.

I know the rest, I saw it in the hospital.

'Tomorrow I return to the roundabout. We will carry his coffin there. A thousand men will pray. He was fifteen.'

'A boy. Hisham …'

'Don't look so afraid. The police won't not cause trouble at a

306

ELECTRIC SOUK

funeral. We have respect in this country, even at these times.'

'I'm not so sure. It always starts like this … Tunisia …'

'I have to be there, Aisling, we are Brothers together.'

'But how will it finish, this Rage? I fear it will burn forever.'

'*Allah Akbar.*'

forty

Laila gives me a strange, sour draft to help me sleep. I am exhausted. A black sea sweeps away the bloodied bodies beneath my eyelids. But not for long. My phone buzzes beside me, wakes me from bitter dreams. I know before I even answer it that it is Tomas.

'Salima? Salima? Help me. I have to get out of here. I heard him. He's here in the hospital, Sheikh Fariq. With soldiers. They're coming to get me.'

'Oh no.'

He hangs up. I stumble around the tent, putting my clothes on, while Laila goes to find Hisham.

They return, Hisham is on his phone. 'It's true. He's left the hospital. The nurse can't find him.'

'I thought he was meant to be sedated.'

We drive at speed once more to the hospital. 'Hisham, the curfew?'

'*Yanni*, I will worry about that if we are stopped. Look, there are still many cars out.'

'Don't they know?'

'They still want to shop, crazy Arabs.'

I laugh. I love how he takes my anxiety and rolls it up into a ball to throw away.

Tomas is there. A few hundred yards down the road from the hospital, sat on the curb, pitiful. He puts up no resistance as Hisham pulls him into the car. As we get to the hospital he pleads suddenly, 'Please don't take me in there, Fariq is there. They will kill me.'

'Hush Tomas, Fariq isn't here, truly. You're tired, you just need to sleep.'

He crumples. We lead him back in, through the waiting room, still as chaotic as it was earlier in the night. We take him back to the cubicle where we left him before, but there is a protester lying asleep on the trolley now. 'Why are we here? This is the wrong place,' Tomas tries to lead us along the corridor.

'You go with him Hisham, I'll find the nurse.'

I go to the nursing station where a weary looking nurse is drinking coffee. I explain that I have brought Tomas back and ask her to help. She looks at me blankly, so I explain again.

'No, no Englishe,' she says. She waves at me to go. 'You go, Missey, go, we busy here, big trouble today.'

I want to scream. The nurse pushes me out into the corridor. I notice the corpse from yesterday is still on the trolley, only now it is groaning.

I wander along the corridor looking for Hisham and Tomas. One of the Filipino nurses I saw earlier comes out from a cubicle. I approach her and repeat my explanation and request for help again. This nurse gives me a shifty look and then denies that Tomas has ever been in the hospital.

'He was here, he was in there.' Jesus, I point to the cubicle.

The nurse walks over to it and pulls back the curtain. 'No; no Mr Tomas, no white mad-man here today. You see, just a student. You go home now Miss, there's a curfew.'

'He saw the psychiatrist.'

'No, no psychiatrist here. Only at the psychiatry hospital. Maybe you go there, tomorrow.'

'You know he was here, and he left and I have found him and brought him back. He is very sick and there'll be trouble because you let a sick man leave.' I look her directly in the eye.

'No, no, only you are trouble Miss.'

The nurse bends over towards me and whispers, 'And you'll be in more trouble if you stay.'

Out in the corridor, a porter with an empty wheelchair pushes past me. What is happening here? Why is everyone being so obstructive? That nurse, the way she looked at me, what does she mean? Is the Sheikh here? A vein throbs at my temple. I touch it and pain shoots at my right eye. Hisham reappears and nods to me to follow him. We walk through to another corridor and then another. This part of the hospital is deathly quiet. Hisham takes me to a small room. Inside, Tomas is now sitting on a box.

'This is where he says he has been.'

'But this is a storeroom. Hisham, something is definitely not right here.' I tell him my experience with the nurses.

As I finish there is a gentle knock at the door and a young woman walks in. She is in a uniform, but not that of a nurse. She tells us she is the pharmacy technician and is here to give Tomas his sedative. I express surprise that he hasn't had it before now.

'I have, I have,' Tomas suddenly springs off the box. 'She injected me, she did, she was here with Fariq and she injected me.' Tomas pulls his shirt up and shows us a plaster and wad of cotton wool on his hip. He tears it off and I can see the puncture wound.

The pharmacist ignores him while she pours a small dose of a white, chalky liquid into a small beaker. She tries to hand it to Tomas, but he won't take it. 'Please, drink this.'

Tomas looks at Hisham and me, he whimpers.

'Tomas, please.' I implore.

He pushes the pharmacist aside and bolts for the door, but Hisham blocks it. The pharmacist hands him the beaker. He gulps it back and sits down heavily on the box.

We ask the pharmacist why Tomas is in this storeroom and why no one is looking after him. We explain that he left the hospital and we found him down the street and brought him back.

'I don't know about that. It's not true … but if you say so.' She tells us as far as she knows he has been in the cupboard all evening. He is here while the nurses find a bed for him on the ward, but with all the casualties, that is proving difficult. 'He can't stay in the casualty room with all those protesters. It's better for a white man to be kept separate.'

'In a cupboard!'

'We'll take him to a ward now.' She goes.

'Hisham, this is all wrong. We should go and take Tomas with us.'

The pharmacist technician returns quickly with a decrepit porter and a wheelchair. She tells us she is taking Tomas to a ward. We follow.

'No, no, you can't come. No visitors at night.'

Hisham asks to speak to whoever is in charge and she tells us to wait while she finds the night doctor.

Tomas and the porter disappear into the elevator. 'We can't leave him, Hisham. I don't like this place. It's not right.'

'Take my keys. Wait for me in the car. I'll get more answers by myself. They won't speak in front of a white woman.' Reluctantly I go and sit in the car, tapping the dashboard. I look at my watch. Ten minutes. I look again, twenty. A car slides past. Two minutes later it is back. Hisham comes round the corner.

He gets into our car. 'It's ok, he's in bed in the ward and already asleep. I saw him.'

'Why was everyone acting like that? I know they must be under pressure today, but still …'

'This is how it is. You have to understand most of those nurses aren't qualified, and they are always afraid of getting into trouble, being deported. This hospital is a shame to our country. You saw what it was like. *Sae, ya*! No organisation. Don't worry, there's nothing bad happening there, just wrong management. It's the same in all government departments. This is why we protest today. Our people deserve better.'

We pull out and drive round the corner to join the road out of the hospital, but as we do, we nearly hit another car driving on the wrong side of the road. It is the car I saw earlier. Hisham swerves sharply and we clip its wing mirror, which spins off across the car park. The car screeches away at speed. 'Crazy drivers!' Hisham yells.

We return home. Hisham cannot risk going to the roundabout, with the curfew in place the roads leading there, if not the malls, will be policed for certain. Laila isn't in the tent, she is inside the villa. She doesn't like to be anywhere alone. 'Habibti,' says Hisham. He pulls me down onto the rug beside him, and holds me close to him for what remains of the dark night hours, until the muezzins begin to call in the distance. I lose myself in his frankincense scent. As dawn steals across the rugs, he leaves me for the roundabout.

☾

It is late in the morning when I wake, with a start of conscience. I promised the psychiatrist I would go to the hospital first thing to sign the papers needed to enable him to assess and move Tomas.

'Laila, Laila,' I call across the yard. 'We have to go to the hospital.'
I find Laila inside the villa, wailing with her sisters. 'What's wrong?
Why are you arguing?'

'We are not arguing. The men, they've gone to the funeral.
We begged them not to go. It's not safe. *Hallas!* What can we do?
They'll not listen to us, women.' I don't want to think about the
horrors today might bring. 'Let's go to the hospital. We can't just
sit here.'

I feel sick returning to the hospital. We go to the ward. Laila
speaks to the clerk. Quickly voices are raised and Laila storms past
the clerk.

'Laila, what's happened?' I hurry after her.

'He said he's not here. He's lying I know it. Hisham says he is
here and I will find him. These people are fools.'

The clerk follows us shouting, while Laila shouts back at him.
She pulls back the curtains of the beds looking for Tomas. Quickly,
several nurses come running down the ward. Soon there is a huge
row ensuing as Laila demands to know where Tomas might be. All
the nurses deny he has ever been there. I pull her away, worried
she is going to get us thrown out. Maybe Hisham got the wrong
ward name. Laila is incensed and certain Hisham has not made a
mistake. We leave the ward and make our way back to the main
entrance while Laila calls Hisham to clarify the ward name.

'La, la, *Shukran.*' She snaps her phone shut. '*Akide*, yes, I was
right. Hisham says Tomas is in that ward. We will go find the
doctora.'

I do not want to return to the ward and face another argument.
Why are all the staff in this hospital being so awkward? Again.
Last night was one thing, but today, once more? This is more
than incompetence. I don't like it at all. 'Let's try the casualty
department.'

In the casualty department the shift has changed. I don't recognise any of the staff. This shift, just like the night before, denies all knowledge of Tomas' admission.

'No record on the computer. He's not been here.'

'But I brought him here myself, twice.'

I ask to see the psychiatrist, but the nurses just ignore me. I tell them the psychiatrist must be here, as he told me he is holding a clinic this morning and will also see his patients in the casualty.

'No psychiatry doctora here, Missy. Go, go.'

We don't know where to turn next. Where is Tomas? We wander around the casualty cubicles, peering in to see if he is there still. Has he run away again? He is so fragile, if he is out too long in this heat he will collapse. A terrible thought scrapes at me. What if he has run away to kill himself? He was so desperate yesterday? Who knows what he might do? He could do anything. How can we find him? The small city suddenly seems vast. We go round to the store cupboard. No, he isn't there.

'Madams, what are you doing?' A shrill voice behind us.

Laila explains to a cross nurse that we are searching for Tomas and that he was last seen in this cupboard last night.

'Rubbish. You're liars. Where do you think you are? Africa? We don't put patients in cupboards.'

'Liar, liar! How dare you? No, no, no! I'll have you terminated right away. You can't speak to me like this. This is *haram*! Where's matron?'

The nurse beats a hasty retreat with Laila following her, invective in full stream, her long thin, boney arms shaking at the nurse as she retreats. I cast one last look at the cupboard, and there on the floor in the corner is a wallet. I pick it up and look inside, just a few riyal notes, credit card and a photo, Salima and baby Gabrielle.

I find a seat in the endless, pale green corridor and wait for Laila. It's as if I'm inside the stem of a long blade of sweet grass, before it's cut. A figure appears at the far end, moving slowly towards me, pushing a dazed looking student in a wheelchair. It is the porter from last night. He is a crinkly old man with his front teeth missing. I stop him and ask where Tomas is. He shakes his head and pretends he doesn't know me, he shuffles off, but I bar the way.

'I know he is here. *Shufi*, look, I have his wallet. He dropped it in the cupboard.'

'La, la, not here, never here.' He won't look at me.

'I'm going to the embassy if I cannot find my friend and then everyone will be in trouble. How will it look if this hospital has lost a sick man, a Westerner? With all this fighting in the city? What if he's lying dead somewhere?' I stop, let him think this over. 'It will be a big scandal. CNN will come and people will lose their jobs. Not people at the top, they never lose their jobs. It will be people like you.' Now the porter looks at me, pained. I feel a pang of guilt at his fear, but he knows more than he is letting on. I am close now, I can sense it, and I'm not going to stop.

'He gone. Gone home.'

'How? How has he gone home?'

'Taxi, he call taxi.'

'No, he has no phone.'

I show him Tomas' phone. The nurses gave it to me yesterday along with his watch and door keys. 'And I have his wallet. See, this is my friend's wife and baby. They're very worried for him.' I shove the picture right in front of him.

'Phone,' the porter points to the corridor phone, further along from us. 'I call psychiatry hospital, find him.' I let him go. He hobbles along to the phone.

Psychiatry hospital? Tomas cannot go there until I sign the papers. The nurses said there is no psychiatrist. This place. The porter replaces the handset carefully in the cradle.

He nods, 'La, la, he's not there. I can't help, I don't know. *Alhamdulillah*.'

I start to walk away. I hear the porter's feet padding off. Slap, slap, slap. Of course. How could this porter know that Tomas needs psychiatric help? When he saw Tomas, he was sleepy in a wheelchair going to a medical ward. I turn back to face him.

'*Hallas*.'

A siren howls.

forty-one

The psychiatric unit is on the other side of the city, beneath a six-lane flyover. We take a winding route as the main roads through the city are closed off. Police at all major junctions. The sky is ashen; the light dull, straining. The immaculate city is strewn with debris, catching in-between railings. Small clusters of men slink between buildings, like souk cats, making their way to the roundabout. Some carry rolled-up tents. Many cover their faces with scarves.

Every road we turn down we are flagged away by the police. At one junction, an officer waves us down, Laila opens her window, he barks at her. 'What did he say?'

'Go home, the streets are no place for women.'

The unit is a concrete urn surrounded by a high, wire fence, barbed along its edges. The urn stands in the middle of a cracked cement slab. The door is open. There is a single desk in the large white tiled reception area. A middle-aged woman sits behind the desk, staring into space; in front of her a ledger. Laila asks to see Tomas.

'No, no Europeans here,' she says without moving her gaze.

'Yes, yes, he is here, the hospital told us.'

'No.'

While Laila questions the woman I glance at the ledger and there it is plain to see, Tomas' name. I point to the ledger. 'See, he is here. I am a psychologist appointed by his embassy and I am here to check on the care of this patient.' Before waiting for a reply I walk off down the main corridor. Bold.

The receptionist is so comatose she doesn't question my audacity. Meanwhile Laila blasts her for her attitude, giving me time to reach some offices. I can hear voices in one of the rooms. I knock on the door and a young woman answers it. Repeating my story I ask to see the doctor looking after Tomas. She takes me two doors along. Here another young woman, who explains she is the psychiatrist looking after Tomas, greets me. She removes her veil to talk with me. I again pretend to be the embassy psychologist and this is not disputed.

'*Yanni*, I'm pleased to meet you. This is very strange for us, to have a white man here. People in your community usually look after cases like this, send the patient home. How has this not happened?'

'The arrangements are being made, but with all the trouble in the city …'

'Ach, yes. It's difficult. It would be better if Mr Tomas goes soon. He upsets the other patients. They think he is a ghost.'

'You can discharge him into my care.' I don't want Tomas out of my sight now, there is some undercurrent I don't understand. The puncture wound, it plays on my mind. All I know is that I need to get Tomas somewhere safe.

'Sorry. It's too late.'

She has already sectioned him for his own safety, as he is suicidal. Now it will take a local judge to agree his discharge and the judge only sits in session once a week. At the very least we will have to wait until Wednesday when the next session is scheduled. Even then Salima will need to attend as his next of kin, as he will have to be discharged into her care. How will we ever get him out?

'Don't worry. Maybe, it is best he is here. He says he will kill himself, before they kill him. He needs supervision, all the time. You can't look after him.'

'They?'

'Who knows? Delusions. You agree?'

'Yes. How did he get here?'

'This is very strange too. He came in a taxi. He had nothing, just some riyals in his hand.'

'So he wasn't admitted by the casualty on-call psychiatrist?'

'No, I am afraid we have no such doctor.'

Who was the psychiatrist that Hisham and I spoke to the night before? Who put Tomas in a taxi to get him here and gave him money? Why is everyone denying his existence, even the zombie receptionist? Who wants him hidden away? My mind races; scratch, scratch. The doctor tells me that if someone is in mental distress the best they can hope is that if he arrives at the hospital then the casualty nurses will put him in an ambulance and send him to the psychiatric unit. This is the normal procedure.

'We are alone here, no one cares about these people, they send them and forget.'

She tells me none of the staff have been paid for the last month. The rations for the patients are running low, no fresh vegetables for several days. The staff are bringing in whatever supplies from home they can spare. 'This is the life now. His Highness spends all his time in Europe and does not think of our poor people, our sick. Our whole country, our life, is sick now. We are dying, all dying. I pray to Allah to save us all.'

She leads me to the ward to see Tomas. To access the ward, we are admitted through three sets of locked doors. There are twenty-six male patients on the ward, all housed in small rooms with just a metal bedstead, mattress and blanket, and a small table with a plastic jug and mug. Many of the patients are lying silent and still in their beds, but a few are roaming the corridor and a space at the end of the ward. There are no pictures, no entertainment of any sort, no colour. The patients are dressed in beige thawbs, made from a cheap shiny nylon. They are all painfully thin and those wandering the corridors are moaning. One is running around, waving his arms above him and clucking loudly, his eyes throb. A nurse follows, trying to calm him. The doctor points to two men tied to their beds in one shared cell,

'They've been in there for sixteen years. No one visits.'

The air in the unit is stale, although the unit itself is clean, sterile. My eyes sting. Tomas is in a room at the far end, locked in. The nurse explains he is locked in because he is shouting a lot and disturbing the other patients. As the nurse unlocks the door, he bolts out. His hair is on end and he is dripping sweat. He is dressed in a beige thawb. He has a cut lip. The nurse says he tried to bite another patient, who lashed back. He sees me and stops dead still. He drops to the floor.

'She's come to kill me. Whore. Stop her.'

This pathetic spectacle, my heart rips. How can Tomas believe such terrible things of me? But it is not Tomas. It looks like Tomas, and I have to tell myself my friend is gone from this shell. These words come from his mouth, in his voice still, but they are not his words. How can I make him remember me? How can I bring back the real Tomas?

I bend down to him and try to reassure him that I am trying to help, but he just rocks on the floor. The man who is running around pretending to be a hen runs over and asks Tomas, pointing to the doctor.

'Who is this? Your grandmother?'

Tomas laughs. He gets up and goes back into his room, where he sits on the bed. The doctor says we should leave. I can't bear to go, but I can't bear to stay any longer either. I go into the room to say goodbye.

'Tomas, I'll come back soon. I'll get you out of here.'

He looks up at me, the wild look in his eyes gone. 'No, you mustn't do that. It's safest for me, for you, the only way now.' Quickly he looks away and shouts, 'She's going to kill me. She's going to kill me.'

The nurse hurries me out and locks the door. I'm dazed. Did I really see that?

'Miss, he'll be ok.' He seems like a kindly soul, as do the other nurses who are treating their charges with tenderness. I want to believe him. I tell the doctor I will return later with as much food as I can, and clothes and books for Tomas.

'Thank you. But no books. The patients will eat them.'

☪

I rejoin Laila, who is waiting for me in the foyer. She is circling the moribund receptionist, her steps clap against the concrete. We walk back out to the car. Laila searches in her bag for her keys while I trace the fissures in the cement slab. Gravel chips are caught in the fractures. I bend down to wiggle one free, but it is stuck fast. I have to call Hisham. I shout down the line as there is so much noise at his end.

'Hisham, they're forgotten. They need food. They need help. No one should live like that. Chained to a bed for sixteen years.'

'We must film this, to show our people. They must see the truth of this regime. I will meet you there in an hour.' He rings off.

C·

Laila and I go over to Tomas' villa to pick up some clothes for him. As we drive we hear horns blaring in the distance, and every now and then a plume of black smoke twists about a tower block.

Laila sighs. 'These are the end of our days. This is as Allah said it would be.'

The gates at Tomas' villa are unlocked and clanking back and forth an inch or two, in the odd hot gust of wind. The grounds of the villa are austere. The pool is half empty and the water is green, flies buzz at it. We approach the large wooden doors of the villa. Near the lock there are some scratch marks. I insert the key, but the lock is already turned, I push.

The doors open onto a large hallway, brightly coloured bricks and balls are scattered everywhere. We pick our way across the hall to the kitchen. It is a mess. Drawers and cupboards are open, their contents spewing onto the floor. In the sink is a stack of dirty dishes.

'How could Mr Thomas live like this? He should have a maid to look after him, it would be better for him.' Laila draws her *abaya* close, avoiding the greasy surfaces. From the kitchen we walk through the dining room and main lounge. These rooms are as chaotic, furniture up-ended, drapes on the floor.

'*Wallah*, what has happened here?' I pick up a ragdoll, as I do, my eyes line up with the skirting and I see the telephone sockets are ripped from the walls.

'Let's get what we need and get out of here fast.'

We head again for the psychiatric unit. We filled the car with as much food stuff as we could find at the villa.

'We have to get Tomas out of the country. I don't know what's real any more.' That moment, did I see the real Tomas just then? And if I did ..?

'Hisham will find a way.'

'Those sockets. Did he do that? He said he was being bugged, you know. Or ...'

Laila points across at a building site, a field of rubble. On the far side is one of the main highways. Empty.

'They have closed it. It goes to the border.'

But there is something. We watch. A serrated edge slowly spans the horizon, saws at the sky, severing us from heaven. Tanks.

'From over the border. The Prime Minister must have called for help from our neighbours. Aaii, I'm dying inside, dying!'

As we get closer to the psychiatric unit the streets get more crowded. The last kilometre takes us nearly an hour as we squeeze the car through. At least there are no police here. The bare yard of the unit is now thronging.

'La, what is this?' asks Laila. She winds down the window and speaks to some men in the crowd.

They tell us people are gathering about the unit to protect it. The doctors and nurses have been treating the wounded all afternoon, after the hospital closed its door on the orders of the army. Ambulances are being prevented from reaching the electric souk roundabout and the soldiers are beating the paramedics if they try to approach.

'Oh God, what has happened at the roundabout?'

The army has forgotten about the psychiatric unit. Word has

quickly got round that the doctors and nurses here are ready and willing to help the injured. Battered bodies are turning up in carts, wheelie bins and carried in arms.

'Sister, we have to get Tomas out now, he cannot stay. Who knows what will happen when the army get here.'

I can see patients in the crowd, distinctive in their beige thawbs. They are tearing up sheets for bandages. I text Hisham. *We are here*. Laila calls over one of the nurses and starts to pass him the food we have brought. Men in the crowd help him carry the bags and boxes. Men knock on the windows of the car. The car rocks. We are trapped.

'La, la, stop, stop,' Laila shouts to them, but they are laughing, shouting.

'*Shukran*, Sister of the Revolution.' Praising Allah for the supplies. I am not a Sister of the Revolution. I saw the tanks, I am scared through. When will they get here?

A growing commotion at the main doors of the unit catches the attention of the crowd. They surge towards it. The car steadies. A man, a doctor, I judge by his white coat, emerges from the building. Beside him I recognise Tomas' young psychiatrist. The doctor is bloodied about his head, a deep gash across his crown. Quickly the crowd lifts him up. Someone hands him a loud hailer. 'The regime has broken something inside of me. All of you people have something broken in you.' He places his hand across his heart. 'Today I was at the roundabout. I was treating the wounded in a tent, our Brothers. The army, the government, they did this.' He rubs his hand across his forehead, blood covering his fingers. 'They tore down the tent. They hit me with a metal pole.' The crowd stiffens. 'Brothers, Sisters, you will win your rights and your dignity. What they have done to you will be avenged.' The crowd pitches towards him and roars, 'Victory for the people.'

Through the crowd, behind the doctor, I see him. I clamber out of the car and onto the scorching metal of the bonnet, but I don't care, I barely register the pain. I try to shout, but my voice cannot be heard above the crowd. I wave. He sees me. He pushes through the crowd, pulling a dazed Tomas with him.

'*Hisham.*' We kiss, public.

'*Yallah.*'

Back in the car, we inch our way out of the unit's yard. A helicopter buzzes overhead. Tomas screams.

'They're coming to get me.' He cowers in the back.

A fog descends around the car. Hisham slams off the aircon. 'Cover your faces,' he shouts. The crowd around us scatters away, people choking and scrapping at their eyes, bent double.

forty-two

Laila and I lie in the tent, our bodies torpid; but, our thoughts, prayers and terrors are racing through the drifts of smoke to the tents at the electric souk roundabout. Through the night our ears keen every minute for the rumble of tanks. They are in the suburbs, we hear them crunching over the barricades of dining room chairs, clawing against villa walls. There is no mobile signal, no television. The fighter jets scream over this morning at eleven, our new call to prayers.

☪

Three long days pass. Still there is no Hisham. I want to go to the roundabout, but even if I could get there through the cordons, there are no women in the ranks of the protesters. Still the strict divide. The heat has swelled, now there is hardly any room to breathe. Martial law is in place. Nothing we hold in our hands stays in one piece, dread breaks everything. We have all become splinters, our senses sliced.

Even though there is no news, no pictures, to follow on the

television, we know what is happening. Canisters of news fill our tent, as the canisters of tear gas continue to fill the streets. We keep vinegar to hand.

I want to Skype, call, text Grandaddy and Mammy, but I can't. No line. I feel sick thinking of them on their knees in St.John's, praying, fretting. Grandaddy in his chair, beside the fire, awake all night.

Sami arrives at dusk, his face grimy. He tells us about the events of the days before. The police fired several shots at the funeral of the young student. More protesters were killed, at least five. Rocks were thrown. So, it started, the running battle between the mourners and protesters, and the police. Buildings were set on fire. Then the army came, smashed through the tents at the Electric Souk roundabout. Sami showers and leaves.

'Hisham?' I beg the angels.

Despite the curfew, people nip from house-to-house and mosque-to-mosque to share the latest snippets. The villa murmurs each day with the comings and goings of Laila's relatives. The street fights have staggered on for almost five days, although today we hear that the crowds are thinning. Bread is short; people are worn through. The heat. Forty-three degrees. We are told many people have been shot, and hundreds more hurt. We are getting used to the sound of sirens throughout the night. Today a warship from a neighbouring state anchored off the coast.

Tomas is with the Prof, who has him lightly sedated and confined within his villa. He sends a note, says he is silent, spends his time watching children's DVDs or sleeping. Sami comes at dusk. We don't ask after Hisham, we dare not. He goes. We comfort ourselves that if something terrible has occurred we would by now know, surely. Tomorrow we will hear. *Inshallah*. Always *inshallah*.

Sami returns again today, flat.

'The curfew is to be lifted tomorrow. Government workers are ordered to go back to their offices.'

'This is all? The revolution is over?' Laila asks.

'*Bismillah*.'

'All this blood for nothing.'

☪

Next day we go to work, as ordered. Street sweepers are out. Glaziers measure up. Queues for bread. Life restarts, goes on. The office is quiet, but alert, in every room ears pricked ready to catch the next rumour. We keep our door closed. No one knocks. The morning passes. We go home.

☪

Another day, much the same as the one before. Heat hangs over the city, smothering. The city stays quiet, uneasy. We shuffle papers. Wait for email. Still no lines, no signals. Watch the hours pass on the clock. Go home. Don't sleep.

☪

Now it cracks. First one, then two, then a steady trickle of people drop by our office to ask if we know where Mr Tomas might be. On each enquiry we feign ignorance.

'No more, Laila. I'm tired of this. Let's put a sign on the door saying meeting in progress, do not disturb.' We do this and get an hour's respite.

The door flings open, clipping into the wall.

'Some meeting?' A pop of gum.

'You're back.'

'Mr Brian needs me.'

'Get out.'

'Not until you tell me what's going on with Mr Tomas.'

'Mozah, I'm sure you know as much as I do.'

'Clever, what a clever answer,' Brian steps into the room behind Mozah.

Laila begins to squawk, as she doesn't have her veil on. I push Mozah and Brian out of the room and slam the door shut on them. I turn the lock and lean against the wood. Brian's voice penetrates the door.

'You'll be sorry, Aisling, you'll be very sorry.' Tears roll down my cheeks.

An hour passes. Bang. An explosion, gunfire? I run to the window. A huge crack of lightning slashes up the sky. A few heavy drops pelt the office window. Rain, just rain. The first rain I have seen in the desert. 'Rain, Laila, rain! *Yallah, yallah!*' I grab Laila by the hand and we run down the stairs and out into the car park. I spread my arms out to the heavens. I catch a huge splash in my hand, and then the rain stops, as fast as that. We return to the office. Our mobiles are buzzing in our handbags.

'The network is back!' I answer my phone.

'*Habibti.*' His voice. The line goes dead.

'*Habibi*'. My reply dries on my lips.

☪

The television signal is working. We sit in the tent and watch the news, if you can call it that. Footage shows leading dissidents being arrested, accused of collaborating with foreign insurgents to bring down the regime. Protesters throwing Molotov cocktails are rounded up, they speak with foreign accents, Iraqi, Yemeni, Afghani, Laila tells me. Sami pokes his head into the tent, 'Come quickly, I've got the papers, we need to get them typed and signed and then we are ready.'

'Aaii.'

'Hisham sent these.'

☪

We drive to a far suburb of the city. I don't know where I am. I have never been to this part of the city before. Sami points to a long, low slung building. He tells me it is a police station and that when the papers are ready we have to get them signed there to confirm Tomas, a good German citizen, has no outstanding debts, or rather, Dieter Muller, as Tomas is now to be known, has no outstanding debts. The papers Sami shows me look genuine, but how can I tell? I feel my pulse pick up. I have to do this, be brave. I follow Sami to a series of tiny wooden huts lined up alongside the fence of the police station. The clacking of ancient typewriters can be heard coming from the row of huts. Sami explains that the forms have to be typed and not hand-written.

We enter one of the huts. A sinewy black man is squatting over a typewriter on a wooden crate. He is hitting at keys furiously. He doesn't look up as we enter, but just sticks out his hand. Sami thrusts some notes at him. The man pockets the notes and then sticks out his hand again, Sami hands him the papers. Again he doesn't look up. He just takes the paper he is working on out of the typewriter and instead winds in our papers. I look around the hut. Other than the typewriter and crate there is just the shell of a dented filing cabinet, no drawers. A fan is perched on top of the cabinet. The hut is oven-hot. I stand at the doorway, desperate for air. Sami tells me the airport is opening tomorrow and already long lines of expats are forming at the terminal. Some European governments are due to send emergency planes tomorrow to evacuate their citizens. The plan is to get Tomas on the plane sent by the German authorities. We need these fake papers.

Ten minutes later and we have our forms.

'Here, take these. You go into the police station, turn left, and give them the papers for signing.'

'You're not coming with me?'

'I can't come in. They'll be suspicious, ask questions.'

'But I don't speak enough Arabic.'

'They speak English. You'll be fine.'

'I can't do this.' I have to.

Sami hands me a fake ID card. It has my photo. I am now Anja Muller, the wife of Dieter Muller.

'I need a wedding ring.'

'*Wallah*! I didn't think of that.'

I take the ring Laila gave me and turn its stone into my palm. I walk into the police station. A small queue of four expat men are waiting for the two officers at the booths to call them. The ceiling is low and the aircon gurgles, it's not working properly. The stench of middle-aged male body odour drenches the room. One of the officers looks up as I join the queue. He says something to the man in front of him, who immediately steps aside. He waves me over, I walk past the queue, one of the men mutters. The officer signals to me to give him the papers. It is uncomfortable queue jumping like this, but it is the norm for women to be given preferential treatment everywhere.

'ID please, Madam.'

The card is acid in my hand. I pass it over. He smiles and then starts jabbing at buttons on his computer. My breath is shallow and I concentrate hard not to shake visibly. I stand statue. Occasionally the officer looks up at me. Each time I smile weakly. The stone in my ring is pressing into my palm. Every now and again he frowns and peers at the screen. Whenever this happens I am sure he is about to tell me he knows the papers are false. Finally, with a resounding clunk of the official stamp, he hands me back the papers. I look at them, unable to believe we have pulled it off. The officer looks up at me, brushes me on.

☪

Through the open flap of the tent Laila and I watch plane after plane circle over our heads.

'Do you wish you were on one of those airplanes, Sister? This life, our life, is broken. I'm afraid all the time. You must want to be back with your family and friends.'

My family and friends. In the brief moments the network is back up I text home to say I am 'fine', 'don't worry', 'no trouble near me', and 'it must look worse on TV than it is.' Please let Grandaddy sleep now. The British and Irish governments have yet to charter any flights. The tanks are on the streets, there will be no more trouble. Hold tight, is the official advice.

'This is my life now. You, Hisham, are my family too.' We lock our arms together, and look back to the sky. On one of those flights Tomas is on his way out.

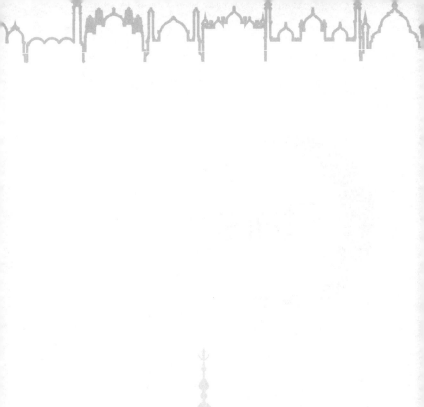

Stars

forty-three

The streets have been quiet for weeks, but still we all listen for the crack of gunfire. No one believes the trouble is over yet; it is there, smouldering behind the darkened windows, in the shadowy cafes of the souk. The sunny mummies have gone and the pools in the villa compounds are drained. The airport car park is full of abandoned cars, buried in thick dust. Those expats who have stayed still go to the Celestine on Friday for brunch, but only a trickle of champagne flows; everyone wants to keep a clear head. They have a case packed by the front door. Brian and the Rex thugs have retreated to London, along with many of the minor Royals. We see the Royals in the newspapers at Ascot, Wimbledon and garden parties; convincing the world all is well; just a blip, keep investing. The local newspapers are reduced to a few pages of these photos and advertisements.

I tune to the BBC World Service; as the Jasmine Spring becomes summer, fetid with the death of thousands. Those early hopes of a people's revolution sweeping liberation across North Africa and into Arabia are crushed as brutal civil war erupts in one country after another, and there is no end in sight to the bloodshed and chaos. NATO bombard Libya, in Yemen there is an assasination attempt on President Saleh, and the country rises up in Syria but Assad's forces attack with chemical weapons. Humanity blisters.

After the streets hushed, Hisham returned. He was bruised, limping, a blackened eye. He would not speak of what had happened. Now, he is at the villa very little. Since the riots he will not use his phone. He has a new one, he will not share its number with us, safer for us not to use it, he says. Every day we hear murmurs of another activist arrested. Hisham comes even less. His eyes are distant, lit by the fires in Syria, Libya and Yemen. We are worried sick by his increasing involvement with the rebel cause. Laila's sisters accuse Hisham of recklessness, it is not just his neck he risks but the whole extended family. Vengeance here is never just an eye for an eye; the regime, the Royals will want the whole body, every sinuous tendon. Laila pleads with him, when we do see him, to come home, come back to our tent. They quarrel, sometimes bitterly. I try to stop them.

'Keep out of this Aisling. I will not fight with you as well as her.'
Laila curls up amongst the cushions on the tent floor.

'But look, you are making her cry.'

'You take her side?'

'No, no.'

'My family should stand with me, stand with the people.'

'She is scared. Scared for the family, for you. I am too.'

'You are stronger than this.'

'Hisham, it's only natural, for God's sake.'

'The Irish people, your family, fought for many years for their freedom. Are you of their blood?'

'How dare you!'

'Allah tells us to be strong, brave. He will protect. *Allah Akbar*.'

Where once we talked for hours, now our talk is trimmed; he cuts me to a word with his rallying call to his God.

Laila stands, pulls me away. I go from the tent and into the villa. I shower off our anger. I sit before the mirror, in an emerald silk wrap, one Hisham gave me weeks back.

'The colour of home,' I said as I thanked him.

'The holy colour,' he replied.

I towel dry my hair, its lustre has dulled, stripped brittle by the desert. The door opens and Hisham enters, he crosses to me and takes a damp strand, curls it around his fingers.

'Come with me to the village.'

We go.

☪

Hisham lights a fire by the shore as I dip in the thermal water of the sea. We have made love, urgently but not spoken. We didn't talk all the way here. As we drove, he took one call on his mobile after another, growing more agitated with each. After the last call, he slapped the dashboard,

'We will cut off their heads,' he yells.

'Hisham?'

But he ignored me, dialing a comrade.

He waves me to return to the beach, the mint tea boiled. I step out of the water, pick the silk wrap up and tie it about me again, but he rips it from me and, pacing out into the waves, scrunches it up and throws it.

'What are you doing?'

The wrap slinks beneath the ripples. I scramble for a bathing towel and cover myself fast. I don't like how his eyes mock my nakedness.

'I can only think of your home when you wear it. How you will go back there.'

'Hisham, I am here with you.'

'You will go.'

'I will go! You are the one who has left.'

'What do you mean?'

'I don't know you any more. The Hisham I knew has gone. Once you talked of justice; ending poverty, repression. Now, it's blood, killing…'

'I thought you loved me. You understood, were with us, with me, you didn't think like them.'

'Them?'

'Westerners.' He spits, '*Kaffar.*'

A kick in the stomach would have winded me less.

'How can you use that word with me? This revolution, you've changed, so hard.'

'*Mounia …*'

'No, don't call me that any more. Dream … this is no dream. You pick fights with me to push me away. It is you who doesn't love me, you only love to fight.'

I stoop down to put on my sandals, hiding my lips, their tremble, 'Take me back.' He stamps out the fire.

forty-four

As dusk falls we hear the cannons fire, the scholars have squinted at the pearly disc, plotted its arc through a million supplications and signaled the first night of Ramadan. I haven't spoken with Hisham since that last night at the abandoned village. That was nine days ago; I count every day. I unthread.

When Hisham has appeared during these last nine days, it has been in the small hours of the night, his visits are fleeting and the family instantly surrounds him. I am out at the edge; with no legitimate place in his life, no claim to his attention at these times. It is so hard to see him, to be so close, just a few feet away, and yet be nothing more than a dropped stitch in the tent.

The villa is a hubbub of children tonight, all getting ready to go to mosque to celebrate the first night of Ramadan. In the melee, I miss Hisham. Every now and then I catch sight of him surrounded by little nephews, throwing one up in the air and catching him. But he slips from room to room before I can reach him, back to the men's quarters. This is family time, holy time.

I retreat to the tent. Just before the family leave for mosque, Laila comes in to find me.

'All will be well now. This is our special time to pray and be close to Allah. This is a peaceful time. No one will do anything bad during Ramadan.'

The family return from mosque, but Hisham is not with them. I hoped he would forget his anger with me tonight; we would celebrate Ramadan together. I leave the family to their festivities and go to the tent; I need to sleep. My dreams distort with the screams of ghosts chained to beds, blood spilling through the streets, filling the Bay. That weight, pressing me to the rock, my ribs breaking. Sour breath, I can taste it. My stomach cramps, wakes me.

I get up, the night is silent. The family have gone to bed. I pace once more about the yard, lit in stark strips by the neons of the street tailor shack next door. The gate opens. I know every line of the silhouette. I cross to *him*.

I remember his touch, I reach out, yearn. He catches my hands and holds me back. We are in stasis for a moment. I walk away from him, desolate as the pole star.

As I reach the tent, I turn back to him. He is standing by the gate watching me. 'I am with you, Hisham.' The gate closes behind him.

☪

I like the stillness of the Ramadan day. Mostly, everywhere is shut-up and asleep. A balm for the city. Life at work is slow, quiet. Many people have taken leave and those who are left, mainly slump at their desks. I am as apathetic as my colleagues, we all have headaches from fasting. I am fasting as well, in respect of my hosts; but I barely notice my physical hunger. The first few days of the fast are always like this, always hard they say, then it dulls.

It isn't the same for my fast though, for me the pain does not ease over time, it sharpens.

At night the world leaps awake, like hail bouncing on parched land. The neon is more dazzling, the traffic reckless, parties feverish; all the more so this year, Laila tells me. Each night we break Iftar with a magnificent feast of dishes and the by now inevitable macaroni cheese. Each night there are grand Iftar parties in massive tents at the luxury hotels. Have we all forgotten these last few weeks? Conscious amnesia, the only way to go on.

☪

After tonight's Iftar Sami hands me a memory stick. We are alone in the tent. He has sent Laila into the villa, saying her mother needs her. 'Hisham asks if you will send the files on this stick to the western media, you have the contacts?'

'Can't I do more than this?'

'Guns, mortars, tanks. These things destroy, so no one will remember. What we need is words, words that will record this butchery, forever.' Sami pauses, 'You must be clever, send them from a computer that cannot be traced to you, to us.'

'Ok.'

Hisham needs me.

I'm a step closer to him.

☪

After work I go to the Celestine. There are a few kiosks with free internet. Two children are playing games on one of the computers, there is no one else. I attach the memory stick. I know the face immediately, despite the swollen, purple cheeks and the torn eyebrow. It is the young psychiatrist who was in charge of Tomas' care at the psychiatric unit. I click through the images. Doctors, nurses, patients, all the same, battered. Bullet holes riddle the walls of the wards behind them. Broken furniture, smears of blood on the paintwork. My chest is tight. I return to the young doctor. I want to see her kind eyes, but I cannot. Her eyelids are red and puffy. I have cried so much in this country but as I look at the ravaged sight of this beautiful, gentle doctor I have no tears left.

My hands do not shake today as I set up a fake email account. I read the testimonials.

Today we received reports that our Sister, Dr Saraa, has been tortured under the orders of the The Prime Minister's cousin Sheikha Hana, a senior official in the Palace police. Saraa is a psychiatric doctor. She was arrested during the first week of the protests in the psychiatric unit. No one has seen her since. The Sheikha watched while her officers applied electric shocks to Saraa's face, spat in her mouth and beat her.

Six twitter users were today each sentenced in a closed court to a year in prison for comments deemed insulting to our Royal Family. We recall that Esmat Al Mosawi, a veteran journalist, recently tweeted: 'I got sacked from my work for demanding democracy and I have never thought that 140 characters on Twitter will give me so much more liberty to express my views than a full column on a government censored newspapers.'

For more than twenty days eleven-year-old Abdul has been imprisoned. He was picked up with eight other youngsters playing in the street and detained under the laws preventing 'illegal gatherings' in the street. Brothers, these are our children!

I load the press release.

'Attention: News Editors

Our hospitals are places to be feared. Our doctors and nurses are being targeted because they have evidence of atrocities committed by the authorities, security forces and riot police. The military has taken over the hospital, psychiatric unit and many health centres. Soldiers and police conduct interrogations and detentions inside the health facilities. Protestors are arrested if they seek treatment. At least thirty-two healthcare professionals have been detained since martial law was declared. Their families do not know where they are held and are denied any contact. Physicians, medical staff and patients have been attacked with weapons, beatings and tear gas. These attacks violate the principle of medical neutrality and are grave breaches of international law.

We call on the United Nations to prosecute.'

My hand cannot waver; I hit the send button.

☪

I return to the villa. It is empty, as the family has gone to the mosque. I go into the tent. He is sitting on the floor. I sit down. He says nothing, does not move.

'I know, you can't leave, Hisham. You can't love me now.'

'Would you believe me if I said I did?'

I want to say yes, but I hesitate and before I can answer he says, 'You're not ready to trust me. Not ready to trust yourself that you can be loved.'

☪

It is the last day of Ramadan, a month of fasting has passed.

Laila bursts into the tent excited. 'Tonight we have a great treat.' She will not say more, and the sisters tease me.

I try hard to feign delight, but I don't want to leave the tent.

Sometimes I think I can still just catch his frankincense in the fabric of the cushions and drapes. The girls dress me in my beautiful red silk gown, plait small white jasmine blossoms in my hair and wind sparkling, jangling bangles around my arms. They are all dressed like exotic birds in silks and feathers. The night air is heavy with oud perfume as they fragrance our hair.

Fairy lights of every colour bob from the palm trees that line the road to the Celestine. We have come to the grandest Iftar party of them all. The girls are so high-spirited. Two colossal marquees have been erected in the forecourt, one for the women and the other for the men. As we enter the women's tent we are swept through a narrow pathway between two sand dunes. Through the dunes we are in a magical tropical land, with birds of paradise flowers and a thousand tiny stars in the canopy. Drumming can just be heard above the excitement of the women, clacking their tongues and chattering. The pounding becomes stronger, the rhythm inescapable. The lights go out, the room hushes, and a single spotlight trains across the marquee and lights a figure on the stage. A voice as old as time, and with the regret of a thousand wars, soars through the darkness. The room is still; rapture. The woman sings for all infinity. She is a grand, handsome woman, vast, weighed down with heavy gold chains and a towering turban. I close my eyes, a tear drops. Hisham is in the men's tent.

The beat changes. The women clap and then cover their exotic dresses under their *abayas*. Veils are replaced. Laila shakes a pashmina about my shoulders as a man dressed in a brightly striped robe leaps onto the stage. He whizzes around and around like a spinning top, holding a fist of streamers above his head. He runs ever faster, his robe spread out around him in a circle. The heat in the marquee spikes and disco lights swing and lurch.

I slip out to the quiet and dark of the forecourt, shaking the shawl off to feel a tiny quiver of breeze. I find a scrubby patch of grass and sit down for a while trying to rattle the dervish from my mind. A tank is parked across the forecourt. I look across to the men's tent, I can see a small knot of men sitting outside, smoking. I think I see Hisham there. He is laughing and jostling with his companions. I come from a tiny village by a grey ocean. He only knows a lunar slither of me. We exist only in the moments when I lie in his arms, and when we split apart… our Iftar, break…fast…

I return to the marquee. The feasting is underway. One of Laila's older sisters calls to me as I approach the table.

'Ah, there you are Sister. Laila is trying to find you. We want you to meet someone special to our family.' She ushers forward a tall, cool beauty. She mumbles something to Laila's sister,

'You must excuse her, she doesn't speak much English.'

'I'm sure her English is no worse than my little Arabic.'

Laila's sister translates and the hint of a smile shimmers on the girl's elegant, long face. 'But la, I haven't introduced you. This is Nabeela, she will be our dear brother Hisham's wife.'

The girl kisses me distantly. I whisper my congratulations. '*Mabruk*.'

A wave of nausea sweeps me. One of the sisters pulls me to a seat.

'*Shufi*, look the great Rana is back and is going to sing.' The great Rana is formidable but, as the lights dim, she sings with the frailty of all our broken hopes.

forty-five

Cannon fire signals the end of Ramadan. Before we break for Eid, Sheikh Fariq announces that he is going to restructure the Board and he is calling in experts from London to help him with this task. They will arrive imminently. Blackheath & Company. Mozah strides into my office, two secretaries clutching notepads in her wake.

'Here, I want the desk moved, and a filing cabinet there.'

She completely ignores me. Laila says something to the two secretaries and they giggle nervously.

'Mozah, what are you doing?'

She continues as if she hasn't heard me. 'They will want a big round table over here for meetings. Get rid of the plants.'

'Mozah, I'm asking you again, what's going on here?'

She smirks. 'Sheikh Fariq wants this office for his new restructuring team. They move in after Eid.' She picks up Laila's little sparkly ornaments on our coffee and sweets table. She tosses them in the bin, 'And get rid of all this trash.'

'How dare you? Who gives you the permission to act like this?' Laila hisses.

'You're being reassigned. You're going to be a secretary in the Works department.' She leaves.

'*Wallah*! Is this true do you think?'

'I have a bad feeling about this Laila. I think I can guess who this new team might be.'

I nip down to the office, which was once Tomas' and now is home to the Prof. I want to ask him about this new team. No one questions where Tomas is these days. There is an uncharacteristic silence on the matter, as if everyone wants to deny Tomas ever existed. The Prof is just finishing a call as I walk in.

'I have to go Aisling. An overseas delegation is transiting through the airport on their way East. I must go and greet them. I'll see you after Eid.' He places his hand on his heart and leaves. The room, the building, everything is desolate.

I wander back out to the corridor. I don't know what I am doing here anymore. I want to feel the cold wind on my face. I want be in the cafe by the Liffey, sipping hot chocolate, warming my hands on the mug. I want to look out and see the Mary Street traders, with their rackety old silver cross prams bouncing with bananas and fags, chased by a bored Garda. I miss the scudding clouds, I want to be able to skim life.

☪

'Sure enough.' I speak out loud to myself. Laila isn't with me today. She hasn't returned after Eid, but has gone off sick in protest at her re-assignment to the Works department. My office key no longer turns in the lock and outside the door is a bin bag full of my remaining files and papers, those that survived the shredding. I leave the bags where they are and go to camp out in the Prof's office. He isn't there. I sit and wait.

'So this is where we are hiding, is it?' Brian walks in carrying a bin bag, which he throws on the floor. Papers spill out. 'Our new restructuring expert, I presume?' My laugh is bitter.

'I gave you your chance, Aisling. You could have been top-dog in the Sheikh's office by now, instead, here you are, a miserable mongrel we have no use for.'

I raise my hand. No, don't make it easy for him. Breathe. He takes a step closer to me, his eyes goad.

A tea boy hurries into the room. 'Mr Brian sir, Sheikh Fariq is calling for you, please come now.'

'Maybe I'll make you my filing clerk, yah.'

I type up my resignation letter and wait for the Prof to appear. I don't want to go to Sheikh Fariq's office alone, I need some moral support. I wait all day. No show, I go to the mall.

☪

'It's time. I must go home now.' I lean against the hood of the phone booth in the mall. 'I've just had enough, Patrick. I've written my resignation letter. I'll give it in tomorrow, before they fire me. It's coming, I'm sure. I won't give them the satisfaction.'

'Well, now that's a fine plan, but they might not accept it, you know. You signed a three year contract.'

'Surely I can give notice?'

'You can try; just don't hold your breath. A contract is a contract out here, no notice period.'

'Fariq, Brian, they can keep me here?' This is a worse scenario than being fired, deported. He will keep me, I realize. This is why it hasn't happened yet. It's not going to. Three years of contracted torment.

'You have to get me out, Patrick.'

'We've been a little busy lately. I'm working on it.'

I rip up my resignation letter. He won't have the pleasure of declining it. Laughing at me.

☾

I sit alone at the desk in the Prof's office. I have no work to do, almost a week has passed since Rex returned and I ripped up my resignation letter. Grandaddy has finally mastered the Skype, detecting the soft note of despair in my voice at the other end of the phone line. I cannot explain any of this to him; he knows, he tells me about Father Brendan's gout, the dog stealing washing off the rotaries about the village, the hurling score, and Mammy's latest batch of stone scones.

'Jesus, the only woman who can't bake a scone in Ireland, and in my house.'

I feel sick all the time, and exhausted. I just stare into space. Every now and again a couple of *nikab*-clad women poke their heads around the door. The faceless watch me, no one pretends anymore. A few paces along from the office a man sits on a stool all day, brooding. If I leave the office for any reason he follows me wherever I go, even waiting outside the female bathrooms for me. One time I hiss at him as I walk past, Laila-style, but his expression does not change. Where is the Prof? He hasn't returned to the office after Eid. I try calling his mobile, but it is switched off.

The office door opens. I don't bother to look up. I know it will be one of my minders, but someone comes in. Dr Mouna. Although she is fully veiled I recognize her. I realise at this moment, when everything feels so out of tune, how in tune I have become with this hidden world. I can recognize my friends, Laila, her sisters, the princesses, Dr Mouna, all veiled. I know their individual gaits, steps, postures. I work with my intuition, it has switched on like another sense, as habitual, more so than the other five.

'Sister Aisling. I will speak quickly, *yanni*.'

'You'll get into trouble.'

'Tch. Allah protects me. I answer only to him. *Yanni*, Aisling. This is serious, my dear, the National Audit Board is preparing a case, a very big case. Financial mismanagement, maybe worse, criminal charges. The state auditors will come soon and start interviewing staff. Arrests will happen. If you can go now Sister, go and don't delay. Find a way.'

'But, I haven't done anything.'

'No, but you could be a witness. They'll keep you here for many years. Our courts are slow. You're here alone. It'll be hard for you. Who knows how a case can turn, and a witness can become the accused.'

'The Professor?'

'Take care, my dear.' She leaves.

☾

Straight from work after this warning, I go to the mall again. Find a phone. Call Patrick.

'It's not easy Aisling. I need a few more days.' I hear the catch in his voice, he is trying to sound calm.

'I don't think I have a few more days.'

☾

Laila comes back late from a party at Nabeela's villa. The sisters are all full of the news that Hisham and Nabeela will marry within the month. Tomorrow the builders arrive to refashion a suite of rooms in the family villa for the newly weds. Laila is vexed by this, as it means she will lose one of her rooms. 'Where will we sit in the evening now in winter, when it is too cold to be in the tent?'

'Laila, my room will be free soon,' I am hardly able to say the words.

'What do you mean?'

'I think I have to go home now.' I have to protect *us*.

'No, no, how can you say this? This is your home now, here with us, you are my Sister now.'

'I have to go.'

'You cannot leave me. Is this because of Nabeela? She'll be the first wife. But Hisham loves you.'

'You think? He has forgotten me.' Second choice, once more. My heart can't even register this pain, this time. All I can think now is of going.

'No. Trust me, I know my brother.'

'But Laila, even so, I have no choice.'

I tell her of Dr Mouna's caution.

'Stay here.'

She leaves the room, coming back moments later with Hisham. I didn't realise he is at the villa, he never comes to greet me anymore.

He mumbles an acknowledgment to me, but looks only at the floor.

'Tell Hisham,' says Laila.

I repeat the warning. Hisham sits down heavily and leans back, looking heavenward,

'I wish you hadn't told me this.' A dart of fear pierces me. 'We can't ignore this. It's not safe. She's right, she has to go.'

'Brother, how can you say this?'

'She brings attention to our family. I don't need this. I've more important concerns.'

He jumps up. 'We'll help. No, Laila, we will. She goes. I'll get you papers, like Tomas.' One of the little nephews clatters into the room, crying that his brother has hit him. Laila picks him up and hustles out of the room.

'Hisham …'

'I can't say the words to you that you want to hear, Aisling.'

He looks at me. At last.

'I can't.'

forty-six

I don't want to be here, but Hisham insisted.

'Go to work tomorrow, give them no reason to think you know anything.'

No one speaks to me. My email flickers on and off, some messages come and go without my touching a key. They want me to know they are watching. You are ours.

I can't keep still, and stand up from the desk every few minutes to pace the office. Smoke creeps into the room. I look out of the window. There is a skip below and I can see tea boys throwing in bags of papers and files.

'I can't.' It scratches round and round in my head.

༄

After work I take a taxi to the Bay and board a water taxi to cross to the other side. I need to be at sea, away from the battalions of skyscrapers and the traffic growling about them. No one really uses these battered wooden water taxi; just the odd tourist. I pay to go back and forth across the Bay twice, much to the bewilderment of the ticket boy. But in the end he just chews on some khat while I sit huddled at the back, numb. Fear has a taste, it is metallic, every swallow, razor sharp. I ask the boy if I can borrow his phone. I say mine has run out of battery. I stuff some notes in his hand. I ring Patrick and tell him I am getting some papers.

'If I can get to the border, can you meet me on the other side?'

'This Hisham guy, can you trust him?'

'I think so … '

'Grand. Just let me know when.'

'Patrick, I've got too close. To everything.'

☪

Later, Hisham takes me to the souk. His contact needs to take a passport photo of me. The souk is silent, many of the stalls are bordered up. No shisha hangs in the air tonight, just the reek of cat urine.

'Where is everyone?'

'Home, waiting.'

'Waiting?'

'They arrested the foreign journalists today.'

'So the world doesn't see what comes next.'

'Tonight there will be raids. Tomorrow the doctors and nurses in prison are going on hunger strike.'

'I'm sorry, I'm getting in the way.'

'Come, we need to be quick. I have a meeting tonight. We're organising a general strike. Twenty thousand government workers will walk out later this week at our signal. The Rage awakens.'

☪

Next day. Fifty degrees. The planet is melting away. The morning is gristly and my mobile has started whistling whenever I try to use it. I want to know that Hisham is safe after last night's raids, but I dare not call, text. The phone in the office and the computer are gone. One of the princesses comes to the office bearing a plate of cupcakes. My minder follows her into the room.

'Sister Aisling, it's my birthday, so we should celebrate.' She shoos the minder out.

'What did you say to him?'

'I told him I wanted to eat cake with you and remove my veil and he can't see me, it is *haram*. Now start eating cake, we won't have long before he brings one of those *djinn* to spy on us.' I pick at a glittering cupcake.

'We're angry. Sheikh Fariq's a bad man. He's sent many people home, told them not to come back. His men are here now. But they'll not work. What do they care about the health of the people? They're here to sit in offices, read newspapers and smoke. It is shameful. Mr Brian's going around the office and ordering the computers and telephones be taken out. Who is this man? He's wicked. We don't like how you are being treated, like a prisoner, Miss Aisling. We think they'll terminate you soon. If they do, don't fear, we'll all leave early and no one will mock you, not like the others.'

Tears smart my eyes, 'You shouldn't be in here talking to me.'

The princess laughs, '*Yanni*, not me, they can't touch me. My family is a noble, we are cousins to His Highness, don't be afraid for me.' She kisses me. 'And now, these are the days to be brave, to speak. Today a poet was put in prison. What is this regime? To be afraid of a poet.'

I can hear footsteps along the corridor. I look to the door.

'I must tell you. The talk. The Professor has been arrested. He's in a prison in the desert.'

The door opens and in walk my two veiled watchers. An angry exchange breaks out between the women and my princess flounces out, screaming and throwing a cupcake at one of them. This woman spits at me.

☾

An hour passes. Yusef comes to my office and barks, 'Come with me Miss Aisling, this minute.'

My feet barely register on the marble floor as he marches me to Sheikh Fariq's office. The door to the office is open. I can see Sheikh Fariq sitting one side of the vast oil slick desk, looking at some papers. On the other side are Brian and Mozah, with an empty chair between them. Yusef calls out to Sheikh Fariq. He looks up and waves me in, pointing to the chair. I sit down. Mozah and Brian slaver.

'Miss Aisling, tell me where is the Professor?' Fariq's voice, harsh.

'I don't know.' I am determined to say very little, I am afraid my voice will waver, give me away.

'Mm. Where are the Professor's files?'

'I don't know.'

'You don't know much, do you? Why don't you know? You're the Professor's assistant. You're in charge of those files.'

'No, his office manager is in charge of his files.' Sheikh Fariq looks over to Mozah. She chews her lip, no gum today.

'Miss Mozah is that true? You have been examining how the Professor organises his office.'

'I understand that Miss Aisling, unofficially, managed the office for the Professor.' She emphasizes the 'unofficially'.

I open my mouth to reply, but before I can, Brian butts in.

'Some twenty confidential files appear to be missing, Sheikh Fariq. Miss Aisling moved a number of bags of files out of the office I am now occupying.'

I glare at Brian, but he just stares steadfastly ahead at the Sheikh.

'This is unwelcome news Mr Brian. As you know the National Audit Board are coming to look over the Professor's files. I don't know what they'll say when we tell them that the files are missing.' Brian draws breath in over his feral teeth. 'It will be vital evidence that's missing,' he pauses 'tampered with.' Now he turns to look at me. 'Miss Aisling should really try to recall what she did with those files.' The Sheikh continues, 'It's a bad situation, isn't it? And these complaints as well.' He points to some papers on the desk. 'Why is it that all the directors complain that you write secret reports about them for the Professor? Really, they think you are a spy, a troublemaker and none of them like you. They call for you to be terminated. See here, I have a letter of complaint, signed by them all.'

Brian takes the letter and places it in my lap. Dr Mouna's signature is at the top. I try not to let any emotion flick across my face. I know Dr Mouna and the others must have been made to sign, but it still stings to see those signatures. No one can support me now. Sheikh Fariq stands up and holds up a pile of cuttings from Arabic newspapers. 'Do you know what these are?' I shake my head. He throws them at me, they explode about me like a crowd of dirty pigeons. 'Lies. Foreign lies. Saying we have beaten, tortured, killed our brothers and sisters, our doctors, our nurses. Made up stories and actors in make-up, pretending to have injuries.'

A soft Scottish voice behind me, 'Where did they come from Aisling, Finn? Who gave out these facts?' He places both his hands on my shoulders, close to my neckline. His fingers claw at my collarbone. I stand up to leave, enough.

The Sheikh shouts, 'Sit down Miss Aisling, I did not say you could leave.' Mozah grips my wrist and pulls me back into my chair.

Brian continues, 'I also regret to inform you Sheikh that Miss Aisling is known to try to influence the girls in the office with her anti-government propaganda.' Mozah digs her nails in. I purse my lips tight. 'As you know Miss Aisling vacated her generously provided government apartment and is rumoured to be living with a known insurgent and his sister. CID are on their way to pick up these conspirators.'

Oh God, Hisham, Laila.

'This is a very serious charge, Miss Aisling. I will need to discuss this tonight with my colleagues in the CID. I expect they'll issue a warrant for your arrest. I want a written statement from you by tomorrow morning explaining where the Professor's files are, what's in those files and details about the insurgents and foreign agents you collude with. You will write down the names of the girls in this office who have helped you. Tomorrow morning you will bring your statement to me at eight o'clock and I'll decide what we should do with you.'

I sit still, unable to take in these accusations and threats. Sheikh Fariq slams his prayer beads down on the glass table, they crack against the glass like a gun shot, 'Go.'

I run from the room. Yusef and his coffee cronies watch me. Yusef whistles slightly. I run back along the corridors, snatching for breath. I trip over the legs of my minder, who is slumbering on his stool. He swears as I slam my office door shut. The tears are unstoppable. I try to call Laila, but the phone whistles and clicks. I can't stop shaking. Why have they let me go? Why did they not arrest me here and now? What game is this? Laila? Hisham? I look out on the skip of ashes.

The villa is deserted when I finally reach it. It's taken me ages to get a taxi and get here. I run through the rooms, calling for Laila and Hisham. No reply. Where is everyone? Please don't let CID have been here already. I go out to the tent. I touch the door flap, ready to push it aside, but I can't go in. I sink my head into the folds. I smell smoke, cigarette smoke. I push open the flap. It is dim inside, but I can see a figure sat on the far side, as he always is.

'Hisham.'

'Aisling, girl.'

'You.'

'I thought you might need some help writing your work of fiction tonight.'

'Where are the family? Where's Laila? Hisham?'

'You need time to think, alone. That's why we gave you tonight. To really think. The night is long.'

'I intend to have a good night's sleep.'

'I advise you to write the report. We will have the names.'

'Never.'

'I could offer you a reprieve. Give me the names and you can choose one to spare. Now which will you choose, the sister or the brother?'

I will not answer.

'Ha! You are tempted.'

'Drop dead.'

'The Sheikh will expect his report first thing tomorrow morning. On the desk. Of course, we could put something else on the desk for him, yah.'

'Enough of these games, Brian.'

He throws a packet at me. 'What's this?'

'Funny, I was going to ask you the same thing, girl. It's a passport and an exit visa for a Mary Doyle, with your photo. So are you Mary or Aisling? Or maybe you'd prefer an Arabic name now? Mounia perhaps?

'Bastard! And who are you Brian? What are you?'

'Sharp one like you and you haven't worked it out yet? I'm just a gun for hire.'

'A mercenary.Here?'

'The game's up. I admit, not as much fun to be had here as we had in Iraq, but it's early days and there's great money to be made from civil unrest, once you've stirred it up. And the game's up for you too, Aisling. Why do you think no one's here? You've been betrayed.'

He stands up, comes over to me. He pulls a pack of cigarettes from his pocket and lights one, his teeth flash, takes a long drag, and exhales the smoke.

Betrayed. I won't believe it. Lies. The darkness will not creep in.

'Want one?'

But those turned-down eyes, was there guilt in your eyes, Hisham? Is that what you didn't want me to see? I cannot, I cannot. Scratch.

'White skin. It's a novelty at first, but they always go back to their own. And they'll do anything to protect the family.'

His laugh, a snarl. He rises, comes towards me.

'I'm your only friend now.'

He lunges to kiss me. I bite his lip hard.

His fist knocks me back through the flap into the yard. I fall heavily on my hip, my ribs. My head crunches on the grit. I shield my stomach, curl over, fearing his boot. His shadow, above me in the yard; his arm strikes dark across the blazing orb.

Running footsteps towards me.

'Sister!'

'Habibti!'

My eyes won't open. I open my mouth, no sound comes out. I think I hear a shout, a scream. Thud. The blood runs thick in my head, my ears. The pain sears. I feel hands on my body. I am being pulled up. I try again to open my eyes. I see him.

'Hisham.'

He is half carrying me. Other hands hold me up. Laila.

'Stop, stop, let me breathe.'

'We have to go.'

'Laila, hold her. I'll get the car.'

'Quick, they will come. They'll come.'

My eyes focus. 'Laila, you're safe. I thought you'd been arrested. Where were you?'

'At Nabeela's, a family gathering, for the wedding plans.'

'CID, Sheikh Fariq …'

'We know. Yusef called me. We came as soon as we heard.'

'Yusef?'

'You have friends, Sister.'

'Brian, oh God.' I am facing the gate. I try to turn around. Laila holds me tight.

'Where is he?'

'Don't look, don't look.'

I struggle with her, I see the pool of blood beyond her shoulder. His body prostrate in the yard. His guts in the dust.

☾

We drive south on the highway. A long convoy of army vehicles heads north, to the city. A flare gashes the sky.

'Rockets.' The sand *djinn* will have her due. We turn off the highway, pass small desert towns. Lights out.

I can see the shoreline, just darkness beyond, no moon tonight.

'Mr Patrick will meet you on the other side. I called him' says Laila.

We see a hut. 'Here, we are here.'

We get out of the car and walk to the edge of the sea. My ribs ache, my jaw throbs. I can see a tiny rowing boat. Hisham goes into the hut, brings out some oars and a lantern. He wades out, pulls the little boat closer. It's a wreck. He throws the oars in. Laila passes him a white pashmina.

'Come.'

He hands me up and in. Pushes the boat out a bit.

'Hisham.'

He is hugging Laila on the shore. She moves away from the waterline.

'Laila.' I call to her. Her back is to me. Hisham wades to the boat. He clambers in.

'It's too old. It will only take the weight of two,' he says.

'But then take Laila first and come back for me.'

'This boat has one last time if Allah pleases, then it will be finished. I can't risk it. I have to take you.'

'Sister.' I call again. She turns, wavers, runs into the water. My arms are round her.

'Aisling, Sister, my true Sister.'

She lets me go, steps back.

Hisham pulls away sharply on the oars. Laila stands in the water, a tiny star, swallowed by the night.

When we can no longer see her, Hisham weeps. I stroke his hands as he rows onwards. 'They'll kill her. An eye for an eye.'

'Hisham, we have to go back, we have to fetch her or I have to stay.'

He will not answer and continues to row. I try to wrestle the oar off him, but he pushes me back. Occasionally, he rests his arms and when he does he takes my hands.

After a time I can see the shoreline, Hisham lights a lantern. Now I can see the headlights of a car.

'You made it then, you do realise I missed the big match tonight.' Patrick helps me out of the boat.

'You may need this, Fariq will not honour borders.' Hisham hands me the shawl.

It is wrapped around something. I unfold it; I can smell Laila's jasmine perfume. There is a slim, handbag gun.

'Hisham?'

'I can't leave her. Laila and I will face our fates together.'

'Hisham.'

Patrick tries to hold me back while Hisham pulls away in the boat, but I tear free and run out into the sea. The water is about my waist when I catch his oar. I reach across the boat and clasp his hand.

'Hisham, I ...'

He cries, 'I know you do. And me ... *habibti*.'

I don't need those words any more; I put my lips to his. Inside me a small heart beats with ours. A life for a life.

The lantern blinks, just a small curl of smoke over the lapping waters.

He pulls away.

Acknowledgements

While I wrote at my desk looking out at the shimmer of the Arabic Gulf, I never thought I would see my writing in print. At times it has felt like struggling up a sand dune in forty degrees, with djinn at my heels. Now my novel is in my hands there are some special people to say Shukran for chasing away those djinn.

First my parents, Paul and Cheryl, and brother, Neil, for your love, always being there and nurturing my love of reading and writing through sunshine and rain. My friends for their unfaltering belief and telling me I was a writer way before I ever dared think I was. My NHS colleagues whose practical, as well as emotional, support has created the space for me to write. The inspiration I found at the West Cork Literary Festival, Listowel Writers' Week and the Margate Bookie.

Above all, my Faber Falcons writing group, every single one who has sharpened my writing, widened my reading, given me inspiration, courage and love like I have not known before and who I treasure – all incredible writers to watch: Laura Arends, Fiona Campbell, Mia Fenwick, Karen Hamilton, Joe Kershaw,

Rohan McLachlan, Antonia Parker-Jones, Jessica Rachid, Roger Smith, Margaret Sutherland, Phil Willians, and Helen Irene Young.

Writing is one thing, getting published quite another and there are friends to extend a special Shukran. Allana Hansell, who insisted my novel must be published, took me to the first publishing workshop I ever attended and has been with me every step of the way. Jacki Kelly, a fine writer who I met in my first writing class in Bantry, and gave me confidence to read out my first piece. Kirstin Zhang whose generous advice set me on the path to being a writer. My beta readers for their passion for Electric Souk: Mia Fenwick, Karen Hamilton, Joe Kershaw, Pippa Rance and Helen Irene Young. Amanda Saint for the wine, wisdom and hope. Sophie Duffy and Paul McVeigh for the eureka moment on Chesil beach when I saw the truth submerged in the first page of my novel. Isabel Costello for the resilience you inspire. My brave publisher, Matthew Smith, for his vision in bringing us fresh writing, letting Souk breathe and his commitment to readers. The Urbanites for being such a welcoming community.

My mentor, Peter Horn, who took my calls at midnight in the desert and clears my cloudy skies. Catherine Walker, Eleanor Hubbard, Juliet Payne, Sandra de Souza, Anna Callinan, Irene Milligan, Eva Horgan, Rose Morris, Paula Grace, Demelza Penberth, Deborah Homa, Sue Baldwin, Kathy Walters, Jackie and John Constable for your hearts of gold and the cocktails.

Richard Skinner, without you my novel would have drifted away in Bantry Bay. Thank you for restoring my faith, changing my life by encouraging me to join the Faber Academy and making me write the novel I always wanted to write.

IC, for the dreams.

My dear friends in the Middle East who will always be in my heart, mae habbi.

Rose McGinty lives in England and works for the NHS. She studied at Trinity College Dublin and is an alumna of the Faber Academy. She has worked overseas, including the Middle East. She has won a number of writing competitions.

URBANE

Urbane Publications is dedicated to
developing new author voices, and publishing
fiction and non-fiction that challenges, thrills and
fascinates.

From page-turning novels to innovative
reference books, our goal is to publish what
YOU want to read.

Find out more at
urbanepublications.com